Praise for *The Madw*

An Edgar Awards Finalist for Best Novel

A *Woman's World* Book Club pick

A Historical Novel Society Editor's Choice pick

"This engrossing novel explores all the different ways that young women are exploited and told they should appreciate the attention. . . . The novel is well-written, thought-provoking, and immersive. . . . A must-read for those interested in the treatment of women and the ethics of medicine. Highly recommend."

—Historical Novel Society

"[Jennifer Cody] Epstein has achieved her goal of immersing readers in the 'stranger-than-fiction' universe of late-19th century Paris. At a time when women's reproductive rights are under threat and people with unexplained medical conditions are routinely gaslit, *The Madwomen of Paris* provides a fascinating look back at a condition with modern-day resonance."

—*Science Magazine*

"This haunting story of the cruel and misogynistic mental health system of late 19th-century Paris . . . makes the gruesome details of what women had to endure at the infamous Salpêtrière all the more horrifying."

—*Paste Magazine*

"Laure and Josephine's story reflects the raging obsession that people had with hysteria. . . . It speaks of the dangers of treatments used on patients and the vulnerable positions in which they were placed. . . . A gripping historical novel that describes the treatment patients received from Dr. Charcot at the Salpêtrière."

—*Booklist*

BY JENNIFER CODY EPSTEIN

The Madwomen of Paris
Wunderland
The Gods of Heavenly Punishment
The Painter from Shanghai

THE MADWOMEN OF PARIS

THE
MADWOMEN
OF PARIS

A Novel

Jennifer Cody Epstein

BALLANTINE BOOKS
NEW YORK

2024 Ballantine Books Trade Paperback Edition

Published in the United States by Ballantine Books, an imprint of Random House, a division of Penguin Random House LLC, New York.

BALLANTINE BOOKS & colophon are registered trademarks of Penguin Random House LLC.
RANDOM HOUSE BOOK CLUB and colophon are trademarks of Penguin Random House LLC.

Originally published in hardcover in the United States by Ballantine Books, an imprint of Random House, a division of Penguin Random House LLC, in 2023.

Grateful acknowledgment is made to Robert Lee Brewer and WritersDigest.com for permission to reprint "Jennifer Cody Epstein: On Finding the Bravery to Write Critically About the Past in Fiction" by Robert Lee Brewer, posted on WritersDigest.com on July 13, 2023. Used by permission.

LIBRARY OF CONGRESS CATALOGING-IN-PUBLICATION DATA
Names: Epstein, Jennifer Cody, author.
Title: The madwomen of Paris: a novel / Jennifer Cody Epstein.
Description: First edition. | New York: Ballantine Group, [2023]
Identifiers: LCCN 2022058012 (print) | LCCN 2022058013 (ebook) |
ISBN 9780593158029 (trade paperback; acid-free paper) | ISBN 9780593158012 (ebook)
Subjects: LCSH: Charcot, J. M. (Jean Martin), 1825-1893—Fiction. | Salpêtrière (Hospital)—Fiction. | Psychiatric hospitals—Fiction. | Psychiatric hospital patients—Fiction. | Mentally ill women—Fiction. | Hysteria—Fiction. | Paris (France)—Fiction. | LCGFT: Biographical fiction. | Thrillers (Fiction). | Novels.
Classification: LCC PS3605.P646 M33 2023 (print) | LCC PS3605.P646 (ebook) |
DDC 813/.6—dc23/eng/20221213
LC record available at https://lccn.loc.gov/2022058012
LC ebook record available at https://lccn.loc.gov/2022058013

Printed in the United States of America on acid-free paper

randomhousebooks.com
randomhousebookclub.com

1st Printing

Book design by Diane Hobbing

FOR STEVE AND ROZANNE

WE ARE ALL HYSTERICAL.
—Guy de Maupassant

IT'S THE TRUTH EVEN IF IT DIDN'T HAPPEN.
—Ken Kesey

I ACCEPT THE GRAND ADVENTURE
OF BEING MYSELF.

—Simone de Beauvoir

THE MADWOMEN OF PARIS

Chapter One

I didn't see her the day she came to the asylum.

Looking back, this sometimes strikes me as unlikely. Impossible, even, given how utterly her arrival would upend the already chaotic order of things at the Salpêtrière—not to mention change the course of my own life there. At times I even forget I *wasn't* present at that pivotal moment, for I can see it so clearly in my mind's eye: The blood-streaked clothing and skin. The wild eyes and unkempt hair. The slim legs, bare of stockings, covered with bruises and mud. That single bare foot—for she'd lost her boot at some point—as white and fragile as an unshelled egg. My mind replays her screams as the orderlies drag her from the ambulance, an otherworldly mix of falcon and banshee interspersed with strangled pleas: *Nonono don't TOUCH me* and *I will kill myself* and—most chillingly of all: *They are coming! Do you hear me? THEY ARE COMING!* I marvel at the sheer physical strength I saw—or think I saw—her displaying, at the way she fought so viciously against the men attempting to drag her into the admissions building that they had to briefly lay her down to attend to a wrist she'd bitten, a cheek she'd scratched, a kick she'd successfully landed to a loathsome man's privates. . . . It's all etched into my head with such clarity that, more than once, I've consulted the journal I kept at the time, scanning through its scribbled pages to affirm that these "memories" are, in fact, not memories at all. That rather, they are imaginative reconstructions, woven together from various medical reports and doctors' musings, and from snippets gleaned from those who did witness her arrival—or else were party to it, and bore the injuries to prove it.

Given my own history with mental disorders, I should perhaps find such self-deception troubling. And yet the truth is, I value these false reminiscences far more than I do my "valid" memories from that period, which to this day remain the bleakest of my life. Indeed, I sometimes suspect my mind of re-creating her spectacular arrival as a kind of defense against those same drab realities, to remind me that something better was coming. And, perhaps, to give me that much more of her to hold on to.

I'd been at the Salpêtrière—the largest women's asylum in France, and perhaps all Europe—for roughly a year by that point. But I'd only recently ceased being one of its patients, having been pronounced cured of the illness that had kept me sealed in its infamous hysteria ward for virtually all my nineteenth year of life. The verdict had come as little relief, for beyond the asylum I had nowhere to go, having lost both my parents, my home to my father's creditors, and—as I'd only recently learned—my beloved sister, Amélie, to France's byzantine foster care system. In desperation, I'd done what many penniless Salpêtrière "graduates" did to keep a roof over their heads: accepted a job as an asylum *fille de service*, or attendant, in the same gloomy and malodorous ward from which I'd just been discharged. It was thankless, menial work, my supervisor despised me, and the weekly wage was just a little under two francs—half of what male attendants were paid. That day, however, I had reason to believe I might be on the verge of escaping these miserable circumstances—and, hopefully, of finding my sister, about whom I was desperately worried. For Babette—Hysteria's hatchet-faced head nurse—had handed me a letter that afternoon.

"From a *notaire*," she'd noted cryptically. "Have you gotten yourself into trouble, Bissonnet?"

Though she'd clearly expected alarm on my part, I felt my heart leap with excitement. It was all I could do to not snatch the missive right out of her arthritic hand.

"No, Madame," I said as levelly as I could, and dropped the envelope into my apron pocket until she'd hurried off to check on one of the ward's epileptics. Only when she'd fully disappeared from view did I pull the letter out again, checking its sender's address to confirm that it matched that of my late father's notary, to whom I'd written several weeks earlier, and from whom I'd almost given up on hearing back. And—yes!—there it was: *Étude de M. François LaBarge, Notaire,* scripted in an even and methodical hand.

My heart beating slightly faster, I turned the envelope back over, inspecting the equally neatly printed mailing address:

> *Laure Bissonnet*
> *La Salpêtrière*
> *Hospice de la Vieillesse (Femmes)*
> *Boulevard de l'Hôpital, 47*
> *Paris*

Laure Bissonnet / La Salpêtrière. It still seemed strange to me that this was how the world now knew me, where it thought I really belonged. That it knew nothing of the modest flat in Chaussée d'Antin where Amélie and I were born and our parents both died; the apartment from which—barely a year earlier—I'd been dragged, trembling and jerking and biting my tongue hard enough that to this day, it bears a deep groove near its tip. Some other family lived there now, propping the balcony door open in the summer, kindling flames in the parlor fireplace in the winter. I, of course, knew this to be true. Yet trying to imagine it felt oddly disorienting, like tumbling through space with nothing to grasp on to, no way to ground myself.

I'd had the same unsettling response to the one other letter addressed to me at the Salpêtrière by that point. This one had been from the Paris Hospice des Enfants, where my sister had been taken by the city right after I'd fallen ill. Shortly before my discharge I'd written the orphanage's director, requesting he pass along a note I'd enclosed for Amélie: *I'm sorry, so very sorry for leaving you. I am well again now, and I think they'll let me leave soon. I'll come for you. Please wait a little longer.*

Unlike Maître LaBarge's, that response had arrived promptly, and my spirits soared when I saw that it also was accompanied by an enclosed note. My elation evaporated, however, upon discovering that the note was not from Amélie after all. Instead, it was my own note to her, returned unopened. Even worse, the brief letter from the orphanage informed me that Amélie was no longer at the orphanage; that in fact, no one actually knew *where* she was. Upon becoming a ward of France she'd been sent to a foster home in the Morvan region, in those days a full day's train ride from Paris or more. *Our records show,* the orphanage's director informed me brusquely, *that she was then removed from the original home some months after her placement. There is no indication of her current location.*

In other words, my sister had disappeared.

I'd stared down at this hastily scrawled note in disbelief, struggling to process what I'd just read. How could the state, having made itself Amélie's legal guardian, have then *lost* her in Burgundy a few months later? And yet according to Bernadette, a dark-eyed hysteric who swung wildly between pious mania and sensual excess, and who'd been raised in a convent orphanage herself, Parisian orphans were often quietly placed with farming families in those regions.

"They say it's to keep them from the sinful temptations of the city," she noted, her needle darting above and below the wooden frame of her tambour. "But it's really to keep all those farms in business. With so many leaving the countryside for Paris these days, there's more need for meat, cheese, wheat, and wine here than ever—but no one left on the farms to help provide it. They fill the gap by shipping in all those little orphaned Parisians and putting them to work."

Orphan labor, she explained, could be a double windfall; not only did it mean more working bodies for the farms, but foster parents were paid an annual bonus for the care and feeding of *les petits de*

Paris. Once those orphans turned twelve, though, both the bonuses and the annual check-ins from L'Assistance Publique stopped—and some families washed their hands of their young wards altogether.

"But if they don't know where she is, how can they know she's safe?" I asked, a thousand terrifying images rushing into my mind: Amélie thrown into a workhouse somewhere. Amélie begging on a street. Amélie whipped—or worse—by some cruel and villainous new "parent." She'd always been tiny for her age; it had seemed a miracle to me that she'd survived the scarlet fever that often killed children in those days, while our father had unexpectedly succumbed to it.

"They don't." Bernadette gave me one of her sweetly serene smiles. "Those fosters could have shipped your sister to Algiers in a barrel. No one at L'Assistance Publique would know—or even care."

"But they knew I was still in the city!" I'd protested. "They must have known I'd come for her."

Bernadette had looked up at me, her needle still in constant motion, a silverfish traversing a silken sea. "You're not 'in the city,' Laure," she said gently, almost pityingly. "You're at the Salpêtrière. You might as well be living on the moon."

"What do you mean, I can't have it? It's *mine!*"

The voice was distraught, whistle-shrill, and dispiritingly familiar. Pulled from my thoughts, I turned to see Babette—apparently done with her epileptic—now facing off with a statuesque young woman whose full cheeks were flushed with fury. From the latter's imperious expression one might have mistaken her for a doyenne taking a servant to task. In fact, she was a patient—though not just any patient. Rosalie Chardon, lovingly dubbed "The Alsatian" by the Parisian press, had by then become the most celebrated hysteric in France. She had also become my central responsibility as a Hysteria *fille de service;* a fact underscored as Babette curtly beckoned me over.

"Come, Bissonnet," she barked. "*This instant.*"

"It has nothing to do with her!" Rosalie protested.

"I'll decide what's to do with who here," the old nurse snapped back.

Sighing, I slid the letter back into my pocket and began making my way across the room, my heart sinking a little with each step. Living with Rosalie as a fellow patient had been challenging enough. But living with her as a ward attendant was a whole new order of exhausting. I was now tasked with actually *tending* to her continual complaints and demands, her nightly screams and stomach ailments, and the injury done to herself and others during her fits. It was also my job to temper the hot flame of her seemingly endless ire, whether over an imagined smirk by a male orderly, a spot of mold on her breakfast bread, or a trinket she claimed had been stolen by a fellow wardmate but that inevitably turned up in her own pocket or beneath her bed.

Drawing even with her now, though, I saw that this latest eruption had been sparked by something both softer and sweeter. That is, it had been sparked by fruit; an enormous (and clearly costly) basket of greenhouse grapes, peaches, and apples had mysteriously appeared on her cot.

"It's from the marquis," Babette informed me. I knew at once who she meant: an elderly nobleman as renowned for his myriad mistresses as he was for his lavish spending.

"And it's scandalous," she went on, turning back to Rosalie. "I won't have it in my ward."

"You think everything's a scandal," Rosalie said, pouting. "I might as well live in a convent."

"At least in a convent you'd be safe from lecherous old degenerates," Babette responded. "You've no idea what that man is really like."

"Of course I don't," Rosalie retorted. "You won't give me an opportunity to find out."

Babette's face tightened, a weathered purse with its strings pulled. "You're a patient in an asylum," she snapped, "not an actress at the Comédie-Française. Even if he first saw you onstage."

"It wasn't onstage," Rosalie noted sullenly. "It was at the ball." She was at that point being regularly presented as a medical subject in lectures given by the Salpêtrière's director, the world-renowned doctor and neurologist Jean-Martin Charcot. But the marquis had indeed first laid eyes on her at the Bal des Folles, an annual Lenten event in which the most privileged members of Parisian society paid to mingle with the asylum's inmates. Rosalie had gone that year as a musketeer, her yellow curls cascading out from beneath a handsome plumed hat, her shapely legs sheathed in blue satin tights from Le Bon Marché that must have cost close to half the ward's modest costume budget. I myself, attending in my itchy new staff uniform, had seen the old man's face light up when he spotted her. He'd looked like a magpie spotting a coin in a dust heap. The gifts—flowers, fancy wines, cut-glass bottles of scent—began arriving soon after, with Babette intercepting them as doggedly as a fencer foiling an opponent's thrusts and advances.

"It doesn't *matter*," the head nurse said now. "You can't simply go gallivanting around Paris like some fine lady of leisure." Turning on me again, she added: "And *you*! Why didn't you tell me about this? I've specifically told you to notify me when such things are delivered."

"I—I didn't see it until now," I stammered.

"So now you're blind as well as useless?" She expelled a scornful sigh.

Stung, I looked away. The old woman's dislike of Rosalie was easy enough to understand. That she seemed to loathe me as well, however, mystified me—especially since I'd always made every effort to be deferential toward her, as both patient and subordinate. While still the former, I'd thought she perhaps doubted the extent of my illness, for there were few hysterics who earned Babette's disgust more than those whom she suspected of feigning fits and outlandish symptoms in competitive bids for the doctors' attentions. And yet, my transition from patient to ward attendant only seemed to have deepened her disdain.

It was Bernadette who had suggested another theory. "She's afraid you'll show her up in front of the doctors," she'd said, looking up from a cushion cover on which she was painstakingly embroidering Christina of Spoleto as her body was torn bloodily apart by iron hooks. "After all, you've been to boarding school, and been a tutor to wealthy families. Most of all, though, you're the daughter of a doctor. She thinks you know more than she does."

And as absurd as I initially found this explanation, I had to admit it made a sort of sense. The Salpêtrière was a public hospital, after all, which meant that the vast majority of its patients came from much harder backgrounds than I did: florists, laundresses, seamstresses, and the like. Many of them had never even seen a physician before being committed, much less had one as a parent.

"I'm sorry, Madame," I muttered. "I've been very busy."

This was true: In addition to having had three hysterical attacks since the midday meal, Rosalie—who clearly saw me more as lady's maid than medical caregiver—had commanded me to massage liniment into the knuckles and wrist of her right hand, which for some reason always contracted when she seized. She'd also had me file down a snag in one of her fingernails, wash and set her hair in preparation for her appearance on Charcot's stage the following day, and run to the asylum market for the sugary *dragées* she liked to snack on between meals and which the shopkeeper gave her free of charge. From there she'd led me on a grounds-wide but ultimately unsuccessful hunt for the latest issue of *Le petit journal,* which supposedly featured her own image on its cover, in color.

"We're all busy," Babette snapped. "It's no excuse for negligence." Snatching the gift off Rosalie's cot, she hooked its handle over her thin arm. "Either way, this is completely unacceptable."

"But it's only *fruit!*" Rosalie wailed, lunging after the disputed produce.

"It most certainly is not," Babette countered, swinging the basket beyond her patient's reach while holding aloft two crisp hundred-franc bills I assumed she'd discovered amid the straw packing. "It's a down payment, is what it is. And the director has made it clear you're to have nothing more to do with that man."

"I've had nothing to do with him to start with!" Rosalie cried. "It's not *my* fault he keeps sending me things!"

Babette snorted. "No more than it's your fault that you were caught all but clambering into his lap the other day, I suppose."

"I told you," the Alsatian said indignantly. "I don't remember *any* of that." The prior week she'd been discovered by an intern while attempting to slip off asylum grounds, in what she'd claimed was a state of "spontaneous delusion." It later came out that the marquis had been waiting in his landau just outside the Salpêtrière's arched stone gateway, a bouquet of exotic roses—the same cerulean blue as Rosalie's eyes—in hand. No one knew how he'd arranged the rendezvous, though there was speculation he was paying one of the orderlies to ferry notes and trinkets through Babette's daunting wall of defense. It was thanks to that thwarted attempt that, to Rosalie's annoyance and my dismay, I'd been designated her primary chaperone.

"This is not the Opéra," the old nurse continued, ignoring the denial and tucking the bills into her apron pocket. "A man can't just *buy* himself a hysteric as he would a dancer. I don't care what title he tacks on to his name."

At this Rosalie's face flushed almost as darkly as one of her soon-to-be-commandeered grapes. *Don't respond,* I willed her wearily, fingering the envelope in my own pocket. *Let it go. Let me go—if only for a few minutes.*

But of course, she did not.

"How *dare* you, you stupid codfish," she spat. Lunging for the basket again, she jerked it enough that a peach tumbled to the floor. She was a strong girl, broad of shoulder and wide of hip, renowned for her ability to hold challenging hysterical postures for long stretches of time. But she was no match for Babette, who despite being at least four decades older, a full head shorter, and as wiry as a whippet, snatched the gift back with enough force that Rosalie fell forward, landing on all fours on the floor next to the now-bruised piece of fruit.

"*Now* look what you've done!" she cried out. "I've twisted my ankle! I'll have to *limp* onto the stage tomorrow!"

"You'll recover," Babette said shortly. Hooking her forearm beneath the basket's rush handle, she turned back toward her desk.

But Rosalie wasn't done. Snatching the fallen peach up, she hurled it at the nurse's retreating form with the same sturdy arm that had made her the ward's reigning *jeu de boules* champion. Perhaps if she'd been hurling a heavy wooden *boule cloutée* instead of a stone fruit, her aim might have been more precise. The peach, however, merely flew a few meters before landing in the next row of beds, moistly but harmlessly.

Stopping in her tracks, Babette turned slowly around again. She stared first at the soggy missile, then back toward the panting girl who'd launched it.

Had anyone else in Hysteria done what Rosalie had just done—or spoken to the asylum's longest-serving nurse as she just had—the consequences would have been as swift as they would have been unsparing. Rosalie, however, clearly felt herself immune to such retaliation—and for good reason. Dr. Charcot had begun featuring her in his weekly "Friday Lessons" some eighteen months earlier. Since then lecture attendance had tripled, swelling from a handful of somber colleagues and dozing medical students to a thronging crowd of civilians, social elites, and journalists covering the events for Parisian papers, often rhapsodizing over Rosalie's golden hair, sapphire eyes, and a bosom that, at least according to one *Le Petit Parisien* editorial, "rivaled that of any ship's figurehead."

Charcot already had a towering international reputation, having clinically demystified other baffling neurological diseases such as Parkinson's, multiple sclerosis, and amyotrophic lateral sclerosis earlier in his career. Thanks to all the media attention, he was now widely seen as the nation's foremost expert on hysteria as well, ensuring the Salpêtrière a widening stream of public monies that, under his direction, went toward cutting-edge additions like the asylum's new hydrotherapy and electrotherapy units, its gleaming new amphitheater, and a state-of-the-art photography studio. In short, Rosalie was now a major asset to both the Salpêtrière and its most esteemed doctor. And for all her fits and delusions, she knew it.

I held my breath as the aged nurse and the young hysteric locked gazes, Rosalie's much-lauded bosom heaving beneath her bodice. Still kneeling on the floor, she straightened her spine, threw back her shoulders, and lifted her dimpled chin in defiance. An expectant hush fell over the close, dark room. Two girls playing *bésigue* by the window looked up from their game. Bernadette dropped the worn copy of *Lives of the Saints* she was reading onto her lap, while Madame Chambon— a stocky matron of about sixty—stopped singing to the little doll she'd been cradling and covered its painted eyes with her plump palm.

Removing a handkerchief from her sleeve, Babette bent and picked the ruined fruit up with it. Slowly and deliberately, she stepped to a nearby waste bin and dropped the peach into its depths, where it landed with another wet-sounding *thunk*.

"Mark my words," she said quietly, turning back to face Rosalie. "If you're not careful you'll end up the same way."

"End up what way?" Rosalie sneered.

"Done. Discarded. You think that because he favors you now, you're untouchable."

"*He?*" The Alsatian's azure eyes narrowed. "Who?"

"The doctor. The marquis. Either. Both." Babette shrugged. "You may have caught the interest of important men for now. But you're the same as everyone else in this place in the end—just another penniless madwoman."

"I'm not mad," Rosalie countered hotly. "I'm a *hysteric*. You of all people should know the difference."

"You still call a madhouse your home," Babette retorted. "It's right here on the man's card." She flicked the marquis's card with her gnarled finger. Then she flicked her cold gaze back to me. "Clean that up," she ordered, jerking her chin at the pulpy imprint the peach had left on the floor.

And with that she marched off toward her desk.

Rosalie stared after her, her chest still heaving and her rosebud mouth slightly ajar. Then—without warning—she torqued herself onto her stomach and began pounding the floor with her fists. "Stupid cow!" she shrieked. "Ugly *trout*! Wicked old *trollop*!"

"Be not quick in your spirit to become angry," Bernadette admonished her, her tone prim but carrying over the racket. "Anger lodges in the breasts of fools."

Rosalie paused in her paroxysm, her yellow hair awry and her face smudged with tears and floor grime. "You're one to speak of breasts," she hissed.

'Nadette—who in a fit of religious mortification had once snipped off her own left nipple with sewing scissors—just smiled beatifically and returned to her saints. I took a rag from a nearby cleaning bucket and knelt to clean up the juice-slicked spot.

"It's only fruit, Rosalie," I said mildly. "You don't even *like* fruit." After having several plates I'd had made for her indignantly rejected, I knew better than most that the Alsatian favored pungent and strong-tasting foods: pickled herring and garlic, or sardines, everything heavily salted and sauced, and usually consumed with enormous amounts of bread. She attributed these cravings to her continual ether treatments; while leaving her ravenous, they apparently also dulled her sense of taste.

"What would *you* know about my likes and dislikes, you skinny little sausage," she snapped.

Sighing again, I tossed the rag back into the bucket and set about retrieving the scattered hairpins she'd just shaken free from her chignon. The sharpness of her tongue still sometimes caught me off guard. It also puzzled me, for Bernadette often remarked on how different the Alsatian had been when she first arrived in Hysteria. Not as a patient, but as a *fille de service* like I was now. In those days, she'd been known as a softhearted girl who passionately loved birds, and who still sobbed sometimes over the death of her mother and infant sisters years earlier. "She was actually *kind*," 'Nadette recalled, shaking her dark head in bemusement. "She'd wash my dress for me if I soiled it during a fit, even though Babette said I was to wash it myself. When I broke my rosary, she bought me a new one—with her own wages!"

Needless to say, I never saw that version of Rosalie, since less than a year into her employment in Hysteria, she began exhibiting hysterical symptoms herself. These soon expanded to include all four of the hysterical stages that Charcot had determined to be characteristic of the disease—usually in the precise order (epileptoid, clonic, passionate poses, delirium) in which he'd determined they naturally unfolded. It was upon discovering that he could hypnotically prompt this same "classic" hysterical sequence at his convenience that the renowned doctor began featuring Rosalie in his lectures and scholarly papers, launching her own rise to celebrity. Strangely, though, neither the fame nor the continual medical attentions bestowed on her seemed to have done much to alleviate Rosalie's actual hysteria. By the time I met her, she was having more attacks than ever. She'd even set the ward's daily record the prior week, succumbing to a full hundred and fourteen fits in thirteen hours.

Her living standard, on the other hand, had improved vastly: Along with a personal attendant (me), the lion's share of Babette's ether and amyl nitrate supplies, and a secondhand silk dress for the stage, Rosalie enjoyed extra food to keep her strength up, extra time to sleep in the mornings, and a steady stream of fawning notes and gifts from her growing circle of male admirers—not all of which Babette was able to block, as the string of paste pearls the Alsatian wore today attested. She was also excused from the work that was generally required of inmates deemed mentally and physically capable of doing it, whether it be in the laundry facility, the sewing workshop, one of its three vegetable gardens, or—God forbid—its pig farm. One would have thought such preferential treatment would have further sweetened the girl's temperament. Apparently, though, it had had the opposite effect.

"Here," I said, holding out a handful of hairpins as a kind of prickly peace offering.

"Never *mind* those." She snatched them from me impatiently. "I'm *starving*. And thanks to the old witch, I have nothing to eat. Go to the kitchen for me."

I glanced at the ward clock. It was now barely an hour before suppertime, and on top of the *dragées* I'd fetched her, she'd had extra helpings at both breakfast and lunch. As she pulled herself unsteadily to her feet, though, her face wan but her gaze defiant, I understood that the command had less to do with hunger pangs than bruised pride. It also dawned on me that the added errand was a blessing in disguise. The Salpêtrière's kitchen was a cavernous, clattering place with grease-coated walls, three huge cast-iron stoves, and a small army of cooks and aides to attend them. It was also notoriously slow—especially with special requests. Once I put the order in, I'd easily have a good twenty minutes to finally—*finally*—discover the contents of my letter . . . and hopefully, my fate.

"Fine," I said. "I'll have them make a plate. The usual?"

"More sardines this time," she replied regally. "A whole jar, if they have it. And don't let them forget—*extra* vinegar."

Nodding, I turned away, scanning for another *fille de service* to keep an eye on her while I was gone. Usually there were at least two other attendants assigned to the fifty-odd patients in our section. Now, though, there were no others in sight. Biting the inside of my cheek, I looked back to where Babette sat reconciling the ward's ether supply logs with its dispensing records. I was loath to approach her, given her seeming mission to mock and denigrate nearly everything I did under her watch. But I was also under strict orders not to leave Rosalie unattended.

I made my way over to her desk, unease unspooling in my belly and the letter seeming to pulse through my skirt and petticoat like a paper heart.

"What now?" the nurse muttered when I reached her, her eyes still fixed on her ledger.

"She wants another plate."

Babette looked at the clock, clearly making the same mealtime calculation I had. But she didn't argue. Charcot himself had decreed that Rosalie be allowed to order freely from the kitchen whenever she liked.

"Be quick about it, then," she snapped instead. "I'm short-staffed right now. In case you haven't noticed that either."

I felt my cheeks heat. "Weren't Claudine and Julienne working this morning?"

"Claudine's assisting a feeding. I sent Julienne off to help with a new *internée*. Even more of a spitfire than that one, it seems," she added, nodding in Rosalie's direction. "Some *flics* dragged her off the edge of the Pont Neuf this morning."

And there it was: the very first time I heard mention of the girl who would reshape my world.

This, in my mind, is where I always seem to recall the harbingers of her arrival: The snorts and whinnies of spooked horses thundering up the asylum drive. The frenetic ringing of ambulance bells. The girl herself screaming as she was dragged down from the carriage (*NONONO don't TOUCH me THEY ARE COMING!*). The shouts and whistles of attendants trying to subdue her. I even imagine I heard the indignant shrieks of Julienne as the girl's flung fist connected with her lower lip. And yet as none of this appears in my journal entry from that night, it seems likely that I heard nothing out of the ordinary.

Which is not, of course, to say that I heard nothing, for the Salpêtrière was an unremittingly noisy place. How could it not have been, housing as it did some three thousand women in various states of mental distress; two hundred children in its reformatory schools; six hundred doctors, surgeons, *internes* and *externes*, nurses, and various other assistants; and over a dozen on-site workshops making everything from copper tools to iron horseshoes to wooden clogs for its patients? It was effectively a small, mad city, with a rotating roster of daily workers (masons, carpenters, plumbers, mechanics) and its own trolley line to clatter goods from site to site. It had a massive inmate-staffed laundry that took in sheets, uniforms, and towels from every hospital in Paris. In addition to its pig farm it boasted a butchery, a post office, a tobacco shop, and a bakery. It even had its own *marchand de vin*, where the staff and patients mingled and drank together whenever it hadn't been closed down following some incident—like the time two of Charcot's protégés, after consuming a bottle or two, hypnotized Bernadette into kissing the asylum priest on the lips.

The result was that even at its most serene, the place operated amid continual din: muffled shouts and scuffling feet, shrill screams and obscene curses, ringing bells and clattering carriages, all of it periodically interspersed with spirited debates between the doctors, rounds of bawdy chorus by the medical interns, and the chatter of public tour groups those same interns often led about for extra cash. After a few weeks or months living there, though, it all melded into a subdued mélange of background noise that most of us all but ceased to notice.

"Is there no one to watch her, then?" I asked.

"She'll be fine," Babette said, glancing back to where Rosalie now sat perched on her bed. "She'll need an hour at least to primp now, anyway."

Following her gaze, I saw the Alsatian painstakingly redoing her coiffure with the aid of the heavily ornamented hand mirror—another illicit gift from a suitor—that she kept by her bedside. Charcot considered vanity such a common symptom of hysteria that he often noted it on medical charts, though it had never appeared on mine. Rosalie, by contrast, had become so fixated on her appearance that it could paralyze her as effectively as any cataleptic fit. If her stays weren't tight enough, or her cheek marred by some pimple or scratch, she would simply refuse to leave the ward until the perceived flaw was either fixed or concealed. I'd even seen her hide in the linen closet once, after one of the interns led his tour group into the ward without advance notice.

"Is the new patient another hysteric?" I asked, turning back. "Where will we put her?" We were at the height of Paris's hysteria epidemic then, and easily taking in more new patients than were being discharged, being transferred to the lunacy ward, or (as was unfortunately not uncommon) dying from illness or self-inflicted injury. I wasn't sure we even had a spare bed.

"Her diagnosis is none of your concern," Babette retorted. "Stop dawdling. Get the plate."

Bobbing a hasty curtsy, I turned back toward the ward's double doors, consciously working to keep myself from running. I'd barely made it two steps, though, before I heard my name barked out yet again: "Bissonnet!"

I turned back around.

"You may as well take that with you." Babette pointed her pencil stub at the basket, which sat perched on a pile of folders on the corner of her desk.

"To the kitchen?" I asked, confused. "What will they do with it?"

She rolled her eyes. "It's food, isn't it? They'll find some use for it." Sitting back in her chair, she glared at me until I took the thing. "*Incroyable*," she muttered, as if to herself. "You'd think a physician's daughter would have more sense."

A quarter hour or so later, having duly put in Rosalie's order and handed over the disputed fruit, I made my way to the one place at the asylum where I could usually find at least relative quiet and solitude: its chapel, Saint-Louis de la Salpêtrière.

I had mixed feelings about faith in those days. At my mother's insistence, Amélie and I had attended weekly mass for most of my childhood, while my father—like many of his profession, a self-proclaimed atheist who put his faith in the laws of science rather than those of God—usually managed to beg off. Following our mother's death in childbirth when I was twelve and Amélie five, Papa's tolerance of formal religion waned even further; apart from on Christmas Eve and Easter morning, he rarely bothered marching us the six short blocks to our neighborhood place of worship.

Since arriving at the Salpêtrière, I'd come to share his ambivalence. As I saw little point in worshipping a Being who'd so cruelly stripped me of everything I'd ever valued—including, for a time, my own sanity. I was therefore grateful to have arrived well after the asylum had done away with both the rule requiring *internées* to attend daily mass, and the white-wimpled *soeurs-infirmières* who'd for centuries enforced it.

Yet I'd still come to see this sleepy little church as one of my few refuges in that miserable place. The serene faces of its statues were a welcome change from the tortured grimaces and manic grins I lived among and now tended, their stillness a respite from the spasming bodies and jerking limbs of the ward. Even the damage and neglect many had sustained—the Madone at the front altar sported a chipped nose, and the Saint Anne above the confessional had enough dust on her robed shoulders that she looked draped in dingy cloth— was comforting. It somehow made them seem more human.

Settling myself into the last pew, I pulled out the letter, setting it on my lap. Then—more surreptitiously—I took out my handkerchief, unfolding it to reveal three grapes I'd slipped from Rosalie's basket before handing it to a confused-looking kitchen attendant. Taking one between my fingers, I rolled it around, studying its unmarred, maroon complexion. On the rare occasions we'd had grapes at home, Amélie and I had both known to eat the fruit as our mother had taught us, discreetly stripping away the sour skin first.

But I didn't bother doing that now. I popped the round globes into my mouth one after another, chewing carefully to avoid the pips. I ate all three of them that way, spitting the bitter seeds back into my handkerchief.

As I finished off the last one, a memory came to me as if released from the fruit's pulpy flesh: Amélie, her hair brown like mine but thicker and leavened by glints of red. Her eyes like pools of warm coffee, tinged with cream, shining as she dropped seeds from an orange we must have just shared into a little ceramic pot, then smoothing dirt over the pips as though covering a newborn with a soft blanket. She'd even sung them a little song: *Fais dodo, colas mon p'tits frères, fais dodo.* "Don't you see, Laure?" she'd said, when I laughingly asked what she was doing. "I'll keep them in the sun, and when they grow into trees we'll have oranges whenever we like!"

Squeezing my eyes shut, I struggled to place that luminous moment. It couldn't have been in the final year or so before my father's death—or if it had, it wouldn't have been an orange he'd have bought himself. By that time, poor money management—including a disastrous investment in a doomed venture providing milk transfusions to surgical patients (often killing them in the process)—had left our bank account empty, Papa's client list diminished, and our pantry pared down to the most basic of sustenance: Eggs and bread, cheese and butter. Meat twice a week if we were lucky. If we'd had fruit, it would almost certainly have been at someone else's largesse; an offering from some grateful associate or patient, or a gift from one of the families I tutored. I did recall that Amélie's pips never sprouted. But the memory of it—her childish faith in seed and soil, in a future filled with tree-born treats—was as sweet as the gritty grape essence on my tongue. It almost felt like a good omen.

Heartened, I tucked the handkerchief back into my pocket and turned my attention back to Maître LaBarge's letter. Though I'd never met the man, he'd been my father's notary for decades, and had settled Papa's affairs after his death. It was based on that intimacy that I'd written him, making my case for what I wanted with the same careful eloquence that had earned me praise from my *lycee* teachers. I'd drafted and redrafted my request in my journal before copying it meticulously onto stationery slipped from Babette's desk: *I know most of our possessions have already been auctioned off,* I'd written. *I'm asking only for whatever might be left—whatever wasn't wanted by anyone else but that might still be worth a little bit of money. Surely you can see how even such a small gesture might help alleviate the cruelty of our current circumstances. I beg you to consider it, as you'd wish it to be considered were your own daughters to experience the same kind of misfortune as have we.* After sealing this message into its Salpêtrière-embossed envelope, I'd handed it to the surly postmaster at the tiny asylum post office with a curious sensation in my stomach, one I only later recognized as hope.

Despite myself, I felt that sensation once more, like butterfly wings brushing against the inside of my belly. My need for funds had only grown more urgent since learning of Amélie's disappearance, for trying to find her was sure to be costly. What an unfathomable relief it would be if LaBarge had written me that *yes,* there was some money left; that *of course* I was entitled to a little of it or—who knew?— perhaps even more than a little. Maybe there were even one or two things of sentimental value from our home that I'd be allowed to take back; our parents' wedding photo, for instance. I couldn't imagine anyone else would want that, after all. And yet to me at this point, being able to again see their faces would feel like a treasure in and of itself.

The last time I'd prayed had been at the rushed funeral service for my father, in the antiseptic-smelling chapel at the Hôtel-Dieu. Now, though, I glanced at the chipped-nosed Mary, sending her a single, silent appeal: *Please.*

Then, taking a deep breath, I broke the seal, catching every crumb of red wax in my palm as though it, too, might be of monetary value before easing out the folded page inside.

My first thought was how brief LaBarge's response was. And yet, I reminded myself, he was a busy man—his long silence had implied as much. Just because he hadn't written in detail didn't mean he was writing with bad news.

Breath still bated, I began reading.

> *Mademoiselle Bissonnet:*
>
> *Given the extent of your late father's debts, what you request is— simply put—impossible. Under French law, were I to bequeath to you any item from Dr. Bissonnet's estate it would render you person- ally responsible for the entirety of his financial obligations. In other words, it would land you in circumstances I can assure you would be significantly crueler than any you are experiencing at present. It might very well land you in debtor's prison.*

I read the curt paragraph twice, then a third time, the words more devastatingly blunt and brutal each time:

Impossible.

Crueler.

Prison.

I had to steel myself before forcing my gaze down to the commu- niqué's final line, telling myself it couldn't be any more punishing than the curt lines preceding it. But as it turned out, I was wrong about that as well.

> *I do not have a daughter. But if I did, and she were—by some un- fathomable twist of fortune or fate—to find herself in your position,*

my advice to her would be to remain where she is. Given the dire cir-
cumstances under which your father so negligently left you, you should
consider yourself lucky to be at the Salpêtrière—not to mention under
the care of a celebrated physician such as Dr. Jean-Martin Charcot.

Cordially,
François LaBarge, Notary

Chapter Two

I jolted awake early the next morning to the yowls and shrieks of mating cats.

It was a common enough sound there in those days that I normally barely took notice of it. That morning, though—it was a little before six—I found myself listening to the undulating duet intently, as though there might be some secret message embedded in the despairing wail of the hapless female, the triumphant howl of the male. And perhaps there was, for upon shutting my eyes to try to steal a little more sleep, I was instead overtaken by another memory of Amélie.

This one involved a little porcelain cat Papa had brought home for my sister when she was perhaps five or six and had been pestering him for a real-life pet for months. After naming it "Miaou," Amélie dragged it across the floorboards of our flat at the end of a tattered blue ribbon. She also gave it "checkups" modeled on those our father gave his patients, claiming that one day she was going to be a doctor just like he was. On the fine spring morning I remembered, though, we'd been playing *marelle* in our courtyard, peeling off our shoes and stockings in order to feel the sun-warmed pavers beneath our feet. Before hopping her way through the circular "snail" we'd chalked, Amélie tucked the toy into the toe of her little slipper. "Just to be sure she won't run off," she said.

"Where would she run to?" I teased. "After some prowling porcelain tom?"

"I don't know." Amélie stroked the toy's hard little head. "I just don't want her to be separated from me and end up all alone. It would scare her so much she might die."

Perhaps because I was still half asleep, this memory—unlike the one in the chapel—was so vivid it felt less like a recollection than a relocation in time, disorienting enough that I actually felt dizzied by how closely it mirrored my present fears (*all alone, she might die*). I tried my best to tamp it back into that dark, sealed-off part of my mind into which I crammed all thoughts of my past life. I knew all too well the dangerous path down which they could lead me, one remembrance unspooling into another, entangling me in an incapacitating web of nostalgia.

I shut my eyes again, searching for something safer to ponder. My mind quickly landed on Monsieur LaBarge's letter, which I'd slipped into my journal the prior night before tucking the little book beneath my pillow. I was tempted to reread it now, as though its message might have somehow softened overnight like the lentils the kitchen attendants soaked in bathtub-sized vats. Instead, I returned to the calculation I'd begun mentally making as I'd dragged myself out of the chapel yesterday: how much it would realistically cost for me to leave the Salpêtrière and begin my search for Amélie. I usually enjoyed doing sums—at boarding school, it had been one of my strongest subjects. This, though, was proving to be an unusually dispiriting exercise: Thirty francs for a train ticket to Avallon by way of Nuits-sous-Ravières—for according to the old atlas I'd found in the asylum library, Avallon was one of the largest towns in the region, and probably had an Assistance Publique local agency in charge of placing Paris orphans at surrounding farms and businesses. Seventy francs for a boardinghouse, assuming I'd need to stay there for several weeks at least. An additional fifty francs to cover transportation and sundries during that stay, and—ideally—another fifty on hand as emergency funds.

The grand total I arrived at now was the same one I'd reached yesterday—and every bit as discouraging: two hundred francs. It was a sum most of Papa's clients would barely have blinked at. Indeed, most of them spent more than that on a barrel of good Bordeaux. In my current situation, though, and given my pitiful weekly wages, it could take years to scrape together.

Clearly, if I wanted to find Amélie, I needed to make more money—lots more of it. And yet I could conceive of no way to do this, of no other position for which I was qualified that would cover meals and a safe roof over my head while still allowing me to save. Before Papa had sickened, I'd tutored the children of one or two of his wealthier clients. Even if I could find similar work now, though, my recent institutionalization would disqualify me from it. Rich Parisians happily paid to gawk at hysterics at the Bal des Folles, as well as on asylum tours and Charcot's gleaming new stage. But they'd never pay one to teach their own children. And without the funds I'd hoped Maître LaBarge would help me reclaim, there was no way to even begin finding Amélie. I might be trapped in this place until I became as aged and gnarled as the asylum's *reposantes*, the ancient lunatics who spent their days outside on benches, knitting and cackling and spitting cheerful obscenities at passersby.

The thought was so discouraging that all I wanted in that instant was to pull my threadbare covers over my head, to let my miserable world churn on without me. Then I saw Babette. The old woman was already up, dressed and coiffed, making her way between the rows of slumbering women in order to wake the *filles de service* for their morning chores.

More eager than usual to avoid the bony press of her fingers, I forced myself from my bed, thrusting my journal into a slit I'd made for it in my mattress as I hastily made up the sheets. Then I checked on Rosalie. She'd had another difficult night—which of course meant I had too. I'd had to get up three times: first to refill her water cup after she'd drained it, then to retrieve the coverlet she'd tossed to the floor, then to clean the mess she'd made after tripping over the chamber pot she'd had to use after drinking the water. Now, though, she slept quietly, one hand flung across her forehead and a faint saw-

THE MADWOMEN OF PARIS {27}

ing sound sifting from her parted lips. I knew from experience that she'd stay that way until I woke her at eight to begin preparing for that morning's medical lecture.

Stifling a yawn, I shuffled over to the rusting washstand I shared with six others, passing a clammy rag over my face and beneath my arms before pulling on my stockings, stays, and woolen work gown, and tossing my threadbare shawl over my shoulders. Knowing Babette would tell me to do it anyway, I emptied the chamber pots in my section, then picked up the slops bucket by its wire handle to leave outside for the groundskeepers.

By the time I passed Babette's desk, she'd already seated herself and was working away at her staff ledgers. I lifted a hand in greeting, more out of reflex than goodwill. If she noticed the gesture, she gave no sign.

'Nadette was right, I thought glumly, continuing on with my foul-smelling cargo. *I might as well be living on the moon.*

My bleak mood endured as I dragged myself to staff breakfast, the holes in my asylum-issue wrap doing little to shield me from the bite of the early April air. Upon seating myself in the refectory, I found myself next to Julienne, the *fille de service* who'd assisted with the "spitfire" patient's intake the prior day. As usual, we didn't acknowledge each other. I took some bread from the basket, listening with half an ear as the other workers exchanged the usual gossip: which interns were supposedly sleeping with which patients and who'd been seen slipping together into the "softs"—padded, soundproof cells built to isolate violent inmates, which sometimes doubled as spots for amorous assignations. One of the housekeepers also recounted seeing Charcot explode in outrage upon learning a long-standing rival of his—a lead doctor at the University of Nancy—had published a paper in which he accused Charcot of hypnotically "coaching" Rosalie so that her hysterical symptoms aligned with his theories on the disease.

"He shattered an ink pot!" the maid said. "Threw it right against the wall! Thank the saints he missed the window. And that the wall's already black."

"I never understood that," said one of the orderlies. "Why paint a perfectly good wall black? So gloomy."

The housekeeper shrugged. "To better set off all those spooky pictures and paintings of his, I suppose." Charcot was an avid collector of anatomical sketches of seizing women, as well as of religious paintings—especially ones depicting exorcisms and demonic possessions. But he was also, I'd heard, an avid fan of the theater, and I sometimes thought he'd arranged his office to look like one.

There was also talk about Rosalie's fruit basket. Not just the extravagance of its contents—which the kitchen staff had quickly devoured—but speculation about how the marquis had managed to get it past Babette and onto Rosalie's pillow. "I'm telling you," said one of the orderlies, "the man's got someone in his pay. It's how he got her to meet him last week—and probably how he found out her real name as well." As with all the patients he presented publicly, Charcot introduced Rosalie under a pseudonym: Hers was "Blanche W."

"This one should know who it is," said Julienne, jerking her chin in my direction. She finally turned to face me, and I saw with a start that her lower lip was scabbed over with blackened blood.

"She knows *everything* about our Alsatian these days," Julienne went on caustically, digging her sharp elbow into my ribs. "Come on, Laure. Tell us all his name."

I hated being the center of attention—and Julienne knew it. "All I know is that it's not me," I mumbled, picking off a piece of my crust.

"We know it's not you," Julienne laughed. "I said *he*, didn't I? You don't look *that* much like a man."

I dropped my eyes, feeling my ears flush. The comment recalled a cruel rumor that had circulated when I first started at my girls' boarding school: It was whispered that I was a boy in disguise. I have no idea how the story began; perhaps because I was thin and plain, or because thanks to my father's library (which included medical books in German and Latin) I had an unusually strong foundation in those languages for someone of my sex. But for days after my arrival at l'École Roseline de Villeneuve, I was followed by speculative whispers, and the girls with whom I shared my room refused to dress or undress until I turned my back to them. It wasn't until we all took our first communal bath that the rumor subsided—though of course, by then they'd found other things to mock me for. It actually came as a relief when my father brought me home before the end of my second year there. To help with Amélie, he said at first, though it was actually because he could no longer afford the tuition.

"Surely there wasn't *that* much blood!"

I glanced up as the kitchen server that morning—a languid-limbed girl named Céline with a cleft upper lip—sloshed weak, lukewarm coffee into my cup, though since she was looking at Julienne and not the cup, a good amount splattered onto the table.

"Her apron was more red than white with it," Julienne replied. "The cops attributed it to a cut on her hand. It looked more to me like she'd butchered one of the pigs."

It took a moment to realize that the conversation had turned to the new patient Babette had mentioned to me yesterday—the one the police had dragged off the Pont Neuf.

"Even then, it still apparently wasn't enough blood for her," Julienne went on, gingerly touching her own lower lip. "She needed to bloody *me* up as well. The chit's as skinny as a broom handle, and screaming for her mother like a little child. And yet she packs a punch like a circus strongman. It took two brigadiers and Claude to get her inside—and even then we had to drop her once."

"What, she's that heavy?" Céline asked, frowning.

"Not heavy. *Wild*. She caught Claude in the jewels with one of her kicks."

Several of the other girls smirked. Claude was a black-haired giant of a Basque who never failed to let fly some off-color comment or invitation when he passed almost anyone of the opposite sex, often accompanied by a backside pinch. A few weeks earlier he'd tried to back me into the Hysteria linen closet with him, though he'd abandoned the effort when Babette swept by, pinning us both with her withering glare. If the new girl had managed to take both him and Julienne down a notch, she'd earned my respect already.

"What I don't understand," Julienne went on, "is why the *flics* didn't get her into a jacket while she was still in the ambulance. It would have made things so much easier."

"They didn't think they needed one," offered a male attendant sitting across from us, a lanky youth with protruding ears and hair that for some reason always reminded me of mouse fur. "Fellow I spoke to said she was out the whole trip. Fell to the ground insensible soon as they pried her off the balustrades. Like she'd been hit in the head with a mallet." He shrugged. "Seems she was missing her stockings as well as a boot, and was covered with bruises and scrapes." He gave a leering wink. "Didn't *look* like she'd be much of a problem, in that state."

This detail—the bare legs, that one bare foot—caught my attention too. At first I recalled that waking image I'd had of Amélie, skipping barefoot in our courtyard. But it was also impossible not to imagine the kinds of violating acts that had led to the girl's bruised and bare-legged condition. That no one at the table bothered to say as much was a testament to just how common such injuries were in incoming patients to Hysteria. Indeed, in my experience, nearly every woman in our ward had suffered them in some form or another. In lucid conversation, hysterics referred to these traumas obliquely, eyes averted, voices hushed. During their fits, though, they screamed and wailed and sobbed openly about them, reliving them in their minds. Rosalie's reenactments of her own ordeal—involving the man who'd taken her virginity at fourteen—were especially wrenching to witness.

Curiously, Charcot himself took little interest in these agonized articulations, dismissing them as further evidence of the hysteric's voracious need for attention. "A lot of noise over nothing," he'd pronounce as whichever *internée* he happened to be discussing or examining wept and ranted at his feet. What interested him, rather, was the language of the female *body*, its corporeal expressions of temperature, heart rate, pulse. Its secretions. Its sensitivity—or lack thereof—to needles and probes, or the influences of various magnets and metals. This language he listened to with the attentiveness of a priest in a confessional booth, or of Samuel listening to God.

For my part, after hearing so many of these women's accounts, though—horrifically different in detail but brutally alike at their core—I had come to see them differently. I'd also begun taking them down in my journal, translating my wardmates' frenzied words and flailing limbs into the events they seemed to be struggling so desperately to depict, just as I'd written—in meticulous detail—about my own suffering in losing my home and family. I wasn't quite sure why I felt compelled to take down these narratives. I only knew they somehow *mattered;* that those who screamed or cried or whispered of their miseries did so because they needed to be heard.

"Did you hear what happened once they got her to Hydrotherapy?" Céline was saying, distractedly offering me a tarnished spoon without seeming to have noticed that she hadn't yet given me any porridge.

"No, what?" asked Julienne.

"Disaster. The minute the jets hit her she broke free from the chair. Just pulled right out of the cuffs."

"Really?" Julienne lifted a brow. "I've never heard of a *folle* doing *that.*"

I hadn't either. I'd experienced the hoses myself when I was admitted, and while my memories of that time remain as muddled as subaquatic dreams, I remember the paralyzing force of that icy water all too well. It had left me with barely the strength to draw a breath, much less break free from my restraints.

"It's true," the maid said. "She's got a contraction in one foot, mind you. But she still ran—stark naked—for the door, slipping and sliding. The technician had to sit on her to keep her still."

"I'd have thought she'd have liked the water," the mouse-haired attendant mused. "She was going on about it when they brought her in, wasn't she? About wanting to throw herself into the Seine?"

"I'll throw her in," Julienne muttered, touching her handkerchief to her lip. "Just give me half the chance." Setting the blood-dotted little cloth back down, she picked up her mug, attempting to take a sip from it before wincing and setting it back down as well. "The little tramp," she said, pouting. "I'll likely need a stitch."

"Which ward is she to be sent to?" I asked.

Julienne blinked, as though she'd forgotten I was there and was mildly annoyed by the reminder that I was. She'd been one of Babette's personal hires—I think they were distantly related—and I sensed that she shared the old woman's view that my former social standing and education somehow constituted a threat to her.

"They still haven't been able to assess her," she said. "She won't even give anyone her name. Just kept screeching *don't touch me* and *they are coming* over and over. After the hoses, she stopped talking altogether. Just more of that awful screaming." Glumly, she dunked her roll into her coffee. "They finally had the sense to etherize and jacket her—that's the only way they could get her to the softs. And, of course, I'm the one Babette assigns to bring her meals there. I've half a mind to let her skip breakfast altogether."

"You mean not bring it to her?"

"Why should I wait on her like a lady's maid, given what she's done to me?"

"The doctors won't like that."

"Oh, so *you* know what the doctors like and don't like now?" she shot back archly. "I'll just say I brought it. It's not as if they'll take her word over mine."

She glared at me, daring me to contradict or snitch on her. But I'd long ago learned that where Julienne was concerned, it was better to keep a low profile.

Instead—and somewhat to my own surprise—I said: "I can do it."

Julienne frowned over her dripping bread. "Do what?"

"Breakfast. I can bring it to her."

She narrowed her eyes. Black as pitch and heavily lashed, they served to soften what was otherwise a decidedly foxlike face. Men found her pretty, though I'd long stopped seeing it.

"Why would you want to do that?" she asked.

I was already asking myself the same question. I had so much work already, and so few moments to myself, that I already half regretted the offer. And yet the girl's story had piqued my interest—and Julienne's vows of revenge on her stuck in my throat like a lump of swallowed chalk. I had little doubt, moreover, that Julienne would follow through on them, given how vicious she could be toward patients in general. She'd once laughingly told one of the *reposantes* outside—an old lunatic who insisted her long-dead poodle was still attached to the end of the filthy leash she carried around—that the animal had been crushed to death beneath the laundry trolley's iron wheels. "Look," Julienne had said, offering up a chicken bone she'd saved from lunch, seemingly expressly for this purpose. "This was all that was left of the poor creature."

And she'd laughed as the old woman's face crumpled in grief.

"I have to go to the kitchen anyway, to order Rosalie's breakfast," I told her now. This was true: On lecture days Rosalie demanded (and was granted) yet another special meal in the ward. "If I bring the new one's tray to the softs afterward, you can go to the infirmary. You do look like you might need a stitch."

I was almost sure she'd refuse, if only out of spite. There was in general a kind of wall between the ward girls who, like myself, were former Salpêtrière patients and those who, like Julienne, had never been "inside." The simple truth was that we didn't trust one another. Those who had never been patients had little faith in those of us who had, perhaps suspecting that our true loyalties still lay with our former fellow *internées*. And they weren't entirely wrong—at least, not in my case.

Now, though, Julienne nodded curtly. "Fine," she said. "She's in number three. No cutlery."

"How is she supposed to eat?"

"Should I care?" Julienne snapped. "She should have thought of that before trying to tear my face off."

I considered rescinding my offer, unsure whether I wanted to have anything to do with a patient so desperate, dangerous, and apparently doomed. Looking back now, I sometimes wonder what path my life would have taken had I done so. Would I still be in Hysteria, dutifully emptying bedpans and dispensing ether, as sealed away in my own misery as any unfortunate locked in a cell? Or would she have found some other way into my narrow and pathetic universe, completely turning it on end?

It's something I'll never know, since Julienne was already clambering to her feet. "Don't forget to tell Babette I'm in the infirmary," she called over her shoulder. "I don't want her to think I'm being a sluggard."

"I won't," I called back, though I was sorely tempted to do just that.

A short time later I found myself carrying a tray of bread and soup to the isolation unit below the lunacy ward. The area had once housed the old loges—dank, cavelike cells in which lunatics had languished, chained to the walls, their bare toes dragging in puddles and gnawed at by rats, their cellblocks guarded by jailers with dogs. The area had been renovated since then. But it was still a rank, gloomy place, lit only by the kerosene lamps hung at intervals along the brick wall.

When I got there, I saw to my dismay that Claude—the Basque attendant whom the new girl had reportedly kicked in the groin— was on duty, and as lecherous as ever. After he'd inspected the tray to confirm its lack of forks, spoons, and knives, he lifted my skirt with the same leisurely ease with which he'd lifted the tin plate to look beneath it.

"Too good for me, Princesse?" he asked when I slapped his hand away. It was a nickname he'd given me upon learning that I'd been at boarding school.

"I have work," I snapped back, stepping out of range. "Key, please?"

Shrugging, he detached the key for the cell's food slot and flipped it onto the tray. "Careful. She's a she-wolf, that one. Split Julienne's lip right open." He made no mention of his supposedly damaged "jewels."

Turning, I carried the tray and key a few steps farther down the ward hallway as he settled heavily back into his chair. Setting the tray on the floor, I pressed my ear against the steel door of the cell that had a large black *No. 3* painted above the frame. I heard no sound but the Basque's heavy breathing behind me.

I had to kneel to fit the key's jagged teeth into the lock. After wrestling the rusted slat cover open, it took a minute for my sight to adjust to the weak light within. When it did, at first I could only see a patch of dirty, canvas-padded wall. It was only upon angling my gaze to the right that I made out a small, still shape pressed into the room's darkest corner.

For a confused instant I thought Julienne had sent me to the wrong room. This girl—if it even was a girl; it was that hard to tell—looked nothing at all like the ruthless warrioress described at breakfast. Her frame looked slight, almost frail, her hair not wild and red but dark and stringy. And the straitjacket Julienne had mentioned was nowhere to be seen, though maybe she'd gotten that part wrong. For all the ingenuity of her various cruelties the girl wasn't the sharpest blade in the kitchen.

"Good morning," I called softly. "I have breakfast, if you're hungry."

There was no response, and for an instant I feared the girl had found a way to make good on her threats to do away with herself, even stripped (as I knew she was) of any belts, hairpins, or shoelaces that she might have used for that purpose. Or perhaps, I thought, she'd been killed by the violence of her own spasms. It happened on occasion: *malignant catatonia*, the doctors called it. I'd written that down in my journal as well.

I tried again. "Hello? Would you like something to eat?"

Barely discernibly, the shape stiffened, the movement dislodging a wad of heavy fabric the girl had been using as a pillow. Recognizing the straitjacket, I felt another prickling of unease. I'd never known a patient able to free herself from one.

For a second time I considered fleeing back to the more familiar derangements of the hysteria ward. Then, though, the girl turned toward me. Something about her—the raw bewilderment, the vulnerability, or perhaps the faint outline of one bare, filthy foot—kept me rooted to the spot.

"Who are you?" she whispered.

"My name is Laure," I replied. "I work here."

"Where am I?"

"The Salpêtrière."

She stared at me blankly. I clarified: "The women's asylum."

She said nothing, though it seemed to me that I could see her turning the word—*asylum*—over in her mind, gingerly touching her lip with her little finger. As my eyes adjusted further I saw her wrist and forearm were covered with angry blue-black bruises, many of them no larger than a thumb tip.

I felt my breath catch: I knew those bruises. I'd seen them on so many of the girls who came here.

"How long . . ." Her voice trailed off.

"You came in last night." I peered at her. "You don't remember anything?"

"I remember the bell."

"What bell?"

She opened her mouth to speak. Then she shut it, her expression turning opaque. "It's all blank," she said. "As if I've never lived before now."

I looked back at Claude. He appeared to have fallen asleep, eyes closed, big head lolling against the ward wall.

"You don't remember the ambulance?" I asked, dropping my voice to a near-whisper. "Or the river?" Recalling Julienne's description of the startling state of the girl's apron upon arriving, I added: "Not the blood? They said your apron was covered in it."

At *blood* she winced, glancing down at her left hand. It was wrapped in a dingy-looking bandage through which blood appeared to have seeped heavily at one point, though it had dried into a brownish smear now.

"No," she said. "Nothing at all."

"It's all right," I told her quickly. "A lot of girls here forget things."

Which was true. I myself have no clear memory of my own admission to the Salpêtrière, though I remember all too clearly the desperate days leading to it. Remember how, exhausted from nursing and then burying Papa, and then nursing Amélie when she fell ill shortly thereafter, I'd creep out early enough to elude the creditors who seemed always to lie in wait for us outside, circumventing the growing pile of payment notices they left in their wake. How each time I left I took with me some item from Papa's office—a leather-bound anatomy book, a boxed medical scale—to bring to a nearby *mont-de-piété* in exchange for a salmon-colored ticket and a few francs to keep the two of us fed and the kitchen stove fueled for another day. How I methodically worked my way through my father's poorly organized accounts, visiting clients who still owed him for his services and—when they refused payment (as, incredibly, all of them did)— begging for any sort of work they might be able to offer me, a request that was also dismissed.

What I don't remember: coming back one day after yet another rejection and realizing there was no food with which to feed my sister, and no money with which to buy more food. I don't remember collapsing, and seizing, and hitting my head against the grate so hard it left a lump the size of a quail egg. Nor do I recall being carried out; nor the week I'm told I spent in the hysteria ward during which I obsessively tended some phantom patient whom only I, in my delirium, could see.

Perhaps strangely, though, I do remember Amélie's cries, begging the police she'd summoned not to take me, not to leave her alone. It was the last time I'd hear her voice in our home.

My next memory is waking woozily in the ward, racked with nausea, the metallic tang of ether on my tongue. Babette stood over me, and her craggy features swirled and spun before my eyes for a moment before falling into a recognizable pattern, like crystals settling in a kaleidoscope.

"Ah," she said. "You've come back."

"Where . . . where am I?" I stammered, just as this girl just had.

The old woman's nearly hairless brows twitched as if the question amused her. "You're at the Salpêtrière. You've been here a full week."

And in that instant it had felt as if the bed had dropped out from beneath me, shackles and all.

"Are you hungry?" I asked the new girl now. "I have your breakfast here. I'm afraid that you'll have to use your fingers."

She shook her head.

"You should try," I coaxed her. "I know you're probably feeling sick from the ether. But if you don't eat on your own, they'll force you to."

She just tightened her lips. Sighing, I tried a new tack. "Anyway, you'll need energy for the next part of the process."

Her brow creased. "What next part?"

"Your assessment. They'll examine you and decide on your diagnosis."

"My *diagnosis*?" She gave a short, bleak-sounding laugh. "Isn't that why I'm here? Because they think I'm mad?"

"There are different kinds of madness," I said carefully.

She gave me an odd look. "Mad," she said, "is mad."

I hesitated, wondering if she'd truly never heard anything about the great Charcot and his hospital. If she had, she'd have known that here—of all places—mad was never simply mad.

"Anyway," she continued, "what does it even matter what kind of mad they think I am?"

Her voice was listless, all but toneless. But she seemed to be sitting just a little bit straighter now. Brushing her tangled hair back off her forehead, she also seemed for the first time to be trying to make my own features out through the slot. I could finally see hers clearly: Her face was heart-shaped; her nose small, fine, and turned up delicately at the end; her skin sprinkled generously with tea-toned freckles. I felt my breath hitch again: Even in that dim, dank light, and covered in grime and the bruises, she was heart-stoppingly lovely. For a moment I almost couldn't speak.

"It matters," I said, collecting myself. "Especially when you're a patient."

"How would you know? You're not a patient."

"I was, though. Until just recently."

"And being here made you better?"

I hesitated again. "Better enough."

Outside, the chapel bell tolled the half hour, reminding me that Babette would be wondering where I was, and that Rosalie—if not already awake of her own accord—would need to be roused. I'd impulsively wanted to help this girl, yes. But it wasn't worth risking my position. Not when I had nowhere else to go, and needed a plan to find my sister.

I angled the tray into the slot, the tin cup just barely clearing its metal edge. "Last chance," I murmured. "I'm needed back in my ward."

Silence. I could tell she still hadn't moved.

"All right, then, don't eat. But at least take some advice."

She turned toward me, her face wary.

"Don't hurt anyone else," I said. "*Especially* not the male attendants. They'll only find ways to hurt you back. And it'll increase the odds of your ending up in the lunacy ward."

"Lunacy?" She repeated the word as though having heard it for the first time. "Aren't all the wards here for lunacy?"

I bit my lip, wondering how to even begin explaining it to her: The vast difference between Lunacy and Hysteria. That the two were as far apart as hell and heaven. That Lunacy, located in the tumble-down Rambuteau building, was a place of unwashed bodies and decay-filled mouths, of a sick-sweet scent I recall to this day even though I've never smelled it anywhere else. It was a place of mean-ingless movements signaling drawn-out deaths: the tremblings and quakings of the Parkinson's patients, the demented ravings and foot-slapping walks of the syphilitics. And that was before one even reached the foul-smelling, triple-locked back rooms of the *unité des incurables*—the dreaded incurables unit, where they kept the truly hopeless cases.

Hysteria, by contrast—situated in the slightly less shabby Esquirol facility—was a place of unpredictable rhythms: one minute as hum-drum and uneventful as a convent, the next filled with contorting bodies and screeching voices. It could be nerve-shatteringly noisy, mind-bogglingly petty—even physically dangerous if you got too close to a flailing limb, a spasm-jerked skull, or one of Rosalie's increasingly violent tantrums. But it was also a place of unexpected freedom. Unlike the vast majority of its lunatics, most of Salpêtrière's hysterics had free run of the asylum grounds. They worked in its workshops, took exercise in its gymnasium, roamed the campus with friends and family on visiting days. Rosalie was even allowed shopping excursions in the city—though only when supervised by an attendant (I myself had taken her to Bon Marché two weeks earlier, to have her fitted for a new corset).

Hysteria was even a place of a certain kind of pride. For hadn't Charcot himself—the most famous doctor in all of France—made our malady the focus of his current study? And didn't he often use us as subjects in his famed Friday Lessons? And didn't the younger doctors who worshipped him—future luminaries including Georges Gilles de la Tourette, Joseph Babinski, Pierre Janet, and Sigmund Freud—spend hours examining, experimenting on, and writing about us, using our symptoms as quivering rungs on a ladder by which they could clamber to the very tops of their respective fields?

Behind me, the Basque gave a theatrical yawn. "You're still here, Princesse?"

"I was just trying to get her to take the food."

"If she won't take it, take it back. That's the rule."

I sighed, though I knew he was right. Just as I began withdrawing the tray, though, it jerked suddenly in my hands: She'd come to take it after all. As it disappeared into the cell, I quickly lowered my face to the slot.

She was right on the other side now, close enough that I could smell her—a mixture of stale breath and dried sweat, but also something faintly floral, like almond blossom. I could see now that there were angry-looking bruises around her neck as well. The sight made my own throat tighten almost painfully.

But it was her gaze I felt the most. It was like a physical slap, wide and clear and startlingly green. As our eyes locked I felt my cheeks heat, felt a tingling jolt make its way through my body. As though I were connected to one of Charcot's electrotherapy wires.

I heard the Basque's heavy footsteps approaching upon the tiled floor. "Now, Princesse," he said. "Don't get too close. You heard what she did to Julienne, didn't you?"

When I looked up he was hovering over me, glancing suspiciously between the open meal slot and my unsettled expression. "What are you two chatting about, anyway?" he asked, scratching his groin and wincing slightly.

"Nothing." Slamming the slot cover back into place, I set about locking it. For some reason my hands were trembling. "I was—I was explaining she'd have to eat without utensils."

As I climbed to my feet, he gave me another bemused look before giving the metal door a rap with his keys. The resulting *crack* was so sudden and sharp that it sounded like a rifle retort.

"Mark my words," he said, grinning. "That's going to be the least of her troubles in this place."

Chapter Three

"As if that's not enough, she's apparently deaf, too," Rosalie scoffed.

About two hours had passed. The Alsatian was staring balefully out to where Charcot stood in the stage lights, stooping over his lecture's first subject. Clotilde, a whey-haired slip of a hysteric whose arms and legs were dotted with cigar-tip-shaped scars, sat slumped in a wooden chair, her head lolling to one side.

"Mademoiselle," Charcot repeated, lifting his voice slightly. "I asked whether you can hear me."

Clotilde shifted sleepily. "*Oui, Docteur,*" she said. The words emerged thickly, as though it required enormous effort to push them through her slackened lips.

"Do you know where you are?"

"In the amphitheater," she said drowsily. "On the stage."

"Correct," Charcot affirmed. "Do you know what it was that woke you?"

"Why, you did."

"No. You were awoken by a sudden pain on your arm." Taking her wrist, Charcot held it up, brushing a spot just past her elbow with his thumb. "Here," he said decisively. "It hurts because I am holding a candle above it. The candle is dripping hot wax right on this spot. Can you feel it?"

Clotilde jerked up in her seat. "*Ah*," she cried. "Yes! Take it away!" Her voice was shrill enough that I started. I noticed several others in the audience did as well.

The hysteric tried to pull her arm back, but Charcot held her fast. "Can you feel the wax?" he intoned, as calmly as though he were making an observation about the weather. "Your skin is very soft in that spot. I'm sure it must be quite painful."

"It is," Clotilde said. Her eyes were fully open now, unfocused but wide in distress. "It is! Why won't you take it away?"

Charcot didn't seem to hear her. Still holding her firmly, he stared down at the spot he'd indicated, his eyes narrowing in concentration. As Clotilde continued to writhe and protest, some audience members gazed around in puzzlement, as though unsure how they were supposed to be responding. My own stomach tightened uncomfortably, even though I knew Charcot was merely highlighting an intriguing symptom of his subject's illness, as he'd done with countless other symptoms and subjects before her. His protégés were clearly taking the exercise in the same way; most seemed more focused on jotting down the great man's words than questioning what he was actually doing.

Rosalie, for her part, merely seemed further annoyed. "So much *whining*," she muttered, wrinkling her powdered nose. "You'd think he was slicing off her whole arm." But I saw that her gaze was no longer on Clotilde but on a spot in the front row of the seating pit. Those seats were usually reserved for members of the medical community and other "special guests"—including, in past weeks, the author Guy de Maupassant, who'd written about hypnosis, hysteria, and even Charcot himself in several of his short stories.

But the spot that Rosalie was looking at now was occupied not by the famous and rather dashing author but by a coarse-faced man in livery of pale blue and mustard yellow. He was energetically blowing his nose, looking distinctly out of place amid the doctors, interns, and assorted medical students with their cigars, aprons, and battered evening hats.

"Do you know whose man that is?" I murmured. "In the blue-and-yellow uniform?"

"Why would I?" she retorted.

But she avoided my eyes as she said it. My inner alarm grew louder.

"Please!" Clotilde's tone was turning tearful. "Why are you hurting me like this? Why do men always *hurt* me?"

"Sometimes the treatment seems more painful than the ailment," Charcot said briskly, his dark eyes still fixed on her skin. "But trust me. You will feel better soon enough."

He seemed to be waiting for something, and though I had no idea what it was, I found myself holding my breath.

Then he grunted, his eyes brightening. "*Et voilà!*" he proclaimed.

Lifting Clotilde's arm like a trophy, he turned back to his audience. "As I noted earlier, while there was evidence of other burns on this arm prior to this exercise, there was no such mark in the spot in question. Now, however, there appears to be a newly irritated area on the patient's forearm of approximately two to three centimeters in diameter. It bears all the hallmarks of a superficial burn. I expect there will be blistering there within a few hours."

The audience gasped in astonishment. Those in the three front rows were scribbling furiously on their clipboards and notebook pages, while those behind them, in the general seating area, whispered in muted wonder.

I fully understood their amazement. Not even two years earlier I, too, would have been stunned if I'd witnessed what they just had. The truth was that before becoming hysterical myself, all I'd known about the malady was what I'd read about it in the newspapers or heard from my father, who, like all doctors in the city, had confronted a dramatic rise in hysteria cases in recent years.

Like Charcot, my father had seen hysteria as at least in part a reflection of the dizzying pace at which modern society operated, the result of our inability to keep up with the hurtling speed with which we now traveled from one place to the next, and the even more hurtling speed with which information, image, and sound passed through telegraph wires, gramophone speakers, and the very air itself. Papa's prescription to his wealthy hysterics, however, was in stark contrast to Charcot's mandated regime for his far poorer ones: a "rest cure" involving no physical or mental exertion and lots of bland and milk-based foods. Many of them took it in the country estates they maintained, or else leased for that purpose.

All this I knew, of course. But before entering the Salpêtrière, I'd had no idea of the astonishing *range* of conditions associated with hysteria—conditions that to me, at least, often bordered on the fantastical. I'd seen bellies swell during hysterical pregnancies and breasts that expressed hysterical milk. I'd seen girls become so rigid that they could be laid across the backs of two chairs like logs, and hysterics push darning needles through numbed palms without flinching. (Even Bernadette claimed to have felt "nothing, nothing at all" when she'd clipped her nipple from her breast some years earlier.) Other hysterics suffered hysterical "yawns" that lasted days, leaving them wandering about with mouths stretched wide, like tortured figures from a Munch painting. I'd seen the palms of hysterical hands and the soles of hysterical feet weep real tears of blood, which—when wiped away—revealed no sign of any wounds. I'd even tended a patient who'd inexplicably forgotten her French and could only communicate (haltingly) in German, which she claimed to have never studied. I still have no explanation for these events, any more than I can explain why some hysterics lost their contractions when they seized, while others, like Rosalie, suffered contractions solely during their fits. Or, for that matter, why I was one of the very few of all these poor women who'd actually and fully recovered from the disease.

What I do know—what I will go to my grave averring—is that with very few exceptions, the symptoms I witnessed there were *real*. They were not, as Charcot's critics were even then beginning to charge, the result of trickery on our parts, or subconscious coercion on his. They may have been unpredictable in duration and presentation—it wasn't uncommon for a hysteric to go to sleep with one symptom and awake with another, a contracted arm replaced by a numbed tongue, blindness inexplicably morphing into dumbness. But the illness underlying them all was the same: some strange, alchemical interaction between our tortured psyches and our abused bodies, between the intolerable experiences we struggled to banish from our thoughts and the fragile physiques that fell victim to that struggle.

Above all else, though, it was *real*. Just as the events I lay out for you in these pages are real. They were improbable—incredible, even. But they happened.

Rosalie, however, was clearly less than impressed by Clotilde's remotely induced wound. "A *superficial* burn!" she sniffed. "Why, I'd have blistered ten times as badly. They'd have had to carry me straight to the infirmary. I don't know why he even used her in the first place. Last week, he said he was going to write about *my* stigmatic symptoms for that English journal—what was it? *The Lancelot?*"

"*The Lancet,*" I said, correcting her. My father had kept every biannual issue—bound in gleaming brown leather—dating back to his École de Médecine days. "And I'm sure you would have done better. Perhaps he only chose Clotilde for this because he didn't want to overtax you—he's probably putting you in a much bigger and more important exercise."

I had no idea if this was true, but I was hoping to placate her before her stage appearance. Even by her own violently mercurial standards, Rosalie had been exceptionally bad-tempered all morning. When Babette announced that Clotilde had been added last minute to the lecture's program, the Alsatian had seemingly taken it as a personal insult, declaring she had half a mind not to go onstage at all if she had to share it with a "little lying nobody." I'd only gotten her to the amphitheater by pointing out that boycotting it would result in Clotilde's being featured in any newspaper coverage of the lecture, rather than Rosalie herself. She adored seeing herself in the news.

"Besides," I added, again hoping to appeal to her vanity, "do you *want* a scar on your arm? Your skin is so lovely."

She ignored me, watching with narrowed eyes as Dr. Babinski, the

tallest and handsomest of Charcot's interns, finished counting Clotilde down from her trance and began helping the groggy but now-
lucid girl to her feet.

"As I noted earlier," Charcot said, resuming his lecture, "the pain
suffered by hysterics is often unaccompanied by any correlating signs
of physical trauma." He'd absently tucked his hand into the opening
of his vest as he spoke, a conscious or unconscious echoing of Napoléon the First, whom some said he resembled. "In this case, however, our hypnotic suggestion did produce a minor wound on the
subject's arm. One of the many mysteries of this curious disease re-
lates to why such stigmata appear in some cases but not others. A
larger question, though, is why do *any* of these symptoms appear?
And who is most likely to suffer from them? It is my belief that
hysteria—much like other neurological disorders—does not grow all
by itself, like a mushroom. It is, rather, *hereditarily transmitted*. A kind of
cellular Sword of Damocles that lurks not overhead but in the blood,
awaiting a triggering event. I will explain this theory by introducing
my next subject."

Turning his head, Charcot caught my eye and nodded: our cue.

"You're on," I whispered. Taking hold of Rosalie's arm, I took a
hurried step toward the stage—only to find myself anchored firmly
in place.

She wasn't moving.

"Come," I murmured. Thinking she somehow hadn't heard, I
tugged her arm. She still didn't respond, the dense weight of her as
fixed in place as if her feet were rooted to the wooden floor.

"What are you *doing*?" I whispered.

She just stared past me, her gaze empty of expression. Could she
be having another fit? I grasped her wrist to check her pulse, my own
pulse beating thickly in my ears. Rosalie's seemed a little fast, but not
very much more so than usual. I shook her shoulder again. "Rosalie!" I hissed. "You'll make him angry!"

Normally, the mere thought of sparking Charcot's infamous temper struck fear in the heart of anyone in his orbit. But it had abso-

lutely no impact on Rosalie now. She merely gazed ahead blankly, her lips tight and her pointed chin lifted.

By now my heart was racing. If I couldn't get her onstage immediately Charcot would almost certainly fire me. He'd dismissed other attendants for far less. I'd end up on the streets, without a sou to my name, and lose even whatever slim chance I had at finding Amélie.

I gave Rosalie another shake. Then, desperate, I slapped her rouged cheek. It wasn't a particularly hard slap—more a kind of forceful tap. But she reacted, letting out a little scream I was sure the audience could hear. Clearly Charcot had, for out of the corner of my eye I saw his white head swivel in our direction, and felt his dark eyes burning into us both.

"*Shhhh!*" I hushed her frantically. "He wants you now. Let's *go!*" And taking her arm, I attempted once more to lead her out into the spotlights.

"Don't *touch* me," she hissed, jerking from my grasp.

She seemed to waver then, and for an instant I thought she'd turn and flee back out the passageway. Instead, she set off onto the stage at a virtual sprint, her strong legs pumping beneath her skirts like a working girl competing in the annual Parisien Race of the Midinettes. I started after her, then stopped again abruptly, realizing that the two of us stumbling out like drunken marauders would look even worse than Rosalie's careening onto the stage on her own.

At a loss, I looked across the stage to where Charcot's secretary, Pierre Marie, had just settled Clotilde into a chair near the interns. He frowned and held a hand up: *Stay there.*

By now the audience had spotted the Salpêtrière's star hysteric. I heard another explosion of gasps and excited whispers, as though Rita Sangalli had just leapt onto the Opéra's stage in her *pointes.* "That's *her,*" I heard. "The Alsatian!" Even in the midst of my dismay, I couldn't help marveling at the way the mood in the room had instantaneously shifted. It was more attentive, even, than it had been with Clotilde—and another crowd entirely from the one that had sat through the lecture's first hour, which Charcot had devoted to railway spine. Like all of his presentations, it had been impressive, delivered with the force and flow of a well-rehearsed play, peppered with Shakespearian references and deft asides in Charcot's fluent Italian, German, English, and Latin. He'd mimicked symptoms of other disorders—the shuffling gait of advanced syphilis, the vacant gaze of Parkinson's disease—so realistically he'd seemed to briefly transform into his own patients. All the while, the audience had looked on with polite appreciation. But there had been none of the barely suppressed excitement that filled the room now like the electric pause before a storm. *This* was the moment for which all these people had come today, piling into the auditorium with the giddiness of circus-goers.

As Rosalie tripped toward center stage every eye in the room seemed glued to her, every breath bated as the audience awaited her next move. I knew she relished that attention. I also knew that I would never experience it myself, for I would never be on Charcot's stage. That much had been made clear from my first encounter with the great doctor—or at least, the first one I remembered after emerging from my weeklong mental fugue. It was there, shivering in my shift before a row of white-aproned men who'd just poked and prodded me in every way imaginable, that the full bleakness of my predicament had been explained to me: Not only was I an orphan, newly destitute, separated indefinitely from my sister, and cursed with one of the most puzzling diseases of our time.

But I was also, as it turned out, incapable of being hypnotized.

The news was delivered with the grim solemnity of a courtroom "guilty" verdict, after a series of doctors—Babinski, Janet, Gilles de la Tourette, and finally Charcot himself—had held ringing tuning forks by my ears and winking mirrors before my eyes. After it had become amply clear that for all their suggestions that I felt my *eyelids becoming heavy,* that I was *becoming sleepy,* that I was, *in fact, now fast asleep,* I was in fact none of those things. I was merely bereft, baffled, and teeth-chatteringly cold from standing in the February air in my undershift. When they finally sent me back to Hysteria, I felt little more than relief.

What I hadn't realized then—what would only dawn on me in the months that followed—was that I'd just failed a central test of my worth at the Salpêtrière. It was a lesson I came to understand quickly enough, though, for never once did Charcot summon me back to his clinic for further evaluation, or to illustrate some notable symptom to his students or his steady stream of distinguished visitors. And he certainly never selected me for his Friday morning lectures. Even my seemingly inexplicable recovery from hysteria a year later held scant interest for the man who was, by then, considered the world's leading expert on the famously impenetrable disease. On the day of my release, he perfunctorily checked my pulse, heart rate, and temperature, then discharged me with a gruff instruction: *Keep your thoughts in the here and now, Laure. The past can be dangerous territory for those suffering nervous disorders.*

And with that, he'd hurried off to examine a new patient who claimed to be a man trapped inside a woman's body.

In the bleak months that followed, as I ferried sloshing chamber pots and emptied fetid slops buckets and stripped soiled bedsheets and scrubbed grime from the splinter-worn floorboards, Babette's hard-as-steel eyes following me at every turn, I was unable to shake the feeling that my recovery was not, in fact, something to celebrate, but confirmation of my utter *failure* as a hysteric. That somehow, of all the shameful things I'd experienced in those bleak months as a patient—the unpredictable fits and self-inflicted scrapes, bruises, and injuries; the humiliating incontinence, the terrifying helplessness of coming to see my own body as a weapon deployed against itself—my inability to be entranced was the most shameful of all.

Stopping short by the chair Clotilde had just vacated, Rosalie wobbled a moment, as though thrown off-balance by the drama of her own entrance. Charcot's dark gaze flicked in her direction, registering her belated appearance. But he did nothing to acknowledge it.

"In the old days," he went on instead, as though nothing had happened, "hysteria was thought to be caused by the uterus in its barren state, roaming about the female body in search of purpose. The ancient Greeks believed it could be lured back to its rightful post by placing appealing smells—spices or flowers, for instance—near the vaginal cavity, and placing offensive smells near the nose and mouth." He paused briefly before adding, with perfect raconteur timing: "Inducing sneezing was also thought to be efficacious."

The audience chuckled. I was still trying to steady my breathing, certain that the worst was over. But another rippling of whispers drew my gaze back to the stage. To my dismay, Rosalie had not, as I'd anticipated, seated herself in the chair Clotilde had vacated. Instead, she'd positioned herself directly *next* to Charcot, as one of his interns might have. Her chin was lifted, her lips curved in the slightest hint of a smile, like a schoolboy testing a new schoolmaster.

Charcot, however, continued to ignore her. "Needless to say," he declared, "our understanding of the malady has evolved." He motioned to Monsieur Londe, a heavyset and luxuriantly bearded man who headed the asylum's new photography studio, and who now stood by a kind of electrical lantern he'd developed to project photographs onto a canvas screen. Looking faintly confused, the latter slipped a plate into his "megascope" and turned the device on. The crowd let out a collective gasp, as it almost always did at this moment. Few of them had ever seen photographs projected in this manner—much less photographs of the Salpêtrière's startling hysterics. This one was of Rosalie, her gaze turned upward, her left hand lifted as if in entreaty. Her right hand, though, remained clenched at her side and jutting out at a painful-looking angle from her wrist, as it always was during her seizures.

The photo was likely taken by another of Monsieur Londe's inventions, an enormous camera sporting nine winking lenses and connected to a ticking metronome via a snarl of electrical wiring that he'd christened the "photoelectric," though it reminded me less of a camera than of the hundred-eyed Argus of Greek mythology. I'd heard Charcot was delighted with the thing, though, as it allowed him to break a hysteric's frenzied spasms and postures into a neat sequence of still images that he could later examine at his leisure.

"Here is a patient," he announced now. "We shall call her Blanche W." He gestured toward Rosalie as he used her stage name, as unperturbed by her location as if he'd instructed her to stand shoulder-to-shoulder with him himself. "She arrived at our institution some five years ago," he went on, "in the position of ward attendant in our hysteria and epilepsy ward. Initially, she displayed no sign of hysteria herself, so it might be tempting to conclude she simply 'caught' her own case of it from the hysterics she was then attending. With careful interrogation, however, we can trace the true roots of her disorder to the prior generation."

He nodded at Rosalie. "Tell us about your mother and father, if you please."

Rosalie cocked her head thoughtfully, her golden hair gleaming in the stage lights. She licked her lips. I felt the audience leaning forward again, as though she were Cassandra about to deliver a prophecy.

Then—to my astonishment—she shook her head.

There was an audible storm of gasps across the room then, like the sound of scores of rubber balloons deflating. *She's going through with it,* I thought incredulously. *She's sabotaging his lecture.* For all her earlier threats to do just that, the idea was shocking to me.

Charcot repeated his question, his tone and inflection unchanged. Once more, Rosalie shook her head. She wasn't even looking at him. Her eyes were fixed on an enormous painting that hung on the amphitheater's back wall, a reproduction of one that had caused a stir at the Paris Salon two years earlier, *A Clinical Lesson at the Salpêtrière.* In it, Rosalie, with her shirtwaist down and her corset unlaced, swooned into Babinski's strong arms. The painted Charcot stood nearby, his hand outstretched like a pontiff giving a benediction, his expression sanguine.

His real-life counterpart, however, looked distinctly less pleased. After shooting Rosalie a cold glance, he turned back to face his audience. "What we appear to have here," he said crisply, "is an example of hysterical defiance. As with many hysterical behaviors, it is largely intended as a tactic to draw attention to the hysteric herself, for as I've often noted, hysterics *thrive* on attention. The best response on the practitioner's part is to simply pay it no heed. Once a hysteric recognizes a trick is failing to work, they will usually choose another from their arsenal—which is invariably well supplied."

He said all this with his usual authoritative delivery, as though Rosalie's rebellion were nothing more than a preplanned aspect of his lecture. I saw her blue eyes shift uncertainly, then widen as they settled somewhere on the front row. Looking there myself, I caught my breath again: The horse-faced servant had disappeared. In his place was an elderly man in a sateen suit and matching top hat. His eyes—one glinting behind a silver-rimmed monocle, but both so pale that from where I stood they appeared almost colorless—were locked unblinkingly on to Rosalie's cornflower-blue ones.

I'd seen the marquis once before, when a Venetian mask had covered half his face. But it hadn't covered those weirdly colorless eyes; the same eyes that, back in March, had remained fixed on Rosalie throughout the whole of the Bal des Folles, through every giggle and simpering dance step. It was clearly the same man—the attempted landau abductor, the sender of the forbidden fruit basket and all the other gifts that Babette had more successfully intercepted. Even now, there was something blue glimmering between his gray-gloved fingers; some trinket, I supposed, that he intended to try to slip to Rosalie directly. Rosalie had clearly spotted it too, for her small smile deepened.

"Happily," Charcot was intoning, "I can supply the information our patient seems peculiarly determined to withhold. I can tell you, for instance, that her father died of syphilis when she was an infant. Her mother, meanwhile, suffered from melancholia and alcoholism before passing away when the patient was fourteen. All three of these conditions are, in my opinion, hereditarily linked to hysteria. Which means the subject likely had an *inherited proclivity* to hysteria from birth, which was then 'triggered' by a series of events: first, the trauma of losing her mother, followed by what she has said were the unwelcome attentions of an employer who took her in in the wake of her mother's death. Shortly thereafter, in her new employment here at the Salpêtrière, she was exposed to what are doubtlessly some of the most violent forms of hysteria to exist. These, I believe, proved to be the final straw."

He'd turned to face Rosalie as he spoke, and was now glowering down at her from above his large and slightly hawklike nose. Tearing her eyes from the marquis, she took a faltering step back.

"What is particularly useful in this patient's case," Charcot went on, "is that while her illness manifests in a typically broad array of symptoms, when she is hypnotized these symptoms can be isolated, and even slowed down, for more in-depth examination. Moreover, they almost always present in the four-stage sequence I've identified as centrally characteristic to hysteria. This makes her a valuable subject for the study of this perplexing disease."

He gestured again to Babinski, who nodded and moved toward Rosalie, withdrawing a small, long-handled mirror from the pocket of his long white apron. She watched his approach inscrutably, her eyes flitting between Charcot and his mentee. I braced myself, though I'm not sure what I was expecting—that Rosalie would snatch the mirror from his grasp and fling it out into the seating gallery? Or to the floor, shattering it into a thousand slivered pieces?

To my surprise, though, it was Charcot who reached over and plucked the tool from the younger doctor's hand.

"I will now hypnotize our patient myself," he declared.

Babinski blinked. He almost always hypnotized Charcot's hysterics for him, both onstage and in Charcot's office. I'm not sure why this was, though I suspect it was connected to Charcot's general disinclination to touch any of his patients physically unless he had to.

Turning to face Rosalie directly, he lifted the mirror so it was even with her eyes and began moving it in a slow arc back and forth. By that point, Rosalie was so accustomed to being entranced that she could fall into the state in under thirty seconds. Now, though, she seemed to be having as little response to Charcot's mirror as she had to his questions.

Charcot dropped the device to his side, muttering something to the younger doctor. Nodding, Babinski produced from his apron pocket a silver tuning fork about the size of his hand, the same one he'd used on Clotilde, and handed it to his mentor. Holding the tool next to Rosalie's ear, Charcot pulled a stylus from his own pocket and gave the fork a sharp rap. A pristine hum pierced the room, the very air seeming to shiver. But Rosalie continued to stare past them both, her lips still curved in a victorious smile—though what exactly she thought she was winning for herself I couldn't imagine.

Charcot rapped the tuning fork a second time, then a third, the silvered tones overlapping like icy waves on a beach. As the last note dissolved into the close amphitheater air and Rosalie's face and posture remained unchanged, Charcot turned back to Babinski, his expression grim. The two conferred again briefly. Then Charcot turned back toward the auditorium.

"As some of you may have observed," he said, "our subject for this lesson does not, at the moment, appear to be responding to our hypnotic efforts. I will remind you that animal experiments performed before an audience often give different results than those seen in the laboratory."

Despite my mounting distress, I couldn't help wondering to which "laboratory" he was referring. It was well known that Charcot adored animals and had several of them at home, including two dogs and a monkey gifted to him by the emperor of Brazil, who was one of his former patients. He also had a sign in his office that Madame Charcot—an amateur painter—had made for him: *You will find no dog laboratory here.*

"We will make one more attempt," he went on now. "If we do not get the desired result, it will still be a significant lesson for you—as, I assure you, it will be for the patient herself."

The threat to Rosalie was unmistakable now. My stomach tightened again as Charcot struck the tuning fork a fourth time, placing it so close to her left ear that it almost touched the delicate extremity. As its tooth-tingling tune dissipated, I found myself pleading in silence: *Just do it. Just do what he wants.*

And as if she'd heard me, she did. Her eyes slid shut. A moment later she was swaying on her feet, collapsing just slowly enough for Babinski to race around and catch her in his arms before lowering her carefully to the ground.

"A-*ha*," Charcot pronounced. "And now we shall attempt to induce the first stage of hysteria, which is usually comprised of a series of physical seizures similar in nature to those witnessed in epilepsy. This, of course, accounts for the name this disease has come to be known by: hystero-epilepsy."

He nodded at Babinski. Kneeling before Rosalie's prone form, the young doctor supported her back with one hand while pressing firmly into her pelvic region with his opposite fist. Almost immediately she threw back her head, giving the same, strangled cry she always gave before launching into an attack. I sighed quietly in relief.

"The epileptoid phase," Charcot continued, "can be divided into tonic and clonic portions. What we usually see with this patient now is of the clonic variety."

He paused, watching coolly as Rosalie began trembling, her booted feet kicking and her body vibrating with the almost automated rapidity it always displayed when she seized. This time, though, there was something about it that felt vaguely different, though I couldn't put my finger on what it was.

"The clonic phase," Charcot continued, "is distinguishable by the spasmodic jerking and twitching of the patient's limbs. Now we press her ovarian region once more—for as I have often noted, most hysterics have a region of particular hysterogenic sensitivity. And while this is by no means always located in the ovarian area itself, pressure upon it will often suffice to start or stop a fit."

He nodded at Babinski, who moved so that he was straddling Rosalie's thrashing form. After straightening the paper covers on his sleeves, the younger doctor held her shoulder down with one hand while once more thrusting his fist deeply into the flesh just above her left hip bone. It was an action that, at first glance, appeared unsettlingly violent. But it had its desired effect: Rosalie's thrashing stopped. As Babinski clambered off her, she lay like a corpse, one hand pressed against her damp forehead, the other flung out against the floorboards. Then, with a low moan, she pulled her feet toward her, propping her knees up toward the ceiling, the blue skirt falling around them like a gleaming tent.

Charcot gazed down at her, his heavy brows drawing together briefly. At first it seemed to me that he was about to say something to her. But then he turned his gaze back to the seating gallery. "Do this procedure with a real epileptic," he said crisply, "and nothing will happen. But in this case, my colleague's actions cause an observable reaction: a brief respite in the patient's convulsions, before she moves into the phase I call 'exotic' movements. These are often marked by extreme muscle spasms causing a backward arching of the head, neck, and spine—almost as we see in cases of tetanus."

Rosalie uttered another strangled groan. Then she thrust her hips toward the ceiling with enough force that the back of her head fully lifted off the ground, her weight shifting until her entire body was tremblingly balanced between her toes and the top of her head. I heard murmurs of recognition ripple through the room.

"This, of course, is the famous *arc de cercle*," Charcot noted. "It is a pose requiring exceptional physical stamina. And yet when a hysteric performs this move—even for an extended period—she will wake from her fit with no sign of fatigue." He waved vaguely at Babinski, who once more slipped his hand under the silken curve of Rosalie's back while pressing his fist into her ovarian area. She collapsed and lay panting on the floor.

"And now," Charcot said, "we enter what I refer to as the 'passionate poses' phase of the event, during which the hysteric will relive painful or powerful experiences from their past. A brief word of warning: This particular patient will often do so in a manner that is overtly voluptuous. This is not uncharacteristic, and I would ask that you keep in mind that this is not a willful act of lewdness but a *physiological reflex* that is driven by her illness."

Rosalie sat up, and the room fell so silent I heard two of her hairpins drop with silvery *ping*s to the floor. Slowly and dramatically, she rose to her knees, staring wide-eyed at the ceiling. Even the cigar smoke that hung like an odorous cloud above the top hats and derbies seemed to stop swirling for a moment in anticipation.

Clasping her hands together, Rosalie lifted them upward in a gesture faintly evocative of the one that was still projected onto Monsieur Londe's screen. "*Maman*," she exclaimed. "Don't leave me—I'm so frightened!"

It was in that moment that it hit me, what was different from her usual seizures: Her left hand wasn't contracted. Not even a little bit. It was as flexible and functional as her right.

Stunned, I glanced back at Charcot, who had to have caught the discrepancy as well. And yet he merely gazed down without expression as Rosalie continued reaching weepily toward the lights. "Here," he said, "we have vocalizations, which as the Bard said are merely so much sound and fury, signifying nothing." He stroked his chin briefly. "What matters is the *physical* expression of her illness. Which, with a little prompting, we should now witness as well."

Babinski knelt before Rosalie once more, bracing her by putting a hand on her shoulder before pushing his fist into her hip region yet again. She was crying openly now; the tears were coursing down her pale cheeks as the room continued to wait breathlessly for her to make her "voluptuous" move. Instead, throwing her head back, she let out an almost feral-sounding howl, her lips stretching as wide as those of patients trapped in hysterical yawns. Her screech filled the amphitheater as undammed water pours into a reservoir: rushing and relentless, drowning everything in its path. Several audience members started, looking about uneasily. A few even covered their ears.

Rosalie repeated the screech, her hands clawing at her hair and her back arching so violently that the small of my own back twinged in sympathy. Then she collapsed backward on the stage, motionless but for the ragged rise and fall of her chest.

Charcot gazed down at her again, rocking slightly on his feet. After a moment he looked back up at the pendulum wall clock. It was quarter to twelve, the point in his lecture when he'd normally conclude his comments and take questions from the audience. But he merely stroked his chin, his eyes boring into the timepiece's round face as though he suspected it of lying about the hour.

After a moment, he turned back toward the gallery.

"Gentlemen," he said, disregarding the women in the crowd, "this concludes the morning's second lesson. I hope you've found it instructive."

He made his way toward the stage's rear, pausing by Dr. Marie to murmur something to the secretary before scooping his top hat up from the small table where he'd set it, pushing past into the now-empty passageway, and disappearing from sight.

Throughout all this, Rosalie had still been lying in a puddle of petticoats and blue silk. Now, though, she began to sit up, blearily straightening her sweat-stained bodice and smoothing her hair. She glanced toward the marquis's seat, and following her gaze I saw with another start that it was empty. Somehow the look of stricken bewilderment on her face as she registered this vacancy erased all my earlier resentment. I hurried to her side, gathering up the spilled hairpins and helping her to her feet. As I guided her toward the passageway, I heard a low chorus of discontented murmurs and whispers, a far cry from the rhapsodic reaction that normally greeted her appearances. Then again, she hadn't done much more than scream at the ceiling before falling into a faint. It seemed her audience had expected more.

And yet it was clear that the past forty-five minutes had thoroughly depleted her. Her complexion was chalky beneath its rice powder and rouge, her bodice darkened with perspiration. I wanted to get her back to Esquirol as quickly as possible. Not just because she obviously needed to change and rest, but because the marquis's disappearance continued to unnerve me. Ushering her toward the exit, I half expected the nobleman—or perhaps his burly servant—to intercept us.

But it was Marie who caught my arm as we made our way toward the door. "She's to go to his office," he said.

"Like this? Still in her stage dress?"

He nodded curtly.

"Immediately," he said. "He wants her now."

Chapter Four

At Marie's words, Rosalie's face drained even further of color, becoming so ashen that I could make out the fine blue network of veins at her temples. I fully understood her shock. While it was perhaps a stretch to call her the director's "favorite"—I doubted someone like Charcot could be said to even *have* a favorite patient, given his apparent disdain for us as a group—it was true that his famously glacial reserve sometimes softened with the Alsatian in a way it didn't with his other hysterics. I'd actually seen him smile at her several times and chuckle aloud at her prattlings. In addition to the myriad privileges he allowed her, he often gave her little gifts—glass beads, ribbons, licorice, or barley twists—particularly after a long day of hysterical research. I'd even heard him call her *my dear* once or twice, in what for him might have passed as an almost fatherly tone. But even I, who had known Charcot for far less time than Rosalie had, knew better than to read real intimacy into such indulgences.

From the look on her face now, though, it was clear that Rosalie had done just that—and was only now registering the enormity of her mistake. She didn't fight or protest as we made our way across the grounds to his office. But she walked so slowly, literally dragging her feet along the graveled pathway, that I feared she'd further enrage him with the delay. And when we reached the door to Charcot's clinic, she turned on me abruptly.

"Help me, Laure," she breathed. "Come in with me. I don't want to be alone with them."

I promised that I would try. Practically the moment I knocked, though, a harried-looking Marie whisked her into the room. The look of terror Rosalie shot me over her shoulder seemed to land in the pit of my stomach.

I remained outside for a few minutes after Marie shut the door, straining for some hint of what was unfolding behind it. But there was only silence, which somehow felt more menacing than hearing Charcot erupt into one of his notorious fits of bellowing. I coughed faintly, hoping to at least reassure my charge of my proximity. Almost immediately, Marie poked his head out again.

"You may return to Hysteria," he told me. There was a weary curtness in his voice that I'd never heard before.

Flustered, I curtsied. "When—when should I return for her?"

He just shook his head. "We'll send for you if we need you," he said.

I spent the rest of the day completing a string of punitive chores that Babette assigned me: emptying more chamber pots and slops buckets; refilling washstands; scouring a small mountain of thermometers, syringes, spittoons, and basins with soda and brine. She then dumped me with a wad of menses-bloodied rags and a soiled nightshift I recognized as Rosalie's. Normally inmates were responsible for washing their own clothes. But as Babette informed me, she had no idea when Rosalie would be back from Charcot's office. "Or wherever else he might have sent her," she added ominously.

"But won't she need it tonight?" I asked. "It won't be dry."

"I'm sure she'll make do," she said vaguely.

By lights-down, still no summons had come from Marie. Rosalie's cot remained conspicuously unoccupied save for the damp nightshift I'd hung to dry on one of the bedposts and a satin ribbon she'd tried on briefly that morning. She didn't return the following day either, though her nightdress had disappeared from her bed. In fact, most of her things—her hospital gown, her washrag, and the little wooden box in which she kept her hairpins—had vanished as well, though her rouge pot, powder, and hand mirror remained in her bedside table drawer, along with her string of paste pearls.

By that point there were competing rumors about the Alsatian's whereabouts. Julienne swore she'd seen her being dragged out of the hydrotherapy room in her chemise, bedraggled and dripping wet. Claudine, another ward girl, said she'd heard Charcot had sentenced Rosalie to the softs for a full week. Even after having witnessed the amphitheater rebellion firsthand, I found these claims hard to credit. After all, the Alsatian had been immune from all such corrective treatments for as long as I'd known her. On the third day of her absence, though, something happened that made me wonder whether there might be some truth to them.

I'd come back from breakfast to the usual assortment of crises— two seizures, one of them hysterical, the other epileptic. The forced-feeding session of Louise, a habitual self-starver who promptly vomited the gruel we fed her back up the rubber tube. There was a catfight over a length of green ribbon that ended in a King Solomon–like threat on Babette's part to cut the disputed trimming into bits, and a reluctant treaty between the battling hysterics to wear it on alternating days. I also had to deal with Bernadette, who was weeping noisily on her cot in the wake of what she claimed was another nocturnal visit by her secret soulmate, Dr. Babinski.

This had been a continual complaint of 'Nadette's for as long as I'd known her. It apparently dated back to a medical article the young doctor had written on her case some years earlier; 'Nadette maintained Babinski had seduced her during the course of his research for it. Though he staunchly denied this, she'd clearly taken the publication—"Hysteric Nipple Amputation and Its Parallels to Skoptsy-Sect Religious Ritual"—as proof their destinies were entwined.

Personally, I didn't know what to believe—especially since 'Nadette also claimed to have been violated by both demons and dead saints during her fits. But as I've said, liaisons between patients and staff—and as Rosalie's case attested, patients and men with the means to access them—weren't uncommon. In fact, at least one or two girls from Hysteria ended up pregnant every year, to be shuttled away when their times came and then shuttled back weeks later, their wombs emptied and the paternity of their infants further fodder for the asylum's voracious rumor mill. The babies were placed either with relatives or in the same children's hospice where Amélie had briefly been sent, though I'd heard they fared even worse than the older orphans. According to 'Nadette, they were given either donkey's milk or a thin mixture of cow's milk, water, and sugar. As many as one in four died there in their first year, she said, "their little souls freed from this world of mortal pain."

"See, Laure?" she told me now. "Just last night he did this to me. We were like wildcats!" She pulled her dress down at the neckline, just low enough to reveal a perfectly mouth-shaped bruise above the angled plane of her collarbone. "And then on rounds this morning? He wouldn't even meet my eyes!"

I brushed the spot with my thumb. It certainly looked like the sort of *suçon* a lover might leave on one's neck. It was possible she'd pinched herself the way some girls in the ward did in an attempt to catch Charcot's medical interest. 'Nadette, though, had never needed such tricks. Her stigmatic symptoms were extreme and startling enough that for years she'd been a frequent lecture subject of the director's, until her increasingly erratic response to entrancement— along, I suspected, with the unsightliness of her mangled left breast— caused his favor to shift to Rosalie.

"Of course," 'Nadette continued contritely, "my sufferings are nothing compared with those of our Savior. I suppose God allows me to be wounded like this as a reminder to reserve my true love for Him, and Him alone." Clasping an arm weakly around her bedpost, she rolled her dark eyes upward so that she briefly resembled the Vierge Marie in a *carte de visite* of the Annunciation she kept tacked above her headboard. Almost immediately, though, her expression hardened again.

"I hope that that atheist cad gets what's coming to him when he goes to the devil," she spat out. "Which he will. They'll start by cutting off his phallus altogether. Not all at once, mind you. But bit by bit. With tiny nail scissors . . ."

"I'll get the arnica," I said quickly, turning away before she could complete one of her notoriously gruesome afterlife predictions. "That will help with the mark."

"Don't bother," she sighed, her expression beatific once more. "The Lord put it there to bear witness to my shame. I should suffer it without complaint."

I went to the nurse's station anyway, trying to banish the thought of Babinski's meticulous emasculation in hell as I rummaged through the various bottles. Finding the one I needed—a brown vial labeled with a picture of a frail-looking flower—I shook it slightly to see how much was left. As I did, I heard my father's voice in my head, explaining the tincture's purpose in the patient, playful way in which he'd always explained aspects of his work to me and Amélie: *It makes bruises disappear, you see?*

How? Amélie asked gravely.

No one knows, he'd responded with equal solemnity. *Perhaps it's a magic blossom—like the ones Laure tells you about in her little stories.*

I wanted to sink into the memory the way I had the featherbed I'd shared with Amélie since she'd left her bassinet. Remembering Charcot's warning, though, I wrenched it from my mind. The last thing I needed now was a relapse. *Here and now,* I thought, and turned back to 'Nadette.

But I'd barely taken two steps before I heard Babette's familiar rasp. "*Laure!* What are you doing?"

I turned reluctantly to face her. "Treating Bernadette's bruise."

"Don't bother with that. Come here."

Sighing, I returned the little bottle to its shelf and made my way to my supervisor's desk, her lead-gray gaze a weight on every step. When I reached her she pulled something from her apron pocket, her lips as tight with disgust as if she'd been handing me one of the hapless rats from the asylum's basket traps. But it wasn't. It was a bird. Or rather, an image of one, embroidered in gold thread on a velvet bag the color of a robin's egg.

"Claudine found this under Rosalie's pillow when she went to strip the bedclothes yesterday," she said. "Have you seen anyone lurking about recently?"

"Only Claude," I said. "When he came in to help with Félicie."

Félicie was a new *internée*, a petite middle-aged widow who suffered from itching attacks that no amount of scratching seemed able to reach—though her frenzied attempts left her looking as though she'd been attacked by rabid dogs. None of the female attendants had proven strong enough to keep the poor woman from all but skinning herself, so during her last episode Claude had been called to hold her hands behind her back. Even so, she'd struggled so violently that in the end they'd had to jacket her and dose her with ether.

Babette gave me an accusatory look. "I don't trust that big brute. You need to keep a closer eye on him when he's here."

"Yes, madame."

I took the little bag from her as she thrust it at me, hearing something delicate and metallic jingle inside it. Curious, I shook its contents—a delicate gold chain bracelet studded with gleaming blue gems—onto my palm. I barely registered what it was, however, before Babette was snatching both bag and bauble back.

"What are you *doing*?" she hissed. "Don't ogle it in full view of everyone." She slid the bracelet back into the pouch, tightly knotting its silken cord. "*Mon Dieu*," she added disgustedly, handing it back to me. "Use your head."

I pushed the bag into my pocket, my face flushing. "Are those . . . were those sapphires?"

She pursed her lips, nodding. "My guess is the thing's worth four thousand francs. At least."

My God, I thought. I'd never touched an adornment of such value. "Does Rosalie know about it?"

"Of course not," she snapped. "Given the state she's in now, I doubt she even knows her own name."

I glanced back at her quickly, caught off guard by this statement. Was she confirming that Rosalie was indeed now being subjected to the sorts of punitive measures that were rumored? Or was she saying the Alsatian's condition—which as I've said had been steadily worsening—had deteriorated even further?

"Either way," she went on, not giving me an opportunity to ask, "the director wants it returned to where it came from. It's a jeweler's shop by the name of Swallow in the passage des Panoramas. I need you to bring it back there and have the shopkeeper send the money back to the marquis."

"It's from the marquis?" I remembered the blue glint I'd seen between his gloved fingers. "Shouldn't it just go back to him directly?"

"It cannot. The man's done the hospital some significant favors, including using his influence to get the new photography studio funded. Charcot wants it done more discreetly."

"But what's the difference between returning it to the shop and to his home?"

She rolled her eyes as though I'd asked her the difference between salicin and arsenic. "His *wife*," she said.

"Oh," I said, feeling my cheeks heat again.

The marquise in question was as famed for her jealous temper as her husband was for his roving eye. She'd once had one of the marquis's then-mistresses—a bit-part actress at the Théâtre des Variétés—thrown into Saint-Lazare on suspicion of theft. It was a full six months before the poor girl was cleared of the charges and released, and by that point neither the marquis nor the theater would take her back. I'd heard she'd ended up at a seedy *bordel* in the Grands Boulevards area, eking out a living by selling favors to sailors and common laborers.

"Thank heavens Rosalie never saw it," Babette went on. "It would have made her transfer even more difficult."

"Her transfer?" I looked back at her in confusion.

She nodded. "Charcot has decided to move her to the lunacy division for the time being."

I gasped. "He's sent Rosalie to *Lunacy*?" Imagining Charcot's prize hysteric in Hydrotherapy had been difficult. Picturing her in the lunacy ward was all but impossible. "For how long?"

"For the foreseeable future, I'd imagine," the old woman said. There was a distinct note of satisfaction in her voice.

I looked back at Rosalie's empty bed, wondering which section of Lunacy she'd been assigned to. Surely Charcot wouldn't have sent her to the dreaded incurables unit—not for what amounted to less than an hour of bad behavior. After all, Bernadette had fled our ward no fewer than four times since I'd been there, once evading discovery for three whole days. They'd finally found her in the chapel belfry, stark naked and drunk on sacramental wine. After spending an afternoon in Hydrotherapy, she'd reappeared in Hysteria as though nothing had happened at all. Then again, I realized, she hadn't challenged Charcot in front of four hundred respected peers, journalists, and members of his admiring public.

I thought of Rosalie as I'd last seen her, her eyes wild, her face white. *Help me, Laure. . . .*

"Do you know which section she's in?" I asked.

"Enough *questions!*" Babette snapped. "Just get going. I need you back by four to take Caroline's body from the morgue to Autopsy with Jacques."

I stifled a groan. I didn't mind Jacques, a towering orderly with protruding, brownish front teeth and hair that looked like wet straw. Morgue duty, though—which entailed confirming the identities of hysterics who'd passed away with the asylum coroner before transporting them to Charcot's foul-smelling autopsy chamber—was the duty I detested the most. In part it was because I knew the gruesome protocol that followed: Charcot and his protégés would not just cut into the lifeless bodies but extract their brains as well, slicing and sampling the pinkish tissue for evidence that hysteria was caused by the same kinds of lesions that Charcot had confirmed caused other neurological illnesses, such as *la sclérose latérale amyotrophique.*

I knew that the dead didn't *feel* these scientific scavengings. And yet the thought of the women I'd lived and slept among having their brains and bodies plundered in this way was nevertheless deeply troubling to me. Delivering Caroline to this fate would be all the harder. I'd had a real fondness for the girl, who had died unexpectedly a few days earlier of diphtheria. With her high-pitched laugh and hands that fluttered like pale birds when she spoke, she'd reminded me a little of Amélie.

Even as I was thinking this, however, something in Babette's previous directive about the bracelet sparked a stirring of recognition. It took a moment to make the link: the passage des Panoramas, a high-end shopping arcade with an arched roof of glazed glass, wasn't at all far from the boulevard Haussmann address on Maître LaBarge's letter. At first, this proximity seemed little more than a coincidence. As I turned it over in my mind, however, an idea began taking shape.

Since I'd tucked the notary's note into my journal, my despair over its contents had softened into a kind of defiant disbelief. After all, France was among the most—if not *the* most—enlightened nations in the world. Surely, its laws wouldn't leave a defenseless young woman to assume the liabilities of a father she'd so painfully lost— much less send her to prison over them. In fact, the more I considered it the more likely it seemed that I hadn't been clear in my letter to the notary, that he'd somehow misunderstood my situation. I'd planned for this reason to write him again, requesting further clarification on the subject and advice on how to improve my and Amélie's circumstances.

Now, though, a better idea struck me: Babette's errand shouldn't take much time. Why not just go to the man's office in person? Not only would I not have to wait a month (or more) for a response, but it would leave less room for confusion than trying to communicate on such complex topics in writing.

"No later than four, do you hear?" My mind was still racing as Babette pulled out her mesh change purse, shaking several centimes into her palm. "For the omnibus," she added, thrusting them at me. "Check on Louise before you go—she may need her compressor tightened."

"Yes, madame." I took the coins, my eyes fixed on the floor so she wouldn't see my excitement over this unexpected opportunity.

Fetching my bonnet and shawl, I hurried over to Louise. She appeared asleep on her bed, her mouth slightly open and her lips and tongue reddened from where the feeding tube had rubbed against them. I bent over her to tighten the compressor, a device Charcot had invented after discovering that applying pressure on a hysteric's ovaries could both start and stop attacks. The thing had never worked on me, and I'd likewise never known it to have any impact on Louise. Still, per Babette's instructions I adjusted the rubber bulb until it was tucked snugly beneath the girl's pelvic bone.

As I stood to go, her coffee-colored eyes popped open.

"Too much?" I asked.

She shook her head groggily. "I barely feel it," she lisped through still-swollen lips. "Where are you going?"

"To the passage des Panoramas. On an errand."

She shut her eyes again. "Oh," she said dreamily. "There's the best chocolate shop there. Bring back rum-filled truffles. They're divine."

Outside, the sun gleamed off the golden dome of the asylum chapel and the newly scythed green grass. I made my way beneath the early-blooming lilacs that lined the pathway, their scent tingeing the chill air like a promise. As I turned onto rue de l'Église, a fat pigeon that had been perched on one of them fluttered down and pecked expectantly at the gravel by my feet. Both its lack of concern at my proximity and its unnaturally pink tail feathers marked it as one of Rosalie's three "*beaux bébés*"—chicks she'd found last spring in an abandoned nest in the chapel courtyard. After marking them with different shades of ink from the Salpêtrière's (dog-free) laboratory, she'd named them after three of her sisters who had passed away as infants. The Alsatian spent hours with the creatures perched on her shoulders and arms, sometimes feeding them crusts of bread with her own lips. Others found this sight to be charming. For my part, it made my skin crawl. My father had always believed pigeons carried many of the diseases he spent his days and nights treating—including, for all I knew, the one that ended up taking his life.

"Shoo, bird," I told the pink-feathered scavenger, feinting a kick in its direction. "I have nothing for you."

The thing flapped off toward the refectory, probably hoping for more success with the waste bins by the kitchen's back doors. I hastened on to the asylum's main entrance, glancing up out of habit at the bronze sculpture of Philippe Pinel liberating the Salpêtrière's lunatics from barbaric madhouse methods of the past. In his gleaming right hand, the famous man held a bit of the chain from which he'd just freed the young girl crouching at his feet.

He wasn't looking at the girl, though. He stared into the middle distance, where chambray-shirted laborers worked with pickaxes to widen boulevard de l'Hôpital to accommodate its ever-increasing flow of traffic. As always, he struck me as vaguely distracted. As though his great metal mind had already moved on to something else.

Some forty minutes later I stood on boulevard Haussmann, woozy with nerves and motion sickness. I traveled by foot in those days when I could, preferring the streets to the cramped and often malodorous omnibus carriages. Given how little time I had to accomplish all I needed to now, however, the bus had seemed the fastest option—until, that is, the one I was on got stuck behind an overturned brewer's cart. There it had remained for a good twenty minutes, mired in stalled lunch-hour traffic and buffeted by impatient shouts and whistles and carriage bells until city workers managed to haul the vehicle upright.

Breathing deeply to clear my nose of yeast fumes, I pushed through the usual scurrying servants, basket-bearing laundresses, and a group of dark-dressed women distributing religious pamphlets. I was just turning onto the busy main avenue when an incensed male bellow froze me in my tracks: "You *whore!*"

Looking over my shoulder, I saw a portly-looking man in a brown suit. He appeared to be wrestling with one of the pamphleteers I'd just passed, though I couldn't fathom why he'd take such offense at a church-related brochure. And yet clearly he had. In fact, as I watched he succeeded in yanking a canvas sack from the woman's shoulder, upturning it, and spilling its contents onto the sidewalk.

"This is *trash*, I tell you," he shouted, flecks of spittle flying from his wet lips. "Pornography and trash. I'm calling the *flics*. Police! Police!"

The woman and her associates scurried to rescue the scattered pages, hampered by the fact that the man was stamping on those within reach of his booted foot.

A small and mostly male crowd had begun gathering by this point, some of them picking up the now-soiled bits of paper and skimming their contents. An elderly priest on the edge of the group shook his white head before disgustedly throwing the thing back on the ground. Meanwhile, the officer the man had summoned had materialized, hand on the hilt of his service saber.

"Arrest these . . . these *degenerates*," the man ordered him breathlessly, clutching at the woman's arm. "She and her fellow witches are out here again, spreading their lies and filth. It can't be tolerated." He handed one of the publications to the officer. "Go ahead," he prompted. "Just read that."

But the officer barely glanced at the flimsy page. Instead, he turned to the woman, still indignantly attempting to pry herself free from the fat man's thick fingers.

"Madame Aubert," said the constable, "we agreed last week that you would limit your activities in this area."

To my astonishment, the woman quite literally laughed in his face—not a high-pitched feminine titter, but a deep and unapologetic peal of scorn.

"I don't recall an *agreement*," she declared. "I recall you ordering us not to distribute our bulletin here, and myself telling you that as it was fully within the bounds of the law, I fully intended to continue doing so."

A murmur of incredulity rippled through the onlookers. The policeman loomed over the little woman. "It's only within the bounds of the law if the distribution is conducted peacefully," he told her.

She stared unflinchingly back up at him. "It *was* peaceful, until this philistine disrupted us!"

She looked to be around forty and was well but simply dressed, with dark hair and eyes that snapped with intelligence. And yet as with her laugh, it was her voice that struck me the most. Low and slightly nasal, it was so otherwise unexceptional that it didn't immediately sink in for me what it was that made it so arresting: It was devoid of fear as well as apology. Devoid, in fact, of any womanly lilt at all. She spoke in the same spirit with which she'd laughed and with which she stood—with the full confidence of a man.

"You know as well as I, Officer, that the free and equal dissemination of ideas is perfectly legal," she added. Disentangling herself from her accuser, she brushed disgustedly at her sleeves, as though his fingertips had left stains.

"It damn well is not!" shouted the man. "Arrest her, I say! Arrest them all! Throw 'em in Saint-Lazare!"

"Actually," the woman retorted, "Saint-Lazare is among the oppressive and misogynistic institutions we address in this issue. You should read it, monsieur." She smiled serenely at him. "If, in fact, you can read."

The man's face deepened from red to something closer to purple. Whirling, he poked a thick finger almost directly into the officer's face. "Are you just going to stand by and *watch* this abuse? Or are you less of a man than she is?"

The policeman's face flushed as well. Grasping the woman's arm, he ducked his head apologetically. "I'm afraid you'll have to come with me now, madame."

"On what charges?" she demanded.

"Disrupting the peace."

"And pornography!" the fat man snapped. I heard scattered grunts of approval from the crowd. A low chant was starting up: "*Arrest them! Arrest them! Arrest them!*"

"The only 'pornography' we traffic in is an honest appraisal of the way the men of France treat their wives, mothers, and daughters," the woman said, raising her voice to be heard over the chanters. Indicating the crowd with her gloved hand, she added: "*They* are the pornographers!" Shaking off the policeman once more, she defiantly resumed picking up the scattered news pages until a half-eaten apple came soaring from somewhere behind the crowd's ranks and hit her in the small of the back.

Spinning around, she put her hands on her hips. "You see?" she cried, her tone victorious. "*I'm* the one under attack. Woman or not, will you protect me?"

"You'll be safe enough in the precinct office," the policeman growled. Recapturing her arm, he signaled a colleague, who came and grasped her from the other side.

"But I've broken no laws!" Madame Aubert cried, struggling with renewed energy. "And if anything, it's the *laws* that are obscene! The laws themselves—written by men, without representative voices from women . . ."

"That's enough from you." The constable nodded to his colleague; together they began to march her off in the opposite direction. A third constable fell in behind them, dragging along the woman's two companions. Neither of the latter struck me as surprised or even particularly resentful of their capture. One even winked at me, pointedly dropping the paper she'd had in her hand at my feet as she was hustled past.

As the small group turned the corner, I bent to pick up a leaflet myself, curious to see what it was that had caused the ruckus. But I'd barely taken in its masthead—*Les citoyennes*—when the brown-suited man gave another shout: "Don't forget that one!"

With a start, I saw that he was pointing directly at me.

"Hey!" he huffed, his small eyes squinting beneath his hat brim. "You forgot one! *Police!*" He made his way toward me, his glowering cohorts in tow.

For a moment I couldn't move. Then, crumpling the pamphlet into my pocket, I hitched my dress and petticoat up with both hands and fled across the bustling avenue, barely avoiding being trampled by a pair of hansom cab horses going in one direction and a furniture delivery wagon in the other. Reaching the other side, I leapt over the mud-filled gutter, dodging an Arab chestnut vendor and two starch-capped nurses pushing perambulators at a maddeningly leisurely pace. After a moment's hesitation, I darted across the busy intersection toward the Palais Garnier, weaving myself between a startled group of German tourists standing outside the Pavilion of the Emperor.

A few minutes later I emerged on rue Scribe. I quickly ducked into the arched entranceway of a stately, sand-colored building and huddled there, my heart thumping as I listened for my pursuers. All I heard was the sound of the street's traffic, the chattering hum of passing pedestrians, and—closer by—two little girls playing *jeu des grâces* on the sidewalk outside. Just to be sure, though, I decided to wait a few minutes.

As my breathing slowed, I realized that I was still clutching the pamphlet that had sparked my flight. My first thought was to get rid of it, lest I get mistaken again for one of Madame Aubert's "pornographers." Then I caught the lead article's headline: "The Legal Enslavement of Women."

I smoothed the pages out again. Below the headline was a black-and-white drawing of what, at first glance, appeared to be a typical wedding scene: a young couple at the altar before a priest. Upon closer examination, though, there was nothing typical about the image, though the young man in his frock coat and top hat looked every inch the standard bridegroom. The woman's frothy gown, however, was offset by the bulky manacles locked on to her wrists. These were attached to a thick chain, the lead end of which the priest appeared to be handing to the groom.

Baffled, I skipped to the bottom of the article. Its author had signed it only with the initials *I. A.* But as I glanced back at the masthead, I spotted a small notice just beneath it: *Isabelle Aubert, Founder and Editor.*

Madame Aubert. That tiny, severe-looking woman the brigadiers had trundled off to their station.

I was tempted to read the article in full then and there, along with the editorial below the fold on "inhumanity and injustice at the Saint-Lazare prison for women." But between the delayed bus and the mob, I was already running later than I should have been: *No later than four,* Babette had said. Even if I went directly to the passage des Panoramas now, I'd be cutting it uncomfortably close.

Folding the paper into my pocket, I turned and hurried back toward boulevard Haussmann. A few minutes later, I was twisting the turnkey bell beneath a polished brass sign reading *LaBarge & Fils, Avocat à la Cour.*

The door was opened by a clerk who may or may not have been the *fils* advertised on the firm's sign, a plumpish young man with pockmarked skin and hair that looked as though he spent most of his days raking it toward the ceiling with his fingers. He listened dubiously as I spilled out a hastily improvised introduction, saying that I was the daughter of one of Maître LaBarge's clients (I didn't mention a dead one), following up on a communication I'd recently received. After looking me over with a faintly dismissive grimace, the youth shrugged and led me to a second-floor office, instructing me to wait outside as he poked his head in.

"You've got a visitor," he said, indicating me with a tip of his double chin.

A man in a checked suit looked up from a pile of papers he'd been annotating. He appeared to be about sixty, with a long face and a narrow nose marked by a distractingly pronounced bump at its bridge. Frowning, he set his pen down, peering over the rim of his spectacles first at me, then at a lantern clock on the mantel of a small fireplace in which embers from the morning's fire still glowed.

"A client?" he asked.

"Says she's the daughter of one."

The notary peered at me again. "I don't have anything in my agenda."

"I only need a few minutes," I said quickly. "I don't have an appointment."

LaBarge's frown deepened, but he nodded at the younger man,

who may or may not have been his son. "Go find that document I mentioned over lunch, will you? I'll need it for Monsieur Dubois."

"Right away." The clerk disappeared.

Smoothing my skirts, I stepped farther into the office, a well-appointed room with wood-paneled walls, gleaming sconces, and a floor-to-ceiling bookshelf filled with leather-bound volumes, their spines tooled in glinting tones of gold and silver. The notary was studying me now, and I suddenly saw myself as he must have: My coarse dress stained from the morning's work in the ward and mud splattered from my race across the street. My hands ungloved and—as I only now noticed—smudged with newsprint. My hair—initially bundled under my squashed bonnet—had half shaken loose as well, and I attempted to tuck it back up as I nervously approached La-Barge's paper-strewn desk. "Thank you for seeing me."

He nodded coldly. "May I inquire to whom I have the pleasure of speaking so unexpectedly?"

It was impossible to miss the irony in his tone. I swallowed. "My name is Laure," I said. "Laure Bissonnet."

At first he just looked puzzled. Then his eyes—which were somewhere between blue and dark pewter in tone—narrowed in recognition. "The physician's daughter. From the madhouse."

Hysteria ward, I thought, but didn't say it. "Yes. My father was Doctor Henri Bissonnet. I wrote you recently regarding his estate."

"And I wrote you back in answer," he said brusquely. "Did you not receive my correspondence?"

"I did," I said quickly. "I just . . ." I hesitated, unsure how to proceed. "I'm just not sure you fully understand the situation," I said at last.

He lifted an eyebrow. "Are you implying I don't know the law?"

"Of course not," I said quickly. "I just don't see how receiving just a *few* things from our father's estate, things no one else wants, could be construed as some sort of . . . of crime."

One of the notary's dark brows shot toward his hairline. "Did I say it was a crime?"

"You said I could end up in prison."

"And so you could," he said shortly. "Or at the very least, the poorhouse. Which wouldn't be much better."

"But *why?*" I felt it now, the same jagged-edged panic I'd felt after reading and rereading the man's letter, though I struggled to keep it from my voice. "I've already lost everything—my home, my prospects, my parents. I've even lost my sister. No one at l'Assistance Publique seems to know where she is. She's only twelve. How could the law want to see me further punished, when all I want is to find her and make sure she's safe?"

He listened to my outburst, his expression impassive but his pen twitching between his thumb and forefinger in annoyance. Its rhythm slowed slightly when I mentioned Amélie's disappearance. But when he spoke again, his tone betrayed not the faintest hint of sympathy.

"The point, mademoiselle, is that *you* didn't lose everything. Your father did. And in fact, he lost far *more* than he had. So much so, in fact, that even after the sale of his estate, his outstanding obligations remain sizable—close to five thousand francs, I believe." He rapped the pen against his desk's edge as he uttered the sum, as if for emphasis. "Even if I could give you anything of any worth, the law is very clear on this point. That sum—five thousand francs"—*rap rap rap* went his pen—"is the amount for which you'd be personally liable. And that's regardless of whether or not you actually find your sister."

The cold skepticism with which he said this—as though my finding Amélie was as likely as my discovering sunken treasure in the Seine—made me flinch. I stumbled on, grasping at the one flimsy straw he seemed to have left me.

"It doesn't have to be something of monetary worth," I protested. "I'd happily take something from our old home—anything, really— that's of no worth at all. There—there was an old photograph, for instance. Of my father and mother, on their wedding day. It was in a brass frame on our parlor mantelpiece; perhaps you saw it. I don't need the frame—just the portrait. Just so Amélie and I can have something to remember them by."

He was looking at me now with a mixture of pity and disdain, the way one might look at a blind beggar outside a church.

"I mean," I went on, flustered, "of course we'll *remember* them. But the way they looked; their faces. My mother's—she died seven years ago—it's already becoming unclear, even for me. And Amélie was so small when she passed away. . . ." My voice trembled. Mortified, I dropped my gaze to the floor, afraid that continuing would lead me to humiliating tears.

When I looked up, LaBarge had his knuckles pressed above his brow, as though my presence was giving him a headache. When he spoke again, it was with the weary overarticulation of a schoolmaster addressing a dim-witted student.

"Mademoiselle Bissonnet," he said. "I am struggling to find a way to put this that you will understand. As I've just explained, there is legally *no way* for me to give you *anything* of your family's—not even a crust of bread—without rendering you responsible for the entirety of your father's debts."

"Yes, but—" I began, but he held a hand up.

"*However.* Even *if* the law were different, or *if* I were willing to break it on your behalf—which, obviously, I am not, any more than your father would have willingly sickened one of his patients—there is quite literally *nothing to physically give*. It has been well over a year since your father died. And in that time, every item that was legally in his name has been sold or otherwise disposed of."

I swallowed. "Everything?"

He gazed back at me coldly. "*Absolument tout.*"

"There's *nothing* left? Nothing at all?"

"Not so much as an empty jam jar." This pronouncement, too, was delivered with complete dispassion. He might have been confirming the barrenness of someone's larder. "And now," he went on briskly, pushing back his desk chair and standing, "I must ask you to leave. I've another client coming soon to discuss business that is actually relevant." He was already looking past me as he spoke, toward the still-open doorway. "François?" he called. "Can you escort Mademoiselle Bissonnet out, please?"

"*Oui*, Papa." The clerk appeared in an eye-blink, as though he'd been lurking just beyond the doorframe. And apparently he had, for after he'd led me back down the stairwell and to the building's central exit, he turned to me with a patronizing smile.

"My advice?" he offered, as if I'd asked for it. "Gussy yourself up a little, to the extent that you can. Find a husband—a tradesman, perhaps a carpenter. Someone who's bound to see a doctor's daughter as a step up—even without looks or a dowry."

And with that, he shut the door in my face.

I was left staring at the same plaque I'd taken in mere moments earlier with a faint but palpable sense of hope. Now, though, there was only a leaden tenderness in my gut, as though I'd somehow taken multiple blows to it without noticing. As I locked gazes with my own reflection in the brass—wavering, distorted, strangely ghostlike— the two LaBarges' words tumbled in my head like sheets in the asylum's laundry vats: *The extent that you can . . . without looks or a dowry . . . the entirety of your father's debts . . .*

"Excuse me."

I turned to see a middle-aged man in a top hat and neatly pressed suit, standing close enough to me that I could smell the wine he'd had at lunch. "*Excuse* me," he repeated sharply, either not registering or disregarding my obvious discomposure at his unexpected proximity. "I've an appointment in this building."

Mumbling an apology, I began making my way back to the street. But rather than waiting for my retreat, he reached around me, enveloping me in an unwelcome half embrace as he briskly twisted the turnkey bell. The door sprang open almost immediately.

"Ah!" exclaimed the younger LaBarge. "Come in, monsieur! My father's been expecting you."

Paying no more attention to me than the visitor had, he held the door wide in welcome. Once the older man was inside, though, the younger one's gaze returned to me behind his back. This time, his expression was distinctly less friendly.

"Go on," he muttered. "You're done here."

He began shutting the door a second time, but not before the other man mumbled something I couldn't make out. I heard LaBarge's answer clearly enough, though: "A girl," he said. "Just a girl."

I stumbled to the sidewalk, my ears ringing with the dismissal as though they'd just been boxed. As the door slammed behind me the bells of Notre-Dame-des-Victoires launched into their latest announcement of the hour: three slow, sonorous chimes. I realized dully that it was even less likely now that I'd complete Babette's errand at the passage des Panoramas and still be back for morgue duty at four. If I was going to try, I had to hurry. And yet rather than urgency, this realization sparked something else: a fury unlike any I'd felt in recent memory, not even after learning Amélie had gone missing.

Heedless of the pedestrians pressing past me on the sidewalk, I slid the bracelet into my palm and stared down at it, strangely repulsed by its glittering blue beauty. What was it Babette had said? *The thing's worth four thousand francs. At least.*

Four thousand francs, I thought. A man Rosalie had danced with once—*once!*—had given her a bauble almost equal in worth to the debt that could legally land me in prison. And yet according to that same law, I wasn't entitled to so much as an empty jam jar from my own home—much less the funds I needed to find my sister.

Closing my hand around the bracelet, I had a sudden urge to turn and toss it into the nearest dustheap, a fantastical offering to the basket-hefting ragpickers who sifted through the city's trash. But then another idea came to me:

What if I just . . . keep it?

The thought was like a bitter-cold breeze against my fevered thoughts. Not only because it was so shocking, but because on some levels it actually made sense. After all, it wasn't as if Babette would personally confirm I'd returned the thing. The marquis would be none the wiser until he managed to see Rosalie, and *that* seemed unlikely to happen anytime soon, now that Charcot had locked her up in Lunacy. Far more likely the old man's famously lecherous eye would land on someone else first, and then he'd forget about both Rosalie and the bracelet altogether.

Meanwhile, I could find a way to sell it. And once I had, I'd simply . . . leave. I'd gather my few possessions and take the first train I could to Nuits-sous-Ravières, and from there to Avallon. Once I got there, I'd have all the time in the world to search for Amélie—without help from LaBarge or anybody else.

One by one, the pieces fell into place—a perfect subversive puzzle. As they did, my rage cooled into a kind of exhilarated terror, something I'd felt only once before, standing on the chalk cliffs of Normandy. Papa had brought Amélie and me to Étretat after Mama and little Louie, our unborn brother, died, an excursion meant to take our minds off our sadness. But for me, that celebrated seascape had had the opposite effect: Rather than being soothed by its raw beauty, I'd wanted nothing more than to become part of it—to hurl myself right off the famous chalk cliffs. I'd felt it so strongly, so compellingly, that my toes curled inside my boots, protesting the image my mind's eye presented: myself, feet pedaling, hair streaming, skirts tangling in the salty airstream.

That prospect terrified me, of course. But it also summoned a strange sense of calm. As a choice, leaping out into that blustery and wetly winking void would almost certainly have been my last. But at least it would have been wholly my own.

Sliding the bracelet back into its pouch, I tucked it into my pocket, beneath the folded issue of Madame Aubert's broadsheet. I'd have to move quickly. But as a plan, it could work. It *had* to work.

And once it did, I'd once more have both a family and a home.

Chapter Five

I set back out for the Salpêtrière in a kind of giddy fugue, as drunk off my own recklessness as Bernadette had been on holy wine when they found her after her last escape. As I made my way to the omni stop, my head filled with thrilling thoughts of my pending re-union with my sister, with luminous visions of how we'd use our new-found windfall. We'd find a little room somewhere, I decided, and stay up late in it as we'd done in our old home, sleepily watching the shifting shadows on our ceiling while I told her stories until she fell asleep. I tried to imagine what four thousand francs (*four thousand francs!*) looked like. What it would feel like to hold in my hands, a fairy-tale fountain of riches clinking through my curling fingers, like the pirate booty Jim Hawkins found on Treasure Island. It seemed a good omen when the first horse bus to pull up was one of the newer and larger ones, and an even better one when I secured a seat on top, thus avoiding the motion sickness I inevitably suffered inside the stuffy carriage, and saving fifteen centimes in the process. Upon set-tling myself onto the bench there, though, I was taken aback to find myself face-to-face with Rosalie's pink-cheeked visage, for the man sitting across from me was reading the same *Petit journal* issue she'd had me so frantically seeking just three days earlier.

The artist had depicted her not on Charcot's stage, but being de-murely led past a row of rumpled beds by an old nurse who looked something like Babette—a setting the Alsatian wouldn't have appreciated. But I knew she'd have been delighted by her image, doubtlessly clipping it out and decorating it with ribbons and sequins before pinning it to the wall by her bed, as she had with the other newspaper and magazine portraits of her. They were still there now, gazing blankly out at her former dominion while Rosalie herself languished in Lunacy.

Help me, Laure. I don't want to be alone with them.

Looking away guiltily, I checked my pocket to make sure her bracelet was still there, only remembering Madame Aubert's broadsheet when I felt its crumpling edge against my fingers. I pulled it out, smoothing it against my knee to study the shackled bride again before moving on to the piece it illustrated, "The Legal Enslavement of Women."

The editorial turned out to be an acerbic comparison of France's marriage laws to those in Algeria, the supposedly "barbaric" nation we'd colonized a half century earlier. One would, of course, have assumed ours to be the more civilized of the two on this and most other fronts. And yet Madame Aubert fiercely set about disproving this notion, point by point, lauding the Arab legalization of polygamy as "honest" in comparison to France, "where men proclaim fidelity while privately practicing its opposite." She also noted that after marriage, an Arab woman kept her family name and received a dowry proportional to her husband's fortune, which was hers to do with as she liked. Her French counterpart, by contrast, forfeited not only her name but any wealth she might have—along with many of her legal rights. *In short,* the editorial concluded, *matrimony in France is a mere means to turn its women into chattel and slaves. And until we have truly abolished the subjugation of a full half of its citizens, we have no right to our self-proclaimed title of "civilized."*

I read the piece a second time, amazed that the tiny woman I'd seen had not only penned this explosive text but deliberately distributed it to the very men it took to task. No wonder she'd sparked a riot! I was still shaking my head as I skimmed a short piece on the deleterious health effects of the corset, before finally reaching the exposé on Saint-Lazare she had mentioned.

I read the first few lines—about the economic demographics of the women interred in the infamous prison (not surprisingly, the vast majority came from dire poverty), as well as the grim accommodations made for those who had children—with a kind of curious detachment. But when I reached the paragraph describing living conditions at the place—the vermin-infested cells, the overflowing buckets of human waste, the solitary-confinement cells kept so dark that being shut up in one was *akin to being buried alive in a coffin*—I felt a chill current of fear: Over the past hour, I'd thought only about how the bracelet could reunite me with Amélie. Only now did I realize that it could also sever us even more irrevocably than my father's death and my illness had. For the fact stood that by pocketing something of such enormous value, I was committing a serious crime—one that could easily land me amid the stomach-turning circumstances about which I was now reading.

Shaken, I refolded the paper, suddenly doubting the rash decision I'd just made. I even considered trying to undo whatever it was that I was doing, giving Babette some excuse for not returning the bracelet to the shop and—presuming I survived her wrath—doing so another time.

But even as I pondered this option, the carriage turned onto boulevard de l'Hôpital, and the asylum came jostling into view. I immediately felt it again: the familiar, creeping dread I'd experienced the last time I was briefly liberated from my wretched life there—taking Rosalie to Bon Marché to shop for her corset—and then faced with the prospect of returning to it. After all, the asylum was a kind of prison too, albeit a more survivable one than Saint-Lazare. Its inmates may have been convicted of lesser crimes, of nervous illnesses and madness rather than theft, prostitution, or murder. But they were imprisoned nonetheless—just as I still was, despite being an employee there. And as of now, the jewels in my pocket were my only means of escaping.

The omni came to a rocking stop. Refolding *Les citoyennes*, I quickly slipped it back into my pocket. As I withdrew my hand, my fingertips brushed the velvet bag, and I thought once more of my dawn-break vision of my sister with her little toy cat.

I just don't want her to be separated from me and end up all alone.

You're not alone, I promised her in my head. *You're not, I promise. Just wait for me a little longer.*

As it turned out, the open-air omnibus ride saved me not only money but time as well, as I had fifteen minutes before I had to be at the morgue. Since I'd missed lunch, I spent the change on some day-old rolls at a nearby *boulangerie*, thinking I'd eat them after delivering Caroline to the autopsy theater, once the cigar-and-formaldehyde stench of the place had left my nostrils. Snack in hand, I set off down rue de l'Infirmerie, waving to the three old *reposantes* who, as usual, sat outside on a bench with their knitting needles clicking, and ignoring the advice of their leader (an ancient hag so inexplicably obsessed with a certain historic square in the fifth arrondissement that it had become her asylum nickname) that I *fuck right off to Place Maubert*. Upon approaching the weathered building in which the asylum morgue was located, though, I was surprised to spot Jacques hurrying in the opposite direction—not toward the morgue, but away from it.

"You're not going to get Caroline?" I called.

"Change of plans," he replied gruffly. "Marie wants me to help in a feeding."

"Not Louise again?" I asked worriedly. She'd already been put through three feedings this week.

But Jacques shook his head. "New one," he said. "That redheaded *folle* they brought in Thursday."

"They're *tubing* her?"

"I guess she's in pretty bad shape." Pausing, he picked something from between his front teeth with a grime-rimmed thumbnail. "That's what she gets, though, acting the hellcat every waking hour. Charcot wants her fed before sending her over to Lunacy."

"Lunacy?" I repeated, unexpectedly stricken. "They've assessed her already, then?"

He snorted. "She won't *let* them assess her. Nearly scratched Claude's eye out when he went to bring her to Charcot this morning. As if booting him in the balls Thursday wasn't enough."

Dismayed, I looked away. This was precisely what I'd tried to warn the girl about: that not only did she have to eat, but any further violence could have dire consequences here. I'd assisted in enough force-feedings to know how brutal they could be. After Louise's first session—which she'd fought tooth and nail—her tongue and gums had bled, and her throat had been so inflamed she couldn't eat or drink of her own volition for two full days. Almost as distressing was the twisted terror on the girl's face as the presiding doctor forced the tube down her throat. I'd heard of another patient who had contracted pneumonia after an inexperienced intern "fed" soup into her lung instead of her stomach. Yet another had had her jaw broken by the block Claude, with far too much enthusiasm, had jammed between her teeth to prop her mouth open.

"Anyway," Jacques said, "I'm off. They'll have my hide if I'm late." And turning, he set off toward the kitchen.

"Wait," I called after him. "Am I still expected in the morgue, then?"

"No one said anything about you," he said, shrugging. "Just that I'm to go fetch the gruel and meet Claude in the feeding room."

"Claude?" My heart sank further. "He's assisting too?"

"He is," Jacques confirmed. "Said he's looking forward to it too."

As he strode off toward the kitchen I stared after him apprehensively, trying to decide what to do. It was safe to assume that Babette still expected me at the morgue, and I was loath to defy her a second time. I was, after all, by nature so conflict-averse that one of my (kinder) boarding school nicknames had been "Mademoiselle Oui-M'dame."

But as I turned tentatively toward the morgue, I saw the girl again in my mind: Her eyes, the color of sunlit spring leaves. The bruises on her arms and shoulders. I imagined the Basque's heavy hands on her, his leering face as he forced her mouth open for the feeding tube. Something inside me clenched hard, like a fist.

What does it matter, I thought. *I'm going to be gone soon.*

And rolls in hand, I hurried off in the direction of the refectory.

A few minutes later I reached the airless, windowless closet that had been installed like a grim afterthought a little ways from the main dining area. It was already set up for the girl's arrival, the table next to the oaken feeding chair equipped with a wooden block, a tin funnel, a pewter pitcher, and a cheese-colored rubber tube, neatly coiled. I'd just stepped in, holding my breath against the overpowering smell of vinegar, lye, and stale vomit, when I heard scuffling footsteps and agitated voices approaching from the other end of the corridor.

Peering back out into the hallway, I saw the girl being hustled toward me by Claude. She looked even more disheveled than she had in the softs, her red hair tumbling lankly down her back, her eyes red rimmed, as though she'd been crying. Apart from the now filthy bandage wrapping her left hand, she was wearing only a rumpled-looking nightshift. She was also limping noticeably, her left foot dragging behind her slightly as she walked. I remembered what Julienne had said at breakfast about her contraction.

"They sent *you,* Princesse?" Claude narrowed his small and rather wide-set black eyes. "I was expecting Jacques." He glanced at the table. "And where's the gruel?"

"It's coming," I said. "So is Jacques. But I'm—I'm to help."

"*Help?*" He looked me up and down scornfully. "How can you help?"

"I can calm her," I improvised. "So she won't fight the tube." The words sprang from my lips with surprising confidence.

The Basque stared at me dubiously. "Never heard of them doing that," he said. "Sending someone for 'calming.'"

"There's a lot you haven't heard of," I said airily.

To my surprise, he didn't challenge me. He merely dragged the girl over the threshold. I saw her green gaze take in the items in the room: The heavy chair with its six sets of worn leather straps, which buckled at the ankles, wrists, torso, and forehead. The gruel on the little table beside it. The dully gleaming pitcher. The tube coiled like a yellow snake beside it.

"What is this place?" she asked warily.

"I told you," the Basque said. "You're having a treatment."

"What kind of treatment?"

"A *food* treatment," he said, continuing to half lead, half push her toward the chair.

Her gaze darted from the chair to me and then back. If she recognized me, she gave no sign. "The doctor said I could eat when I was ready."

"Doctors say lots of things," he replied brusquely. "But I've got my orders. Come on now; let's get you strapped in."

He pulled her again. Now, though, the girl began to resist him actively. Throwing her slight weight against his, she lunged back toward the hallway, trying to claw his hand from her arm. Her desperation was evident, but there was a feebleness to her movements I hadn't seen in the softs. It was hard to believe that a few days earlier she'd supposedly fought off four grown men in the asylum courtyard.

For his part, Claude—not unexpectedly—seemed to welcome the rebellion. "Oh, we're doing this again?" he drawled as he continued wresting her toward the chair. "We'll see about that!" He flung a hairy arm about her shoulders, trying to get her into a headlock, and her eyes took on a glassy look of terror.

"Get *off*," she cried, twisting away from him. "Let me go!"

The Basque grunted, attempting to wrench her arms behind her back with enough force that I feared he'd dislocate them. She raked her nails across his cheek, leaving behind a trio of bright red scratches.

"You *little bitch*!" Bellowing in rage, the orderly kicked the girl's good leg out from under her and wrestled her violently to her knees. Still clawing at the air with her free hand, she flung herself back toward the door, her eyes catching mine for a fleeting second.

"Tell him," she gasped. "Tell him to let me go!"

"Her?" Claude snorted, finally ensnaring her wrists. "She's here to help me, not you. Now get in the damned chair." Using both hands, he tried to haul her back to her feet. But she merely sank heavily back onto her thighs, hardly seeming to notice the painful angle of her arms. "No," she said, squeezing her eyes shut. "*No no no.*"

"*Oh la vache!*" the Basque groaned. Digging his hands into her armpits, he struggled to lift her back up to her feet. Given the difference in their sizes—he was easily twice as heavy as she was, possibly more—it shouldn't have been hard. And yet somehow she managed to keep slipping from his grasp, her slight body going so limp it seemed boneless.

"*Merde,* Laure," he grunted. "Help me to get her back up!"

At the sound of my name the girl opened her eyes, seeming for the first time to fully register that I was the same woman who'd tried to feed her in the softs, who'd given her advice she'd ignored.

"*Laure,*" she cried. Again, she wrenched herself free from the Basque, as though my name alone had somehow renewed her strength.

Cursing, Claude lunged to reinstate his grip. In response, she hurled herself directly at me, throwing her arms around my legs and burying her flushed face against my knees.

"Help me, Laure," she murmured into my skirts.

I stared down at the coppery top of her head and the pale, uneven line of her part, strangely aware of the press of her fingers against my calves. "It's all right," I said, awkwardly touching her copper-bright hair. "It's—it's going to be all right."

"*Nom de Dieu!*" the Basque exclaimed. "It's not going to be all right. Not even close to it. Not unless we get her in the goddamn chair. Take her by the hair if you have to."

Ignoring him, I extricated myself from the girl's grasp and knelt next to her on the floor.

"What the hell are you doing?" Claude demanded, moving toward us both.

I threw a hand up against him. "*Don't touch her,*" I hissed.

And to my amazement he complied again—though more, I think, out of astonishment than conscious deference. He watched in disbelief as I reached back into my pocket, pulling one of the rolls from its wrinkled depths. I heard more footsteps outside, along with two familiar male voices. One of them was Marie's, the other Jacques's. "I told them to hurry it up," the latter was saying, his voice slightly petulant. "But they take forever in there. I thought that girl had forgotten me entirely."

"It's fine," Marie said. "I still have time, so long as Claude has everything set up for us."

"They're here," Claude snapped. "Enough of this nonsense." He lunged at us again, once more reaching for the girl's arm and cursing as I slapped his hand away, hard. "What the devil was *that?*" he exclaimed. He sounded almost wounded, as though the blow constituted some sort of betrayal. "Have you gone mad again, too?"

Perhaps I had. And yet strangely enough, in that moment I actually felt more lucid than I could remember feeling since arriving at the Salpêtrière—more lucid, possibly, than I'd ever felt in my life.

Turning back to the girl, I took her right hand—the uninjured one—and placed one of the rolls directly in it. Then, locking gazes with her, I brought the other roll to my lips.

I took a bite.

"Go on," I murmured.

She stared at me, her eyes lichen colored and wide.

Outside, Marie was still speaking, his voice low enough that I couldn't make out the words. This time, to my alarm, it wasn't Jacques who answered.

"It's no trouble at all, Doctor," Babette said crisply. "I need to set up for Louise's next feeding anyway. Always happy to be of use when I can be. . . ."

My mouth went suddenly dry. But I forced myself to take another bite of bread, indicating the roll in the girl's hand with my chin. "*Please,*" I whispered between chews. "You must trust me."

She stared back at me blankly. It was as if I hadn't spoken a word.

Suppressing a groan, I swallowed my bite, tensing as Babette's familiar shrill sounded from the doorway. "What is *happening* here? Laure? Why are *you* here? You're supposed to be in the morgue!"

Glancing back, I saw her poised just beyond the threshold, her hands on her bony hips, Marie and Jacques standing just behind her. "And *you*!" Babette glared at the Basque. "Why isn't the girl in the chair?"

"She told me to hold off," Claude said, jerking his head in my direction. "To calm her."

"To *calm* her?" Babette's voice rose even higher in disbelief. "What goes on in that big southern skull of yours? Bissonnet, get up this very instant. There will be consequences for this. And you!" She glowered at Jacques. "You're an orderly, not a waiter at Café de la Paix. Get that girl into a chair and strap her down." Sighing in exasperation, she made to step into the room. But Marie set a hand on her shoulder.

"No," he said. "Wait."

His blue eyes were fixed on the girl. Following his gaze, I saw with relief that she was slowly—almost experimentally—bringing the roll I'd given her to her lips. We all fell silent as she paused midway, as if contemplating whether or not to proceed. At last, though, she took a small bite of the bread, chewed, and swallowed, the muscles of her throat contracting delicately and the bruises there undulating, like shifting black-blue shadows. Closing her eyes, she sat still for a moment, as if mentally tracing the bite's progress into her stomach. Then she took another bite. And another, until the roll was completely gone.

Opening her eyes then, she looked at me.

"Is there more?"

Wordlessly, I handed my roll to her. This one she ate quickly, as though the first had only served to make her aware of her hunger. Marie watched her intently. Then he shifted his attention to me.

"You brought her the bread?"

"I did," I said, climbing shakily to my feet.

"You had time to stop at a bakery but not at the morgue as I told you?" Babette shrilled, her thin face pink with anger. "Did you—"

I swallowed again, sure she was about to ask about the bracelet. Thankfully, Marie interrupted her. "Let's be glad she did," he said, pushing past her. "I think we can skip the tubing, with the patient eating of her own volition."

"It's only *bread*," Babette pointed out querulously. "It doesn't constitute a full meal."

"Better bread by choice than gruel by force," the doctor countered. He crouched down next to the girl, peering into her pale, freckled face. "Are you willing to eat more after this, mademoiselle?" he asked. "Say, some soup?"

"I will," she said, swallowing the last of the roll. "If Laure stays with me."

"She also said she'll sit for an assessment now," I added quickly.

Marie frowned. "She told you that?"

"She didn't—" Claude began, but I cut him off.

"Yes," I said firmly. "She did."

"This is true?" Marie asked the girl. "You'll meet—calmly, civilly—with Dr. Charcot for an examination, so he can properly diagnose you?"

The girl looked at me, and I felt the same jolt I'd felt when I'd locked gazes with her in the softs. As though I weren't just looking into the startling green of her eyes but *falling* into them, with a kind of stomach-lurching velocity.

"If Laure stays with me," she repeated. After the frenzied violence of a moment earlier, both her voice and her demeanor struck me as strangely composed, as though she'd arranged the whole encounter with the sole purpose of having it reach this conclusion.

"We'll hold off on the feeding," Marie said decisively, climbing back to his feet.

The Basque looked confused. "Will you still be wanting her in the chair?"

Marie shrugged. "She can sit; it will be easier. But she doesn't need to be strapped in. Fetch another chair from the dining hall, so Laure can sit by her." Glancing down at the bowl of gruel, he added: "And fetch some real food from the kitchen. More bread. Perhaps some soup, or cold pork as well, if there is any."

"Me?" the hulking orderly grumbled. "Why can't Laure go?"

"Laure," Marie said, "will remain with the patient." He smiled slightly beneath his beard. "It appears she does, in fact, have a calming influence. In fact, I'm going to assign the girl to Hysteria for the night. Laure can sleep beside her." He turned to Babette. "I believe Rosalie's cot is still available?"

Babette sniffed in disapproval. "Are you sure you trust her to behave, Doctor? These girls can be wily. And this one's already injured two attendants."

Marie studied the girl again, his sandy brows drawn together in thought. "I think she'll be fine," he said finally. "Won't you, mademoiselle . . ." Tilting his head, he frowned. "Actually, I don't believe we ever got your name. Can you share it with us now?"

"My name?"

He nodded. "You do have one, don't you?"

The girl blinked slowly, her full lips curving into a faint but unmistakable smile, as though the question amused her.

"My name," she said, "is Josephine."

Chapter Six

"He told me to take my dress *off*?"

My new ward's eyes had been closed as I dusted her face with rice powder. Now, though, her lids flew up in alarm, revealing twin pools of dismayed green.

It had been a little over a month since the feeding session Josephine and I had thwarted together, but that one small bite of bread had transformed our lives. Rather than being strapped into a stained chair, she now sat perched on Rosalie's bed while I prepared her for her second appearance on Charcot's stage. I'd already swept her red curls into the sort of simple twist that Rosalie would have refused to even consider, claiming it would make her look like a farmer's wife. Josephine, however, had merely glanced distractedly into the mirror when I was finished, pronouncing it "perfect" before sinking back into her own—seemingly troubled—thoughts.

"*Off?*" she repeated. "Just like that?"

"He said it was because you were at the seaside together, and it was hot." I brushed the rabbit's paw Rosalie had used for powder application between her pale, pinkish-golden brows. "So you were going to go bathing."

The look she gave me fell somewhere between rage and revulsion. Out of instinct I braced myself, even though over the course of the past four weeks she'd shown no sign of turning her now-legendary strength on me. But we all knew what she was capable of. And when we forgot, Julienne still had a faint red mark on her lower lip to remind us.

Now, though, she just grimaced and rolled her eyes.

"*Bathing*," she said contemptuously. "Where was Charcot during all this?"

I frowned, trying to remember. After her first hypnotism she'd asked me—with a strange intensity—to tell her exactly what had happened while she was "under," as well as anything that happened to her in that condition. It was a request that had taken me slightly aback. After all, Rosalie had never seemed to care a whit about what happened to her while mesmerized, apart from the time Charcot—annoyed by her prattle—accidentally paralyzed her tongue by instructing her to "stop flapping" it. For whatever reason, though, Josephine had been insistent. And so I'd agreed. Since then we'd fallen into a pattern of my recounting the details of her time passed under hypnosis with the same regularity with which I'd once told Amélie stories before bed.

This time, I'd been detailing the events of a research session in the director's office the prior day. We'd just reached the point where after entrancing Josephine, one of the interns—a diminutive doctor specializing in verbal tics and syphilitic disorders whom the hysterics had nicknamed "the Gnome"—had taken it upon himself to test how Josephine's natural modesty held up under hypnosis.

"Did Charcot just let him do it?" she persisted now. She'd begun worrying a cuticle beneath her right thumbnail with her left hand, aggravating a spot that was already reddened and raw from hours of prior picking. It seemed a new habit; I hadn't noticed her doing it during her first few weeks in the ward. Then again, she'd spent most of that time sleeping, as though those first fraught days of her commitment—along with whatever terrible trauma had preceded them—had left her too drained for anything else. Now that she'd settled into a daily rhythm here, however, she seemed continually engaged in some sort of anxious movement—chewing her nails, touching her hair, tapping her good foot on the wooden floor. It was as though an uncontainable current of electricity ran through her body, even at rest.

"I don't think he was listening," I said. "He was talking to Marie about getting last week's lecture notes ready for the publisher." I brushed the paw over her left cheekbone, then the right, veiling the spots there with a layer of white that cooled their tawny warmth to something closer to gray. After her triumphant first appearance in the amphitheater two weeks earlier, Charcot had instructed that going forward she was to be powdered as Rosalie had been. It was a few days later that I saw the *Figaro* editorial describing Charcot's newest hysterical muse as *transfixing in every aspect—save, perhaps, for a complexion marred excessively by sun spots.*

Personally, I loved Josephine's freckles. They looked to me like a dusting of cocoa against an expanse of warm milk. There had even been moments—pinning her hair up off her neck, or running a wet washrag across her back when I helped her bathe—when I'd been tempted to taste them with my tongue. But I knew better than to dispute one of Charcot's rulings, particularly when it came to Josephine. The first and last time I'd done so—at Josephine's medical assessment, a day after the roll incident—it had very nearly cost me my position.

"And did I do it?" she asked.

"Do what?"

"Take my *dress* off."

I hesitated. She had listened—at least initially. As the rest of the interns watched (and a few of them smirked), she'd begun hesitantly undoing her bodice. But at the fourth button she'd stopped, staring down at her pale fingers as though she'd just realized they belonged to someone else. Then she started trembling violently, in the way I'd come to recognize was a harbinger of the onset of one of her fits. That was when Marie—apparently only then noticing what was happening—stepped in to reverse the suggestion.

I considered telling her all this now—after all, I had promised to leave nothing from her now near-daily mesmerism sessions out. But I'd seen how profoundly distraught even a hint of improper male attention could make her. She would stoically withstand the most invasive medical examinations by Charcot or the other doctors. Yet an affectionate pinch of her cheek or absent pat on the shoulder afterward could send her into a stiff-limbed panic—or even trigger a hysterical episode, as the "bathing" suggestion very nearly had. She'd had the same reaction to the Basque after our feeding-room tussle with him—and sometimes, to nothing at all. Returning from the laundry with her stage dress earlier, for instance, I'd carried it over to where she'd been standing by her cot. I'd assumed she'd heard my approach. But when I'd laid the dress on her bed she'd whirled around with a little scream, and with such a look of sheer terror on her face that I'd nearly screamed as well.

I hadn't asked her about these reactions. I'm not sure it would have served any purpose, as she still had no memory of her former life, not even her family name. But I still found them unsettling; unspoken affirmations of the terrible story I'd been slowly piecing together about what had sent her to the banks of the Seine that day—and might well have sent her to her death.

"I didn't, did I?" she prompted now, her eyes still pinned to my face.

"No," I said firmly. "You told him the weather felt perfectly pleasant to you, and that if he wanted to bathe he could do it alone." It seemed a small enough detail to soften, given that she hadn't gotten past that fourth bodice button.

Josephine closed her eyes. "Good," she said. "*Mon Dieu*, but I hate that little man."

"You're not alone," I said dryly. Apart from with Charcot—who adored him—Dr. Gilles de la Tourette wasn't popular at the Salpêtrière. This was probably at least somewhat due to the man's unfortunate appearance (sallow skin, irregular features, stubby limbs). But it was more directly a product of the arrogance with which he spoke to patients and colleagues alike. Before now, I'd mostly just pitied him. He'd never been particularly rude to me, after all, and the ridicule he endured at the asylum reminded me of the mockery I'd suffered at my boarding school.

Leaning forward, I swept more powder across Josephine's brow and the five freckles there that reminded me of the Cassiopeia constellation our father had taught us to recognize. As I did, I marveled quietly at how different the experience of preparing her for Charcot's stage was from preparing Rosalie, which more often than not had felt like trying to keep a carriage that was hitched to panicking horses from running off a cliff. There were still challenges in tending Josephine, of course; though her fits occurred less frequently than Rosalie's, her still-surprising (at least, to me) strength made them even more hazardous. I already had deep bruises on both thighs from where her head had slammed into them while I held it in my lap. When Josephine was lucid, though, being with her felt less like tending a patient than spending time with a friend.

A friend. In this place.

The idea seemed strangely fantastical. Like stumbling upon a bluebell in the charred wake of an inferno.

By that point in my life I'd had few real friends, apart from my journals and books. There had been one teacher at school with whom I'd briefly become close, a young woman to whom I'd turned when the other students were cruel and who would comfort me and share her own trials as a schoolgirl. At some point, though, she seemed to have lost interest in our friendship, for while she remained cordial to me in the classroom, she stopped opening her door to me when I visited her chamber alone.

Even 'Nadette—the *internée* to whom I'd become closest in Hysteria—was someone I engaged with as much caution as confidence. In part, this was because she was prone to obscenely detailed descriptions of how everyone around her—including me, sometimes—would one day suffer in hell. But she was also the only one at the asylum with whom I'd shared my dilemma about Amélie—which meant that once I did leave (which I still intended to do as soon as I could manage it), 'Nadette would be the one person to know where I'd gone. I knew she'd never intentionally endanger me. But given how much she talked—in her sleep, in her fits, in her periodic drunken rampages—I had little faith she'd keep those whereabouts to herself.

With Josephine, though, it was different. For all the violence of her arrival, the murkiness of her past, and her periodic descents into flailing insentience, she had an unexpectedly grounding effect on me. Over the past weeks, as I'd introduced her to the daily rhythms and peculiarities of Hysteria and escorted her to and from Charcot's office, that dread-filled, hollow feeling to which I'd awoken daily since arriving at the asylum had been replaced by something else. It wasn't contentment, exactly. It wasn't even optimism, for between worry over the stolen bracelet (the theft of which burned continually in my conscience, no matter how I tried to rationalize it to myself) and the fact that there was still no word on my sister's well-being or whereabouts, my future continued to feel grimly tenuous.

But my present, at least for now, had taken on a kind of clarity and purpose I hadn't felt since the brief but bright period between Amélie's recovering from her sickness and Papa's taking ill. My days had lost the jangling hum of anxiety and annoyance that, between Rosalie's cruel volatility and Babette's contemptuous scrutiny, had been as much a constant for me as the dank ward air.

In fact, I rarely answered to Hysteria's head nurse at all anymore. It was instead Marie—and sometimes Charcot himself—to whom I reported whenever Josephine experienced some change in her symptoms, such as when a week earlier she'd awoken to find the vision in her right eye had shifted so that she now confused red with blue and orange with green. And it was to me, not Babette, that the doctors now turned for updates on everything from the girl's sleep and menstrual cycles to her bowel habits. Not surprisingly, this last change had pushed me even more deeply into the old woman's bad books. I'd heard her muttering to Julienne about how *arrogante* I'd become: "She thinks she's one of those nose-in-the-air lady doctors now," she'd groused.

"So what if she does?" Julienne retorted. "The skinny chit will never be more than what she is—an ugly maid in a madhouse."

But even Julienne's barbed invectives didn't sting as they once had—and this, too, I attributed to Josephine. *She* clearly didn't find me arrogant, or bookish, or boyish. She didn't even seem to find me plain. She marveled at the narrowness of my wrists and the slenderness of my fingers—"like a dancer's," she said once, tracing a tendon from wrist to knuckle to nail. I'd always thought my eyes mud colored and dull, but she insisted they had glints of gold in them, "like treasure buried in the earth." And she said my lashes were the longest she'd ever seen apart from those on a cow or a horse, which she also assured me was a compliment.

Perhaps best of all, though, she wasn't threatened by my social background, my schooling, or my love of reading books. Quite the opposite; she was fascinated by them, having seemingly had little schooling herself. In the precious free moments before lights-down she'd beg me to describe my boarding school to her, as though it were a castle out of some magical tale. She'd ask me to retell stories from books I'd read: Scheherazade spinning tales to save herself from a lustful and murderous king. Phileas Fogg fighting off Sioux warriors on his way to Omaha and rescuing a doomed princess in Bombay. When I recounted the last novel I'd finished, Auguste Villiers de l'Isle-Adam's fantastical *The Future Eve*, she'd laughed incredulously as I explained its premise: A fictional Thomas Edison, seeing only flaws in human females, sets out to invent the perfect "android" woman.

"I think Monsieur Edison and Dr. Charcot would get along very well," she said when I'd finished. Like many of her observations, it was a comment I'd find myself coming back to often in the months and years that followed.

And in the end this was also part of my fascination with Josephine— the universe of contradictions she embodied. She knew as little about herself as a newborn, thanks to her amnesia. And yet she seemed to possess a kind of world-weary wisdom rivaling that of the ancient *reposantes* outside. She could be breathtakingly violent, and yet there was a kind of serenity about her that felt as calming to me as the belladonna drops my father had sometimes prescribed to his nervous patients. Even her eyes were a paradox, one minute as gray as the ocean in winter, the next the color of sun-warmed green sea glass.

"Did he try anything else?" she asked. Her eyes—which now struck me as the color of honey-dipped olives—were still trained on my face.

"Who?"

"The Gnome. After trying to get me out of my clothes."

"Oh," I said. "No. Marie gave him a talking-to. He sulked in the corner for the rest of the session."

She nodded, evidently pleased by this. "And what happened then?"

"Charcot spent the next hour taking you through another one of those card exercises." Setting the powder down, I picked up Rosalie's rouge pot. It still felt strange to be using the Alsatian's things—especially with her sketched likeness staring out at us from the be-ribboned clippings that still hung over her bed. But Babette had instructed me to do so. "It's not as if she needs them where she is at the moment," she'd sniffed. Which was true enough.

I hadn't seen Rosalie since her expulsion from the ward. But I'd heard from Claudine that she looked terrible—thin and wan, the imperious fire that had animated her speech, posture, and gestures doused by long hours in Hydrotherapy. Word also had it she'd been begging for a meeting with Charcot, but that he had refused to engage with her. After his last lecture—which had been the first time he'd presented Josephine—a *Le Temps* journalist asked if Rosalie would return to his stage. Charcot just scowled and moved on to the next question.

"What kind of card exercise?" Josephine asked. "Like the cat card one he did with me?"

The "cat card" exercise was a hypnotic experiment Charcot had introduced his interns to a week prior. He'd begun by showing Josephine—whom as usual he'd entranced—a card that he'd marked inconspicuously on the back so that he alone would recognize it, and to which he'd told Josephine he'd affixed a photograph of a small white cat. In reality the card was blank, as were all the cards in the deck. Astonishingly, though, Josephine was able to quickly find it even after he'd thoroughly shuffled the cards together. Charcot repeated the exercise several times, each time inserting additional cards with different suggested images, and again she was able to not only find each one but describe the various "photographs" they supposedly bore. Even more strangely, she could still clearly see the cat's image on the card upon waking, though she remembered nothing of the experiment itself. She'd liked it so much that she'd asked to keep it, tacking it to the wall over her headboard next to a *Le Figaro* illustration of Rosalie's recoiling in horror at an imagined snake. She'd even given the "cat" a name: Mimi.

This designation had struck me as strangely poignant, perhaps because it made me wonder whether she'd actually *had* a cat named Mimi in her old life, or whether, like Amélie, she'd merely longed for one and been denied it by her parents. This, in turn, had made me wonder about those parents, for where were they now? Surely, I thought, they must be desperately missing their daughter. Had they been searching for her, as my own parents would have done? Had it even occurred to them that she might have ended up at the city's notorious asylum? There was always a steady stream of petitioners to the Salpêtrière's admissions offices: mothers and fathers seeking missing daughters, siblings seeking missing sisters, husbands seeking missing wives. All of them hoping desperately that their spouse or child had ended up here—perhaps mad, but alive—and not in the Paris Morgue.

It was a desperation I understood well, given Amélie's disappearance. In fact, I'd recently invested most of my small store of savings in notices I'd had placed in two Morvan-area periodicals recommended by the man who ran the boulevard de l'Hôpital news kiosk: the *Journal du Morvan*—which was the main regional paper—and a weekly agricultural bulletin called *The Friend of the Good Farmer of the South*.

Recherche, the advertisement read. *Seeking information on the whereabouts of Amélie Bissonnet, age 12. Physically slight, with brown hair and eyes, and a triangular scar of about 4 millimeters just above her right elbow. Send in-*

formation to Laure Bissonnet, at the hysteria ward of the Salpêtrière asylum. The notices had run two weeks ago now, and each day that went by without a response seemed to fuel a new nightmarish scenario about where my sister was, what terrible things might be happening to her.

"Which images did he use?" Josephine asked. "The same ones as before?"

Forcing myself back to the conversation at hand, I shook my head. "There was one new one. Charcot said it was of himself."

"And did I describe it back to him afterward? Like I did the cat?"

"You did."

"And what did I say? Specifically?"

I stifled a sigh. Recounting Josephine's hypnosis sessions to her sometimes reminded me of the endless-seeming conversational loops I'd have with Amélie when she was small, the answer to each question merely sparking another question. "You told him he was wearing a white shirt and a fine dark coat," I told her. "And that he had a Legion of Honor pin on his pocket. You said he was standing with a hand in his vest, like Napoléon."

Though I didn't say it, this had caused a chuckle among Charcot's interns, since as I've said the great man's resemblance to the disgraced emperor was widely remarked upon. One paper had even referred to him as the "Napoléon of neuroses."

"Then what?" Josephine prompted.

"Then you thought a moment and said his hair was darker in the photograph than it was in real life, and that there was more of it in the front, and so he must have taken the portrait some time ago." I gave a short laugh. "I think that caught him off guard."

She tilted her head. "Why? What did he say?"

"He didn't say anything. He just looked . . . surprised." Which, needless to say, didn't happen very often. Capping the rouge, I set it back on the bedside table and handed her Rosalie's little mirror. "Why are you so curious about all this, anyway? They're doctors, after all. Don't you trust them?"

"It's not that." Josephine gazed at herself in the glass, turning her heart-shaped face first one way, then the other, her good foot tapping distractedly against the floor. I was struck, as I often was, by the intensity with which she—like so many of the other ward hysterics—scrutinized her own image. As though examining a piece of fruit for bruises or imperfections. Or a twenty-franc bill for signs of counterfeiting.

"Then what is it?"

"It's more the—" She stopped, creasing her newly powdered brow. "It's the not knowing where I've *been*," she said slowly. "Sometimes when they wake me, it feels like I've simply . . . disappeared. I don't know why, but it's frightening." Setting the mirror down between us, she added, a little sheepishly: "I know it sounds foolish."

"It doesn't," I said. "I understand exactly what you mean."

"Really?" She frowned. "But you said you can't be hypnotized."

I looked away, feeling the self-conscious twinge that I always felt when this particular hysterical "failure" came up—a discomfort only deepened by the fact that Josephine herself had, in these past weeks, proven to be so spectacularly sensitive to entrancement that it had caused a small stir among the doctors. Indeed, the first time she'd been "put under" during her initial assessment with Charcot had marked one of the few other times I'd seen the man caught off guard.

Up until that point, the evaluation had unfolded as they usually did. I'd helped Josephine undress, and under Charcot's direction had placed her by the large window in his office so that the morning light illuminated her pale skin. He'd observed her from his desk, with the piercing and almost unblinking gaze he always used while diagnosing his patients. As though his eyes, like the radiographic rays that a few years later would be utilized in the asylum photography studio, had the power to pass straight through skin. He'd had Josephine limp back and forth a few times, and then perform a series of other movements designed to assess her balance, gait, and overall mobility, seemingly unconcerned by a tour group that had stopped right before the window and gawked through it as though staring into the Ménagerie du Jardin des Plantes monkey house.

Initially, I'd feared this attention might send the girl back into Amazonian battle mode—or at least distract her from Charcot's rapid-fire directives. But she'd followed his commands seamlessly, even gracefully, stretching her arms high, turning in a slow circle, bending over to touch her toes, all with the same placid if faintly removed look she'd worn as she'd silently polished off the rolls I'd given her the day before. This expression hadn't slipped once, not even when Charcot had one of his newer interns—a young clinician who'd just arrived from Vienna—take her temperature vaginally, pinch and prod her pale skin to test for anesthesia, and mark areas of it with grease pencil.

After the physical portion of the assessment, I was allowed to help Josephine back into her shift and her chair, though Charcot directed me to keep her gown and corset off. He consulted with Dr. Freud, who then knelt before Josephine, Charcot's mirror in hand. I'd found myself holding my breath, remembering how profoundly this one moment had shaped my own trajectory at the asylum.

"Keep your eyes on the mirror, please," Freud murmured in his heavily accented French. "Pay attention to its movement and to my voice, but to nothing else. Do you understand?"

Josephine had nodded, the strange, small smile she sometimes wore playing about her pink lips.

As the Austrian doctor began moving the tiny glass back and forth, I'd actually shut my eyes, afraid to watch. I'd been lucky enough to be diagnosed with hysteria despite the fact that Charcot considered hypnotic sensitivity a central feature of the disease. But I'd also presented with many of its other symptoms—the epileptoid fits, the delusions. I'd even suffered from anesthesia in my right hand—and, somewhat strangely, my lips—for several months after my father's death. But I hadn't had Josephine's history of violence toward others and herself—the sort of behavior that led to placement in the lunacy ward. And if she couldn't be entranced, it seemed all too likely to me that that was where she'd end up, despite all my efforts to keep her out of it.

Barely had I closed my eyes, though, when I heard Freud draw a sharp breath.

"Mademoiselle?" he asked uncertainly.

Josephine had fallen forward slightly in her seat. Her eyes were closed, her lips parted. Her chest rose and fell slowly beneath the thin cotton of her chemise.

"*Josephine?*" Freud said. "Can you hear me?"

At first, there was no response. Then she shifted slightly, sluggishly. "Yes," she murmured. The word emerged as though scraped from the bottommost depths of slumber.

Stunned, I leaned forward in my chair. She certainly *sounded* like she'd been entranced, and her countenance had that flat, slackened look I'd learned to associate with hypnosis. But it seemed impossible to me that it could have happened so quickly—and on the very first attempt. Under Charcot's tutelage, I knew, Freud had proven unusually skilled at mesmerizing. Though he'd been here less than a month, it rarely took him more than a minute or two to put a patient fully under—even less time than Babinski, who'd studied the technique for far longer.

In this case, though, it had barely taken a full three passes of his little mirror. I'd never seen anything like it.

The Austrian clearly hadn't either. After exchanging baffled glances with Charcot, he checked Josephine's pulse at her wrist, then her neck. He pulled up first her left eyelid, then her right, leaning over to peer into the dark pools of her pupils. Throughout all of this she didn't so much as flinch. Her breathing continued its slow and peaceful ebb and flow.

"She's fully under?" Charcot lifted a brow.

"She appears to be, yes." Releasing Josephine's eyelid, Freud climbed slowly to his feet. "Though I'll admit I'm . . ." He shook his head without finishing the sentence, returning his mirror to his pocket. "This response doesn't align with hypnotic theory as you've explained it to me."

"Theory is good," Charcot said curtly. "But it's not a substitute for clinical observation."

Rising from his thronelike chair, he shuffled over to where Josephine slumped in her seat, her eyes still closed, that faint smile still on her lips. He repeated Freud's actions, checking her pulse against his pocket watch and peering into her right eye, and then her left. Then, grunting, he turned back to his mentee.

"Take a note for the intake record," he said. "Subject appears very . . . no, perhaps *exceptionally* susceptible to hypnotic inducement."

He spoke with his usual quiet authority, his voice low, the words slow and weighted. And yet I thought I detected a new note in his tone—a vocal spark that, by the end of the morning, had grown into a blaze of visible excitement as he guided Josephine through each of the various stages of hysteria he'd deduced were central to the malady's expression. And from my chair by the door, I could see why. The girl's hysteria didn't unfold that morning in the textbook sequence to which Rosalie's had come to conform. But what her fits lacked in precision they more than made up for in the potent effect they had on those watching them. It's still a hard thing to put words to, but there was something about Josephine's contortions and strangled cries that was almost mesmerizing in its own right, an ineffable combination of strength and vulnerability, of rawness and grace, that I'd never seen in a hysterical episode before. Her epileptoid fits were so violent her teeth chattered, her green eyes rolling so far back in her head that she resembled the possessed in the garish paintings of exorcisms Charcot collected and hung on his office walls, interspersed with photographs and sketches of classic hysterical positions.

Her "exotic" movements were equally striking. As the doctors quickly discovered, not only could she hold the *arc de cercle* for even longer than Rosalie, but she produced the most intricate and demanding physical movements I'd yet seen in a hysteric, torquing her torso as she repeatedly slammed it against the floor, or hurling her legs over her head in a way that made her body seem to fully fold in half before thrusting them straight up in the air and—toes pointed— lowering them to the ground again in a smoothly even arc. This sequence—which she could repeat dozens of times without becoming tired or sore—had a fluidity to it that was almost dancelike; in fact, some of Isadora Duncan's dance moves, when I saw them three decades later, reminded me uncannily of parts of Josephine's "clonic" fits.

But it was the "passionate pose" stage of her episode that day, the phase Charcot had identified as the one in which hysterics act out powerful or traumatic moments from their past, that was at once the most riveting and shocking. Rosalie had earned her notoriety from this stage of episodes, which included graphic reenactments of losing her innocence at fourteen, to a furrier who'd taken her in when she lost her mother. It was clearly a painful memory for her, but the Parisian papers had loved it. *Le monde illustré* had dubbed her *Charcot's hysterical Bernhardt.*

In her fit Josephine, too, clearly relived part of whatever assault it was that had left its brutal marks on her body and mind. Only on that day, her reenactment felt less like a gasp-inducing theater presentation than watching her actually experience the assault as it happened—it was that realistic, that terrifying. As her slight body spasmed, it had so truly seemed to be in response to a vengeful fist that the hairs on my arms and nape actually stiffened. When she flipped from her back to her stomach, it was with such startling violence that I kept looking for the heavy hand that had done it. I think part of me even wanted that—for the shape of an actual man to materialize—if only to make sickening sense of what I was seeing. For I knew the attack wasn't real—that it *couldn't* be real. And yet I felt the same shock and nausea I would have had that brutality been unfolding directly before me. At one point, as Josephine's head was jerked up sharply—as if being pulled by the hair—I could have sworn I felt the fiery sting of the abuse in the follicles on my own scalp, my eyes watering in shocked response.

Stop it, I'd wanted to shout at the two doctors. *This isn't right. Make it stop. Make her stop.*

But neither did. Both Charcot and his disciple merely continued watching the convulsing girl with a kind of intrigued incredulity. Charcot—who had been kneeling beside Josephine during the epileptoid phase of her attack—had half risen to one knee, but seemed to have forgotten that he'd been planning to stand. Freud hovered over him, his clipboard fallen to his side and his dark eyes barely blinking as Josephine wrenched—or was wrenched—from her belly onto her back. Groaning, she jerked both knees toward her chin, as though she'd just taken a heavy kick to the abdomen. A trickle of blood appeared at the corner of her mouth and made its way toward her chin, a crimson thread. "*Stop,*" she gasped, her green eyes fixed glassily on the ceiling. "Stop, monsieur. Please. I beg you. I'll do whatever you want." The words seemed to earn her a brief respite, for she collapsed fully onto the floor, her chest rising and falling sharply beneath her thin undergarment.

All at once, though, her expression shifted from fear to something more approaching intense concentration. She made a sudden swiping motion at her left heel, as though trying to scratch an itch there. Then her limbs stiffened, her eyes rolling back in her head so forcefully that only the whites became visible once more. She was mumbling something under her breath, so quietly that at first I couldn't make out the words, until I could.

"They are coming now," she said. "*They are coming.*"

She repeated the phrase over and over, the words bleeding together and slowly lifting in volume until they became another full-on shriek. The sound of it seemed to lodge in my back teeth: I shut my eyes and blocked my ears, but my damp palms were no match for the ghastly chant. Nor could they shut out the sound of another echoing shriek that made its way slowly into my consciousness. It wasn't Josephine's, but it was just as shrill and terrified:

"*WAKE HER UP!*"

It took me a moment to recognize that second voice as my own—and that I'd leapt to my feet to unleash it. As soon as I did, I dropped my hands to my sides and stood there, my ears ringing so loudly from the force of my own outburst that I didn't at first register that Josephine had finally stopped screaming and was now sobbing violently.

Opening my eyes, I saw both Charcot and Freud were staring at me. The younger doctor looked shocked and slightly dazed, as though I'd just woken him from a trance of his own. As our eyes met, I thought his cheeks reddened beneath his mustache and beard.

Charcot's unfashionably clean-shaven face, however, reflected only rage. "What did you say?" he barked, his eyes burning into mine as he clambered to his feet.

"I . . ." I swallowed, tasted blood on my tongue. "I said nothing."

"Indeed, you did." Charcot's voice shook with fury. "You *shouted* at me."

"I'm sorry, Docteur," I whispered.

For a moment, the close air in his cluttered clinic seemed to draw even closer around me. I was afraid to move, afraid to even breathe. Somewhere outside on the grounds, Tante Maubert gave a gleeful screech: "I respect *la Place Maubert,* you old turds!"

Charcot let out a low, hissing breath.

"I will tell you this exactly once." His voice was so low I had to strain to hear it. Somehow, this felt more ominous than if he'd been shouting into my ear. "Ward girls who don't know their place at the Salpêtrière have no place in its wards."

"I'm sorry," I repeated, dropping my gaze to the floor. "I promise it won't happen again."

By this point, Josephine had pulled herself into a sitting position and buried her face in her knees, her sobs dwindling to soft keening noises. "If I may say so, *maître,*" Freud offered, his French even more thick and labored than usual, "it was an extraordinarily powerful . . . demonstration. I felt its violence myself." He looked shaken, even awed, as though he'd witnessed a vision of the Holy Virgin herself.

Still Charcot said nothing, his hawkish eyes fixed unblinkingly on the now tangled top of Josephine's head. He seemed to be weighing something, the pale fingers of his left hand tapping thoughtfully against his right forearm. He wasn't a small man, but his hands always struck me as strangely dainty, as though whoever had made him had run out of proper-sized parts by the time they got to his wrists.

At last he nodded. "Wake her," he told Freud. "Have her installed in Hysteria. We'll use her in Friday's lecture, after my segment on Parkinson's."

I was so startled by this pronouncement that I barely registered relief at the diagnosis. Friday was in less than three days' time.

Freud looked taken aback too. "Are you sure that's wise, *maître*? You've only entranced her once. And we don't know how she'll respond to the lights, to an outside audience. To . . ."

But Charcot was already making his way back toward his desk. There seemed to me to be a lightness to his gait that hadn't been there when he'd hobbled into the room. "Friday," he repeated firmly. "I'll want her here at ten sharp tomorrow morning. Tell Babette I'll need her for the full day." These last two orders were directed at me, over his shoulder. "And, Laure?"

I froze, still half expecting to be dismissed.

"Have my wife's dress fitted for her." He said it casually, as though Rosalie had never worn it at all.

The next two days were spent almost entirely in his office. In addition to prompting numerous hysterical episodes—and several more chillingly convincing encounters with what appeared to be the same spectral assailant conjured during her assessment—Charcot put Josephine through almost every hypnotic exercise he'd ever conducted on Rosalie, along with several I'd never seen him conduct on anyone. He tested her dermographic sensitivity; her stigmatic response; her anesthesia levels; her vision; her tongue's perception of sour, salty, and sweet. He had her sniff pungent smelling salts and told her it was perfume; he threw a handkerchief at her feet and declared it a snake. He told her it was snowing and had her open her mouth to catch the imagined icy flakes on her tongue, nodding in approval when she said they tasted of sugar. He told her his top hat was an infant who'd been left at the asylum gates and had her rock it to sleep in her arms.

And that Friday, as he'd promised, he put her on his stage, directly after a lecture on the complexities of diagnosing Parkinson's disease in the absence of physical tremors.

Charcot introduced his new hysteric not by an alias, as he usually did with his medical lecture subjects, but as "a new patient of ours, Mademoiselle Josephine." After hypnotizing her himself (another departure from his norm), he then put her through all four hysterical stages—in perfect order.

The audience responded with even more enthusiasm than they had to Rosalie's presentation of the illness, leaning forward in their seats as Josephine seized and shivered and shook, murmuring as she contorted and bent. When she writhed and wept and struggled against her invisible assailant, there were gasps of outright alarm, and when she dissolved into tears and her haunting chant of *they are coming*, I saw several people look about apprehensively, as if half expecting to come under attack themselves.

After finishing this initial exercise, Charcot put her into a state of catalepsy that left Josephine's body so rigid that it could be laid out like a plank between two chairs, her head resting on one of the chair backs and her ankles on the other, her legs and torso suspended between them, as if by magic. He was greeted by collective gasps of amazement, as though he were a wizard who, with a wave of his little mirror, had turned a woman into wood before their eyes. The following day *Le Figaro* ran a rhapsodic editorial on *Mlle. Blanche's apparent successor, Mlle. Josephine, whose slight form variously displays the plasticity of a Chinese acrobat, the physical might of a strongman, and the pathos of Leda battling her swan.*

"It's true," I said now, returning Rosalie's mirror to the bedstand. "I can't be hypnotized. But I know what it's like to wake up without remembering anything that's happened while I've slept."

Josephine tugged absently at a red strand of hair that had fallen onto her forehead. "What do you mean, 'without remembering'? What are you supposed to remember?"

"Dreams," I said shortly. "I don't dream."

"You don't *dream*?" Her lips pursed a little, as though she thought I was teasing her. "You've *never* dreamed?"

"I had dreams before." I stood, brushing rice powder from my skirt. "Before I came here. But after I was admitted they all just . . . stopped."

"How do you know they stopped? Perhaps you're just forgetting them when you wake up."

"I'm not forgetting them," I said. "I'm not sure how I know. But it's—just different than it was before."

And it was. In my old life, I (like most people, I think) did, in fact, forget most of my dreams upon waking. But I somehow still always knew that I'd *had* them. Their shifting landscapes and fantastic plot-lines might have been mostly hidden from my waking self, but they were also never very far from it. I sensed them somehow, shimmering behind my conscious thoughts like watery reflections on the surface of a lake. I'd often go about my days with some surreal detail of them snagged in my mind, a peculiar image or unsettling emotive echo that served as a cryptic clue by which to try to reconstruct them, though I rarely did. Or at least, not fully.

Upon arriving in Hysteria, though—or rather, awaking there after my week of delusional caregiving—I was aware of a strange new emptiness, one that had nothing to do with my father's death or my sudden separation from my sister. It was hard to pinpoint at first, what it was that was missing. But as the days stretched dully into weeks, and the weeks grimly into months, I became aware of that same strange sense Josephine spoke of, of having been *erased* while I slept. It was a feeling entirely different from the hazy and nauseous aftermath of an etherization. It was deeply disorienting, as if some extra dimension I'd taken for granted had simply been rubbed out when I wasn't looking, or some unseen part of me—some invisible limb I'd been unconsciously using for balance—had been inexplica-bly lopped off. I felt it even now as I gazed back at Josephine: a strange emptiness at my core, as blank and lusterless as the lime-washed ward walls.

Turning, I took Rosalie's corset from its hook on the wall, shaking the thing out and unleashing a potent whiff of old sweat, stale laven-der, and the special Savon au Bouquet with which the Alsatian had washed herself before lecture nights. The device fit Josephine well enough around the middle, though it gaped at the bust and hips no matter how tightly I laced it. Still, it was all we had apart from the bulky, laceless asylum girdles patients were assigned to wear with their hospital gowns.

"Here," I said, wrapping the corset around her slender waist and hooking it up in the front for her. As I moved behind her to attend to the laces, she pensively chewed her lower lip, heedless of the rouge I'd just daubed onto them. "I think I'd be glad if my dreams vanished," she mused, sucking in her breath as I tightened her stays. "Most nights they're worse than having nothing."

"You say that," I said. "But you'd feel differently if they did." Reaching under her arms, I adjusted the corset's rim so that it fit as snugly as I could make it beneath her small breasts. "I'd be happy to even have my worst dreams back now. Otherwise, it feels as though I'm just losing everything all over again."

"What do you mean by 'everything'?"

I sighed. "I mean I've already lost everything once. My mother and baby brother, my father and sister. Our home. Now I don't even have them in my dreams."

Josephine looked at me over her shoulder. "You had a sister?"

"Have," I said, correcting her without thinking, then immediately wanted to take it back.

"Really? Where is she?"

I didn't answer, busying myself with her petticoat and Rosalie's sweat-stained bustle pad. Apart from Bernadette, I hadn't told anyone about Amélie. In part this was because I was still worried about being tracked down once the bracelet's theft was discovered. In part it was because of a superstitious but very real fear that the more I talked about my sister, the less likely I'd be to find her alive.

As Josephine turned to face me, though, I realized to my surprise that I actually *wanted* to tell her. Not just about my little sister, but about my whole family, and our flat in Chaussée d'Antin, and the little ceramic cat Amélie had carried in her pocket for weeks. I wanted to tell her about the world I'd lost, to mourn its disappearance with her the way I mourned my vanished dreams. I wanted to tell her about my rage at the city office that had callously shipped Amélie away—and then even more callously lost her. About the endless scenarios in my head that kept me from my dreamless sleep on so many nights. I wanted to tell her about the bracelet, stuffed deep into the straw depths of my mattress. I wanted it all so badly that I all but felt the words in my mouth, fully formed; hot little stones burning against my tongue.

"Is she here too, then?" she was asking. "Your sister?"

"I don't know where she is." My voice cracked as I said that. "But I'm going to find her," I added.

Josephine was still gazing steadily into my eyes. I'm not sure what she saw there, but for a heartbeat neither of us spoke. Reaching out, she touched the back of my hand. It was just a light brush. And yet I seemed to feel it everywhere: In my belly, my lungs. Against the backs of my knees. I was unexpectedly swept by a hot wash of emotion, a confusing, sour-sweet blend of grief and gratitude and shame, and something else that I couldn't—or perhaps was too fearful to—name. I opened my mouth to say something, though I'm not sure what it was. But before I could speak, Babette was standing before us, her eyes snapping, one gnarled finger pointing at the ward clock.

"Do you know what time it is?" she barked. "The girl's due at the amphitheater in twenty minutes! And she doesn't even have the cursed dress on!"

A few weeks earlier, her tirade would have made me jump in my boots. Now, though, I simply sighed. "I'm putting it on now," I said, reaching for Rosalie's gown. "We'll be there with time to spare."

The old woman looked at me coldly. "Think you're more important than Charcot now, don't you," she muttered. "And him the greatest doctor in the world."

As she strode off with a grimace, I turned back to Josephine with the dress, trying not to look at the Alsatian—in that very same gown—staring down at me from her beribboned clipping on the wall above us. As I went to lift the skirt over Josephine's head, though, something in her expression—a strange cross between smugness and suppressed mirth—made me pause.

"What?" I asked.

"She's in love with him."

"Who?"

She rolled her eyes. "Babette," she said. "With Charcot."

"You can't be serious."

"She's as mad over him as Bernadette is over that Dr. Babinski," she said, as matter-of-factly as though confirming the sun had risen that morning. "She probably sleeps with his photograph beneath her pillow."

The idea was so ludicrous—the woman had to be at least a decade older than Charcot, who was well past sixty himself—that I continued staring at her, dumbstruck. I think my mouth actually fell open.

Then I burst out laughing, overcome by the idea of those two sallow-faced creatures—the old doctor and even older nurse—sneaking kisses in the linen closet or scurrying off together for a secret tryst in the softs. Even as I laughed, though, I couldn't help thinking that it also made a strange kind of sense. It explained the way Babette smoothed her hair whenever Charcot's laborious footsteps sounded in the hallway outside, the way she still bobbed girlish curtsies when he left and entered the ward. It explained her reverence for the ovarian compressor (Charcot's invention) and her insistence it be used even on patients like myself and Louise, on whom it clearly had no effect. For the first time, I found myself wondering whether my supervisor had ever known love—and whether it was the lack of love that had made her so bitter and brittle.

"Do you think he knows?" Josephine was asking, lifting her arms so I could ease the gown's skirt over her head.

"He must," I said, carefully pulling it down around her waist and the pads. "He knows everything."

As her face reemerged from the soft blue folds, that strange little smile was playing on her lips.

"No one knows everything," she said.

———

Ten minutes later, we stood in the shadowed passageway to Charcot's stage, awaiting our cue. The *Figaro* piece had clearly sealed Josephine's reputation as Rosalie's successor: There were hardly any free seats in sight. Interestingly, there were also more women than I'd ever seen at a lecture—a half dozen at least. Charcot had just finished answering questions about the first part of his lecture on senile pathology, pausing afterward to check the pendulum clock on the wall. Precisely when it struck eleven, he cleared his throat.

"Our next discussion," he said, "involves some new characteristics we've discovered of an ancient but mysterious disease. That is, hysteria."

The room—which had been rustling and resettling itself after the last hour—stilled abruptly, as it always seemed to do when Charcot spoke that word. He gazed out over the expectant faces, his eyes bright, as though he'd successfully cast a spell on his viewers.

"We have for you today a relatively new case," he continued, "one I believe you will find rather interesting." Turning, he nodded at me. "Please bring out Mademoiselle Josephine."

I heard a sea of murmurs, Josephine's name rising among them like waves splashing against a quiet beach: *That's her! That's Josephine!*

"Let's go," I said, grasping her arm. Unexpectedly, though, she held back. Worried, I glanced down at her, recalling Rosalie in the fateful moment before she'd hurled herself from Charcot's favor.

Rather than racing toward the stage, though, Josephine leaned over. She pressed her lips to my ear.

"You're going to find her," she murmured. "Your sister. I know it. And when you do, you'll find your dreams as well."

Chapter Seven

Josephine's second appearance on Charcot's stage was even more rhapsodically received than her first. Charcot led her seamlessly through the "false photograph" exercise again, having her retrieve and describe "photographs" of a donkey in the Pyrenees, the Venus de Milo, and—probably on the Gnome's suggestion—a scantily dressed woman in a bathing machine. He then guided her through what he described as a "classic four-stage hysterical fit" that culminated in the same shocking pantomime of a horrific assault. As the girl's shrieks and protests mounted, the room's atmosphere tautened so palpably I all but felt it like a stretched sheet against my skin. And as she collapsed senseless on the stage, the audience sat in stunned silence, the air still echoing with her desperate screams of *THEY ARE COMING!*

The applause that followed wouldn't have been out of place at the Opéra de Paris. Even Charcot seemed caught off guard by it, exchanging an arch look with Marie as he handed him lesson notes as he always did after a lecture, accompanied by a stern admonition to *arrange these for publication*. But I could tell he was pleased, just as he surely was pleased by the article that ran in *Le Figaro* the following morning: *Mademoiselle "Josephine,"* its editors wrote, *a lithe redhead with striking green eyes, may be the most mesmerizing of the Salpêtrière's somnambulists yet. Her hysterical sensitivities hint at outright clairvoyance, and her halluci-*

natory episodes are on par with our leading queens of the stage in terms of their drama and passion.

He was clearly less happy, however, with the column's closing observation, a pointedly Parisian note about Josephine's *ill-fitting and somewhat shabby-looking frock,* which the editor claimed stood *in clear contrast with that of her popular—and now mysteriously absent—predecessor, "Blanche W."*

Per Charcot's instructions, of course, Josephine had actually been wearing the same hand-me-down gown of Madame Charcot's that Rosalie always wore in her presentations. The difference was that even with it pinned and tucked about her slight form, the girl still looked like a child playing dress-up in it—especially since it was paired with Rosalie's too-big corset and the grubby hospital-issued *sabots* that were now Josephine's only pair of shoes. The very day the piece ran, Charcot pulled me aside after his morning session with Josephine, handing me a note authorizing La Samaritaine's cashiers to charge his store account for a new outfit. "And make sure it all *fits,*" he snapped.

Rosalie, of course, would have been beside herself at this instruction; she'd long complained that the blue dress was becoming ragged at the cuffs, and that its bustle was unfashionably oversized. Josephine, however, merely watched Charcot shuffle away until he was out of hearing. Then she turned to me with that smile that always struck me as somehow amused and mournful at once.

"Odd," she said.

"What?" I asked.

"That he cares so much," she said. "Given that he thinks hysterics are the vain ones."

The following day she perched beside me on a crowded omnibus, her legs crossed beneath her skirts, her good foot jiggling like a small restless animal. She'd seemed in good enough spirits as we left the asylum. After we'd changed buses at Bastille, though, she'd grown somber, her heart-shaped face taking on that look of troubled contemplation I'd been noticing of late. As the team of dappled Percherons pulled us parallel to the river on Quai Saint-Bernard, the morning light through the glazed glass window revealed how fatigued she looked.

This wasn't surprising. She'd been having violent nightmares since being put on Charcot's stage, dreams that—unlike her hypnotic episodes—she recalled in terrifying detail: She was being trampled by horses. Falling into a roaring fire. Sinking helplessly to the sludge-covered bottom of some dank body of water, her lungs aching to inhale. I'd become so attuned to these nocturnal terrors that I often found myself by her bedside before I was fully awake myself, speaking soothingly, stroking her damp brow. It was partly why I was also exhausted. Though of course, there was another reason as well: The marquis's bracelet was still buried within the ticking of my mattress, its illicit presence a source of such rumination and worry that even when Josephine slept quietly I found myself twisting and turning in my sheets, a ship caught in a cottony storm. And it wasn't only out of fear my theft would be discovered before I escaped the asylum. It was also over how, exactly, to navigate that departure, for I now feared selling it wasn't as straightforward as I'd anticipated. The shop it had come from, the Swallow, was actually somewhat famous in Paris, its wares—as I'd since discovered to my dismay—advertised in many of the city's papers. I feared that any respectable pawnbroker in Paris might recognize where the bracelet had come from, and wonder how it had ended up in the chapped hands of a Salpêtrière *fille de service*. It would only take one serious inquiry to trace the thing back to the marquis. And once that happened I was as good as arrested.

And yet the longer the bejeweled trinket remained in its current hiding place, the more I worried about its discovery there. I'd almost been tempted to bring it shopping with us today, for fear Babette, Julienne, or one of the patients in the ward would rifle through my things out of curiosity, spite, or sheer boredom. In short, I felt as effectively manacled to the accessory as I'd once been to my ward bed, as afraid of selling it as I was of *not* selling it. At times I feared my mounting anxiety alone would give me away, like the beating of Monsieur Poe's telltale heart.

The omni swerved as the *cocher* turned his team to avoid some obstacle or pothole on the road. Lurching sideways with the motion, I felt a familiar bitterness bloom in the back of my throat. *Find something fixed in place,* my father had always instructed me when my travel sickness hit. *Something that isn't moving or changing. Keep your eyes on it, and breathe deeply.*

Ever the obedient daughter, I fastened my gaze on a weathered poster for a wild tiger act in Le Nouveau Cirque, starring "Fearless Jeanne," a buxom, whip-wielding woman—*raised on tigress milk and danger!*—whose muscular calves were on full display beneath her knee-length skirts.

"Are you all right?"

Turning, I saw Josephine gazing at me in concern. I felt my throat tighten unexpectedly. Such a mundane question: *Est-ce que tu vas bien?* And yet it felt like a lifetime since anyone had asked that of me—at least in a context that wasn't entirely clinical.

"I'm fine," I said. "I just wish we'd gotten one of the bigger buses. We could have sat outside."

"It's a foolish rule," she said dismissively.

I shrugged. "It's for efficiency as well as safety. Women take too long to climb ladders—and it's more dangerous for us, since we have to do it in dresses. My father treated lots of broken limbs and concussions due to falls from omnibus ladders. Though my mother thought it was dangerous for other reasons."

"What reasons?"

I laughed. "She always said most men in Paris were pigs and was sure they'd look up our skirts if we climbed up."

She nodded thoughtfully, as though evaluating this hypothesis rather than finding it amusing, as I'd intended. As she turned her gaze back to the river I leaned my head back against the carriage wall, thoughts still circling my family. When would they last have had that argument? It would obviously have to have been before Maman died, so I wouldn't have been older than twelve. Closing my eyes, I tried to picture the scene: My father with his pipe and his newspaper, sitting in the worn armchair by our fireplace. My mother on the chaise longue, her needlework in a lap that was perhaps already being crowded out by her growing belly—a belly that would, in a few months, give fruit not to new life, but to two untimely deaths. Where would Amélie have been at that moment? Asleep already in our room? At our mother's swollen feet, pressing the bell of Papa's stethoscope against the sawdust-stuffed chest of one of her dolls? I imagined her solemn, high-pitched voice, delivering one of her typically rambling prognoses: *You will live, but you must go to bed on time each night, and eat lots of jam and butter, and apply leeches and mustard to your backside for ten years.*

For a few seconds it was as if warm honey were flowing through my veins; the memory was that achingly sweet. Then I remembered where I was now—and that I didn't know where my sister was. That she might already be injured, or trapped, or undergoing the horrific kind of abuse that Josephine and so many others in Hysteria had. That for all I knew, she might even be dead. For, I reflected, wasn't that the one flaw in my father's logic? In the end, *nothing* is fixed. *Everything* changes. It takes so shockingly little to shatter the fragile walls of the present, to splinter the comforting illusion of permanence to which we all cling.

And in that moment, I made my decision: I had waited long enough. I had to start my search. If I couldn't sell the bracelet in Paris, I'd sell it en route to Morvan, somewhere that, between my wages and the little savings I had left after placing the advertisements, I could get to on my own. I'd have to get my hands on a map somehow and research possibilities. Or perhaps just ask at the Gare de Lyon when I got there.

The thought gave me a slight pang, for it would be hard to leave Josephine. But I knew she'd survive here without me. She was clearly on her way to great things, fully on track to an even higher place in Charcot's esteem than the lofty one Rosalie had occupied. She'd easily find someone else to provide the services I'd been providing her—to help her wash and dress, to calm her at night. To exhaustively fill in (or selectively leave out) details of all that happened to her while she was entranced. She'd almost certainly be fine, I reassured myself. Amélie, however, might not be—and the longer I waited, the more at risk she'd be.

The resolution had the effect of one of the tonics my father prescribed his patients for dyspepsia: Almost at once my queasiness eased. Spirits buoyed, I turned back to Josephine to ask her whether she wanted to visit the shoe department or the dress gallery first. The question congealed in my mouth, though, when I saw how dramatically her aspect had suddenly changed. She was trembling, her eyes wide and unfocused, her lips pressed together so tightly they almost seemed to disappear.

"What is it?" I asked, alarmed.

She squeezed her eyes shut, her hands flying to her throat as they sometimes did before her fits. I quickly reached into my pocket for the vial of ether I'd negotiated from Babette for the trip. But when Josephine opened her eyes again there was no sign in them of the strange blankness that signaled the onset of an attack. They were instead filled with the same wild panic I'd seen in them as the Basque had dragged her toward the feeding chair.

"What's wrong?" I repeated, putting my hand on her arm.

She shook her head violently. "Off," she gasped. "I have to get *off*." She was staring at the carriage door, which the conductor was pulling shut after allowing a passenger off. Her expression was that of a drowning woman watching her lifeline disappear.

I leapt to my feet. "Monsieur!" I called to the conductor. "Wait, please!"

Gripping Josephine's arm, I helped her navigate the thicket of laps, knees, and outstretched feet until we reached the exit. The conductor hauled the door open for us with an eye-roll, pursing his lips as I herded Josephine down the platform steps to the curb. "Pay more attention next time," he snapped as we fell back onto the sidewalk.

With that he slammed the door shut, and the bus lurched its way back onto rue de Rivoli. Panting a little, I turned again to Josephine, who was gasping as though she'd just finished a sprint. I looked about for a bench, a crate, even an upturned bucket for her to rest on. Seeing nothing, I helped her toward the bridge so we could at least lean against its stone *balcon* to catch our breath.

My instinct, as we stood together beneath the stern steel gaze of Henri IV, was to soothe her as I would have after one of her night terrors: by stroking her arm or shoulder, or perhaps even embracing her. But something about her in that moment—an agitation that seemed almost to radiate off her skin—kept me from doing so. And so we remained as we were, my hand hovering tentatively by the small of her back, her hands covering her face in seeming despair.

I waited until her breathing seemed to finally slow a little before asking a third time: "What is it?"

The look she gave me when she lifted her eyes was disoriented at first—as if she'd forgotten I was even there.

"I've remembered," she said slowly. "Why I was here, on the bridge. Why I wanted to jump."

I stared at her, a sudden chill sweeping through me as I belatedly made the connection. Because of course, it was from this very bridge—the Pont Neuf—that she'd been dragged the day of her arrival. How could I have forgotten?

"I remember almost all of it now," she continued. "It's been coming back to me, bit by bit. But just now, on the bus—I remembered the worst part of all." She took a shuddering breath.

"What was that?"

"How it *felt*. Standing here. Thinking that that"—she waved a trembling hand toward the glinting water—"was the only way to escape them. To escape all of them."

I knew hysterics with amnesia usually regained their memories with time. Somehow, though, I hadn't expected hers to return—or at least, to return so soon. Or perhaps it was more that I didn't *want* hers to return, for the same reason I didn't want to recount the less savory elements of the doctors' experiments on her: I wanted her to be spared the pain of that knowledge. Even now, part of me wanted what she was saying to not be true.

And yet it all made sense: Her increasingly somber mood, even as she gained the favor of Charcot, his junior doctors, and all of Paris. The increasingly agitated fidgeting; the jumpiness. The nightmares . . .

"When did you begin to remember?" I asked her.

"Perhaps two weeks ago."

I nodded slowly, thinking back. The night terrors had begun worsening about two weeks earlier. "And they chased you to the river? Those men who attacked you?"

"I thought men were chasing me," she said. "But not *that* man."

"Which man?"

"*That* man," she repeated, shuddering. "The man who—who did all those things to me."

"So there was only one?"

She gave me a strange look. "Isn't one enough?"

"Of course." I looked away, cheeks flushing. "I only—you always speak of *they* when you seize. You say, '*They are coming.*' I assumed you meant whoever had hurt you."

"I didn't," she said grimly, turning her gaze to the water. "I meant someone else."

"Who?"

She hesitated before answering. "The *flics*."

"The *police*?"

She nodded, tearing at a piece of thumbnail with her front teeth. "I was so frightened, Laure. I was half mad, really, after what I'd just done. I was sure they were right on my heels. And when they pulled me down from the railing I was certain they were taking me to prison. Perhaps even the guillotine. It was only later that I realized that it didn't make any sense. They wouldn't have found him that quickly."

"Found who?" I asked, confused.

Another pause; a much longer one this time.

"The man I murdered," she answered at last.

"The man you *what?*" She'd said it so quietly, and with so little expression, that I was certain I'd misheard.

"Murdered," she repeated. "Killed. I killed him, Laure."

My lips suddenly felt misshapen, locked, my tongue a numb weight in my mouth. "When?" I finally managed to say.

"That morning," she said. "The day they brought me to the hospital."

"Why?"

"Because he *deserved* it." This time there was no hesitation at all.

I swallowed, unnerved by the cold satisfaction in her voice. It was a tone I'd never heard from her before. "He—he was the one who caused all those injuries?" I asked. "The one you see when you have your attacks?"

She nodded. "He'd been abusing me for weeks. Though it had started out as something else."

"As what?"

"As friendship." Her lips twisted bitterly. "Or at least, that's what I thought. He said I was clever, and 'underappreciated.' He was going to help me rise through the servants' ranks at the house where I worked. He even said he'd teach me to read and write better. But instead of giving me lessons he began trying to get me to do . . . other things with him."

She dropped her gaze to her hands, clasping and unclasping them against the worn, polished stone. "I kept asking him to stop. But he wouldn't. Instead, he became violent, forcing me when I tried to pull away. I couldn't think of any other way to make it end. So I hid a knife in my boot. And that last time, when he went to—when he—"

She bit her lip, leaving the sentence unfinished, taking a deep breath before resuming. "I waited until he was on top of me. Then I did it. I—I stabbed him. I plunged the knife right into his body. And I kept it there until I knew for sure that he was dead."

Her eyes were on the Square du Vert-Galant below us. The little park was filled with pedestrians out enjoying the sunshine, its manicured edges bursting with new green growth. Two small girls in white dresses chased hoops through the dappling shade, followed by a frazzled-looking caregiver. I stared at them unseeingly, struggling to process what it was I was hearing.

I knew I should be horrified: If what Josephine was saying was true, she was a murderess. And yet, any horror I felt was not for what it was that she had done, but for what she'd had to endure before doing it: The dangled reward. The deception. The devastating abuse. Even that she'd had to endure killing him—lying there beneath her abuser's loathsome, shuddering body as he expired—struck me as less her own crime than a horrific consequence of his.

"Who was he?" I asked, after what felt like a very long time.

"My employer," she said. "A judge. After my father left us—I was still a baby—my mother had started working for him in the kitchen. She'd brought me with her sometimes when I was small. When I was older, she'd bring me in to help wash the dishes on days I wasn't working at the laundry where she'd placed me. He'd made no secret of his admiration for her. I guess that at some point he'd decided he liked the looks of me too."

She paused, shakily pushing her hair back with one hand.

"One day she came home and told me another girl who'd worked for him had left, and that he'd offered me the position. He said he needed someone to keep his office tidy for him. He'd pay twice what I was making laundering clothes." Her lips twisted into something too mirthless to be called a smile. "She made it sound like such good news."

There was a strange stillness to her as she recounted this, not just in her expression but in her demeanor. The cascade of restless movements I was so used to seeing when she was lucid—the absent touching of her hair, the unconscious worrying of a torn cuticle—had stopped. It was as if all her energy was being poured into telling her story.

"At first it seemed like heaven," she went on. "The house was so grand—I'd always thought it looked like a castle. And the work was so much easier than hauling scalding water back and forth and burning myself pressing other people's underthings. And he was . . . he seemed so *kind*, in the beginning. I actually looked forward to hearing the service bell ring, summoning me to his office." She spoke with a kind of awe, as if still amazed at her own naïveté.

"What happened after he rang it?"

"In the beginning? We'd talk. He'd tell me about his travels. He'd bring back things for me when he went on trips. He said I was so good at what I did that he could easily see me working my way to head housekeeper, and making enough to move into a little house of my own with Maman." She bit her lower lip. "Looking back on it now, there were signs. I just didn't know how to read them."

"What sort of signs?"

"The way the other servants looked at me when I arrived. With a kind of . . . of *pity*. The way you'd look at an animal that was about to be butchered. But the way they looked at Maman was even worse. It was as if she . . . disgusted them, somehow." She winced. "When I asked her about it she said they were just envious, because the master had given her a promotion in the kitchen. I didn't understand the real reason for several weeks."

I swallowed. "Did he—fancy your mother? Was that it?"

"No. I mean, he had, at one point. But at some point he'd stopped. He wanted me—he wanted me to replace her." Another deep breath. "I had no idea, of course. I'd never been a chambermaid before. I thought this was how it always worked—that it was normal for the master to summon me to his office every day, to have me clean it around him. To have me polish the mirror even when there wasn't a single mark on it. Or plump the chaise cushions when it was clear no one had touched them since the last time I'd done so. Then one day, he had me take all the law books from his shelves and dust their spines, and then put them back in alphabetical order. He stood so close behind me when I did that I felt his breath on my neck, felt his—felt his body, pressing against my back." She shut her eyes, her face tightening in disgust—as if the scene were playing out before her. "I froze at first—I literally couldn't move. I was so shocked, so afraid of offending him. Of embarrassing Maman. He finally moved away again, as though nothing had happened. And I told myself nothing had." She opened her eyes. "I see now that he was testing me."

"Testing you how?"

"To see if I'd complain. Or push him away. And when I didn't, he began doing . . . the other things. He began hurting me. At first I thought it wasn't on purpose. But then I realized it was—that he actually enjoyed doing it. Inflicting damage."

I nodded dully. I'd seen that "damage" with my own eyes, not just in the painful legacy of bruises it had left behind, but in Josephine's visceral reenactments of the attacks she'd endured. In some ways, I felt as if I'd already met this monstrous man, for I'd seen the imprint of his hands on her body, the scrapes and abrasions that had scabbed over and sloughed off when I'd helped her bathe. The bruises that had lightened as the days passed, from blue-black to bilious yellow, before disappearing like small, noxious sunsets. I'd seen him, too, as I'd watched her struggling through her horrific hallucinations—had witnessed her body shuddering with the impact of his invisible fists. Seen her head jerk with the force of those unseen slaps.

Below us, one of the girls had kicked off her boots and stockings and was gleefully running across the pavers on bare feet, the nurse-maid simultaneously scolding her and racing to pick up the discarded footwear. I watched them as Josephine went on, still in that eerily flat voice, describing how she'd kept trying to dissuade her attacker. How she kept pleading for him to leave her alone, to take pity on her, but how this only ever made him angrier. He called her ungrateful, after he'd gone through so much trouble to give her and her mother a decent wage, a good life. He'd told her that the whole reason he'd promoted her mother was to get Josephine in return, and that her mother had agreed to this transaction. He said that since the two of them had been living for months now on his largesse they were in his debt, and doing what he wished was the only way to pay him back. "He said," she concluded bitterly, "that he knew the law well enough to ruin us both in a heartbeat, if he chose. That he could send both of us to prison and ensure that neither of us got out of it in our life-times."

"What could he have sent you to prison for?" I asked, incredulous.

"I asked him that too," she said dully. "He laughed. *I'm a judge,* he said. *Rest assured, I'll find something.*"

Her eyes were fixed now on the scaffolded form of the Palais de Justice, still under repair after the Communards burned it down years earlier. "I stopped arguing, finally," she continued quietly. "I couldn't see a way not to. And I thought perhaps he'd go easier on me that way."

"But he didn't."

She shook her head. "It was as if he began using me—using my body—to take revenge for all the wrongs he felt the world had done him—his 'cold-blooded' wife. His sickly son, whose care he said was costing him a fortune. The people he said were always bothering him for money. I think he owed many people." Glancing down, she picked at a loose thread on the cuff of her hospital gown. "I kept thinking that if I could just finally please him, it would be better, that he'd become gentler. But if anything, he just got angrier and angrier. The way he looked at me sometimes, Laure . . ." She shuddered again.

Down in the Square du Vert-Galant, one of the little girls screamed, a long note of what may have been shivering joy, or shrill indigna-tion over being forced to put her shoes back on. I felt the hairs on the back of my neck stiffen. Josephine seemed unsettled too; shading her eyes, she gazed over to where the girls were being dragged back toward the bridge's staircase by their minder.

"And your mother?" I asked. "She knew about all this and did nothing?"

Her jaw tightened. "When I finally told her what had been hap-pening, that I wanted to find another position, she was furious."

"With him."

"No. With *me.*" She gave a short, brittle-sounding laugh. "She said if I left she'd lose her position too. At best, we'd be penniless. At worst, he'd have us both thrown into prison, just as he'd said. I just had to endure it, she told me. For both of our sakes. It was just the way of things, for women like us." She squeezed her eyes shut. "I'm such a fool, Laure," she said softly. "I couldn't believe it at first. But I see it now—he was right. She'd done those things with him too. And then, when his interest shifted to me, she went along with it. She presented me to him like a bunch of flowers. Or a basket of fruit."

I recalled the basket the marquis had tried sending to Rosalie, the pulpy, bruised peach on the ward floor. The thought brought a faint surge of nausea, as if the sour fruit were lodged in my own stomach.

Up until that point, I think, the horror I'd felt over her terrible story had at least been somewhat familiar. I'd heard so many variations on it already over the past year, after all. And yet hearing the role Josephine's own *mother* had played in her abuse added a new and acrid edge to my revulsion. The craven cynicism behind the woman's words and actions, the stinging indifference to her daughter's terrible dilemma—it all landed in my gut like a series of sickening kicks. What sort of a mother said these things, *did* these things, to a child? What else had this girl suffered at her hands?

"So does she know that you . . ." I'd been intending to say *that you killed him,* but the words seemed to stick thickly in my throat. "Does she know what happened?" I asked instead. "Your mother?"

"She must. Though she wasn't in the house when I—when he rang for me that day. I think she was at the market."

"But wouldn't she have come looking for you? Once you went missing?"

"Her?" She snorted in disgust. "All she cares about is her own skin. She's probably halfway to England or America by now."

There it was again, that bleakness I'd heard in her voice as she recounted her mother's unspeakable response to the vile attacks on her daughter—attacks she'd helped orchestrate. And yet, I suddenly also remembered something else Julienne had said at that staff breakfast the morning after Josephine's arrival: *She was screaming for her mother like a little child.*

I looked back toward the little girls. The one who'd taken off her shoes and stockings was being forcibly maneuvered back into them again, pouting as her caregiver brushed gravel from her toes. I thought about how instinctive it is, the trust we place in those who call themselves our protectors. How easily that trust turns into a trap.

"Couldn't you just have left them both?"

"With what?" she asked bitterly. "I had no letter of reference and no money. He was paying her for my . . . work." She pronounced that word—*travail*—with grim wryness. "There was no way to escape. No one to help me stop him. I had to do it myself."

"So you brought a knife to work," I said slowly. "To stop him from attacking you."

"No." The look she gave me fell between bemusement and pity. "I brought the knife to *kill* him."

Clasping her hands together again, she pressed her knuckles into the soft skin beneath her chin for a moment before dropping them back to the *balcon*. "I wasn't sure I'd have the strength—or even the courage. But it turns out I did. I didn't even hesitate when the moment arrived." She looked as though she still couldn't quite believe this herself. "I pushed that blade right into him, Laure. It was actually easy, the stabbing part. Much easier than getting the cursed thing out of my boot."

I nodded, remembering the strange movement she sometimes made in the midst of her delusions, the way her left hand would reach toward her left heel, her fingers scrabbling at her ankle, her lips stretching into a grimace with the effort.

"Where did you do it?" I asked.

"I told you. In his office."

"No. I mean, where did you stab him? Where on his body?" I was vaguely astonished at my own composure as I asked this: I might have been asking whether she wanted light or dark meat for dinner. Perhaps I was simply in shock. And yet looking back on it now, I don't think that I was. I felt remarkably clear-headed. Far more so than I'd felt on the jostling omnibus.

"I'm not sure," she replied. "I was trying for his heart. But I think it ended up lower—closer to his belly. Either way, he collapsed on top of me." She passed a hand tiredly over her eyes. "The blood—Laure, there was so much *blood*. And it was so *warm*. I remember thinking it almost felt comforting—like a compress." She moved her hand up to her forehead and pressed it against her skull, as though trying to force the ghastly memory back into her mind. "I think that's when the madness set in, because I don't remember much after that. I obviously got out—out from beneath him, out of the house. I have a vague memory of running down the streets. And I remember that at some point I heard a police bell clanging. I thought it meant they were coming for me already."

I dropped my own gaze back to my hands. It made nauseating sense—all of it. Especially given what I'd heard of her condition when she arrived, half shod, blood covered, fighting as if for her life—which she clearly had thought she was doing. She must have assumed the brigadiers who pulled her down from this spot were there to punish her for what she'd just done. Her symptoms supported her story too—at least, based on what I'd come to understand about such things. The hand that had been wounded was the one she'd used to stab the man, the knife pulled from the boot that had been lost. She must have cut herself when she grasped for it, kicked the boot off in her frenzy. Or else reached for it somehow, once it and her stockings had been ripped off her. And now the foot that had been in that boot, that had been next to that knife, was contracted. I didn't fully understand how hysterical contractures worked—to be honest, I wasn't sure even Charcot himself did, though of course he would never have admitted as much. But I knew they often affected the parts of the body that their sufferers associated with traumatic occurrences. It was a connection that was fully driven home for me when Charcot—having established my loss of sensation in my lips and left hand—asked whether these things might in some way be connected to my father's death. Baffled, I'd said no. It was only later that I remembered stroking Papa's brow after the doctor confirmed he was gone. Planting my lips on it one last time, as it cooled.

"That's what I don't understand," she continued. "Why haven't they?"

"Why haven't they what?" I turned to face her, trying to push through the chaotic tangle of my thoughts.

"Come for me," she said. "The police. Someone must have found his body that day. They would have been called. And it would have been easy to deduce who'd done it. I'm fairly sure I left the knife there—and for all I know, my boot as well." She looked searchingly into my eyes. "So why haven't they come to arrest me?"

I shook my head, once more at a loss. Why *hadn't* anyone come for her, if she'd left the man the way she said she had? Surely the police would have at least wanted Josephine for questioning. And if they hadn't found her in the house, or in whatever rooms she and her mother lived in, they would surely have made their way to the Salpêtrière. Detectives often consulted the asylum records office when trying to track down someone of interest to them. Just as they checked at the Paris Morgue.

"I don't know," I said slowly. "Maybe they did, during those first days after your arrival. But since you spent those in the softs, and you hadn't officially been admitted, there wouldn't have been any record. So maybe they weren't able to connect you with . . ." I still found myself unable to say it: *the murder*. "With the accident," I finished lamely.

"It wasn't an accident," she said fiercely.

The hair on the back of my neck stiffened again. I glanced around anxiously, afraid she'd be overheard.

"Either way," I said, lowering my voice, "there's no address, no date of birth. No parental information. They don't even have a full name, beyond your given one." I glanced at her sidelong. "Josephine *is* your given name?"

"Of course," she said indignantly. "What else would it be?"

"And—and your family name? That's come back as well?"

Did I imagine it, or did something—the barest hint of indecision—flicker in her eyes? But then she nodded.

"Garreau," she said.

"And . . . and how old are you?"

"Seventeen." This she said without hesitation.

Josephine Garreau, I thought. *Seventeen years old.* And despite everything, there was a small thrill. As though in telling me her true name and age, she'd held her heart out to me, raw and beating, in her palm.

Hard on its heels, though, came another and far more sobering realization: that the entire reason we were here at all was that Josephine had already been mentioned, by name, in numerous Paris newspapers. Granted, most readers would assume that "Josephine," like "Blanche," was a stage name, since Charcot—perhaps concluding the absence of a known surname was anonymity enough—had decided to use it as such. But the breathless descriptions of her "lithe" figure and "flaming" hair, of her "complexion marred excessively with sun spots," would surely stand out to anyone actively looking for her—and there would almost certainly be more such salacious descriptions to follow in coming months. At least, I thought, none of the papers had included her portrait—yet. Just this week, though, she'd had her first session in Monsieur Londe's photography studio, where she'd proven to be as natural a photography subject as Rosalie had been stiff and awkward. This meant that on top of the hundreds who'd already seen Josephine firsthand in the Salpêtrière's amphitheater, the hundreds more who would see her in future presentations, and the *further* hundreds who would read her descriptions in the press, hundreds *more* would soon see her photographed in the asylum's popular publication *Nouvelle iconographie de la Salpêtrière*—presented from a variety of angles, thanks to Monsieur Londe's multilensed photoelectric.

God help us, I thought. If everything Josephine Garreau had just told me was true, they *would* be coming for her. They had to—the odds were far greater that she'd be recognized than not. And once they did, she was doomed. She would certainly face imprisonment—possibly worse. Murder was a capital offense.

I shut my eyes again, trying and failing not to see it: Policemen pounding into Hysteria, or Charcot's office, or even onto the amphitheater stage. Shackling Josephine's hands before her; dragging her, stumbling and limping, to their lorry. Rifling through her bed in search of evidence—and perhaps my bed as well, since I was her caregiver. What if they found the marquis's bracelet? Even worse, what if they came *looking* for the bracelet, and upon finding Josephine in the ward too made the connection between her and the judge's slaying? My own crime would effectively have led them to hers.

I was aware of a cool pressure on my hand, which was still on her arm: She'd covered it with her own. When I opened my eyes, I found her once more gazing steadily into them.

"What should I do?" she asked.

"Maybe—maybe you should tell him." The words were out before I'd fully articulated the thought.

She frowned. "Who?"

"Charcot."

"Tell him *what?*"

"The truth. He's appeared in court before as a special witness in cases involving hysterics. His testimony got one girl—she was accused of stealing—out of prison."

She tilted her head. "How?"

"After examining her, he found that she was a hysteric. Which meant she could have been hypnotized by someone into committing the crime, since he says only hysterics can be hypnotized. In the end, the court sent her to Hysteria instead of Saint-Lazare."

This was true, though it was also true that more recently (and far more famously), Charcot had also testified that another woman—one accused of murdering a bailiff with her lover—was *not* a hysteric, and therefore could not have been entranced into the crime by her lover as she'd claimed. The testimony put her behind bars for two decades. She still fared better than the lover, who was separated from his head.

"What had she stolen?" Josephine asked now. "The girl he got off?"

"A blanket," I said lamely.

"Laure." She stared at me as if I'd just suggested she hurl herself at the Seine again, right this minute. "I *killed a man*. Charcot will turn me over to the police himself if he learns of it."

"You don't know that," I countered. "He's not a monster. And you'd been terribly attacked. Everyone agrees upon that."

She snorted. "The demon could have skinned me and had my flesh made into a new evening hat. It wouldn't have mattered. Both he and my mother were right about that much, at least." She seemed to be speaking more to herself than to me. "No, I can't say anything about it. Not to anyone but you. I just have to keep pretending not to remember."

I opened my mouth to protest. Then I shut it again; deep down I knew she was right. She was a poor girl who'd murdered a wealthy man, and no court in France would care a whit about her reasons. Nor would Charcot, whose own wealth and power rested on the mad fiefdom he'd now spent decades building. One hysteric's freedom—and maybe even her life—meant nothing against all that.

"What happens if you . . . reenact the murder? During one of your trances?" I asked, thinking again of that telling grasping motion she made with her hand. Without context, it wouldn't mean much to anyone who didn't know the full, gruesome story. But what if she unconsciously acted out the next steps—extracting the "knife"? Thrusting it upward? Fleeing the scene of her crime?

"I can't," she said shortly. "If I do you must stop me somehow."

"*Stop* you? How?"

"You did it once. That first time in Charcot's office."

And nearly lost my position over it, I thought, but didn't say it.

"I think that would be a mistake," I said instead, carefully.

She pursed her lips. "Why?"

"Because if I did that—if I intervened—it would only make him angry again. And that would draw more attention to you—which is the last thing we want. There's too much attention on you as it is."

"But how do we keep from drawing attention to me when he keeps putting me onstage?" She wrung her hands together again helplessly. "Isn't that exactly what he wants—to *draw attention* to me?"

"I suppose it is," I said uncertainly.

"Then how are we supposed to stop him?"

I didn't have an answer: The situation felt as hopeless to me as it clearly did to her. Even more so, I realized suddenly, because if I left to find Amélie now I'd also be leaving Josephine alone, to face her own fate.

I can't do that, I thought, feeling sickened again. *I'm all that she has.*

And yet what would staying accomplish? Charcot seemed determined to make Josephine as much of a hysterical celebrity as he'd made Rosalie before banishing her to Lunacy. Nothing I could do would change that. In fact, anything I *tried* to do might only hasten Josephine's downfall—and very possibly mine, too. And then Amélie would have no one left in the world to find her. To *save* her. No, as much as I'd grown to care for Josephine, and as wrenching as her situation was, changing my own course of action wouldn't change what had happened to her—or even what *would* happen to her in coming days. It might even make things worse.

I would proceed as I'd planned.

"Laure?" I could feel Josephine's gaze against my cheek, as insistent as the brushed touch of a fingertip. "There's something else."

"What?" I turned back toward her warily. What more could there possibly be?

"I'm—I'm afraid someone here might know," she said in a low voice.

I glanced behind us at the bustling bridge, at the rushing pedestrians, the rumbling carriages and carts.

"Not here." She bit her lip. "I mean . . . someone in Hysteria."

I frowned. "How could anyone there possibly know? You didn't even know yourself until two weeks ago."

"I'm not sure." She pressed a hand to her cheek. "Perhaps it's just in my head. But last Friday—right before we got ready for the amphitheater—I found something. On my pillow."

It came back to me then: How startled she'd been when I'd returned from the laundry building with her dress. How she'd whirled around at the sound of my footsteps, her face as white and frightened as it was now.

"What did you find?"

She reached into her dress pocket, pulled something from its depths, and slipped it into my hand. I saw that I was holding a small and slightly tarnished-looking silver medallion, upon which was embossed an image of a woman in flowing robes. Hands clasped, she hovered over what looked like a flowing spring, holy rays emanating from her slender figure. Kneeling before her was another figure, a young girl, from whose also-clasped hands dangled a rosary.

I knew the scene well—everyone did. It depicted the legendary vision of the Virgin Mary that a young miller's daughter claimed to have had almost four decades earlier, in the late 1850s. People initially thought the girl mad; there were even calls to put her in an asylum. But when she continued seeing the Virgin, and the grotto's muddy spring water suddenly ran clear for the first time in anyone's memory, the place became a holy destination. Now thousands of pilgrims set out for it every year, believing its springs could cure everything from blindness to tuberculosis.

I looked back up again, frowning. "This is from Lourdes."

Josephine nodded. "It's exactly like the one he—Monsieur Guillaume, my employer—tried to give me, after they'd gone there on a family trip. I wouldn't take it."

"But . . . you said he's dead."

"He *is*," she said, sounding impatient again. "That's why I think someone in the asylum must know." She peered down at the glimmering keepsake. "What if it's the same one?"

I turned the thing slowly between my fingers. "But how would it have gotten onto your pillow?"

"Perhaps it was put there by someone who knows—or suspects—that I killed him. To scare me. Or just to let me know that *they* know what I did. It's possible, don't you think?"

Murder. Madness. And now, seemingly, magic medallions. I shook my head again, less in denial than to try to clear it. "Who in Hysteria would even know he tried to give it to you? Especially if no one else was there to see him do it?"

"I don't *know*," she said wearily, her gaze still fixed on the round ornament in my palm.

I was struck again by how exhausted she looked, her eyes red with lack of sleep, underscored with bluish, half-moon-shaped shadows. And little wonder, given all she'd been through. Not only had she been brutally abused before coming to the asylum, but she was being forced to relive that abuse over and over in Charcot's office, on his stage. To have such terrible memories return now on top of all of that—it was little wonder she wasn't thinking clearly. "I think," I said gently, "that it could have come from anywhere."

Taking her hand in mine, I pressed the medallion back into it. "They must sell thousands of such things there. 'Nadette alone probably has a handful—she's obsessed with Bernadette of Lourdes, since they share a name. Charcot might have one too, for that matter. He's been to that spring many times." Charcot was famously fascinated by the "miracle cures" that supposedly took place at religious sites. He'd even published a paper postulating that those whose injuries and illnesses were alleviated after such pilgrimages hadn't been suffering from them in the traditional medical sense. Rather, he speculated, they were hysterical symptoms caused by extreme religious manias like Bernadette's, which disappeared only because their bearers *thought* they were being cured. By this logic, of course, it might have made sense to allow 'Nadette to visit Lourdes herself to cure her hysteria, as she'd asked to do many times. To date, however, he'd refused, saying it would only intensify the girl's delusions while giving her ample opportunity to run off again.

"Perhaps it was one of theirs," I went on, holding the medallion to the light, "and it simply ended up on your bed by accident. We can ask them, if you like."

"*No!*" Josephine shook her head violently. "If it's not theirs, it could connect me to the crime."

I swallowed, unsettled as much by her vehemence as by the questionable logic of this statement, which struck me as almost bordering on paranoia. "Either way," I said, "I don't think you should think too much on it. In all likelihood it's little more than a coincidence."

She didn't look convinced. But she also didn't argue. She only sighed and turned her gaze back out to the Square du Vert-Galant. "So what should I do?"

"I don't know," I said truthfully, scanning again for the little girls in white. But they and their minder had disappeared. "I'll try to think of something. For now, though, more than anything else, we must avoid drawing unnecessary attention. That means doing *everything* Charcot tells us. Including what he told us to do today."

"You can't mean . . ." She turned her head and looked at me in bleak bemusement, as though I'd just suggested we go out dancing.

"Exactly," I said grimly, linking my arm through hers. "Charcot said we're to buy you a new dress and boots. So right now, we are going to go shopping."

Chapter Eight

An hour or so later we stood in La Samaritaine's second-floor ladies' fitting parlor, a shopgirl tugging the folds of a ready-made skirt around Josephine's slim waist and thighs.

"The tweed is quite practical," the clerk noted, straightening the dress's bodice. "It's elegant, but also modest enough to wear to morning mass or confession."

Josephine just nodded, staring at herself in the gilt-framed, triptych-style mirror. I couldn't read her expression.

"The green underdress also provides for a nice contrast," the clerk—a gangly girl with dark hair and the sort of startled-looking, bulging eyes my father had taught me were symptomatic of thyroid disease—continued. "And it suits mademoiselle's . . ."

She hesitated, as if searching for a tactful way to describe something that was slightly gauche. "It suits mademoiselle's *unusual* coloring," she concluded delicately.

Josephine's lips tightened. But she didn't respond.

She'd remained silent on the short walk from Pont Neuf to the department store as well, as though still processing the enormity of what her memory had just revealed to her. As we made our way through La Samaritaine's crowded ground level, with its chrome-edged counters, lavender-scented air, and elaborate displays of everything from lace to ladies' gloves, she'd barely paid attention to any of it. All her energy had seemed to home in on simply getting to our destination—and even then she'd moved more slowly than usual, stumbling once as we ascended the store's enormous spiral staircase, and nearly falling backward in a way that would surely have resulted in injury had I not had a firm grip on her elbow. Worried, I'd suggested stopping to rest. But she'd shaken her head and climbed unsteadily on.

It wasn't until we'd reached the third-floor gallery that she'd seemed to fully take note of our surroundings—the gleaming chandeliers and rich carpets, the rows of mannequins sheathed in pristine poplin, silk, and wool. "I've never had a new dress," she'd mused, pausing before a wasp-waisted tailor's dummy sporting a day costume of coral sateen. "I've never even tried on one that hadn't been worn by someone else first. Even the chambermaid's uniform Maman bought me for my position at Maître Guillaume's came from the *dépôt-vente*." Pausing, she bit her lip. "What would they have done with them?" she asked me.

"With what?"

"My uniform and apron. My boots—" She stopped, corrected herself. "Boot."

I frowned; I hadn't thought about this. Ordinarily when a patient was committed to the Salpêtrière, any belongings deemed unnecessary or detrimental to life in the wards were warehoused in a dank facility near the stables, ready to be collected on the day their owners were discharged—presuming, of course, that the day ever came. Surely, though, they wouldn't have simply stored Josephine's bloodstained gown and apron—or, for that matter, a single boot. And if they had, that was actually yet another cause for concern: If the police did arrive and asked to see her things, those clothes would be as good as a confession.

"They probably burned them," I said, making a mental note to check if this was true. "I think that's what they do when *internées* arrive in clothes that are too filthy to save."

Something that might have been sadness but just as possibly could have been relief crossed her face at this. But she didn't comment. Turning away from the mannequin, she took my arm.

"We'll buy the first thing that fits," she'd said shortly.

The shopgirl smoothed the bodice over the voluminous skirt. Then she stepped back, cocking her dark head and studying Josephine, lips pursed like Charcot's were when he puzzled out a diagnosis. "It is, perhaps, a little plain," she observed. "But for a mere sixty francs you can't expect much in the way of trimming."

"Plain is fine," Josephine said. "It's only for a medical lecture."

I winced. Given the danger she was in, my instinct now was to share as little about her identity as possible, with anyone—which was why I'd been heartened when, a few moments earlier, this same clerk had scanned Charcot's cashier's note without any noticeable reaction to the famous name scrawled in black ink on its bottom.

Now, though, she looked up from fiddling with Josephine's cuff, her interest piqued. "Do you mean one of Dr. Charcot's lectures?" she exclaimed. "I've heard about those! They say the madwomen over there do the most *extraordinary* things. And that Charcot controls them like puppets. Through *hypnosis*."

She dropped her voice conspiratorially on the word *l'hypnose*, pedaling her hands before her as though maneuvering a puppeteer's control stick.

"I'm not mad," Josephine said tersely. "I'm a hysteric."

The girl's eyes darted back to Josephine's face. "Is she the one from Alsace?" She directed the question at me, looking dubious. "The one everyone says is such a beauty?"

"No," I said quickly. "She's hardly been onstage at all." Catching Josephine's eye in the glass, I shook my head faintly in warning. "I'm not even sure whether she'll be on anytime soon," I added.

The girl lifted a penciled brow. "Why else would she need a new dress?"

I groaned inwardly. *Why* had Josephine mentioned the medical lectures? For all we knew, this idiot clerk would now go about telling all her customers how she'd dressed one of Charcot's famous hysterics—probably complete with a description of Josephine's "*unusual* coloring" and complexion. What if one of those customers had somehow known the judge, and knew the details of his unsolved murder?

"Perhaps he wants it for someone with a similar figure," I said vaguely. And then, in an effort to change the subject: "Do you think the corset is snug enough?" I pointed to the new stays the girl had—with a theatrical little shudder—promptly sent for upon seeing Josephine's bulky asylum-issue corset.

But the clerk wouldn't be dissuaded. "He *must* plan on bringing her onto his stage," she said decisively. "Otherwise why would he send her here?"

I shrugged helplessly, having no answer to this.

"And if that's indeed the case," she chirped on, "I have something *far* more suitable for appearing before a large audience. I knew there was a reason I pulled it!" She was already on her feet, riffling through the assortment of gowns she'd selected for us earlier while Josephine was being fitted for her new corset. "Here," she said a moment later, turning back to us with the skirt and bodice of an emerald-colored silk day dress draped over her forearms. "*This* will be very fetching—especially under stage lights." She held the bodice up beneath Josephine's chin. "Every eye in the room will be on her!" Her own round, protruding eyes were noticeably brighter—doubtlessly at the prospect of a significantly higher commission.

"How much is it?" I asked warily.

"I believe this style is a little over a hundred. *But,*" she added, upon taking in my appalled expression, "your note did say you're to buy *whatever you need* on Dr. and Madame Charcot's store account. There was no limit mentioned. None at all."

I sighed. "No. But . . ."

I'd been planning to point out that Charcot wouldn't be happy if his lecture subject's attire drew more attention than the lecture itself. Then, though, I saw Josephine's face. The glazed look she'd been wearing throughout the other fittings had vanished, replaced by something else as she reached up to stroke the shining material—very gently. As though it were green glass that might shatter at her touch.

"I could at least try it on," she said hesitantly.

I blinked at her. Hadn't we just decided that, going forward, we'd do everything we could to avoid too much attention? And this dress was nothing if not too much. It was all the *too*s: Too expensive. Too bright. Too *fetching*.

And yet even as I was thinking this, I was also remembering what she'd whispered to me as we entered the gallery: *I've never had a new dress. I've never even tried on one that hadn't been worn by someone else first.*

I recognized the expression on her face. It was the way I'd felt in my old life, staring into the windows of the stationers' shops in our neighborhood, as dazzled by their Italian marbled–cover notebooks, gleaming pens, and flower-filled glass paperweights as I'd ever been by any magic lantern show. The difference was that in a few weeks, I'd be able to covet such things whenever and for as long as I liked— and even buy them, if I wanted to. Whereas Josephine might never have this opportunity again.

"I suppose we can at least see how it looks," I conceded.

I watched as the clerk adjusted the shining fabric up around Josephine's narrow waist, now made even narrower thanks to the new steam-molded corset. After finishing with the skirt, the girl arranged the matching bodice around Josephine's neck and shoulders with the concentration of a sculptor putting final touches on a statue. When she was done she stepped back, gloved hands clasped to her chest.

"*There*," she exclaimed. "Very striking! You'll make *quite* an impression in this one."

Which, of course, was precisely the opposite of what we wanted. I started to say as much. Yet when I looked back at Josephine, I was struck dumb by how the gown had transformed her. It set her hair off to fiery effect, made her eyes shine like freshly poured absinthe. It made her pale skin glow in a way that looked almost pearlescent, her freckles gleam like tiny spots of pure gold. Even more remarkably, the gown fit her like a glove even without alteration, the new corset subtly imbuing her slight form with curves and swells that caused me to catch my breath with a feeling I couldn't recall ever having felt before, something between awe and envy, between longing and shame.

Throughout the other two fittings, Josephine had barely moved. Now, though, she dipped and twisted before the triptych-style mirror, performing a stern tarantella with herself in triplicate, her lips curved into that tight, slightly mysterious smile she sometimes had. Watching her, I found myself thinking back to a comment she'd made as I'd helped her prepare for her first appearance in one of Charcot's lectures some three weeks earlier.

I'd been getting her dressed that morning, and had noticed a stain on the sleeve of Rosalie's blue stage dress that the laundry had either missed or else failed to remove—an oversight that would have enraged the Alsatian. When I pointed it out, though, Josephine had just shrugged. "It's not like they're coming to see my arms," she'd said.

I couldn't help commenting on how different Rosalie's response would have been, how she might well have refused to wear the thing at all. "It's why there are no full mirrors in the ward now," I'd told her. "Charcot said she was spending too much time in front of them. He believes that when women pay such excessive attention to appearance, it's a symptom of a weakening mind."

"Perhaps," Josephine had replied thoughtfully. "But perhaps it's the opposite."

I looked up from the black woolen stocking I'd been rolling up over her contracted foot. "What do you mean?"

"There are so few things we can control here," Josephine said, waving a hand toward where Félicie lay straitjacketed on her cot to keep from scratching, and Louise sat screwed into a compressor on hers. Bernadette lay behind them, etherized into a stupor after having spent the night locked in one of her crucifix positions: arms flung out to the sides, legs rigidly pressed together, chin resting on her disfigured chest in pious sorrow.

"Perhaps she just wanted to control what little she could," Josephine had continued, musingly. "How others saw her. How she looked to herself. If so, I don't really think that's weakness. Do you?"

Now our gazes met in the mirror—the first full-length mirror she'd looked into since arriving at the Salpêtrière. There was something in her eyes, a kind of determination that almost bordered on anger.

"I want it," she said. There was no hesitance in her voice now.

It made no sense at all to buy such an extravagant dress when we'd agreed to try not to draw attention—or Charcot's censure. And yet even as it arose, my objection seemed to disintegrate on my tongue like an unpleasant aftertaste. What did it matter, in the end, what Josephine wore to the man's cursed lectures? It wouldn't change what she had done—or the fact that some twelve hundred people had already seen her in the Salpêtrière amphitheater. It wouldn't change the reality that after the next *Figaro* piece more people would flock to see her Friday, that even more newsmen would rush to cover the event. That even *more* people would order the next volume of *Nouvelle iconographie de la Salpêtrière* in order to possess her anguished, seizure-racked form for themselves. Wearing one color, one fabric, one style, over another was meaningless. I'd only imagined it wasn't, for the same reason Rosalie had imagined what she wore had any sort of significance: because doing so made me feel as if I had some control over this impossible situation.

"It looks *lovely*," the clerk gushed, sensing opportunity in my silence. "Really. It is simply stunning." She tilted her head. "And now that I think of it, I have a tartan wrap that would work beautifully with that color. In case, for instance, the lecture stage gets drafty."

This made even less sense than this absurdly glorious dress— a shawl for Charcot's stuffy amphitheater, just in time for a summer the almanacs were already predicting would be unusually warm. But as Josephine looked wistfully at herself, still dancing her subtle, swaying little dance, the last fragile reserves of my resistance collapsed. She'd had so few joys in her short life up until now, and likely had even fewer ahead. The least I could do was to make her present a little easier, a little happier. To protect her in small ways, if not large, before I left.

Before I left.

"We'll see the shawl," I said.

An hour later we made our way back to rue de Rivoli, Josephine's old *sabots* in a brown string box and a pair of plain but well-crafted boots on her feet. She had begged to wear them directly out of the ladies' footwear department, claiming that they were easier to walk in than her clogs, and as with the dress (and in the end, the shawl too), I hadn't been able to bring myself to deny her. The dress, shawl, and corset, plus a pair of black netted stockings and a small horsehair *tournure* (to add, as the clerk had noted, "just a touch of fullness in the back,") had all been sent off to be boxed for delivery to the asylum that evening. To take my mind off the small fortune we'd just spent— not to mention Josephine's gruesome revelation—I impulsively sug- gested a visit to the store's top-floor *salon de thé*, where we shared a pot of tea and a decadent Mont Blanc pastry. The indulgence left no time for a hoped-for visit to the stationer's department, nor money for the new journal I'd planned to buy there. But after over a year of bland asylum food, the buttery sweetness of the confection on my tongue seemed almost worth the rashness of the purchase.

Throughout the little meal Josephine remained in strangely high spirits—as though her dark mood had been shipped off along with her new stage ensemble. Despite myself, I felt my own mood lift a little as well. For a time, in fact, I was almost able to forget who and what we both really were—madhouse parolees; a murderess and thief—and pretend we were girls of the sort Amélie and I had once been and would hopefully be again: girls with nothing on their minds but the purchase of a dress and boots, and the even distribution of the last scooped spoonful of sweet chestnut.

As we made our way back to the omni stop, however, my appre- hension reconstituted in my belly like a malevolent tumor. As first one and then another Bastille-bound omni rumbled by with its seats up and downstairs already full, my mood soured further, for as pleasant as our surreptitious tearoom stop had been, it wasn't worth Babette's ire if we missed dinner. When an older bus finally stopped for us, I heaved a sigh of relief. Helping Josephine up the platform steps, I began steering her toward the carriage cabin. After barely taking a step, though, she balked, pulling back and digging her new heels into the platform floor.

"There's no room," she said, indicating the inside benches with a jerk of her chin.

"They wouldn't have let us on if there wasn't room," I said, though I had to admit that the carriage looked even more crowded than the one we'd taken that morning. Still, as the conductor signaled the *cocher* to move on I made out some space in the farthest row of seats inside the cabin, between a paint-splattered tradesman who seemed dead asleep and a heavyset man immersed in a week-old issue of the *Revue illustrée,* which he'd spread out before him almost as widely as he'd spread his barrel-thick thighs.

"There," I said, pointing. "He's easily taking up three spaces. We'll just ask him to move."

I moved toward the carriage door again, realizing only when I'd reached it that she was still resisting me. Annoyed, I turned back toward her, bracing myself as the carriage swerved bumpily back into traffic. "Don't you want to sit?"

"Yes. But not *there,*" she whispered. "The fat one will crush us both. And the other's drunk as a donkey." She wrinkled her nose. "I can smell him from here."

As if to prove the point the tradesman began slowly tipping sideways where he sat, his cloth cap slipping over one red-lidded eye. After glancing at him sidelong, the man with the paper edged over slightly, leaving just enough room for his slumbering neighbor to half recline between them.

Sighing, I turned back to Josephine. "Well, we can't just get off. I've no money left for another ticket."

"There was room on the roof." She jerked her chin upward. "And you like sitting outside better anyway."

"We're not allowed on the roof." I pointed to the sign by the ladder that stated as much. "Not on these older omnibuses."

Josephine glanced at the conductor, who stood on the edge of the platform sorting the tickets he'd collected. "What can they do? Throw us off?"

I actually didn't know what they could do. It had never occurred to me to test the no-women-on-the-ladders rule, though given my father's experiences it didn't strike me as a good idea in the best of circumstances. It seemed even less so now that we were trying not to attract undue attention. What if they called the police on us?

I glanced back at the conductor. To my relief, he'd clearly spotted the drunk and was now moving purposefully toward the cabin. "There," I said, stepping back to let him press past us. "He'll make room."

Out of the corner of my eye I saw Josephine stepping back as well. Then, though, I saw her dart forward again—not toward the door the conductor was now opening, but toward the ladder beside it. "What are you *doing*?" I exclaimed.

She threw an arch look over her shoulder. "It's a *foolish* rule," she declared.

And with that she was clambering her way up the iron rungs, her contracted foot little if any hindrance and her stocking-clad calves in full sight for all to see.

"Josephine!" I called after her in dismay. "Don't! You'll fall!"

But she'd already disappeared from view.

Setting my jaw, I peered back into the carriage. The conductor was attempting to prod the drunkard back into an upright position—only to see him lurch forward off the seat completely and land sprawlingly on the carriage floor, sparking a chorus of disgusted exclamations. No one seemed to have noticed Josephine's transgression. I glanced up toward the roof again, hoping vainly that she'd reappear even though backing *down* the ladder now, with the omnibus in full motion, was arguably riskier than climbing up it. When she didn't, I threw one last wary glance at the *conducteur*. Then, teeth gritted in annoyance, I secured the shoebox string to my wrist and began cautiously scaling the narrow, rusted ladder myself, grimacing as the heavy package swung and slammed against my thigh.

I reached the top to see Josephine had already traversed the short expanse of the roof to settle directly behind the coachman's seat, as though daring him to contest her presence. I made my way toward her, ignoring the affronted gazes and mutterings of the male passengers I had to squeeze by. When I reached her, she patted the empty space beside her. "You see?" she said. "Plenty of room. Fresh air. No stinking drunks."

What is wrong with you, I wanted to exclaim. But I simply sank down beside her, hoping the *cocher,* at least, hadn't noticed our invasion.

Clearly, however, he had. "Can't you read?" he grumbled, peering over his shoulder at us from beneath his dust-encrusted derby as he lightly slapped his team with his extra-long leather reins. "You're not to be up here."

"Of course I can read," Josephine retorted indignantly, and seemed about to say more until I quietly kicked her beneath the bench.

"I'm sorry," I said, turning back to the coachman. "My friend isn't feeling well."

He looked narrowly at Josephine. "Looks fine to me," he said. "What's wrong with her?"

I considered pleading motion sickness, then thought the better of it. "A nervous illness," I said, opting instead for the truth. "Hysteria."

"Ah. *L'hystérie.*" The *cocher* rolled his eyes. "Seems half the women in Paris have that nowadays."

"Actually, I've heard one in five," a heavily bearded young man seated near to us offered. Both he and the youth next to him wore day jackets paired with the sort of faintly ragged-looking evening hats popular among university students at the time.

"*L'épidémie de l'âge,* they're calling it," he went on conversationally. "Just saw a talk on it last week. Didn't we, Laurent? Fascinating stuff."

Oh no, I thought, instantly regretting my candor.

"Fascinating or no," the *cocher* was grumbling, "it don't change the rules."

He pulled up on his reins, and at first I assumed he was stopping the coach to order us off. Then, though, came the click and clatter of the carriage door's opening, and I realized that he was allowing passengers—including the drunk from the carriage—off at Jardin des Plantes. I glanced back at the students, willing them to get off as well. But they stayed put, the one who'd addressed us leaning over to murmur into his friend's ear.

"Where are you girls headed, then?" the *cocher* was asking.

I hesitated, then—seeing no way to lie—answered: "The Salpêtrière."

"Not much point in moving you now, then," he said gruffly. He urged the team back out into traffic, swerving slightly to avoid a lumbering water cart from which city workers were hosing down the dusty street.

Stifling a sigh, I turned back around too. The student who'd spoken was still eyeing Josephine, his expression now brightly inquisitive. "You're from the Salpêtrière?" he asked.

"We're getting off there," I said vaguely, though Josephine's dark hospital gown was a dead giveaway that we were more than simply visiting the asylum. I feigned intent interest in the busy street below us, hoping to put an end to the exchange. But my coolness seemed only to intensify his curiosity.

"I was right, Laurent!" he exclaimed. "What did I tell you? It's her—*la rousse* we saw Friday. On Dr. Charcot's stage."

It was as if my earlier motion sickness reclaimed me in one fell swoop, my stomach clenching, my throat turning sour. "No," I said tightly. "You're mistaken. She hasn't been onstage."

The student gave an incredulous laugh. "But of course she has! I'd have recognized her anywhere. That hair. Those *charming* freckles . . ." Jutting out his chin, he indicated the area around the hem of Josephine's skirt. "But it's the limp that sealed it. From her contracted foot—the left one. Correct? Dr. Charcot gave an excellent explanation of how hysterical contractures work. He's really an extraordinary lecturer, isn't he? Watching him identify the various symptoms and illnesses is magnificent. It's like—" He paused, waving his gloved hand before his face, as though trying to snatch the simile from the air like it was a bug. "Why, it's like watching Adam name the animals!" he concluded effusively.

The student's friend had been ignoring the exchange up until this point. Now, though, he closed his book, allowing me to see the title: *Surgical Diagnosis: A Manual for Students and Practitioners.* Fixing his gaze on Josephine, he unhooked the wire earpieces of the tinted sun spectacles he was wearing and tucked them into his breast pocket. His eyes looked small and slightly bloodshot without the lenses.

"Mademoiselle Josephine, wasn't it?" he asked.

Catching my eye, Josephine lifted a brow. I could only shrug helplessly in return.

"I *knew* it!" the first student crowed. "You were extraordinary up there too, you know. We were talking about you all night at *chez* Lipp!"

I all but rolled my eyes at this. But when I looked at Josephine she was wearing the small smile she wore when Charcot introduced her to his audiences—a cross between shyness, awe, and an almost girlish excitement. For all her dislike of male attention—which I now fully understood—she didn't seem to entirely *dislike* having caught the admiring eyes of these two well-to-do young men.

Something cold and faintly acrid seemed to suddenly be pressing against my lungs.

"That *mariage à trois* trick had us arguing for hours," his friend agreed, slapping his forehead in feigned bafflement. "Neither of us could deduce how the devil you did it!"

Josephine's smile faltered. "*Mariage à trois?*" she repeated, glancing back at me in confusion. "Which one was that?"

I stared back at her, unable to speak.

"You mean to say you don't remember?" the first student exclaimed. "I would have thought a performance like that would be impossible to forget!"

"Ah, but they *can't* remember when they've been hypnotized," his friend said, chiding him. "Dr. Charcot explained that too, remember? They're in such a completely different state from their waking selves that it's as if they've been in the deepest of dreams."

Josephine turned to look at me again, her pale brows drawing together accusatorially. I looked away, the apprehension in my gut unfurling into full-fledged guilt.

Mariage à trois was another experiment Gilles de la Tourette had come up with, building on the discovery that Josephine suffered from different symptoms on different sides of her body. When she was hot, the doctors had deduced, she perspired only on her right side, while the left side remained completely dry. When exposed to cold— something the doctors tested by running ice chips over her bare arms and legs—goosebumps appeared only on the right half of her body. They'd even found that when her skin was pricked with needles, only those wounds on her right side bled, while the left remained almost eerily bloodless.

All this was in the charts that hung from the foot of her bed, which I read and explained to her faithfully. But the "test" the doctors had devised to explore this duality was one of the ones I'd deemed too potentially upsetting to explain to her in full detail, settling instead on a vaguer, safer version. I offered it again now, hoping to end the discussion.

"It was the one where they . . . examine the different sides of your body," I told her. "To see how the reactions compare." I turned back to the students, hoping to shift the conversation to a safer track. "But it's not nearly as interesting as the blank card exercise the doctors have her do. Have you—"

But the youth wasn't having it. "*Examine?*" he snorted. "I wish *my* examinations this term were as pleasurable!"

Josephine turned back to me sharply. "What's he talking about?"

The omni came to another jostling stop. I swallowed, struggling to think of a response—any response—that wouldn't expose my stammering half truth for what it was.

"To be fair," the bearded student offered in my stead, "it's a little hard to describe. But we'd be happy to help refresh your memory."

He slapped his thighs. "Actually, I have a brilliant idea! Laurent and I can perform a reenactment for you! You hysterics know all about reenactments, right?" He winked.

"Fantastic suggestion!" His clean-shaven friend leapt up as well. "I'll be the left-side husband. You can be the right."

"*Husband?*" Josephine repeated the word as though it were in some foreign language.

"Don't worry," the bearded student said reassuringly. "It's not as scandalous as it might seem."

"Well, it's a *little* scandalous," his friend said, correcting him with another wink.

From down on the street came the sound of more passengers getting off and on: A woman indignantly accusing someone of pushing her. A child crying over a picture book left behind. *Get off*, I thought numbly. *You need to get her off. Right now.*

But the bus lurched back into motion and I remained rooted in place, watching with a kind of paralyzing dismay as the students made their swaying way over to us. The bearded one planted himself close to Josephine's free side. As the he did, his friend—the red-eyed one—hovered above me expectantly. "Excuse me, mademoiselle," he said, gesturing for me to move away from Josephine. "You don't mind making room, do you?"

"You can't do it now," I said desperately. "It only works when she's entranced."

"We're not trying to replicate it *precisely*," he said, as though explaining an obvious truth to an infant. "We're just showing her what those other fellows from the audience did to her."

"Fellows," Josephine repeated flatly, her eyes flicking toward me. I couldn't read their expression.

"Mademoiselle?" the standing student prompted me, once more gesturing at the seat. "We're not going to *eat* her, you know," he added when I neither answered nor moved. He sounded faintly wounded.

"What *fellows*?" Josephine repeated, and now there was a note of icy fury in her tone. "What *fellows* does he mean?"

"Very lucky fellows, if I might say so." The student beside her grinned again. "Can't say I caught their names. But the idea, as I recall it, is that *this* half of you—your left half—is married to me. That means I get to touch it as a husband touches his wife. Like *this,* for example . . ."

He placed his hand on Josephine's left knee.

For a moment she simply stared at it. Then her body went ramrod straight. I saw her lashes quiver as they did right before a seizure. Felt my breath catch like a dry bone in my throat.

What happened next happened so quickly—and so instinctively on my part—that I'm still not sure of the specifics. All I remember is my own rage, as bright and violent as an anarchist's bomb. I felt the string box flying through the air like an unwieldy whip, heard the bearded student yelp like a dog that had taken a boot-tip to the belly. Heard the coachman shouting something about *rules* and *ladies* and *not safe*.

And after that, my own voice, whistle-shrill, shaking: "Don't *touch* her!"

And then Josephine and I were on our feet, and I was half pushing, half dragging her away, my heart hammering so loudly that I couldn't hear anything beyond it. Miraculously, she didn't go into a fit, and I somehow got us both down that flimsy, slippery ladder in one piece, past the surprised-looking conductor who was once more standing on the platform, and into the carriage. There we flopped onto the bench two schoolboys in double-breasted jackets and knee pants had just vacated.

Still panting a little, I stared out the glazed glass window at the platform, ignoring the alarmed looks our ungainly entrance had elicited from the other passengers. I half expected the medical students to give chase—or at least, for the conductor to storm in and eject us as he had the drunk. Instead, however, he disappeared up the ladder himself, summoned by the *cocher*'s aggrieved shout.

I held my breath as the argument escalated audibly, the coachman going on about *decency* and *young ruffians* and *no sense of shame,* the students' voices lifted defensively: *We were just explaining how it went,* I heard one say. And then: Mon Dieu, *the women in this city really* are *going mad.*

A few seconds later the conductor was poking his head into the cabin.

"Are you ladies all right?"

Josephine—sitting ramrod straight in her new seat—didn't answer. I nodded, my cheeks heating.

"You should've followed the sign," he said darkly. And shutting the door, he returned to the ladder. As he did it dawned on me all of a sudden that I'd left Josephine's boot box on the roof.

"Ah," I exclaimed. "Your clogs. I'll ask him to fetch them for us. . . ."

But I'd barely gotten to my feet when I felt her hand on my arm. Her touch wasn't gentle as it had been on the ride to the store, when she'd asked me if I was all right. It was so viselike that I felt five points of painful pressure on my forearm, hard enough to leave bruises. Before I'd fully registered what was happening, she'd yanked me down onto the bench again, so forcefully the air was briefly knocked from my chest.

There were two pink spots high on Josephine's cheeks. Her eyes were as hard as green-gray stones. She leaned close, and for a shocked instant I thought she might strike me. An image of the judge's dead body—her blade plunged into his gut—flashed before me. Instinctively, I cowered back.

But she made no further move toward me. "*Mariage à trois,*" she said, in that same low, cold voice. "Tell me. Tell me all of it."

We were just a few minutes from turning onto boulevard de l'Hôpital now—which meant a few minutes from losing her clogs altogether. Babette would be furious. And yet I knew I had no choice: If I refused her this, I would lose her as completely as if the *agents de police* had already trundled her off to prison.

I took a deep breath. Then, my eyes fixed on the dirty wooden floorboards, her hand still clamping my forearm, I told her about it: *mariage à trois.*

I told her all of it. How, after putting her into the third and deepest stage of hypnosis, Charcot had selected two young men from the audience, seating Josephine between them. How he'd explained to her that her left side was married to the man sitting to her left, her right to the man sitting to the right. How her task had been to keep the left- and right-hand husbands happy with their respective "wives"—but under *no* circumstances to allow either of them to touch the other's.

I told her how I was worried at first that this setup would send her straight into a seizure, as Gilles de la Tourette's "seaside" suggestion nearly had (and yes, I described that as well). But once entranced, Josephine had merely nodded serenely as Charcot laid out the exercise's rules: Each man, he said, was allowed to freely caress and tickle their respective side of Josephine's body as though caressing his actual wife. But if his hand strayed over her midline, attempting to touch the side belonging to the other "husband," she wasn't to allow it.

I told her how it was a test that—like virtually all the tests Charcot gave her—she'd passed with flying colors: how every time either of the men's hands crossed her median—even slightly—she would immediately slap them away. How the man on the right would walk his fingers just past where her navel was, and *slap!* Or the man on the right stroked her left thigh: *Slap! Slap!* ("How *dare* you!") How if the man on the left tucked a curl behind her left ear, she would smile in approval, but if he attempted to do the same with the right, she'd cry (*slap!*), "*Stop* that! I'm *married*!"

I told her how as the "game" went on, the men grew bolder, laughing along with the audience as Josephine slapped and pushed their hands back with increasing rapidity, the look on her face becoming more distressed, her deflections more and more agitated. How by the end, she almost seemed to be playing some nightmarish form of the clapping games I'd played with Amélie, or attempting to beat off a swarm of attacking birds. How it had indeed been—as the bearded student on the omni roof had noted—an astounding performance, all the more so because while Josephine never looked directly at either of her "husbands," she also never missed when one of them crossed her invisible median, even by a hair. How, on those few occasions when the men's hands crossed it simultaneously, she rebuffed them just as quickly, grasping not one but both of their thick wrists in her surprisingly strong grasp, returning the men's hands to their "proper" spots on her left and right thighs.

I told her that Charcot had seemed as delighted by the exercise as his viewers clearly were, speculating afterward that the ease with which "both the hysteric's mind and her body could be so neatly cleaved in half" might prove useful in exploring "whether and how the human brain is divided into different functional regions, as has been recently speculated." That there was the usual flurry of impressed nods, the usual patter of words scribbled onto notebooks. That as the audience members filed out, they were still chattering excitedly about it. "I wish *my* wife was that faithful," I heard one man quip—and I told her that too.

What I didn't tell her was how leaving the amphitheater, a creeping revulsion had seemed to ripple through me, as though it hadn't just been Josephine's limbs but my own offered laughingly to the groping hands of strangers. It felt suddenly shameful, like admitting my hands, too, had also made their way across her entranced form. In some ways, I realized, it was almost as if they had—for the whole thing had only come about because *I'd* brought her to the doctor's attention. Nor did I share with her a new and even more sickening realization that swept me as I continued confessing: that if the police did trace their way to her, whether through one of the dead judge's friends who'd ended up in the audience or through the rhapsodic newspaper sketches and descriptions—that would clearly be my fault as well.

All I said was, "I'm sorry. I was afraid it would be too upsetting for you to hear."

Still unable to meet her gaze, I continued staring at the floor. I think I was hoping that even if she couldn't fully forgive me, she'd give some sign that she at least understood that my duplicity had not been born of malice, but a fierce instinct to protect her.

But she did neither. She simply stared past me out the window, at passing traffic and pedestrians. At the slow-dimming spring sky.

By the time we'd reached boulevard de l'Hôpital she still hadn't spoken a word. Sighing, I signaled the *conducteur* that we needed to get off. But as the carriage rocked to a halt, she made no move to get up.

"We're here," I said. But when I went to take her arm she slapped away my hand as she had those of her errant "husbands," only hard enough that I felt the sting of it in my teeth.

"Don't touch me," she said hotly.

And then: "I *trusted* you."

She barely murmured the words, yet it felt as though she'd plunged them straight into my belly.

Climbing to her feet, she limped out onto the platform alone, giving the conductor her arm so he could help her down the steps. She staggered on ahead of me through the arched entrance to the asylum and past Pinel's steely gaze and the cowering girl at his feet. Given how laboriously she moved, it took effort to not catch up with her, to take her arm and steady her as I usually did. Suppressing the impulse, I trailed behind her all the way to Esquirol, throbbing with shock and shame.

Chapter Nine

In the days that followed, Josephine still wouldn't speak to me, or even look at me when she could help it. She stared off into the distance as I did her hair and laced her new boots, responding to anything I said with a cryptic nod, head shake, or shrug. She did the same as I recounted to her every exercise and experiment the doctors put her through while she was "under." Needless to say, I did so now with excruciating care, often including details of no possible significance ("Babinski smelled like a distillery," "the Gnome went to the latrine twice," "Freud had salad stuck between his front teeth") to be certain I omitted nothing.

And yet these meticulous reconstructions did nothing to soften her stony disdain for me, or to ease her overall agitation. If anything, she seemed even more jumpy and anxious than she had before our La Samaritaine trip, starting at sudden noises and stiffening at the sound of male voices approaching inside the asylum corridors. She seemed particularly wary of Claude, freezing in place if she saw him coming and sometimes even making up excuses to go in the opposite direction. All of this made sense, given both what she'd confessed to me by the river and the brutal way the Basque had handled her in the feeding room. And yet her anxiety troubled me. Not just because she was so clearly terrified beyond her wits, but because I was sure she regretted having entrusted me with her confession—and perhaps even feared I'd betray her to the doctors myself. After all, I'd already betrayed her once.

And it *was* a betrayal. I saw that now. No matter how I tried to rationalize my actions to myself, the fact remained that she'd trusted me to protect her in the asylum, just as she'd trusted her mother to protect her at the judge's. And like her mother, I'd thrown that trust in her face. It mattered little that she had no memory of having been "wed" to two strange men in front of (quite literally) a thousand eyes, or that there was little I could have done to prevent those faux unions from taking place. That I'd kept her in the dark about Charcot's *mariage à trois* exercise was clearly as upsetting to her as the fact that it had happened at all, and that I hadn't anticipated this was a painful source of regret.

Equally painful was her reaction after I went to her during one of her nightmares the night after our trip to La Samaritaine. When I awoke to her ragged shriek, Josephine was already bolt upright in her cot, staring at the shuttered window by her bed with the glazed eyes of someone trapped in a terrifying dream. "How?" I heard her whisper in the slurred speech of the sleep talker. "How is it possible? How is he with—that *beast*?"

Knowing better than to try to wake her, I instead attempted to gently ease her back onto her bed. It was something I'd done dozens of times before. This time, though, when I touched her she jerked away as violently as if I'd touched her skin with a hot fire poker.

"Josephine," I whispered. "Shhh. It's *me*."

I watched the dread drain from her face, the glaze of sleep dissipate from her gaze. Our eyes met, and she slowly registered my fingers on her shoulder. For a moment, I thought she might fall into my arms, as she'd sometimes done in the past.

Instead, she struck my hand down.

"Don't touch me," she hissed, just as she had on the omni.

And turning her back, she lay down again, curling away from me for the rest of the night.

———

I had hoped that with time, this iciness would melt back into the easy warmth we'd begun sharing before the bus debacle; that wordless affection and trust that, for a few short weeks, had transformed my asylum duties from numbing labor into purposeful action, and Hysteria itself into a place almost approaching a home. But the days passed, and she showed no sign of letting me back into her good graces. Instead, we fell into a kind of uncomfortable and lopsided alliance, with me continually attempting to regain her goodwill—clipping pictures I knew she'd like from the newspapers, or buying her barley twists from the asylum market, or suggesting new ways to do her hair—and her rebuffing every one of those attempts.

As one and then another full week passed in this agonizing fashion, I was forced to confront two harsh realities: First, that whatever bright thing had been growing between us had been irrevocably uprooted by my actions—or lack thereof. And second, that without Josephine's affection, the Salpêtrière once more became a place of hopelessness and drudgery, of madness and despair, no more a home than it had been during my own commitment. In some ways it was even worse, for before Josephine's arrival I'd sometimes been able to take my mind off all the good things in my life that I'd lost. Now, though, tied as I was to her side day and night, I was forced to continually confront the fact that she had become another one of them.

Then—impossibly—everything changed.

Two weeks after the omnibus incident, I arrived back from a breakfast consumed in silence next to Josephine (as had become the norm) to find Babette hovering by my cot.

"Who do you know in Vault-de-Lugny, Bissonnet?" she asked, eyeing me with suspicion.

"No one," I said, baffled.

She snorted. "Of course you don't. You don't know your nose from your toe." And pulling a letter from her apron, she tossed it onto my cot with a familiar snort of disdain. I stared after her as she stalked off, mystified both by the letter and by the faint bell that that name—Vault-de-Lugny—rang in my recollection.

Then I remembered: Vault-de-Lugny was one of the villages I'd circled on the map of Morvan that I'd ripped from an old guidebook in the asylum's dilapidated (and generally deserted) library. I'd circled it because it was near Avallon, the largest city in the region where Amélie was. Or at least, where she had been.

I waited until my supervisor was safely out of view before snatching the envelope up. I didn't recognize the sender's name or address:

> *Madame Alphonsine Granger*
> *4 rue de Château*
> *Vault-de-Lugny*

Barely daring to breathe, I broke the seal and withdrew a short note that had been enclosed along with a longer, neatly-folded letter. *Dear Mademoiselle Bissonnet,* it read in a neat and even hand. *Enclosed please find a letter your sister, Amélie—who has been living under my care for the past month—asked me to send on her behalf. I hope for the chance to meet soon. Cordially, Alphonsine Granger.*

I clutched the letter to my chest, a lightness coursing through me with such buoyant force that I thought it would lift me straight off the floor. I wanted to shout with joy, to weep with relief, to stamp my feet and clap my hands until they smarted. Most of all, I wanted to drag Josephine from where she now sat on Bernadette's cot, her back conspicuously turned toward me, and wrap my arms around her neck.

When I looked back up, though, Babette was still watching me from her desk with a look of malevolent interest. Afraid she was about to assign me some further pointless, punitive task—or worse, demand to see the letter herself—I stuffed it into my apron pocket and busied myself with refolding Josephine's nightshift until the old woman's attention had moved on to something else. Then I hurried to the washroom, where I pulled the letter out fully. As I took in its familiar script—the inconsistent slants and wobbly *a*'s, *e*'s, and *i*'s—it was as if some invisible inner tourniquet that had been knotted around my lungs had miraculously been ripped away.

My sister had written, a little over a month earlier:

Dear Laure, I hope that this message finds you. I am sorry that I have not written you before. Things have been very confused since you were taken away to the asylum and I was sent to the Hospice des Enfants Assistés. But I have been thinking of you every day and hoping that the doctors have been able to help you, and that you are no longer hysterical. As for me: I am safe, and for the last two months have been living with a good woman, Madame Granger.

The year before that, however, was strange, and often trying, which is why it was difficult for me to write. I don't believe that the family the agency placed me with at first—the Martins—are unkind people. But they were very busy, and the dairy farm they owned took a lot of work to run. I don't think it made much of a profit, for even with five of us fosters working there all day, there often wasn't enough for everyone to eat a full meal. The rule there was that the harder workers— mainly, the boys—were entitled to extra helpings, which was perhaps not unfair. But it meant that many nights I had to go to bed hungry.

Still, I probably could have borne living there if it hadn't been for the other foster children. From the moment I arrived they all seemed to take a disliking to me—and not just because I couldn't do my fair share of work (though they continually mocked me for that). They also seemed to think that I "put on airs." Madame Granger thinks this was because I wasn't a "found" or "abandoned" child like the others were, but someone who for most of my life had a family, and a father in a prestigious profession. Either way, not only did they tease and complain about me to our foster parents, but they went out of their way to make my life harder, purposefully spilling my bucket during milking and stealing my blanket at night. A boy named Pierre was the worst of them all; when the Martins weren't looking he would often pull my hair or pinch me hard enough to leave bruises.

But then Madame Martin sent for a midwife because she was nearing her confinement. And that's when I met Madame Granger. She needed a girl to help her, and Madame Martin assigned me to her after saying I was useless at almost everything else.

As it turned out, though, I wasn't so useless at helping birth a baby! On top of fetching and boiling water, I knew how to apply poultices and bandages thanks to Papa, as well as how to check Madame Martin's pulse. I even surprised Madame Granger by knowing about Dr. Pasteur's germ theory and Dr. Lister's antiseptic techniques. After it was all over—it was a boy, healthy and very big at nearly five kilos!—Madame Granger was so pleased that she told the Martins I had the makings of a good midwife's apprentice, and that since they seemingly didn't have much use for me on the farm she was happy to waive her fee and instead bring me back with her to Vault-de-Lugny, where she lives. She later told me that she'd also been concerned by how thin I was, and by the bruises she'd seen on my arms and legs. Either way, it seems the Martins were only too happy to be rid of me, since they readily agreed.

Since then, I've been much happier. Vault-de-Lugny is very small, but it's quite close to Avallon, which has some lovely old buildings and churches and a pretty central square. I haven't made any friends here yet and am sometimes quite lonely. But Madame Granger is kind and very wise and is teaching me interesting things—not just about birthing babies, but about growing herbs and medicinal plants, and treating fevers and rashes and imbalances of the digestive system. She says I can become a midwife myself one day, if I work hard. And she says that when you are well enough you must come visit us, and perhaps even move nearby so we can be together.

I must go now—Madame Granger has a patient downstairs whose baby is in something called a "transverse lie," which means it is more or less sideways, like little Louie was. She wants to show me different ways to try to turn it. She knows so much, Madame Granger! I sometimes think that if she'd been the one attending Maman that day, she and Louie would still be alive, though Madame Granger says there's no point in thinking such things. "Le passé est le passé," she says. Still, I think of you, and our old home, every single day. Please, please write me and tell me how you are, and whether you can come soon. I still miss you and Papa so terribly—especially at night.

With all my love, and a thousand kisses,

Amélie

I read the letter once, then a second and third time, still feeling that searing, almost painful sense of buoyancy, as if my veins had been straining these past months to pump lead instead of blood, which had suddenly been replaced by liquid light. It was only after I'd finished it a fourth time that I found myself breaking into laughter so abrupt and uncontrolled that I probably sounded like one of the old *folles* with their knitting needles and ghostly pets.

And in truth, I felt like one—or at the very least like a fool. For I'd just realized that for all the careful detail of her letter, my sister had made no mention of the notices I'd so frantically placed in Morvan-area newspapers. She hadn't seen them and hadn't needed to. Of course she hadn't.

She'd known where I was all along.

That afternoon I sat in my usual spot by the door of Charcot's clinic as he and Dr. Janet—a sharp-featured intern whose arched brows and prematurely retreating hairline gave him a perpetual look of owlish surprise—prepared for their second research experiment of the afternoon. The first, which they'd just finished, had involved shining different colored lights on Josephine and taking note of her reactions, which seemed to vary by hue: Blue light made her shiver, green sent her into an abrupt rage. Yellow had caused her to assume a posture of religious ecstasy that was, I noticed, strikingly similar to one Bernadette often assumed in her fits: falling onto her knees, clasped hands and worshipful gaze lifted toward the ceiling. Janet had recorded each on his clipboard with typical diligence, musing about a possible future paper on the emotive influence of color on the brain.

Now he was arranging Josephine's bare legs beneath the little table at which he'd seated her as matter-of-factly as he might have arranged flower stems in a vase. Charcot sat hunched over his desk, smoking one of his American cigars while studying a set of magnets he'd laid out on top of his papers and folders. When I shifted slightly in my seat—I'd sat for over an hour as motionlessly as I could, but my backside was beginning to numb—he threw me a sharp glance, as if to remind me he hadn't forgotten my outburst nearly two months earlier. At one time that glare would have made me cower as surely as if he'd flung a surgical blade at my head. Now, though, I barely registered it—any more than I'd registered Babette's carping when I returned from reading Amélie's glorious letter in the latrine. Even Josephine's cold remove as I'd helped her undress for the doctors had felt less like a wound than a morphine injection, a temporary discomfort that was easy to endure, since I knew a far, far better feeling would follow.

For I'd made my decision: I'd leave the Salpêtrière the following Saturday—just after collecting my wages. Combined with what I'd make from selling my stash of novels to the Seine-side *bouquiniste* from whom I'd bought them (along with a few carefully chosen tomes from the asylum library that no one was likely to notice if they went missing), I'd have just enough money—and time, I hoped—to get to Dijon, where I'd hopefully be able to sell the bracelet before continuing on to Vault-de-Lugny. I'd already written my sister to expect me. The letter was in my pocket right now, as light and luminous-feeling as a promise, and I would take it to the asylum post office as soon as I could slip away unobserved. If all went according to plan, I might even reach Amélie and her midwife before it did.

I did feel torn over the prospect of leaving Josephine. But as her behavior attested, she still clearly wanted nothing to do with me, and Claudine or Julienne could easily take over her care. I would miss her, I knew—would miss that brief and wondrous span when Josephine Garreau had been the best—and perhaps the one real—friend I'd ever had. But it was amply clear that she'd be happier with me gone.

"Perhaps this one, to start?" Charcot leveraged himself to his feet, holding out one of the magnets he'd been studying. Horseshoe-shaped, it was roughly the size of his hand. "I believe it's the same one Babinski used to temporarily transfer Rosalie's contraction to Caroline a few months back, no?"

I looked at Janet in surprise. I knew the doctors had been experimenting with metallotherapy, using magnets and various metals to treat hysterical symptoms. But I'd had no idea that they'd used it to move symptoms *between* hysterics. The idea was faintly unsettling. For some reason it brought to mind the hapless doctor in Madame Shelley's novel, cobbling together a monstrous human from different body parts.

Janet nodded. "It is indeed. And a good place to begin. We can work our way down to the smaller ones from there."

"And there's nothing else that might interfere . . . ?"

"I've double-checked. With her dress and stays off, there is no metal of any sort left. I've taken out her hairpins as well."

"Good." Charcot gave a short nod toward Josephine's legs. "And why did you remove her stockings?"

Janet cleared his throat. "There seems," he said, "to be mounting evidence that the more skin is exposed, the more pronounced the magnetic response."

Charcot's hawk's eyes fixed once more on Josephine's scantily clad form. For a moment I worried he'd order me to strip her of her shift as well, which he hadn't required of her since her initial evaluation. But he just nodded, slipping the U-shaped piece of iron into his apron pocket as Janet finished his arrangement of Josephine's limbs. The younger doctor had positioned her with her left thigh crossed over her right, her right arm resting on the little table's surface. After studying her further, he bent the arm at the elbow and lifted her right forearm and hand, as if she were lazily signaling a café server for the bill.

"There," he said, inspecting his handiwork. "That should do nicely."

Tearing off a piece of foolscap from his pad, Janet set it down by Josephine's elbow and stepped back as Charcot lumbered over to stand by his patient.

"How are you feeling?" Charcot asked her.

She looked up at him hazily. "Must I sit like this?"

"Are you uncomfortable?"

"Comfortable enough." Her speech was slow and drowsy-sounding, as it always was when she was entranced. Like Rosalie, she could sustain entire conversations in this state, exchanges she'd have no recollection of upon waking, and which might seem fully sentient to someone who didn't know the other signs of her entrancement: The subtle slackening of her muscles. The disappearance of the restless little movements that had become even more pronounced over the past two weeks. The distant, blank look that appeared on her face, as though an invisible iron had smoothed it of expression.

"I was just wondering," she said now, dreamily.

"What are you wondering?"

"Why I must sit like this."

"Ah, that," Charcot said. "It is because you are having your portrait painted. See, there's the portrait artist over there. Right behind his easel." He waved a hand in the direction of the far wall of his office, to a space occupied not by a man in a billowing smock but by a wax sculpture of an old woman, fully nude, with flat, sagging breasts and a look of confusion on her seamed face. Josephine followed the motion, her eyes landing on the waxen crone without any sign that she saw anything amiss at first. Then, though, her brow puckered.

"He's painting me like this?" she asked. "In nothing more than my shift?"

"No, no," said Janet quickly. "You are wearing a—a very handsome gown. And matching slippers. Can't you see them?"

Josephine glanced down at her lap. Then she smiled her small, Mona Lisa–esque smile.

"Yes," she said tranquilly. "The dress is peacock blue, like the one I saw in that old copy of *Le moniteur de la mode* Marthe's mother left in the ward after Visiting Day last week."

"It is exactly that dress," Charcot confirmed. He had quietly retrieved the magnet from his pocket and was holding it up to Josephine's left side, out of her field of vision but near enough to her head that if she'd tipped it back even slightly she'd have knocked right into it. "And it's a very fine dress," he continued. "You'll wear it to dinner tonight and make all the other girls jealous."

"I shall," Josephine agreed. "And next Friday in the amphitheater, as well."

She'd started swaying very slightly in her seat. It was a subtle enough movement that had we been anywhere else I doubt I would even have noted it. But both Janet and Charcot were watching her closely, with the kind of bated-breath excitement with which a child might watch a *diable en boîte* while cranking the box's handle.

"A good idea," Charcot said. "Perhaps you'd like a matching ribbon to wear with it? Madame Charcot can buy one for you on her next shopping expedition." He'd lowered the magnet from just past Josephine's ear to a spot level with her uncorseted waist. Still seemingly unaware of the tool, Josephine appeared to ponder the offer, her eyes still fixed on the "artist" in the corner.

"I think not," she said finally. "It's a medical lecture, after all. There's no need to dress up for it like a Christmas goose." The rocking motion I'd noticed earlier was becoming more pronounced, though her face betrayed no emotion. Suddenly, though, she reversed her position, dropping her right forearm back on the table and lifting her left up instead, switching her legs so that her right now crossed over the left.

Janet's face broke into an elated smile. Charcot moved slowly around Josephine's table, examining her in that bird-of-prey way he had before coming to a stop behind her. "Are you still comfortable?" he asked.

"Yes," she said, frowning. "Why?"

"You changed positions." He lifted the magnet again, this time holding it in a spot just past her bare left elbow.

"I didn't," Josephine said, sounding faintly indignant. "You told me not to." But she was rocking in her seat again, her torso drawing close, and then closer, to the hovering U-shaped tool, until—with the same unconscious fluidity as she'd displayed before—she switched her position back to what it had been.

Charcot's eyes snapped in triumph as they met Janet's. "So I did," he said. "Perhaps I was mistaken. I have an old man's memory now, after all."

"That's nonsense," she retorted. "Everyone knows you've a memory like an elephant's."

I glanced at Charcot's face, worried about how he'd take such impertinence. Unlike Rosalie, Josephine was almost always unfailingly deferential to Charcot, whether entranced or not.

But the doctor just chuckled.

"Perhaps that's why I walk like one," he said. I blinked: It was one of the few times I'd heard him make a joke.

Reaching into his vest pocket, he produced a self-filled fountain pen and set it atop the piece of paper. "I would like you to write something for us," he announced.

"Write?" she repeated dubiously. Much to her own frustration, Josephine's writing skills were—like her reading—limited. She put words to paper with the almost childlike overfocus of someone who has had little call to do so on a regular basis.

"Nothing complicated," Janet assured her now. "We would like you to write out some numbers."

"What numbers?"

"Any numbers you like. Just write them in rows."

Josephine hesitated, then picked up the pen. "It's a lovely pen," she observed.

"A gift from a grateful patient," Charcot said. "You may keep it if you like."

Her face brightened. "Really?"

He nodded. "Just let me or Dr. Janet know whenever it runs out of ink."

"Thank you, Docteur." She unscrewed the cap almost reverently, placing it on the table's far corner. I wondered whether she'd even used such a pen before now. My father had given me one of his own pens—with a black lacquer barrel and a cap painted with delicate golden birds—for my sixteenth birthday. Thinking of it now, I felt a stab of sadness; where had it ended up? Doubtlessly sold to a stranger, like everything else from our flat. I comforted myself with the thought that I could find a new one in Morvan or Avallon—and perhaps one for Amélie as well. After all, we were rich now.

"Just numbers?" Josephine was repositioning herself, propping her left elbow on the table and resting her cheek against the knuckles of her right hand while, with her left hand, she touched the pen's steel nib to the paper's surface.

"Just numbers," Charcot confirmed. "They needn't even be particularly neat."

She nodded, pressing the pen's tip cautiously against the paper a few times to initiate the ink flow. Then, as Charcot looked on over her shoulder, she began to write out what I assumed was a series of random digits.

When she'd finished a line, she looked back up, her cheek still resting on her fist. "Is this right?"

"Very good," Charcot said. "Continue on just like that. Fill the page."

Josephine took a moment to adjust the paper, aligning its bottom edge with the edge of the table before continuing. She was writing with more assurance now, seemingly oblivious to the fact that Charcot was still silently holding his magnet by her left side. For a minute or so there was only the quiet *scritch scritch* of the steel pen tip against the paper. Then the pen, which she'd had lightly gripped in her right hand, seemed to suddenly be twitching toward the left, like the needle on some arrhythmic metronome.

Josephine stared at the writing tool in annoyance, as though it were shaking and trembling of its own accord. Then, all at once, she dropped her left hand from her cheek and switched the pen to its grip, simultaneously planting her right elbow on the table so that she could rest her right cheek against her fist.

Charcot observed this transition without expression. Then he leaned over to peer down at Josephine's page.

"*Fantastique*," he murmured, one thick brow lifting.

"*Maître?*" Janet made his way back over to join him. As he reached Charcot's side, the older doctor turned to face him, shaking his head in bemusement. "Look," he said, indicating Josephine's paper. "What do you see?"

Janet leaned forward. I saw his dark eyes widen in surprise. "Fascinating," he said. "The numbers written with her left hand are written *backward*. As though she's copied them from a mirror."

"Exactly," Charcot concurred. "Extraordinary."

Outside, a grating shriek sounded from somewhere in the direction of the refectory. It was followed by male voices shouting, the heavy clatter of racing footsteps. I heard someone—one of the *reposantes*, perhaps—cackle wildly before letting loose a long howl in response, like a dog baying at the moon. Josephine glanced toward the window, frowning faintly.

"You may stop for the moment," Charcot told her, leaning over to pick the paper up. Handing it to Janet, he made his way back to his desk.

"Remarkable," the younger doctor mused, studying the sheet again. "If the magnets have this impact on her spatial orientation, one wonders what other faculties they might influence."

"Other faculties?" Charcot picked up his cigar, examining its ashy but now unlit end before fumbling in his trouser pocket for his matches. "Such as?"

"There have been studies indicating that everything from vision to emotion, and perhaps even memory itself, might be inflected by changes in the magnetic field," Janet said. "It could be the basis for quite a fascinating paper."

A protest rose in my throat so abruptly I barely managed to swallow it back. It had been unnerving enough to see Josephine's limbs twitch and shift toward Charcot's magnet. The thought of his using it to reorder the contents of her head or to reverse the inclinations of her heart was downright terrifying. What if it somehow affected her resolve to keep her perilous secret, made her confess her crime from Charcot's stage?

For the first time since making my decision to leave the Salpêtrière, I almost found myself questioning it. But I reminded myself that Josephine had shown no sign of revealing her crime while entranced—not even after Charcot handed her an imaginary "pistol"—in reality, a rolled-up newspaper—and had her "shoot" an audience member with it. Lifting the paper cylinder, she'd taken aim with both hands, closing one eye in concentration as she squeezed her imaginary trigger. She'd then frozen in place as her ears registered the nonexistent gunshot retort—in the process neatly proving his stated assertion that hysterics could be sent into catalepsy not just by sudden noise in the mortal world, but by "noises" of their own imagining.

The audience had loved it. So, clearly, had the editors at *Paris illustré*, which two days later ran a front-page image of Josephine wielding her imaginary weapon at a surprised-looking man in a brown bowler. Clearly, though, the editors had missed the point of the exercise, as evidenced by the caption: *The "Napoléon of Neuroses" demonstrates how even the daintiest of hysterics can, when hypnotized, be transformed into a ruthless sharpshooter.*

My musings were interrupted by an explosion of knocks on the clinic door. I glanced at Josephine, half expecting her to be startled into catalepsy again. But she appeared to be engrossed in Charcot's pen.

Hurrying to the door, Janet flung it open to reveal the quivering form of a lunacy ward *fille de service* I knew in passing. Eugénie's round face was pale with worry, gleaming with perspiration. "The—the director," she panted. "He's to come to the kitchen, at once."

"What is it?" Charcot pushed past me to stand next to Janet.

"An emergency," Eugénie said, chest still heaving. "Ismérie told me to tell you you must come."

Ismérie. The name sent a reflexive shudder down my spine. Ismérie Dehainaut was the most notoriously cruel nurse in Lunacy—and it was her section to which Rosalie had been exiled.

"It's Rosalie," Eugénie continued, confirming my fears. "She says she's going to do away with herself."

"Do *away* with herself?" Janet exclaimed. "How?"

"She—she's gotten herself out of Lunacy." Eugénie's voice was trembling. "She slipped off the rope during the afternoon group walk."

"How the devil did she do that?" Charcot boomed.

Eugénie curtsied hastily, seemingly out of reflex. "We were short an attendant, Docteur. Lucien, he was struck by a hansom cab on Monday and now must walk with a crutch. . . ."

"The girl." Charcot waved her on impatiently. "Tell me about the girl."

Eugénie curtsied again, looking cowed. "At first no one noticed. When they did, we couldn't find her. We were searching high and low until word came that she'd shown up in the kitchen and somehow got hold of Cook's butcher knife." She took another shuddering breath. "She says if you won't talk to her—right now—she'll cut open her own throat."

I gasped. Janet was already reaching for his coat. "When was this?" he interrupted.

"Just a few minutes ago, sir," Eugénie said. "Cook's made everyone leave the area except for one of the galley boys."

"Damn it." Charcot's clean-shaven jaw was tight. "She's more trouble than she's worth, that one."

"I can go, *maître*," Janet said.

"We'll both go." Charcot was already pushing past him, shrugging cumbersomely into his coat. "The little idiot's just foolish enough that she might actually hurt herself, whether or not she truly intends to."

Jamming his hat onto his head, he snatched his cane from behind his desk and strode past Eugénie out into the hallway, Janet hard on his heels. The Lunacy attendant made as if to follow them both, but Charcot stopped her with another curt wave.

"Not you," he barked over his hunched shoulder. "Go to the infirmary. Tell Dr. Boudu—I think he's on overnight there—to come right away with his kit. And with plenty of bandages." He thought for a moment before adding: "Have him send a stretcher too. And two attendants."

Eugénie went even paler at this. But she gave a third curtsy before hurrying toward the building's exit. I took a hesitant step after her, the gruesome image—*Rosalie, blade, blood*—swimming in crimson through my thoughts. But Janet laid a hand on my arm.

"Stay here," he told me. "Get Josephine back to Esquirol."

Nodding numbly, I stepped back into Charcot's office, hurrying to the window as the three set off: Eugénie toward the infirmary, Charcot plodding toward the kitchen, Janet loping impatiently alongside him. *Oh, Rosalie,* I thought as the two turned onto rue de la Cuisine and disappeared from sight.

And yet I didn't really believe the Alsatian would follow through on her gruesome threat. It was more likely that she'd staged this spectacle to capture Charcot's attention—and to try to recapture his sympathies. Everyone knew she'd been pleading desperately to see him, to no avail. Far more concerning than the threat itself was that she'd apparently thought it might somehow improve her situation. The old Rosalie would have known that trying to force Charcot's hand was a surefire way to make him lift it even more firmly against her.

Sighing, I turned back to the room. Josephine remained at her little table exactly as I had left her, studying Charcot's fountain pen with a look of faint puzzlement. I felt a flash of annoyance—did she really need to go to such lengths to ignore me?—before realizing with a jolt that she was still deep in the throes of Charcot's hypnotic spell.

Nom de Dieu, I thought. No one had remembered to wake her.

For a moment I felt paralyzed myself, unsure of what to do. Race after the two doctors? But this, I knew, would have been a mistake—not just because Janet had instructed me to stay with Josephine, but because I knew better than to leave her alone in this state. If she were to wander off it would cause a second crisis atop the first—one, moreover, that I'd be blamed for. Right at the very moment I was trying to avoid attention, so that I could make my escape.

I studied Josephine's serene face again, wondering whether I could wake her myself. I had no idea how hypnosis worked. But I'd seen Janet and Charcot break their "spells" scores of times, and described the process to her afterward: *Josephine*, they'd say. *I'm going to count backward. When I reach "one" and snap my fingers, you'll wake up, remembering nothing of what has just passed.* Was there any more to it than that? I tried to remember, but my thoughts were so jumbled from the tumult of the past few minutes that I couldn't recall whether they'd started counting from twenty, or ten, or five. Did it even matter where one started? What happened if I did it wrong, and instead of waking her up put her into an even deeper trance? One even the doctors couldn't get her out of?

No, I decided, shuddering. Better to keep her in the state she was in now. As long as nothing changed she'd be able to hear and see me, and presumably would walk with me back to the ward. Once I got her there I'd have someone get a doctor to wake her properly.

"Come," I told her, taking her free hand. "Let's get dressed."

"Dressed?" she repeated with a hint of the irritability she'd been displaying toward me while lucid. "What are you talking about?"

"Your gown," I said. "We must get you back into it." Taking her elbow, I again tried to pull her to her feet.

"Don't be silly, Laure," she said, shaking me off.

I indicated her chemise. "You want to be seen outside in that? There are tour groups about. There may be newsmen."

"Better they see me like this than in *that* ugly old thing." She jerked her chin at the screen.

For a moment I was mystified. Normally, Josephine was quite modest about her appearance. It made no sense that she'd *want* the world to see her in a semi-sheer cotton shift that left almost nothing to the imagination.

Then I remembered: They'd told her she was dressed for her "portrait." What was it Janet had said? *A very handsome gown. And matching slippers* . . . I pressed a hand to my forehead, dismayed by the doctors' carelessness as well as by how unquestioningly Josephine believed the alternate realities they fashioned for her. Though of course, that was the whole point of hypnotism.

"The dress is lovely," I said cautiously. "But if you wear it out now it will spoil the surprise on Friday. And you might tear it or get it dirty."

"I must keep it on," she said firmly. "Dr. Charcot said I should wear it to dinner."

I bit back a groan. Of course; Charcot had given the command as casually as he might have told her to hold a thermometer beneath her arm.

I gnawed my lower lip, thinking furiously. If I forced Josephine to "change" into her hospital gown now, she might grow agitated, as 'Nadette had after Gilles de la Tourette and Babinski—after entrancing her—told her she had to kiss Père Julien, the asylum priest. Caught off guard by their own success, the two interns had had to physically hold the girl down as she'd clawed and screamed, desperate to get to the chapel. Babinski tried to reverse the suggestion, but it had been so deeply embedded that in the end they finally summoned the cleric to Hysteria. There Bernadette completed her mission with such enthusiasm that I half expected the confused old clergyman to expire on the spot—either from joy or sheer mortification.

"All right," I told Josephine, still keeping my tone carefully neutral. "We will go to dinner. But I must go back to the ward first to fetch something. And I do think you should wear your boots outside. The slippers are silk. The gravel and mud will ruin them."

She frowned, extending one bare white foot while I held my breath, trying to recall whether Charcot had included her "shoes" in his dinner suggestion. Apparently, he hadn't, since she nodded. As she twisted her calf thoughtfully in the waning evening light, I worried that she'd ask me to take her imaginary slippers off for her. I had no idea how I'd manage *that*.

To my relief, though, she pulled the foot—uncontracted now, as it almost always was during her trances—up to her chair seat. With intent focus, she began to pantomime unwinding ribbons, or straps, or whatever it was she saw, from around her bare calves. When she'd done both legs, she sat up, hand extended, thumb and forefinger pinched in a way that suggested she held a pair of light shoes together at the heels.

"Carry those for me," she instructed curtly.

"Of course," I said, exhaling in relief.

Happily, without Josephine's contraction the walk back to Esquirol took half as long as it usually did, though when we arrived at the ward most of the *internées* had already left for dinner. Only Bernadette and Louise remained in our section. The latter was under direct meal supervision after a week's worth of breakfast brioches had been found moldering beneath her bed. 'Nadette, for her part, had lost dining room privileges after somehow managing to post a letter to Dr. Babinski's fiancée in which she'd recounted intimate and occasionally obscene details of her "affair" with the young doctor, as well as reflecting (with her usual wince-inducing specificity) on the eternal tortures both would suffer for these transgressions. The incident had upset the poor lady enough that she'd supposedly called the wedding off entirely. Babinski had refused to step foot in Hysteria since.

Now 'Nadette sat cross-legged on her cot, silver crochet hook flashing as she worked on a spidery length of black silk that she'd earlier informed me was to be a widow's veil, since Babinski's cold neglect had turned her into "the fiancée of Death." Glancing up as we entered, she took in Josephine's ink-smudged shift with wide brown eyes.

"She was out in *that*?" she asked primly.

Another day I might have laughed. 'Nadette herself had been brought back from the grounds wearing less—and drunk off her head to boot. But I merely put a warning finger to my lips before turning to settle Josephine on her cot. As I arranged her pillow behind her back it seemed to me that she was paler than usual, her lips dry, the shadows beneath her eyes almost bruiselike. Was it some sort of side effect of the trance? She'd now been in it for (I calculated quickly) nearly three hours. I couldn't recall Charcot's keeping her under that long before.

Reaching for her wrist, I tried to gauge the flickering blood-beat of her pulse. Without a watch it was hard to tell for sure, but it seemed slower than usual.

"*Alors*, what's wrong with her now?"

Looking up, I saw Julienne hovering by the foot of Josephine's cot, holding a food tray that I guessed was meant for Louise. "The doctors never woke her up after their session today," I said. "They were called to the kitchen. Because of Rosalie."

"Ah, that *pouffiasse*." She rolled her eyes. "They dragged Babette into it as well, leaving me here on my own."

"Her pulse seems slow," I said. "I'm wondering whether I should fetch one of the doctors."

"Because that one's lost in dreamland again?" Julienne threw Josephine a scornful glance. "More fun than being awake in this place, I'd say. But by all means, pester the doctors. You couldn't choose a better moment."

She resumed trudging toward Louise's cot, the soup sloshing in its bowl, the smell of it—salt and onion, acrid fat, and sour broth—wafting greasily in her wake.

"Are we going to dinner soon?" Josephine's eyelids fluttered as if she were having trouble keeping them up.

"Yes," I said, wondering uneasily what happened when someone fell from the "waking" sleep of hypnosis into the blacker oblivion of natural slumber. "But not just yet. The—the doctors want you to take a nap first."

I held my breath as she considered this, half expecting to be challenged. But she merely nodded. "But only for a few minutes. Promise you'll wake me in time."

"I will," I said, lifting her legs onto the bed and reaching for the button hook I now kept in my apron pocket, since she often had to remove her boots two or three times in a day. "I promise. For now, though, shall I take your boots off for you?"

But her eyelids had already slid shut, her lashes twitching in sleep against her cheeks. She didn't move or stir as I eased her fully down onto the mattress. I saw with alarm that her arms were covered with goosebumps, even though the biting chill that tended to linger in the ward from October to May had finally started to ease. Her lips actually looked faintly blue. I draped her new shawl over her and was considering maneuvering her beneath her coverlet as well when I heard the familiar *taptap* of Babette's heels, followed by the shrill ring of her voice: "Why haven't those been filled yet? I quite specifically said they were to be filled and set out before sundown."

Glancing over my shoulder, I spied the old nurse making her way toward her desk, where a dozen new oil lamps were arranged in two neat rows. Registering my presence, though, she stopped short.

"Bissonnet!" she rasped. "Why is she still undressed? And why aren't you both at dinner?"

I hastily explained what had happened: how Charcot and Janet had raced out of their late-afternoon session, leaving Josephine trapped within her trance—as well as unshakably convinced she was sporting a new dress and slippers. "I thought about waking her myself," I said. "But I'm not sure I'd do it correctly—or whether she'd even respond to me in this state."

"You're right about that, at least," she said tartly. "I've no doubt you'd find some way to muck things up." Eyes narrowed, she inspected Josephine's motionless form across the room. Then she shrugged. "Let her be."

"But doesn't she seem pale?" I persisted. "And she was having difficulty speaking before she fell asleep."

"They always sound off when they're under. Any fever?"

"I don't think so. But her pulse feels weak."

Sighing in annoyance, Babette strode over to Josephine's cot and briskly clasped the girl's limp wrist, glaring down at the timepiece she wore around her neck. "Her pulse is slow," she said begrudgingly, dropping Josephine's arm so that it flopped onto her belly. "But it's steady enough. The doctors can wake her on morning rounds, if she doesn't wake on her own first."

"Are you certain?" I glanced back at Josephine's face. Beneath her freckles, her skin had taken on the blue-gray tint of watery milk. "I could go fetch one of the night doctors from the infirmary. . . ."

"Just get her boots off and fetch a counterpane to put atop her," she interrupted. "The doctors have had enough trouble tonight with that Alsatian's latest nonsense."

I nodded. "Is she all right? Eugénie said she had a knife. . . ."

Babette snorted. "Not for long. Claude got it from her fast enough after dosing her, though she knocked over a pot of stew in the process and gave herself a good burn on her leg."

I suppressed a sigh of relief. "Where is she now?"

"Etherized," Babette said shortly. "Though it took four full vials to get her down. She'll stay out a good while, I'd imagine. After that, she'll be kept jacketed in the softs for a few days. And after *that*, we will see." Cocking her gray head, she looked at me quizzically. "Is the interrogation over now?" she added. "Or would you like a report on her vitals as well?"

Flushing, I shook my head. "No," I mumbled. "Thank you."

Not bothering to respond, she snapped her watch shut. Then she turned on her heel, chatelaine clinking as she made her way back to her desk.

Over the next few hours, as Josephine slept her deathlike sleep, I was assigned such a daunting series of chores that it seemed Babette was trying to make up for all the drudgery I'd escaped in past weeks. She had me clean the ward windows with newspaper, the ward walls with balled bread, then tasked me with trimming and filling the lamps I'd seen on her desk, which were apparently to replace the cracked and tarnished ones in the ward. I then spent over an hour looking for Marthe, the ward's newest *internée* (and at twelve by far its youngest), who had already developed a pattern of going missing. I eventually discovered her in the linen closet, wrapped up in a bedsheet and peacefully asleep with her thumb in her mouth.

Throughout all of this Josephine remained atop her cot, as still as a statue on a tomb. Her breathing struck me as so shallow that at one point I surreptitiously held Rosalie's little mirror beneath her nose until it lightly misted over—though far too slowly for my liking. Before retiring to my own cot, I checked it again. To my dismay, it seemed to take even longer.

By that point the ward lights had been lowered, and both Babette and Julienne had turned in, Babette in her room just past the ward's main entrance, Julienne on her cot by the life-sized marble statue of La Madone that had overseen Hysteria for as long as anyone could remember. I briefly considered going to fetch the infirmary doctor on my own. Then I decided against it—less because I feared raising Babette's wrath than because I feared leaving Josephine alone.

The ward was relatively calm that evening, its usual chorus of soft snores punctured by the periodic sobs of Marthe. She kept crying out for her mother, an aging courtesan who'd claimed to have no idea why her child had begun suffering convulsions. It was immediately clear to the rest of us, though, not just from the way Marthe's face colored when she spoke of "Mama's new gentleman friend," but from the fact that after waking from her first fit, she'd had virtually no sensation below her waist. There were also ongoing grunts and protests from Félicie, who'd been strapped to her bed to keep her from reopening the wounds she'd inflicted upon herself during her last scratching attack.

On a normal night in Hysteria, this would have passed for silence. I nevertheless slept poorly, waking every hour or so to worriedly examine Josephine's prone form. Since her confession on the bridge, she'd become even more of a restless sleeper, tossing and thrashing and often whimpering in her dreams, flinging off her covers one moment only to yank them back up the next. Throughout those dark hours, though, she remained in precisely the same position, one arm flung across her belly where Babette had dropped it, the other stiffly tucked against her side. At some point toward dawn I reached out and stroked her bare shoulder, still half expecting her to wake and recoil (*Don't touch me!*). And yet she didn't move. Her skin beneath my fingers felt as cold and smooth as polished stone in winter.

At some point after that I must have fallen into a shallow slumber myself, because when I opened my eyes—or thought I did—I turned to check on her again and caught my breath in horror. She'd disappeared from her cot. In her place was a grinning skull perched atop a haphazard pile of human bones.

I jerked upright, frantically scanning the sleeping ward for her. But there was no sign of her at all. In fact, none of the hysterics—Félicie, Madame Chambon, Clotilde, Bernadette, Marthe—were there. There were only more ghoulish skulls, more moldering bones.

I wasn't in an asylum. I was in a mausoleum.

Terrified, I tried to swing my legs over my bed's edge. But they refused to obey me. Looking down, I saw that my own limbs were becoming bones too. The skin and sinew, the veins and tendons—everything I'd learned about in my father's anatomy books, the fleshly marvels that hold our bodies together—all of it was melting away, like wax liquefying before a flame.

I woke standing upright between Josephine's bed and my own, a choked scream clogging my throat. The ghoulish vision lingered for a few seconds before receding like a slow-slipping shadow, leaving in its wake the familiar rows of living, sleeping women and girls.

It dawned on me then that Josephine's prediction had come true, though not at all in the way I'd expected: I'd found Amélie. And my dreams had returned.

I made out Babette's shadowed form at the far end of the ward, gliding between rows like a dark swan. Still trembling a little, I turned to look at Josephine. Her skin retained that same sickly gray cast. But now both her lips and eyelids were fully blue, as were the fingernails on the hand that rested atop her coverlet. For a moment I was certain I was looking at a corpse, just as I had been in my dream.

"Josephine!" I cried, shaking her hard enough that her head lolled limply against the pillow. *God, no,* I thought. *Please. Please, no . . .* I pressed two fingers against her pale throat. Her skin felt clammy and cool, and for a petrifying moment I felt nothing.

Then—so faintly I might have imagined it—I registered a distant flutter, more echo than beat.

But she was alive. At least for now.

The relief that washed over me was almost suffocating. Still clutching Josephine's wrist, I shouted over my shoulder: "Help! Someone help!"

More *internées* were now stirring, some covering their heads with their pillows in protest at being woken, others sitting up groggily, rubbing sleep from their eyes. I felt a tug on my shift and, looking down, saw Marthe, the rag doll 'Nadette had made for her clutched to her chest.

"Is she dead?" she asked.

"Not—" I began, then stopped myself. I'd been about to say: *Not yet.*

"No," I said as steadily as I could manage. I leaned over, pressing my lips to the delicate whorl of Josephine's ear and inhaling the now-familiar fragrance of her hair, a combination of oily sweetness, sharp-edged soap, and a hint of something else that I could never quite identify, something heady and somehow wild as well. "Wake up," I whispered. "You must wake up."

She still didn't stir.

"What in the Lord's name is happening here?"

I turned to find Babette standing behind me, hand on hip. "Take your hands off her," she snapped. "I told you last night to leave her be."

I swallowed. "I know, madame. But . . ."

"But *what?*"

"She's *dying!*"

The words came out almost a shout. The ward fell into shocked silence. Out of the corner of my eye, I saw 'Nadette cross herself.

Babette glared at me, gray eyes blazing. She lifted her hand, and I shrank back reflexively. But she just pushed me aside and felt Josephine's brow, frowning. Then she tried shaking Josephine's bared shoulder, to as little effect as I had had. Finally, the old nurse leaned over and with the palm of her gnarled hand slapped first one pale, freckled cheek, then the other. She did it lightly at first. But when Josephine still didn't respond, she repeated the blows, hard enough to leave marks. "Josephine," she commanded. "Wake *up,* girl. Stop this nonsense this instant."

No response. Beside me, Marthe let out a small sob. I heard 'Nadette break into murmured prayer: "*Notre Père, qui es aux cieux, que ton nom soit—*"

"Stop that," Babette snapped without bothering to turn around. "Stop your gibbering. Let me *think.*"

She wrenched Josephine's arm over, taking between her thumb and forefinger a span of pale skin just beneath the girl's elbow crease, twisting it like a key in a lock. The pinch was harsh enough to leave a red welt in its wake. But it did nothing to raise Josephine from her sleep.

The old woman shut her eyes. "*Sacré nom de Dieu,*" she muttered. The expletive sparked a round of soft gasps: I'd never known her to curse.

"Get dressed," she commanded, turning on me again. "Don't take your eyes off her." She set off briskly toward the door.

"Where are you going?"

She didn't bother turning around. "Where do you think, you little fool? To fetch a doctor," she called back coldly.

As she disappeared from view I hastily stripped away my rumpled nightshift and thrust myself into my chemise, petticoats, stays, and work dress, twisting my bare feet into a pair of battered hospital clogs I kept under my bed. I was hastily pinning my hair when the overnight physician hurried in, hatless and rumpled, Babette on his heels. A burly man whose thick white beard seemed intended to compensate for the thinning crescent of hair circling his pink pate, Dr. Boudu had clearly been roused from his own hard-earned sleep; he was hatless, and his shirt was misbuttoned. Setting his leather kit on my cot, he withdrew a stethoscope of the older style, the sort that resembled a hearing trumpet, and pressed the cupped end of the wooden cone to Josephine's sternum. Then, taking out a gilded thermometer case, he removed the instrument from it and brusquely inserted it beneath her arm. Upon reading the temperature, he frowned.

"This can't be right," he muttered.

Shaking the mercury back down, he repeated the process— seemingly with the same result, since he quickly pulled each of Josephine's lids up with his thumb and peered worriedly into her eyes. From where I stood, I could see her pupils: huge black pools, barely rimmed in green.

Letting Josephine's eyes close again, Boudu turned to Babette. "Who was with her yesterday? When she came in?"

"That one," she said, waving a hand in my direction.

"And she was definitely entranced when she went to sleep last night?" he asked me.

"Yes. I was with her when Dr. Charcot put her under."

"And what time was that?"

"Around half past two," I said, thinking back. "The doctors worked with her in that state until five. Then they had to leave unexpectedly, so they didn't wake her up as usual."

"So she's been under for . . ." He did a quick calculation, his eyebrows arching in disbelief: "*Seventeen hours?*"

I nodded. "Can—can you bring her back out?"

He shook his head. "I'm not trained in mesmerism," he said. He pronounced *mesmerism* with a hint of disdain, and even in the midst of my mounting fear, this caught me off guard. It was like hearing Père Julien bring up the holy sacrament in a tone of audible skepticism.

Returning to his kit, Boudu took a silver vial from its depths and pulled out the rubber stopper. A waft of ammonia filled the air, potent enough to make my eyes water. He held the smelling salts directly beneath Josephine's nose for a little over ten seconds. Again, no response.

Pursing his lips, the doctor turned back to Babette and murmured something that made her taut face tighten further. She gave a short nod before hurrying toward the door, pausing briefly to give Julienne and Claudine a curt command. As she disappeared through the exit, the two *filles de service* began herding sleep-tousled hysterics toward the washing stations. The infirmary doctor continued studying Josephine's face.

"This is the one they've been talking about, yes?" he asked me. "The one the papers are now writing about, now that the other—the Alsatian—is in Lunacy?"

I nodded.

"They mesmerize her daily?"

"Nearly every day," I said. "Sometimes more than once."

He shook his head. "Madness," he muttered. "Even within a madhouse."

I stared at him, openly stunned. None of Charcot's protégés ever questioned his clinical tactics—let alone critiqued them, implicitly or otherwise. Then again, the Salpêtrière's infirmary doctors operated apart from the asylum doctors. They were physicians not of the brain but of the body, as my father had been. It had never before occurred to me to ponder the differences, any more than it had to question any of Charcot's medical tactics or decisions. Now, though, I suddenly found myself doing both.

I knew Charcot's hysteria work had been coming under increasing scrutiny within the broader medical community. It was said that his rival at the University of Nancy—the same one who'd accused Charcot of hypnotically "coaching" Rosalie to produce her symptoms—had also suggested that by continually hypnotizing them, Charcot was actually *worsening* his patients' hysteria, rather than curing it. I'd always dismissed such allegations as Charcot himself did: as mere products of jealousy and ignorance. Now, though, I wondered: What if Charcot's critics were right? After all, apart from me, few hysterics under his care had actually recovered from their illness. In fact, he'd treated Rosalie more often than any other hysteric in the ward, and her condition had only deteriorated—possibly to the point of madness, if her transfer to Lunacy was any indication. What if Charcot had caused that deterioration, he and the other doctors, by treating her fragile mind like some sort of subconscious savannah they could hunt and plunder at will?

And what if they were doing the same thing to Josephine right now?

It was a blasphemous question, one that only a day earlier I'd have stricken almost reflexively from my mind. Now, though, I didn't. I didn't because I already knew the answer to it, knew it in my very bones: Charcot *was* hurting her. Of course he was. In past weeks he and the doctors had spent more and more time with Josephine, triggering fits; studying symptoms; exposing her mind and body to magnets and metal plates, electrodes and needles; photographing her from red head to contracted toe. Over that same period her seizures had grown not only more frequent but more violent—just as Rosalie's had before her. Even when lucid, Josephine had grown more agitated and fearful, to the point where she was seeing and saying things—like her comment about the Lourdes medallion—that made next to no sense at all. And now here she was lying before me, barely alive. He'd nearly killed her, I realized.

And with that realization came another, as burningly clear as if seared into my thoughts with sulfuric acid: I couldn't leave. Or rather, I couldn't leave *her*—not here. Not when she was only alive because I'd sounded the alarm. And certainly not when, even now, it wasn't at all certain how—or even *if*—she'd recover.

Outside, the chapel bells began tolling again. As the last chime vibrated sonorously I heard the ward doors slam open, heard familiar heavy, shuffling footsteps against the wooden floor.

Turning back around, I saw Charcot and Janet hurrying toward us, Charcot with his top hat slightly askew on his head, his cane slung over his shoulder like an infantryman's rifle. Upon reaching us, he shook hands with Boudu briefly, his eyes trained on Josephine's pallid countenance. "Thank you for coming, Victor," he said briskly. "What have we here?"

"To be truthful, I've never seen anything like it," the white-haired doctor replied. "As of twenty minutes ago her respiration had slowed to four breaths a minute. It looks as if it may be even slower now."

"Temperature?"

"Thirty-four."

"Thirty-*four*?" Frowning, Charcot picked up one of Josephine's hands, studying the darkened moons of her fingernails. "Consistent with hypothermia. As is the apparent cyanosis. No shivering or teeth chattering?"

"Not that I've observed."

"And you?" Charcot threw me a sharp glance. "You've been with her since we left you last night?"

"I haven't noticed any shivering, Docteur," I said, trying to keep my voice level, though in reality I wanted to shout at them both: *Wake her! Just wake her!*

Charcot was already checking Josephine's pulse. When he looked up, his eyes were bright. "Thirty beats per minute," he said, shaking his head slowly. "I suppose we could call it an attack of artificial sleep. Of sorts."

Janet, who had been jotting down Josephine's vitals, nodded. "Almost as if she's put herself into a state of near-death," he said, sounding intrigued.

Put herself? I glanced back at Boudu. His eyes were fixed on the floor.

"Exactly," said Charcot. He turned back to the infirmary doctor. "May I use your thermometer? Madame Botarde intercepted me before I got to my office."

"I did take her temperature twice," Boudu noted, handing over the tool.

"Axillary readings, I assume." Charcot withdrew the thermometer from its case.

Boudu nodded, frowning slightly as Charcot stepped down by Josephine's knees. Briskly lifting her nightdress hem, he inserted the tool's tip into Josephine's sex. An awkward silence descended, with Janet and Charcot both studying the latter's watch and Boudu gazing with renewed interest at the floor.

"Thirty-six," Charcot announced at last, handing the thermometer back to Boudu.

"Interesting," murmured Janet. Boudu dropped both the thermometer and the case back into his leather bag, his expression unreadable.

"An unusually extreme discrepancy," Janet observed. "I wonder what accounts for it."

Seeing that no one else was about to do it, I hurried to Josephine's side and pulled her hem back down over her legs. "I suppose my question now," Boudu said pointedly, "is whether we should bring her out of it. There are, after all, risks of leaving a patient in a hypothermic state indefinitely."

Charcot frowned. "Of course," he said. "Quite right." And to Janet: "Shall we count her down?"

Nodding, Janet crouched next to Josephine's ear. "Josephine," he said. "Can you hear me? It's time to wake up. I'll count backward from ten. *Dix . . . neuf . . . huit . . .*" When he reached *un*, he paused, watching her face closely. Nothing in her expression or position indicated she'd heard him.

Charcot stepped beside his protégé, his frown deepening. Then, without warning, he brought his palms together sharply by Josephine's ear. The clap was loud and sudden enough that I jumped in surprise. A row away, Bernadette—still excluded from group meals—sat bolt upright on her cot and froze. Josephine, however, still didn't move.

Charcot cast his gaze around the bedside, his eyes landing on the cup of water I'd left there the prior evening. As he reached to pick it up, I had the confused thought that he was planning on drinking from it himself. Instead, he flung its contents directly into Josephine's face. Both Babette and I gasped as the liquid streamed down the girl's cheeks, darkening her hair and dampening her pillow. But the dousing didn't spark so much as a lash twitch.

"Extraordinary." Janet looked somewhere between mystified and impressed. "I suppose we can try applying pressure to the hysterogenic zones," he offered, stroking his beard. "That's worked when she's been in catalepsy."

"Good." Charcot nodded. "Give it a go."

Standing over Josephine, Janet gauged her torso. Then, carefully, he pressed two fingers to the outside of Josephine's right breast. At first nothing happened. Then her lashes fluttered, very faintly.

"Perhaps some additional pressure on the right ovary," Charcot suggested.

Nodding, Janet made a fist of his free hand and slowly pressed it against the inside of Josephine's right hip bone. When she still didn't respond, he pushed it more forcefully, his forearm trembling a little with the effort.

Josephine's lashes fluttered, more rapidly this time. Her chest rose and fell—first slowly, then with a quickening pace. Then her eyes and mouth flew open, and she jerked upright with a hoarse-sounding cry. Chest heaving, she gazed at us wildly for a moment, gripping her wet hair with her hands. Then her eyes met mine, and both her terror and her breathing seemed to ease.

The dense mass that had taken shape in my chest these past hours dissolved into giddy relief. I wanted to throw myself on top of her, to feel her breath on my face, her heart beating beneath my chest. To wall her off from these men with my own quivering form. Instead, stepping past the doctors, I reached out and took her hand in my own. I half expected her to jerk away from me, and to be honest I wouldn't have minded if she had, so grateful was I to see her awake, alive. But she merely squeezed my fingers, as thoughtlessly and reflexively as though the omnibus had never happened at all.

"How do you feel, my dear?" Charcot asked her.

Josephine licked her lips. "I feel . . . strange," she said.

"Are you in pain?"

"Not pain." The words emerged softly but with their usual cadence and clarity. It seemed to me that the color was already returning to her cheeks. "But . . ."

She dropped her gaze to her own torso and belly. Her expression shifted to something approaching dismay. At first I thought it was over the fact that her shift—sheer even when dry—had been rendered all but translucent by Charcot's drenching, the dark pink discs of her areolae clearly visible through the sodden fabric.

As she looked up again, though, she struck me as seeming more disappointed than ashamed.

"But where is my new dress?" she asked.

Chapter Ten

"*I AM GOING TO STEAL HER OWN EXISTENCE AWAY FROM HER!*'"

I lifted my voice as I read the declaration, attempting to match the almost comically overwrought capitalization. Beside me, Josephine snorted in amusement.

"Now, how," she asked, "is he going to do that?"

"Just wait," I said, holding up a finger without looking up from the worn book. "He explains it."

I read on, returning my voice to its regular register. "'Making use of modern science, I can capture the grace of her gesture, the fullness of her flesh, the resonance of her voice, the turn of her waist, the light of her eyes . . . her complete identity, in a word. I shall be the murderer of her foolishness, the assassin of her triumphant animal nature.'"

Outside, I heard the sounds of male voices laughing and chattering. I recognized them as belonging to Charcot's interns, probably returning from one of the evening soirées for which Charcot and his wife were known, and at which literary and social luminaries were usually in attendance. As they passed, the men broke into a slurred version of the "interns' anthem," a ditty penned by a former Charcot protégé and sung to the tune of "La Marseillaise":

It is the famous unit of
Old Man Charcot, our leader
The man cannot utter a word
Without the whole universe repeating it
Rows of hysterics, amyotrophics,
Those with Ménière's disease or multiple sclerosis
Fill the wards of the Salpêtrière, the Salpêtrière

Glancing at the rusted carriage clock on the bedside table, I blinked. It felt as though we'd just opened *The Future Eve* a moment earlier. But it was already nearly midnight. If Babette had seen us like this, she'd no doubt have doused the light—and then snatched the book away for good measure.

But Babette couldn't see us—because we were no longer in Hysteria. Or at least, no longer in the downstairs ward, which Josephine had managed to flee from in the middle of the night a week earlier while in the throes of one of her night terrors. She'd been found shivering in the asylum stables two hours later, and had so vehemently resisted Jacques's attempts to bring her back that the orderly ended up with an egg-sized bruise on his head after she threw him into the wooden stall wall.

Normally, Babette simply strapped hysterical sleepwalkers to their bed frames overnight. Charcot, however, had ordered Josephine and me into a private room in Esquirol's old isolation area, instructing me to pull my cot in front of the door at night before locking it for good measure. Babette still frequently materialized in our threshold without warning, doubtlessly hoping to catch me in some infringement or oversight. Overall, though, our new quarters felt gloriously free. Not just from the old woman's shrewd surveillance and my ever-present fears about Rosalie's bracelet (now stuffed deep inside my new mattress), but from the oppressive ambience of Hysteria itself. From the continual threat of outbursts and catfights, of hysterical fits and frozen-in-place female forms that hung over the place like a lowering storm cloud. From that torpid mixture of despair and ennui that so permeated that dark place that it seemed part of the very air we'd breathed there.

To be sure, our new, shared space was in an even greater state of dilapidation than the centuries-old ward that was now below us. It smelled of must and mold and whatever rodents had nested among the surplus furniture and medical equipment that had been stored there. It was separated from Hysteria by a floor so thin that we could still hear Bernadette sermonizing in her sleep.

And yet it felt a whole world apart, as though, like Jules Verne's balloonists, we'd ascended into an entirely new atmosphere. Its flaking walls were free of the newspaper clippings of Rosalie that had remained above Josephine's old bed downstairs (for apparently no one had felt comfortable taking them down) and its one barred window looked out over one of the asylum's overgrown but colorful rose gardens. After I'd finished moving our few things in, Josephine—who'd seemed alternately listless and almost manically energetic throughout the process—had flung herself on her cot, bouncing there a few times in a way that reminded me of Amélie before falling onto her back, her thin arms spread toward the ceiling. "It feels like we've moved into Le Meurice," she'd sighed. "Can we ring a bell and have champagne and beef tenderloin sent up?"

Since her overnight trance, her reserve toward me had vanished as completely as the blue dress she'd still been certain she'd been wearing. She'd said little about the icy reserve with which she'd treated me in those painful days after my omissions to her had been exposed, apart from one short comment on our first night in our new beds. "*Promise* me," she'd commanded, catching on to my wrist as I passed her cot on the way to sleep in my own by the door.

"What?" I'd asked, startled by both the intensity of her tone and the ever-surprising strength of her grip.

"That you'll never lie to me," she said fervently. "Not about *anything*. Ever again."

And equally fervently, I had promised.

"'*The murderer of her foolishness*,'" she repeated now, bemused. "So

Thomas Edison wants to kill this girl, Alicia, because he thinks she's foolish?"

"He isn't actually planning to *kill* her," I explained. "He's only going to re-create her face and body as an android, and give the android a better soul."

"Better according to who?"

I laughed. "To Thomas Edison, I suppose."

She made a skeptical-looking moue. "This Edison. He's American?"

I nodded. "In real life, yes. But the Edison in this book isn't actually Edison himself. He's a fictional version of the real man."

Josephine considered this, absently picking at a blood-crusted line on the inside of her forearm. The looping scab was from a research session two days earlier, the focus of which had been dermography. After entrancing her, Charcot had used his stylus to inscribe *l'hystérie* on the inside of one of her arms and *l'hypnose* on the other. From where I'd sat, the tool's pointed metal tip had barely seemed to brush against Josephine's soft skin, and yet a bright red line of perhaps a millimeter in height had sprung up instantaneously in its wake. Even more astonishingly, Charcot was able to make the letters lightly bleed merely by murmuring the suggestion into Josephine's ear.

"Stop," I told her now, putting my hand over hers. "You'll make it weep again."

She grimaced, pulling her cuff over the shallow wound. "Why would a writer use a real person in a made-up story?"

"It's hard to say," I said. "Perhaps he thinks it's a good way to get his story's ideas across to his audiences."

"The way Charcot uses me to get *his* ideas across to his audiences?"

I frowned, unexpectedly unsettled by this comparison. "He isn't telling *stories*. He's explaining his medical theories. And you're a real person, not a character from some book." Thoughtfully, I drew the book's satin ribbon down to mark our place for next time. "Though I suppose the fact that something didn't happen in real life doesn't mean there isn't truth to it. In fact, I think stories—even untrue ones, or maybe *especially* untrue ones—can teach us things about life that true events can't."

She looked at me sidelong. Her color had mostly returned since the magnet episode, but there were still bruiselike shadows beneath her eyes, products of a continuing and acute lack of sleep. "Then what truth does *The Future Eve* teach us?"

"What do *you* think it teaches us?" I shot back.

She twirled a strand of her hair around a forefinger, tightly enough that the fingertip turned pink. "Not to trust men who work in laboratories."

I laughed, struck not only by how deftly she'd just turned Villiers de l'Isle-Adam's story line on its head (the book's intended villainess, after all, was the impossibly beautiful but unforgivably crass Alicia Clary) but by how precisely she'd given voice to what had preoccupied me since almost losing her completely the prior week.

For I was more convinced than ever that I needed to get her out of the asylum—and soon, our improved sleeping arrangements notwithstanding. I kept seeing her as she'd looked when I'd tried to wake her that morning: The ice-white skin. The blue lips and nails. The shallow breath, barely misting Rosalie's mirror. Nor could I shake the memory of Dr. Boudu's shocking denouncement: *Madness. Even within a madhouse.*

I didn't think Josephine was mad—or at least, not yet. But her increasingly erratic behavior had me more worried than ever: her nightly battle against sleep, the violent nightmares when she succumbed to it, her growing skittishness and agitation during her waking hours. Since moving upstairs, I'd found her studying her Lourdes medallion several times, her expression bordering on panicked. Her fear of Claude had increased as well: After spotting him approaching on one of the grounds' gravel paths a few days earlier, she'd let out a small scream and pulled me into the little rose garden behind the chapel until he'd passed. When I asked her what was the matter—for to my knowledge they'd had no interaction since the feeding room episode well over a month earlier—she'd merely said: "I don't trust that man." But her voice had been shaking.

She'd also begun slipping into my bed at night, sometimes lying there for hours after I turned the light down, staring up at the beamed ceiling, her green eyes defiantly unblinking as she fought against slumber. I did my best to soothe and calm her, using the same technique I'd used when Amélie claimed to be afraid of the dark: telling stories. I'd usually have read aloud to Josephine for a good hour or more already by that point, for she was as voracious a listener of stories as I was a reader of them, and claimed these nightly sessions improved her own reading skills. But I'd still share more quiet narratives aloud in the dark: Sinbad's finding himself atop a sleeping whale or in a diamond-filled valley of elephant-swallowing serpents. Edmond Dantès's escaping the notoriously brutal Château d'If prison, and transforming himself into the rich and powerful Count of Monte Cristo so he could punish those who'd unjustly imprisoned him. Jim Hawkins's perilous voyage on the *Hispaniola* to find buried pirate treasure on a faraway island. Afterward, still determinedly battling sleep, Josephine would pepper me with questions: *Are there really island-sized whales? How did this Edmond disguise himself? Where did Jim learn to shoot a pistol so well?* And once: *Are there no books about girls who have such adventures?* (To my chagrin I couldn't think of any; most of the books I'd read about women were about their tragic lives and misadventures: Nana's sleeping her way through Paris's elite before dying of smallpox. Madame Bovary's sleeping her way through the Normandy countryside before swallowing arsenic. Anna Karenina's destroying her life and marriage for Vronsky before hurling herself beneath the steel wheels of a Russian freight train.)

As I whispered these tales to her, I often had to struggle to stay awake myself. But it seemed to work: Despite her own best efforts, Josephine's eyes would finally drift shut. Her breathing would even, and she'd curl into me like the sleeping cat in the "invisible" photograph she'd pinned over her new bed. As often as not, though, an hour or two later she'd be sitting bolt upright, muttering something about *him,* or *that beast,* or that still-chilling refrain: *They are coming!* Each time this happened, I'd swear again to myself that I'd finally take the last few steps needed to ensure our escape from this place. A few days earlier, in fact, I'd sent a revised version of my initial (and ultimately unsent) response to Amélie, telling her to expect us soon. *I am here*, I'd said, *and I am cured, and I will come in two weeks, if not sooner. I am bringing someone with me, another girl from the hysteria ward. Please tell Madame Granger that we will only impose on her for a night or two—not even that, if she can recommend a safe boardinghouse for women in Vault-de-Lugny or Avallon.*

To date, I'd held off sharing my plans with Josephine herself, not wanting to add to her agitation. Seeing her like this now, though— laughing, playful, as close to relaxed as she'd been in weeks—it seemed to me that it was finally time.

"There's something I need to tell you," I said, turning back to her.

She gave me an arch look. "Let me guess. You want to change out my soul for a better one."

But then our eyes met, and the smile faded from her lips.

"What?" she said, a new note of apprehension in her voice. "What is it?"

I took a deep breath. "I've heard from my sister. She's safe; she's been living with a midwife, in a little village near Avallon. She wants me to go there. To join her."

She didn't move, and for a fleeting moment I had the strange sense that I was looking not at the living girl who'd recently taken Paris by storm, but at one of Monsieur Londe's flat and colorless images of her.

"When?" she asked.

"Two weeks at most. I'd been planning to go sooner, but . . ." I let the words trail off. We both knew well enough what had delayed me. "Anyway," I continued, "I think that together with what I've saved, and by selling some books and a few other things, I have enough to get to Dijon." The "other things" were Rosalie's paste pearls and little hand mirror. Though I felt strange about doing it, I told myself Babette was right: Rosalie certainly didn't need them in the softs or in Hydro, the two places between which Charcot supposedly had her dividing her time since the kitchen incident. And if I bargained well at the *mont-de-piété*—a skill I'd bleakly honed while pawning my father's medical instruments—they'd fetch a decent enough price.

"Dijon?" Josephine repeated.

I nodded. "I'll sell the bracelet there. It's safer, I think, than trying to sell it here. And then I'll buy tickets from there to Avallon. From there it's an hour or so to Vault-de-Lugny, by horse or carriage." I'd shown the bracelet to her after we'd moved rooms, locking our door before retrieving it and the wrinkled copy of *Les citoyennes* from their new hiding place. After asking me about the broadsheet's stories on female "enslavement" and imprisonment, and hearing about the outroar they'd sparked on rue de Richelieu ("They should write about *this* place," she'd said dryly), Josephine had draped the gold chain over her slender wrist, shaking it gently so that the late-morning sunlight transformed the gems into a string of dancing blue flames.

"Oh," she'd half whispered, in something like awe. "I wish someone would give something this lovely to me. Even if it were only paste."

The longing in her voice had caught me off guard. For all the time I'd spent ruminating about that cursed thing—how to steal it, hide it, sell it—I'd never thought of it as something to covet for its own sake. But the sheer delight on Josephine's face had almost tempted me to give it to her on the spot.

Now she stared down at her hands, held loosely clasped in her lap. Their nails had finally lost the purplish tinge they'd taken on while she was in her "sleep of death." The redness and calluses left by months of washing and scrubbing at her old position had all but vanished as well, thanks to Charcot's decree that she be spared the usual asylum work shifts and chores. But a pink scar from the knife she'd used to kill the judge still bisected her left palm.

"That's wonderful," she said. "I'm happy for both of you. I really am." Her voice was as flat as her expression. As though it, like that of the beautiful android in the book we'd just closed, were being generated by one of Thomas Edison's recording cylinders.

"It's not just me!" I exclaimed, taking her hands in mine. "It's you too! I want to take you with me."

"You . . ." Inhaling sharply, she looked up, her expression brightening briefly. Then, a wary shadow crossed her face. "Why would you do that?"

Because I love you.

The words popped into my head, as crisp and clear as if someone had hissed them into my ear. I almost said them aloud, but was stopped by a sudden, urgent sensation in my belly; the same exhilarated and yet bilious feeling I'd felt atop the chalk cliffs of Étretat. As though I were about to plunge headlong into something that might be flight—but might just as easily be death.

"Because," I said instead, a little shakily, "you're not safe here. Surely you see that."

Her brows flew up in surprise. "What do you mean? Charcot says I'm recovering. He said my pulse and temperature are normal again, and that—"

I cut her off. "That's not what I'm talking about."

"Then what *are* you talking about?"

"What they're doing to you," I said. "All these hours of hypnosis in Charcot's office and in his lectures—I don't think it's good for you. I think it might even be dangerous."

"*Dangerous?*" she repeated incredulously. "How?"

"By making your hysteria worse. That's what Dr. Boudu said when he examined you."

"But it's all part of my treatment! It's being done by my own doctors!"

You yourself just said you don't trust them, I thought. But I held off saying it, fearful of upsetting her further, or set off yet another hysterical attack.

"I'm not sure," I said carefully, "that what they're doing has anything to do with curing you. Or any of us, for that matter. I think the goal is simply to learn as much about hysteria as they can. Even if, in the process, they might be making us worse."

"But isn't learning about it the only way to *find* a cure for it?" She was staring at me now, her eyes narrow and her jaw clenched. It was the same look she wore when I recounted things the doctors had done to her during entrancement that she found troubling or upsetting.

"Maybe in the long term," I said. "But I've been here over a year now. I've never seen any of the girls they hypnotize get any better."

"*You* got better."

"But they couldn't entrance me. And once they learned that they couldn't, they all but stopped paying attention to me."

It was an idea that had been taking shape slowly, and one I found increasingly impossible to dismiss. But it still felt strange—nearly sacrilegious—to be putting words to it now. "I don't think the doctors had anything to do with my recovery," I went on, lowering my voice even though no one could hear us. "I think the only reason I *did* get better was that they left me to my own devices."

She stared at me for a moment. Then her shoulders slumped. "But they're not leaving *me* alone," she said, slowly. "They're *never* leaving me alone. Not so long as the audience and the newsmen still like me."

"No," I said quietly. "They aren't."

For a long moment neither of us spoke. Outside, from the direction of the *unité des incurables* came a low, moaning cry that quickly swelled into a full-throated shriek. It made me think of my grandmother's stories about the Salpêtrière during her childhood. She'd died when I was very small, before Amélie was born. But I still remembered her whispering her recollections to me at bedtime sometimes, the way one tells a ghost tale: *Le cri de l'asile,* she called it. *The cry of the asylum.* "It'd start low," she would croon. "Just a few of the real crazies at first. But it would grow by the minute, until it was thousands upon thousands of those awful lunatic voices rising and falling together. As though conducted by Lucifer himself . . ."

The scream stopped with an abruptness that seemed almost as ominous as the despairing howl itself. Despite myself, I shivered. *She can't end up there,* I thought. *She can't.*

"So you see," I said, reaching out to touch her knee. "You need to come with me. Before they do lasting damage to you."

"What if they already have?" Her eyes were locked on the rough weave of the hospital skirt she still hadn't changed out of.

I looked up at her, alarmed. "Why do you say that?"

She toyed with the edge of her cuff. "I keep seeing him, Laure. The judge."

"I know." I touched her knee. "Or at least, I've guessed as much, that it's what your night terrors are about."

She didn't answer right away, just picked distractedly at the L-shaped scratch on her skin. Then she lifted her gaze to meet mine, her eyes glittering beneath the coppery veil of her lashes.

"It's not just when I sleep," she said.

"What?"

"It's not just when I sleep," she repeated. "I've been seeing him when I'm awake, too. Or at least, when I think I'm awake. Ever since that day with the magnets." She passed a hand over her eyes. I saw that it was trembling. "The truth is, I'm not sure I even know anymore whether I'm awake or entranced. It all seems to blur together and change shape in ways I hardly even notice at first—the way places and even faces blur and change inside a dream."

"When?" I asked, my alarm deepening. "Where else have you seen him?"

"All the time." There was a new brittleness to her voice. "Everywhere. I see him in the public tour groups outside and with the doctors on morning rounds. I've seen him twice now at lectures. I've even thought I saw him with Claude at the market—though when I looked again he'd disappeared."

A cold fingertip seemed to be tracing its way down my spine. "And you say this all started after Charcot left you entranced overnight?"

She nodded. "It's *always* after I've been entranced. I realize that now." She wrung her hands together in her lap. "At first I thought it was his ghost, here to haunt me. After all, he looks so strange. Not just in the way he stares at me, with his fat face and piglike little eyes, but in the way his whole—his whole *shape* looks sometimes."

"What does his shape look like?" I asked, already dreading the answer.

"It's hard to describe."

"Try," I prompted her.

She frowned vaguely, as though struggling to recall a receding dream. "It's as though—as though his edges are *melting*, somehow. Like in one of those photographs where people have moved before the photographer told them to." She shook her head. "But maybe that's not it, either. He's been in the very back when I see him, you see. In the shadows."

"In the back of the *amphitheater*?"

She nodded again. "Right beneath that big painting of Rosalie and Dr. Babinski. He was leaning against the wall, smoking. But it wasn't really 'leaning.' It was more like he was—like he was sinking *into* the wall itself, behind all that smoke. And then I'd blink, or look away, and when I looked back he'd be gone entirely, the way he was in the *marché*," she finished. "It was as though the wall had simply . . . swallowed him up."

My heart seemed to drop inside my chest. On the one hand, these visions helped explain Josephine's increasingly odd behavior—not just her refusal to sleep, but her bizarre obsession with the Lourdes medallion and her escalating fear of the Basque. It made sense, too, that she'd have woven Claude into her delusions—he'd been the most physically menacing force toward her in this place.

But it was the hallucinations themselves—the repeated sightings of the dead judge; the fact that he'd "melted" into the amphitheater wall—that were the most alarming. They offered the first real evidence that what I'd feared might happen to her *was* happening, that whatever luminous membrane had separated her consciousness from her unconsciousness had been pierced by the doctors' continual assaults on her mind.

Just as Rosalie's had.

Rosalie. My mind darted to the last time I'd seen her. I'd been hurrying to the kitchen to get Josephine breakfast. The Alsatian had been on one of the shuffling group walks with her fellow lunatics, each woman secured by the wrist to a thick length of rope carried between two orderlies. She'd been in the very back, doubtlessly so that the attendant behind her could keep a close watch on her. I'd been stunned by her transformation: Her milky skin now turned mottled and ashen, her sapphire eyes sunken and dulled. The flaxen hair I'd spent so many hours brushing and pinning was now a matted mass against her head, and she'd walked not with her former quick-stepping impatience, but with the shuffling gait of an ancient *re-posante*. When our eyes met, I'd managed to push past my shock enough to smile faintly. But there hadn't been so much as a flicker of recognition in those cerulean eyes. It had been like looking into the flat blue gaze of one of the tattered newspaper illustrations that still hung above her old bed in the ward.

I squeezed my eyes shut, trying to erase the pitiful image. *We have to go*, I thought. *We have to go* soon. Not in two weeks, as I'd written Amélie. Sooner—much sooner. The very first moment we could.

When I opened my eyes again, Josephine was watching me, worry etched on her face. "You think I'm mad already, don't you."

"No," I said, although I wasn't sure this was fully true. "But I do think we have to leave. Right away."

"Laure—" she began uncertainly, but I cut her off, taking her hand.

"Don't worry," I said. "I'll have enough for both of us by Saturday. We'll have to find you something else to wear, of course. Perhaps we should get you a veil of some sort as well. Given how crowded the lectures have been—and that color portrait in *Paris illustré* last week—we should at least try to cover your hair. . . ."

"*Laure*." She pulled her hand away, her voice sharper now. Tight. "I can't leave now. Not like this."

I blinked, caught off guard by her vehemence. "Why not?"

She looked away, biting her lip. When she looked back at me again there was misery in her gaze. I felt it almost as a physical force, a cold tightening of the air between us.

"Don't you see?" she asked quietly. "I can't go anywhere. I won't escape anything if I do. I'll simply be taking my madness with me. And if I'm going to be mad, I might as well just stay here."

"But once you leave, it will stop!" I insisted. "You've just told me that the visions happen after you've been entranced. Surely that means once they stop hypnotizing you, you'll stop seeing them."

"But what if I *don't*?" She pressed both hands against her forehead, as though trying to physically force her mind into compliance. "What if the damage they've done only leads to other damage? I already can't tell when I see him if I'm dreaming or awake—or even if what I remember him doing to me, and I to him, really happened. What if everything else starts to become uncertain and confused in the same way? What if I stop knowing you're real, I'm real, the very ground beneath our *feet* is real? What if it all just . . . collapses on me, suffocating and crushing me?"

Her hands had dropped to her throat now. Alarmed, I reached for them, thinking she'd worked herself into a fit. But she pulled herself out of my grasp, shaking her head. "I can't go," she repeated. "I can't go without knowing."

"Without knowing *what*?"

In answer she only closed her eyes, squeezing them shut so tightly that creases appeared at their corners. Six faint, fanning lines. Sunbeams inscribed in sun-freckled skin.

"Do you remember," she asked, "when you told me the story about your travel sickness?"

She'd asked me if I'd ever traveled by train (she hadn't), and I'd told her about the first time Papa took me to my old school. It was only five hours from Gare du Nord, but within twenty minutes I'd become so motion sick that I felt as though my insides were spoiling like bad meat. I'd truly thought I was dying. But I had no idea what that had to do with our escape.

"Yes," I said uncertainly.

Josephine opened her eyes again. "Do you remember what you said he told you then?"

"That I was ill because the moving scenery outside was confusing my body, which wasn't moving at all. He said the only way to feel better was to try to find one thing that didn't change or move—some spot on the horizon or inside the train—and focus on it. And then the nausea would pass."

Josephine nodded. "I've been thinking that I need to do the same."

"On the train to Dijon?" I was still confused.

"No." She took a deep breath. "In the house."

"Which house?" I asked, now utterly lost.

"Guillaume's," she said. "The judge's." Leaning forward, she took my hands. "I need to go back there, Laure. I need to see it for myself."

I gaped at her. "But that would be—" I'd been about to say *madness* but stopped myself. "Disastrous," I said instead. "How would you even get inside?"

She shrugged. "The kitchen staff left windows open sometimes, for when they went out to the dance halls at night. But if they were locked I'd find another way."

"But what if someone sees you?" I insisted, aghast at her recklessness. "Someone who knows about the murder? You'd all but be handing them a confession. And I don't see how going back will *change* anything."

"It will for me," she said stubbornly. "I know it will."

"But *how*?"

"In the same way looking at something solid helps you when you're feeling travel sick," she said. "It will give me something real, something unchanging, to focus on when these—visions—come. Something to remind me that I'm not going mad."

She took hold of me again, this time grasping my forearms. "I need proof that what I think happened actually did. That the house is as I remember it. That he's really dead. Something that I can hold on to." Her grip on my arms had tightened, enough that it almost hurt. "Something I know to be true, no matter what tricks my mind is playing on me. I need to know for certain that he can't hurt me anymore. That I'm safe."

"You won't be safe from the police," I pointed out. "You might end up in even more danger. You might end up . . ."

I didn't finish the thought. I didn't need to.

"That's better than going mad," she said simply. "I'd rather risk the guillotine than keep on living like this."

I wouldn't, I thought. *I can't risk losing you.* But once more, I didn't say it.

"Maybe you don't have to risk it either," I said instead.

"What? What do you mean?" She was still holding my arms tightly, and I thought for a moment that I felt her pulse there, dancing lightly above my own.

"I can do it. I'll go to his house for you."

Her brow puckered again. "How would that help? You won't know what to look for. You've never even been there before."

Gently disentangling myself, I turned and pulled the coverlet and sheets back from my mattress, reaching into the slit I'd made there to find my journal and the pencil stub I kept sandwiched in its pages. Pulling both out, I opened the worn little book to a clean page and positioned the lead tip just above it.

"Then tell me," I said. "Tell me everything you can remember."

Chapter Eleven

That night was an especially hard one for me. In part this was because Josephine was even more restless than usual, tossing and turning in her cot before again climbing into mine, demanding I retell de Maupassant's *La parure* to her (she'd become strangely fixated on the short story since I'd first read it to her a few days earlier). But it was also because of the things she'd told me in preparation for my expedition to Marcel Guillaume's home, first methodically describing the house's layout, room by room and floor by floor. Then, in a strangely disembodied tone not unlike that with which she spoke when entranced, she'd led me through the harrowing timeline of her employment there, culminating in that last bloody day in Guillaume's office. By the time she'd finished it was well after two A.M., and despite her best efforts she drifted uneasily into sleep. I, however, found it impossible to do the same, for each time I shut my eyes some horrific aspect of what I'd just heard would return to me.

As I've said, I'd seen her reenact some of what she'd suffered during her fits—as, by that point, had some twelve hundred other Parisians. But hearing her speak of them lucidly that night, and in such matter-of-fact, graphic detail, lent a gruesome vibrancy to my understanding of all that she'd suffered. In my half-sleeping state, it almost seemed to transform her recollections into my own brutal memories as well. I kept picturing Guillaume's face, fleshy, sweat sheened, and pockmarked, straining and grimacing above mine. His wine-sour breath seemed to brush moistly against my cheek, his oily essence to flood my own screaming mouth. I felt his fists against my body, his vicious forays inside my skin. The panicked struggle as I reached for the knife in my boot. I felt his shuddering shock as it slipped into his heaving gut—*as easily as if he were made of butter*, Josephine had reflected dispassionately—and the abrupt bloom of warmth against my own belly as he collapsed onto the blade. I felt the terror and revulsion as he shuddered into stillness on top of me, rendering me an unwilling participant in yet another obscenity—his death. Such images were distressing enough to a waking mind; I could only imagine how much worse they might become when warped into nightmares. It was little wonder Josephine tried so desperately to avoid sleep.

But I was also worried about more pragmatic things: not only how to approach the house and—with luck—gain entrance to it, but finding the time to do so. I hadn't formally had an afternoon off since well before Josephine's arrival at the asylum. In truth I wasn't even sure whom to ask for one, as I no longer reported to Babette (who would have denied the request out of sheer spite anyway). And it seemed impertinent to bother Charcot with such a mundane matter. As dawn began to break, I resolved to unobtrusively ask Dr. Marie for a few hours' leave when I brought Josephine to Charcot's office the following day. Charcot's secretary had always been the kindest of the doctors toward me, after all. I'd say I needed to visit my parents' graves in Montmartre, that it was Papa's birthday and I wanted to mark the occasion. There seemed little way for anyone to check up on the lie.

As it turned out, though, I didn't have to lie—or even ask anyone for permission to go at all. For upon taking Josephine to Charcot's clinic the next day, I was informed by Marie himself that my further presence wouldn't be necessary; apparently there wasn't enough room. Not only were almost all of Charcot's interns in attendance, but Charcot had also invited one of his "special visitors" for the morning. "You can pick her up in Photography before dinner," the young doctor added, taking Josephine's arm.

Normally, Josephine would have balked at being left alone with a half-dozen men. But she merely nodded when I asked in a whisper whether she'd be all right. Still, as Marie led her inside I couldn't help thinking back to a little over a month earlier, when he'd led Rosalie across that threshold for the last time. *Help me, Laure. I don't want to be alone with them.*

Shaking the memory off, I rushed back to Esquirol, comforted by the thought that this would be the last time Josephine had to endure a research session in that grim, black-walled office—and the second-to-last time Charcot would invade the soft gray folds of her mind. In less than two days' time, we'd be on our way south together, by train. We'd be free.

It was on my way back toward boulevard de l'Hôpital—having changed into my day dress, Rosalie's pearls and mirror and several books in a hastily tied bundle by my side (for I'd decided to seize the opportunity to try to sell them)—that my gaze was caught by what at first glance looked like cattail, or some similarly cottony plant part that had snagged itself in the newly scythed spring grass. As I drew closer, though, I saw that it was feathers—some of them unnaturally marked with the pink of laboratory dye.

Whatever had gotten to Rosalie's pigeon—cat? Hawk?—had left little of it behind: I made out only a few pinkish-looking clumps of mangled flesh. Those, and a single claw, clenched in agony or defiance.

A little under an hour later I stood at the intersection of avenue de Villiers and rue Cardinet, studying first the scribbled notes I'd ripped from my diary that morning, and then the house they were meant to describe.

Josephine had told me how, when she was a child, this place with its gabled roof and Grecian columns had always seemed to her like a fairy-tale palace. She'd been particularly fixated on a marble mascaron that she said had hung above the front door: a demonic face with bulging eyes, bloated lips, and ramlike horns springing from the top of its forehead. Initially, it had frightened her so much that she'd refused to even climb up the front steps, though her mother explained that it was meant to ward off evil spirits and not "silly-minded little girls."

In the years after that, Josephine said, she'd mostly stopped noticing it—except for on the last day she reported to work, her body still torn and throbbing from her employer's last assault, a knife from his own kitchen tucked into her boot. On that morning she'd looked up at that horned head as if for the first time, thinking to herself that her mother had been wrong. It was there not to ward off demons but to warn of the real monster residing inside. Studying the thing now, I felt a reflexive revulsion strangely twinned with a sense of relief. The visage was indeed as ugly as sin. But it was also exactly as she'd described it.

Refolding the pages and thrusting them into my pocket, I made my way to the front doorstep, rehearsing the story I'd made up to explain my visit and—in the best scenario—earn me an invitation into the mansion itself. I'd ask to speak with the lady of the house, saying I'd heard she might need a tutor for her son and citing the two families I'd taught for before my father's death—names she might even recognize, given that she and her husband likely traveled in at least some of the same circles. It didn't seem impossible that Madame Guillaume would agree to at least meet me. If so, her attire alone would answer the most pressing question at hand, since if she'd been recently widowed she'd be dressed accordingly, in black. Hopefully, though, I'd also be able to survey the front hallway, or the parlor, or—who knew?—even her husband's office, if she happened to invite me there. But even if she wasn't in, merely peering inside the house from the doorway might offer something to compare with Josephine's memories—black crepe on a portrait, perhaps, or a tray stacked with *cartes de condoléances*.

Upon reaching the large oak door, though, I paused, my hand hovering by the brass knocker as I registered a few weathered-looking correspondences wedged beneath it. Though it was hard to know for sure without disturbing them, they looked less to me like bereavement cards than the same sorts of requests for payment I'd seen piled up on my father's desk in the last years of his life. In some ways this, too, was heartening—for Josephine had mentioned that the household seemed perpetually behind in its payments. But it still struck me as strange that these communications had been allowed to accumulate as they had. It looked as if no one had opened this door in weeks.

Stepping back, I peered up at the building's windows. Josephine had described the place as a nonstop hub of activity, bustling with the movements of a half-dozen servants, the judge's wife, and his young son. Now, though, all was silent, and all the curtains were drawn, with no hint of shifting light or stirring breeze to indicate movement within.

Puzzled, I made my way back down the steps and around to the servants' entrance in the rear of the house, passing a dry-looking garden and an empty carriage house, next to a stable that looked equally abandoned. More past-due notices and calling cards were wedged into the service door's mail slot; one had fallen onto the graveled back pathway. Picking it up, I pushed it quickly into my pocket with my notes before carefully removing the papery backlog from the letter slot. These, too, seemed related to overdue accounts; there was one from a butchery, another from a brewer, yet another from a clearly peeved washer of windows. Pressing my ear against the cleared-out mail slot, I strained to hear any sign of life inside. I heard nothing but the muffled sounds of nearby street traffic.

Stuffing the letters back in, I climbed to my feet, brushing off my skirts as I pondered what I was finding. It was common for the city's elite to keep country homes. I knew many of my father's clients had, for Papa had sometimes traveled there to treat them. The Charcots, for their part, had a villa in Neuilly-sur-Seine. But usually when a family left for their holiday estate they kept one or two of their servants behind—to guard against intruders, send carpets and drapes out for cleaning, and make sure everything was in place when the family returned. At minimum, they'd pay a groundskeeper to keep the garden and courtyard tidy—not to mention to keep the post from piling up as it had here.

But there seemed to be no one at this house at all. The place was as silent as the asylum morgue.

Lifting my gaze, I studied the house's rear façade, remembering Josephine's comments about the windows sometimes being left open. The ones on the lowest level were all shuttered and well beyond my reach. But there was a rain barrel positioned just beneath the one closest to the service door. Following a hunch, I clambered carefully on top of it, balancing precariously on its lid. From this position I found I could pry the shutters apart, revealing a dusty window behind it. It too was shut. But fitting my fingertips beneath the sill, I found it lifted easily.

I glanced back over my shoulder. Being caught breaking in like this would spell certain disaster. Not only would I be arrested, but that arrest might well lead the police to Josephine—not to mention Rosalie's bracelet. It could very well land us both in prison. But apart from a lone cat slinking along the top of the wall that separated this property from the one behind it, there didn't seem to be anyone else around—the whole block had a strange feeling of sleepy stillness about it.

Cautiously, I pulled the window up enough so that I could wriggle through the opening, feet first. From there it was a short drop to the floor.

Inside, I was greeted with a smell of must faintly tinged with decay, as though meat—or perhaps the carcass of a dead mouse or two— were spoiling somewhere in the summer heat. I held my breath, half shocked at my own audacity, my feet still tingling in anticipation of having to flee. It quickly became clear, however, that I was utterly alone. Indeed, with the walls filtering out the sounds of the outdoors the silence was suddenly almost oppressive, unbroken by so much as the steady tick of a pendulum clock.

As noiselessly as I could, I began making my way through the corridor, pausing to peer into a kitchen that also aligned with what I'd jotted down, though the servants' dining table was covered with a layer of dust pronounced enough that I could have etched my name in it as Charcot had inscribed *l'hystérie* on Josephine's skin. As I was turning to head upstairs, my eye was caught by a row of bells mounted on the wall by the table, each one labeled with a destination beneath it: *Petit salon. Grand salon. Bibliothèque. Chambre à coucher. Chambre d'enfant. Cabinet de toilette.*

And beneath that:

Bureau. The master's office.

I felt my mouth go dry. I didn't need to check my notes on this one.

Josephine had described the service bells at length last night, even mimicking the jingling tones they made when rung. She'd recounted, too, the change in her response to that sound: excited and jittery on her first few days of work, but with mounting dread as the nature of her employer's interest in her became clearer and clearer. The day she killed him, she'd waited for the bell's distinctive *ping* with such apprehension that when it finally rang, it felt to her like a small explosion. As she'd described that moment to me, something in my stomach had twisted. I felt it again now, recalling our first exchange that day in the softs: *You don't remember anything?* I'd asked her.

I remember the bell, she'd said.

Swallowing back a surge of nausea, I continued on, passing a scullery with a huge copper pot for clothes-boiling but no other cleaning equipment of note, and a housekeeper's office with a large but empty desk, all in keeping with what she'd told me. Beyond them was a stairwell to the mansion's first floor, where I passed by a darkened library, a dining hall, and the parlor I'd seen from the front window. I thrust my head into each briefly to affirm that they, too, aligned with the descriptions Josephine had given me, and was once more relieved that for the most part they did, though none of the family photographs and portraits she'd described graced the parlor mantelpiece, and it was hard to tell what the furniture looked like, given that all of it was shrouded in sheets. But the grand piano she'd told me of—a mahogany Freudenthaler—was precisely where she'd said it would be, beneath an elaborately branched chandelier that also matched her description, apart from having been stripped of its prisms.

I made my way up the central staircase, careful not to disturb the dust on the oaken banister. Once upstairs, I confirmed the order of rooms as I'd taken them down: washroom, master bedroom, guest bedroom, and—at the hall's end, she'd said—the dreaded office. Here, too, everything was as she'd described it, down to the blue floral runner on the corridor floor. But there was still no sign that anyone had actually passed through these rooms recently. The washroom was large and opulent but smelled close and sour from lack of use. Both Guillaume's and his wife's bedrooms were neatly made up but as clearly unoccupied as everywhere else in the house, with neither soap nor towels by the washstands, and bureaus bare of the sorts of toiletries—shaving stand, hairbrush, comb, hand mirror—one would expect to see in a lived-in space.

Mystified, I made my way back down the hall to the room Josephine had identified as the judge's office. The door was closed, and at first I thought it was locked. Part of me, I think, even hoped it would be. But the tarnished knob turned easily in my hand, and the door swung open as though it had been awaiting me.

And then I was on the threshold, my pulse racing, taking in the chamber before me.

It was a dark room, made darker by the thick velvet curtains half closed over its one window, its walls covered with deep maroon wallpaper embellished with tarnished-looking fleur-de-lis. It smelled of stale tobacco and something fetid, like old yeast. Physically, though, it too matched Josephine's description: leather-bound legal tomes on a bookshelf; a well-stocked liquor stand nearby, complete with cutglass decanters and matching tumblers.

Cautiously, I made my way farther in, my eyes slowly adjusting to the oppressive dimness. The heavy marble mantelpiece was also as Josephine had described it, as was the framed portrait above it. The latter showed a small, pale boy in a sailor suit, a toy sailboat tucked under one arm. Josephine had told me about the other portrait in the room, one hanging on the adjacent wall by the window. Shifting my gaze, I found it as well—and froze again.

The artist had captured Marcel Guillaume from the waist up, in his court uniform: a black gown and white jabot, a black judge's toque held contemplatively in his pale and slightly pudgy hands. He had less facial hair than I'd expected, making it clear his chin was cleft. His neck, too, was less thick than the one my mind had painted. Overall, though, the likeness struck me as akin enough to the visage I'd imagined, based on Josephine's description, that I felt my scalp prickle. The eyes were practically identical: wide-set and slightly piggish, fixed unblinkingly on me as I stood there, immobilized.

Staring back, I recalled Josephine's account of this man's transformation from jovial mentor to pitiless rapist. How he'd plied her with compliments, comparing her favorably to her mother (*I see where you got your looks,* he'd said) and complaining that his wife had been "letting herself go." How he'd stood so closely behind her as she reorganized his books that day that she'd felt his hot breath on her neck, his flesh brushing against the small of her back. How later on, his purred requests for just "one little kiss" soon gave way to red-faced rage when Josephine, shocked and frightened, refused. How on the morning of his first attack he shut and locked the door behind her—something he'd never done before—and then dropped the key into his pocket.

How her heart had seemed to stop then, and fold up inside her chest.

Shuddering, I dragged my gaze down to the mantelpiece above which the painting was hung. Josephine had described a small, ornamental sculpture there of the Virgin; based on my notes, I'd expected a stand-alone statue. What I was seeing, though, was more of a cast-metal scene etched onto the type of box that usually has a music mechanism tucked into its base. The Virgin was indeed depicted, standing over a tiny, iron-sculpted spring. But she wasn't alone. Kneeling before her, on the other side of the little stream, was a young girl with a rosary dangling from her clasped hands.

I lowered my gaze to the inscription that ran around the base itself, though I already knew what it said: *Notre Dame de Lourdes.*

A chill draft seemed to sweep over me. Josephine hadn't mentioned that the ornament—like the medallion she was so obsessed with—depicted the famed scene from Lourdes. Why? The bizarre thought struck me that whoever had put the souvenir on her pillow must have switched the Madonna she'd described with the one I was now studying, though of course that made no sense at all. It was more likely that, in her traumatized state, Josephine had somehow purged from her memory the presence of the young girl who had almost been sent to a madhouse, as she had been. A young girl who, along with the blessed Virgin, had witnessed the judge's repeated, obscene assaults—and Josephine's own desperate crime of self-defense. It made a kind of sense, after all. In some ways, it even helped explain her response to the sight of those same two figures on her medallion, which must be painfully evocative of her trauma.

Unnerved, I backed away from the fireplace, my footsteps unnaturally loud against the musty silence. It took a moment to recognize that the sound pointed to another way in which the room differed from the one Josephine had spoken of last night: her narrative had included a lush Moorish carpet that had doubtlessly cost more than she and her mother made in a year. She'd described it in meticulous detail. Not just how it had looked—deep maroon like the wallpaper and curtains, but patterned intricately with blue and orange blossoms—but how it had felt against her back, the rough wool rubbing her spine raw and red. I'd known instantly that she was telling the truth about that part. I'd seen those angry abrasions myself, had had to wash carefully around them as they healed.

So where had the carpet gone?

I scuffed the floor with the toe of my boot, my eyes scouring the light brown planks for some sign of discoloration, some difference in dust patterns. But it was too dim to make it out in any detail. Moving to the window, I parted the velvet curtains enough to let a broader shaft of late-afternoon sunlight in, illuminating the polished floorboards.

And then I spotted it: a narrow and almost serpentine shadow just off the right front corner of the heavy oak desk. I approached it cautiously—almost as though it were a real snake. It was only when I was standing directly over it that I saw it wasn't a shadow at all. It was a stain: a brownish splatter, tear-shaped on one side but perfectly straight edged on the other. The sort of mark that might have been made by something spilling partly onto a carpet.

A carpet that was later removed.

It could be spilled coffee, I thought, my breath hitching. *Or chocolate. It could be anything at all.* But I was trembling as I knelt and, reaching into my pocket, fumbled past my notes, and the change purse in which I'd stored the proceeds from selling my books and Rosalie's things. Finally finding my handkerchief, I brought it to my lips. My mouth still felt as dry as bark, but I managed to moisten the cloth square with my tongue. Pressing the dampened spot against the stain, I rubbed a few times until some of the stain had transferred onto the white fabric. Then I examined it, holding it up to the light from the window.

The streaks on the soft cloth were faint. But they were unmistakably rust colored.

At once they came pouring back: those "memories" woven from the lurid threads of Josephine's lucid retelling last night, and from her hallucinatory reenactments these past weeks. I felt the judge's thick fingers closing around my throat. His full weight on my body, pinning me to the rough woolen carpet. I seemed even to smell his blood, metallic and sour. For a moment I thought I might vomit. Before I could, though, an explosion of knocks downstairs interrupted my ghastly reverie.

"*Monsieur!*" a rough male voice boomed. "I can see you're home—or someone is! I've come four times already, trying to settle your bill! Come down, or I'll come back with the authorities!"

I froze where I sat, still clutching my stained handkerchief, my heart seeming to knock against my ribs with as much violence as the man's battering fist. For an instant I was washed by real memories of being hounded by Papa's creditors—the grocer, the hot-water deliveryman. The paralyzing panic I'd felt as the booming voices echoed through our unkempt and slowly emptying quarters. That debilitating fear of even breathing in that moment, because it seemed the very air around me belonged to someone else.

Then, inhaling sharply, I reminded myself where I was. That it wasn't *my* debt that this man was bellowingly demanding be settled. It had nothing to do with me at all. What mattered was confirming that the man it did belong to was really and truly dead. Did what I'd just discovered prove that?

"I know you're in there!" the man continued, pounding on the door some more. "I saw the curtains move! You can't fool me!"

Still trembling, I folded the stained cloth up again to put it back in my pocket. As I withdrew my hand something on the floor caught my attention. It was the notice I'd picked up outside—in my agitation, I hadn't noticed its falling from my skirts. As I leaned over to retrieve it, my gaze caught part of the faded letterhead. Once more, something about it felt familiar, though it was still too dark where I stood to read it clearly.

I moved back to Guillaume's desk, where the light was a little stronger, keeping carefully out of range of the window. There, smoothing the envelope out against the dark, polished wood, I strained to make out the sender's address. The ink had been all but washed into illegibility by the elements—as, doubtlessly, had the note inside. But the letterhead was clear enough: *Entreprise des Pompes Funèbres.*

I gasped. I knew that name all too well.

I knew it because I'd communicated with the same entity myself in the hazy days following my father's death—just as he'd done in the wake of my mother's. It was the corporation designated by the city to hygienically handle its deceased, from removing the remains to supplying the coffin to arranging transportation to one of the city cemeteries—all in compliance with Paris's stringent health mandates.

"*MONSIEUR!*" the creditor bawled, his tone now tinged with petulance. "You're a half year behind on your meat bill! It's unacceptable— don't you realize the rest of us must eat too?" The single *thump* that accompanied this complaint had a more aggressive impact to it— as though the man had now resorted to kicking the doorframe. My hand shook again as I peeled the envelope's lip open, carefully pulling out the correspondence inside. Its text was a pale lavender, where it was decipherable at all. But I could make out just enough to sink back against the desk in shock:

> *Our condolences again for this untimely and [illegible] loss. Enclosed, please find an invoice for services rendered for the aforementioned funerary arrangements for [illegible] Marcel Guillaume. While we recognize that this is a time of bereavement, prompt settlement of your account is nevertheless appreciated.*

Looking up, I found myself staring at the Lourdes box again, as amazed as if I were seeing the Madone alive before me.

She killed him, I thought. *She killed him right here.*

Chapter Twelve

Some twenty minutes later I numbly boarded a Salpêtrière-bound omnibus, emotions cycling through me in such rapid succession that I barely had time to identify one before it bled into the next.

My overall feeling, of course, was one of relief, for between the funereal note, the bloodstained handkerchief, and the missing carpet in Guillaume's office (not to mention the fact that everything I'd just seen had matched the details Josephine had shared about the house), I clearly had proof that her memories were intact—which meant she could leave with me Saturday.

But there was also a disorienting and almost giddy amazement over the reality that this discovery affirmed: that Josephine—delicate, thoughtful Josephine—had consciously set out to take a man's life. And then, she had actually *done* it. It wasn't that I'd doubted her when she'd relayed her gruesome history on the bridge. I'd known instinctively even then that she wasn't lying, for it had made sense of everything: the bloodied clothes she'd arrived in, the frenzied attempt on her own life, and—when that failed—the unconscious blotting of that life from her memory. And yet, until I'd seen those smudged words—*untimely loss, funerary arrangements for Marcel Guillaume, bereavement*—I hadn't fully comprehended what they meant.

Now there was simply no way not to.

There was confusion as well, for while it was clear Guillaume was truly dead, I still had no explanation for his missing wife and son, or the half-packed state of his house. Nor could I explain why, more than two months later, the police seemed not to have made the connection between the judge's death and his missing chambermaid.

But what I most remember feeling was not revulsion, or dismay, or apprehension. It was *elation*, a joy so ferocious and filling that when it hit me on the bus it left no room for motion sickness at all.

For this man—this odious man with the little eyes and the cleft chin—had not only believed that what he did to Josephine meant nothing; he'd believed he would get away with it. Of course he'd believed that. Any woman in Hysteria could have told you as much: The men *always* get away with it. It was a central tenet of our time, unwritten and undiscussed, but as incontrovertible as any upheld in an actual court of law. It was also amply evidenced by nearly every case of abuse I knew of: Rosalie's furrier. Marthe's mother's wealthy lover. Clotilde's cigar-wielding suitor. And yet this one time, that law had been broken. The judge *hadn't* gotten away with it—because Josephine hadn't let him. That if she was caught she might end up dying for her crime as he had for his was terrifying—indeed, unbearable. And yet at that moment, what I felt most was a blaze of awe and amazement that she'd achieved the unthinkable: She'd *made him pay* for what he'd done.

This searing satisfaction stayed with me the whole ride back to the asylum. It added a spring to my step as I disembarked from the omni's platform and hurried toward the asylum's arching granite gateway, past the great Philippe Pinel and the groveling girl-child he no longer noticed, and whom the sculptor hadn't even bothered to name. It rang in my breast as the chapel bells chimed half-four and I increased my pace to a quick trot, realizing I still had to change and go fetch Josephine before dinner. It faltered only slightly when, upon passing through the asylum gate, my way was blocked by a heavy figure who'd stepped directly into my path.

"Excuse me," I said, flustered. "I must get through. I work here."

"Oh, I know you work here," said the man. "Right now, though, your job is to come with me."

He was taking my arm as he spoke, and before I'd fully understood what was happening, he was hurrying me back toward boulevard de l'Hôpital. I thought at first, confusedly, that it was the same creditor who'd been pounding on the service door of the house I'd just left, though there had been no one in sight at the time. Panicking, I attempted to pull away, breathlessly exclaiming, "Wait a minute, monsieur. Let me explain—"

"I'm quite sure that you will." He jerked me hard enough that I would have fallen had he not held me upright. "You won't have much choice in the matter." He was propelling me toward a waiting vehicle across the street: a sleek black landau attached to a team of equally sleek black horses. Only then did it dawn on me that the uniform (blue, with mustard-yellow trim) seemed faintly familiar. As was the face (large featured, pockmarked) beneath the feathered tricorn hat.

Then the carriage door was swinging open, and the coachman was actually lifting me off my feet in order to hurl me onto one of the leather-padded benches inside.

For a few stunned seconds I could do nothing but stare up at the unfolded roof of oiled leather, as disoriented as a hooked carp flung onto concrete by one of the old fishermen on the Canal de l'Ourcq. The door slammed, the latch landing with a polished-sounding *click*. The chassis rocked as the driver climbed onto his bench, and the movement helped shake me from my stupor: Wrenching myself around, I pounded on the glazed glass window. This, of course, was to no avail, for the landau was pulling smoothly out onto the street.

Then I heard it: a breathy and strangely high-pitched chuckle, followed by a nasal, male voice I didn't recognize.

"It's a pleasure to finally meet you, mademoiselle."

Slowly, I turned back around. So complete was my confusion that at first I didn't even recognize him, the man who had long been the subject of my greatest fears. Once I did, it knocked the breath out of me all over again.

Rosalie's marquis studied me, his lips twisted into an amused smile. His gaze was opaque beneath a towering stovepipe hat that was just the slightest shade darker gray than his nearly colorless eyes.

He was wearing white trousers of some light summer-weight wool, a matching vest, and a brown frock coat that, while pristine and perfectly pressed, was cut in a style that even I—who rarely noticed such things—knew to be at least a decade out of fashion. He'd also clearly been smoking, for the air in the carriage was so thick with tobacco and some oily sandalwood scent that when I finally managed a breath, I immediately began coughing.

The nobleman took in my watering eyes and reddening face, his half smile in place, as though my choking fit were a performance he was politely pretending to enjoy. When I couldn't seem to stop he tutted quietly, then turned and opened a small compartment in the leather-paneled wall behind him. Reaching inside it, he removed a silver flask.

"Here," he said, unscrewing its cap and extending the container. And when I shook my head: "Drink it, girl. We can hardly have a civil conversation while you're spluttering like a hippopotamus." He then pushed the flask so close to my face that it almost hit me in the nose, affirming that nothing about these circumstances was even remotely "civil."

Accepting the container warily, I forced myself to take a small sip. The alcohol—it was brandy, I think, though I'd had so little liquor in my life by that point that it was hard to be sure—seared its way down my throat like a fire-eater's flame in reverse. Initially it only made me cough harder. But the spasm soon passed, leaving me gasping and flush faced. Shakily, I returned the flask, wiping my damp eyes with the back of my free hand.

Up until that moment I'd only seen the marquis twice, both times from afar. I was almost positive he'd never noticed me. Now, though, he was eyeing me with such piercing recognition that his gaze felt like a cold blade scraping against my face.

I licked my lips, the brandy's aftertaste acridly sweet on my tongue. "Where are you taking me?"

"On a short drive. I've a proposition." Seeing my expression, he gave a derisive laugh. "Oh, don't worry—it's nothing like that. My tastes run in a very . . . *different* direction."

Pulling a handkerchief from his vest pocket, he shook it out with a flourish, meticulously wiping the flask's mouth with it. "Ingenious, the way they make these things nowadays," he said conversationally. "I'm sure Dr. Charcot's father would be astounded. You know he was a carriage maker, yes?"

I nodded faintly. Everyone knew Charcot had come from humble, artisan origins. It was part of what made his legendary ascent in the medical world all the more impressive.

"I particularly like this feature," the marquis went on, replacing the flask in its compartment. "The Hooper representative who convinced me to buy this overpriced contraption said it's one of their most popular features. And I must say it's proven useful. My wife, you see"—he pronounced the word *épouse* with faint distaste, as though it were a concept he didn't entirely condone—"disapproves of my imbibing during drives." He pressed his lips together briefly. "And she is not a woman to be crossed lightly. Not if you value your skin."

Shutting the compartment's little door, he set about refolding his handkerchief. I peered past him out the glazed glass front window, attempting to see around the driver's burly back. We'd now turned onto boulevard de la Gare, and for a wild moment it occurred to me he was planning on murdering me and throwing me into the Seine, the way the city's criminal gangs sometimes disposed of foes. But when we reached Quai d'Austerlitz, the driver turned his team onto it without stopping, proceeding parallel with the water toward the Jardin des Plantes.

"The windows retract," the marquis noted amiably. "On both sides. You see?" He rolled down the one nearest to him partway to demonstrate. "Also very convenient—at least in theory." He frowned faintly. "Though I'm discovering they don't always work as advertised."

"Monsieur." I swallowed, sickened by both the lingering trace of liquor in the back of my throat and the vehicle's rocking. "What is it you want?"

He laughed again. "I'd imagine the more pressing question—for you, at least—is what do *you* want, Mademoiselle *Bissonnet*. Or, more important, what you don't want."

His use of my family name felt like a pin he'd plunged into my skin. "I don't understand," I said unsteadily, mortified by the tremor in my voice.

"Really?" He shook his head. "And I hear you were a tutor. To some rather important families, it seems. I assume you presented a bit more . . . neatly, in those days."

I would have asked him whom he'd been speaking with, but my larynx felt as thoroughly frozen as Rosalie's had been after Charcot entranced her into silence. As though aware of my quandary, the marquis clucked sympathetically again, extracting a silver case and matchbox from another pocket. Selecting a cigarette, he leaned back, his eyes trained on mine as he lit it. "Of course, I can't speak in your place. But I'd imagine someone like you—a girl with at least a few refinements—wouldn't want to end up in prison for the rest of her life. What would your late father think of you now, I wonder." He inhaled appreciatively on his cigarette. "I heard he was quite a decent sort of physician, as far as they go. Had he lived, having a criminal for a daughter would have sunk his career. Or what was left of it, after that unfortunate milk-transfusion business."

I felt my face flush again. "I—I don't know what you're talking about," I managed to say.

"Oh, I think you do." His eyes were now fixed outside, on a pair of *midinettes* in bright skirts and cheaply elaborate bonnets waiting for a chance to cross the road. He inspected them thoughtfully, lips still curved in appreciation. But when he turned back to me, all humor had vanished from his face. "Do you make a habit of stealing from lunatics?" he asked sharply.

I shook my head, my cheeks heating as I thought of the two francs the pawnshop had given me for Rosalie's paste pearls and mirror.

His expression hardened further. "You know I'm among the Salpêtrière's benefactors, yes? Not directly, of course. But I pulled some strings with the city to get that new photography studio funded. Including the newfangled—and very expensive—roof that Londe fellow insisted he needed."

The new studio's ceiling was the brainstorm of Monsieur Londe, who found the noisy magnesium flashes traditionally used for photographic lighting terrified his lunatic subjects when he tried to take their portraits, while startling hysterics straight into catatonia. His solution—replacing the top-floor room's beam-and-plaster ceiling with a massive sheet of frosted glass, which allowed the entire studio to be softly illuminated by natural light throughout the day—had been mounted at an exorbitant cost. Twice over, in fact, as the workmen had shattered the initial pane Charcot had had custom-made on his behalf.

"As an expression of his gratitude," the marquis went on, "your great doctor invited me on a personal tour of the new facility after one of his recent lectures—which was where, by the way, I finally saw for myself that remarkable *rousse* of Charcot's everyone's been buzzing about. Not a classic beauty, exactly. But there is something very *compelling* about her, isn't there? Tell me: Was she truly 'reading' the contents of those vials on her own? Or had Charcot communicated the answers to her beforehand? Some say he does that, you know."

He was referring to an exercise Charcot had conducted twice before—first in his clinic and then on his stage. Called "Medication at a Distance," it involved blindfolding Josephine once she'd been entranced, then holding up vials containing various substances—ipecac, tincture of valerian, and brandy—and having her guess their contents. This she'd done with complete accuracy, not with speech, but by convincingly reacting as though she'd actually *imbibed* each liquid. She'd grown bilious and pale with the ipecac, flush faced and dizzy with the brandy. When the valerian was held up, she'd begun crawling around the stage on her hands and knees, her back arched like a languorous cat, as Charcot sonorously noted the herb's "marked aphrodisiacal effect upon certain subjects." I didn't recall seeing the marquis in the enraptured audience. Then again, I'd been unusually distracted that Friday, having only just received Amélie's letter.

"I heard she photographs strikingly as well," the marquis continued. "Though I didn't get to witness that particular talent, unfortunately. That photographer did take several pictures of another girl,

though—someone with brown hair. Somewhat plump. Very young."
He paused to pick a fleck of tobacco off his tongue. "Marcelle, was
it?" he mused. "Madeleine?"

Marthe, I thought dully. *She's twelve.*

Outside, the late-afternoon traffic thickened with vehicles coming
off the bridge. If we kept going we'd soon reach Île de la Cité—was
he turning me in at the police prefecture headquarters there?

"Whatever her name, she was a little plain, if I'm being fully honest," the marquis continued. "But not a bad figure on her, given her
age. And when the pictures came out—they developed them immediately, you see, for my benefit—it really was remarkable. She might
have been standing outside in broad daylight. Except, of course, that
she was only wearing her underthings."

He extended his cigarette out the window, tapping it against the
edge of the glass to relieve the tip of its extra ash, while I stared at
him with renewed disgust. I'd known his reputation, of course, had
heard Babette's dark mutterings about the man, had seen his shame-
less pursuit of a damaged woman in an asylum. Somehow, though,
the full measure of his odiousness had escaped me until this moment. Now it seemed to pour itself over my skin, a clammy and repugnant slime.

"A photography studio like that could have many uses," he went
on. "Not all of them strictly medical, of course. But potentially quite
lucrative. I didn't get a chance to broach this idea with Charcot,
however. As it turns out, he had something else he wanted to discuss.
Or rather, to confirm."

He leaned back in his seat, his eerily clear eyes fixing on me
again. "You see, a few months back—just before her unfortunate
breakdown—I had a certain gift delivered to poor Mademoiselle
Chardon. Or rather, I *assumed* it had been delivered, since I never
heard anything further on the subject. Not from her. Certainly not
from the shop where I made the purchase."

He was watching me closely now. I stared back, my heart pounding violently enough that I was almost certain he could hear it.

"Imagine my surprise, then," he continued quietly, "when Dr.

Charcot, after asking that I refrain from sending such gifts to his patients in the future, mentioned that my last one had been returned to the jeweler from whom I'd commissioned it. 'You got the money back, didn't you?' he asked. 'I told our ward supervisor to be discreet about it.' That's the word he used: *discrète*."

He gave a mirthless laugh. "I was tempted to tell him outright that it had, indeed, been very discreet. So discreet that I never saw any money from it at all."

Perhaps perversely, now that he'd finally come out with his accusation, my instinct was to simply deny it all. To block my ears and shout *I don't know what you're talking about,* and keep shouting until he stopped this hellish ride and let me out. But I already knew it was pointless to lie. It was obvious—if not from the fact that he'd essentially kidnapped me in broad daylight, then from the triumphant glint in his gaze—that he knew what I'd done. The best I could hope for was to make amends for it.

"It was a mistake," I managed. "Only a mistake. I always meant to return it. But the day I was meant to take it to the shop I—I was delayed. By a personal matter. And since then, I've just been trying to find a way to bring it back that won't—"

"Land you in Saint-Lazare?" The marquis finished the sentence for me, pale eyes glittering. Setting his cigarette carefully on a small ashtray on his armrest, he leaned forward until his lined face was mere centimeters from my own.

"Have you ever been inside that prison, Mademoiselle Bissonnet?" he asked quietly. "I have. I've known—you might even say *intimately* known—other girls who've ended up there."

I swallowed again, remembering the story about his last mistress, the actress his wife had had thrown into Saint-Lazare for half a year by simply accusing her of theft.

"I've seen firsthand what it does, even over the course of short-term sentences," the marquis went on. "Girls who aren't used to its—particular cruelties. It makes your asylum look like a stay at a seaside spa."

He leaned even closer. I felt his sour breath brush against my cheek and ear. "You won't be allowed to bathe—sometimes for months. You'll get lice within the first week. And not just on your head, if you understand. But that's not the worst of it," he went on as I shrank back against the bench. "You'll be among women from the very worst walks of life. Not charming hysterics and harmless lunatics but actual hardened criminals. Very hard indeed, some of them. And the wardenesses are little better." He was all but crooning now, like a beau making love to a sweetheart. "They will do things to you, my dear. They will make you do things to them—things I can't even begin to describe. When you come out—*if* you come out, for many women do not—you will simply not be the same. Nor will you be seen as the same. No one will want you—not as a tutor, not as a ward girl. Not even as a laundress. Certainly not as a wife."

I clenched my jaw, thinking back to that terrifying *La citoyenne* piece I'd just read to Josephine, detailing the infamous prison's dank walls, wood-plank beds, and weeklong stints in tiny rooms so devoid of light that it was like being locked into a coffin. As these things came back to me, something cool and smooth landed on my cheek: the marquis's gloved finger. I sat there, unable to move, as he traced the line of my jaw to my chin, then tilted my face up to meet his.

"I'll ask again," he said quietly. "Is that what you want?"

"I'll get it for you," I breathed. "I can get it for you tonight. I can get it right now, if you'll take me back to the asylum."

He gave another of his short, shrill chuckles, abruptly releasing my chin. "Oh, I don't want the bracelet back."

My head felt strangely light and empty—as though his fingers had been anchoring it in place. "You don't?"

"Not at all." We were both jostled slightly as the carriage wheels trundled over some obstacle on the road. Looking out, I saw the lush green tops of the Jardin des Plantes' Oriental plane trees materialize over the traffic and found myself remembering how, only a few nights earlier, Josephine had asked whether Charcot might let us take an outing there together. We'd talked about seeing one of the Guignol shows she said she loved and maybe sharing a sticky-sweet lemon ice. It seemed like something that had happened in another lifetime.

"No," the marquis was saying, "better you keep it, as far as I'm concerned."

"*Keep* it?" I jerked my gaze back to him. "For what?"

He shrugged. "To wear. To sell. It makes no difference to me."

I stared at him, hardly daring to believe I was hearing correctly. Was he actually, willingly *giving* us the means to escape?

But he wasn't finished. "What I care about," he said, patting his frock coat with his free hand, "is what you do with this."

When he withdrew his hand from his pocket, he was clutching a familiar-looking velvet pouch of robin's-egg blue. It was a little larger than the one I had hidden in my mattress. But the insignia on it was unmistakable—a little bird, outlined in gold thread. Its wings outstretched, its beak pointed toward the sky. Reaching over, the marquis placed it in my lap.

"Go ahead," he prompted. "Take a look."

I unknotted the golden cord, my fingers trembling as I withdrew the bag's contents. It was a necklace. At first glance it seemed a simpler piece than Rosalie's bracelet: a string of small beads on a slender silver chain. But at the base of the chain was a pendant, the center of which was a glass-cut emerald that was bigger than my thumbnail. It was surrounded by small, carefully crafted petals shaped from scores of tiny diamonds. I knew little about jewelry. But my gut told me that if Rosalie's bracelet was worth four thousand francs, this had to be worth even more.

"I tried to have it delivered to her twice last week," the marquis was saying. "But that old battle-axe of a ward nurse intercepted it both times—I think she's on to the chap who runs my little errands for me over there."

I only vaguely registered that he was confirming the rumors I'd heard about his having an "inside man" at the asylum. *It has to be Claude,* I thought numbly. It made sense that the gift wouldn't have made it upstairs at Esquirol. Babette barely let the Basque into Hysteria now, if she could help it.

"But it will suit her, don't you think?" The marquis was lighting another cigarette, watching me with open curiosity.

"Who?" I asked, though we both knew who he meant.

"A doctor's daughter," he said, shaking his head. "A *tutor*. What happens to you girls in that place?"

Biting my lip, I slid the necklace back into the bag, flinching a little as he leaned forward again.

"Listen to me very carefully," he said. "Here is what you are going to do. First: You're to give the girl—Josephine—this tonight. Tell her it's from me. Make sure she's wearing it for tomorrow's lecture." He gave a slow, wolfish smile. "I want to see it against her skin."

The idea of the thing nestling against Josephine's sternum was nearly as vile as the thought of his hands there. I almost retched.

"They'll take it from her," I said desperately. "If they see something this fine on her, they'll know where she got it. They'll realize I allowed her to have it—if not that I gave it to her. Both she and I will be punished."

He made a dismissive motion with his cigarette. "You can tell Charcot's people it's paste. That you bought it for her with your wages." He gave a wry smile. "You're fond enough of the girl, I hear. And no one will bother to look closely. They'll believe it."

This time when I swallowed it actually hurt, as if every hint of moisture had been stripped from my mouth and throat. As if I were swallowing old sand. "And the second?" I whispered.

I felt it before he'd even answered: that slow-twisting nausea I'd felt in the judge's kitchen, looking at the service bell. And then in his office, looking at his piggish painted face.

"The second," the marquis said, "is that you allow her to be brought to me. At a time and a place of my choosing."

For a dizzying instant my vision swam, the carriage's padded leather interior softening into a kind of glossy and suffocating fog. I seemed to hear my own voice somewhere deep in my head, screaming: *No. Nonono.* But when they emerged, the words were barely a murmur:

"I can't."

He lifted a brow. "Oh, you can," he said. "In fact, you can do far *more* than that, living and working in the ward as you do. Going forward, you'll have no trouble at all delivering my messages and gifts to their various recipients there."

Recipients? I thought, bewildered.

Then I understood, and it was as if the air had been sucked from my lungs. It wouldn't be just once with Josephine. And it wouldn't *be* just Josephine. He intended to have me ferry girls and gifts for him indefinitely, at his whim. "I won't do that," I exclaimed, horrified.

He lifted a brow. "You say that as if you have a choice in the matter."

"It's not that. It's—" My thoughts were in such a terrified tangle it was almost impossible to extract a coherent excuse from them. "It's Charcot," I improvised desperately. "He calls hysterics to his clinic all the time. If one isn't available, he'll be suspicious."

"I have ways of assuring the doctor's schedule and mine won't conflict," the marquis said smoothly.

I blinked. Was he implying he had connections within Charcot's inner circle as well? It seemed impossible to believe. And yet, I'd witnessed more than my share of impossible things over the past year.

"But if Josephine leaves hospital grounds without me, I'll lose my position," I said. "My whole job is to keep her from doing that. And then Charcot will lock her up in Lunacy. Like he did with Rosalie, after you tried to get her to run away."

His face darkened abruptly. Leaning forward, he glowered at me in a way that sent a shiver of primal terror down my spine. "That little fool's transfer had nothing to do with me," he hissed. "Her illness became so extreme that she could no longer be controlled by her doctors. I saw it for myself during that pathetic final 'performance.'"

Without turning his head, he flung his cigarette from the window with a motion so abrupt that I flinched as though he'd thrown it straight at me. His sudden vehemence seemed to have caught him off guard as well, for as he exhaled his last pale plume of tobacco smoke he shut his eyes, as if trying to calm himself. His lashes were just as white as his hair, but unusually long for a man of his age. They seemed to soften his craggy face in a way that made it seem years younger. Almost handsome. Then he opened his eyes, and the impression vanished.

"Besides," he said, calmly now, as if we'd been conversing companionably this whole time, "who says we have to leave the asylum?"

He'd been rubbing his thighs with his palms as he spoke, as though trying to revive circulation there. All I could see was those hands on Josephine—on *my* Josephine—twined in her shining hair. Wrapped around her white waist, her slender neck. Doing all the things to her that the judge had done in his office.

Only this time, her mother wouldn't be the one handing her over. I would.

The nausea surged back, a solid block building up behind my tongue that was as palpable to me in that instant as the *boule hystérique*—the "hysterical ball"—that used to rise in my throat at the onset of an attack.

"No," I whispered. "No. I won't do it. You can't make me."

He looked amused again. "What will you tell them, then? Your great Charcot? The police? The judge in whatever court they put you in?"

"I'll—I'll say I returned it," I said with far less certainty than I wanted to. "That you are lying."

"And you think the courts will take your word—that of an orphaned ward girl and former madwoman—against that of two well-respected men?"

They always get away with it.

I was so close to vomiting now that I could almost feel the spasms starting, taste the bile on the back of my tongue. Taking a deep breath, I lowered my eyes to the rug on the carriage floor. *Something fixed in place,* I thought. *Something not moving.* But the only thing fixed, I realized, was me: I was utterly trapped. As trapped as Josephine had been when the judge shut and locked the door to his office. As trapped as she would be when the marquis came for her.

The carriage slowed, pulling over to the curb as a trio of fire trucks thundered past, alarm bells clanging, stallions straining at their yokes. I heard the marquis's driver call out to his own team—*Steady, girls! Steady!*—before pulling back into the resumed traffic and taking yet another left. I was able to make out that we were now back on boulevard de l'Hôpital, headed for the Salpêtrière gates. They'd essentially taken me in a large loop.

"You understand, then," the marquis was saying. "What you are to do."

His colorless eyes were again locked on my face, and again I seemed to feel them there, forcing my chin toward my chest. I resisted for barely a second before nodding.

"I want to hear you say it."

"I—I understand what I am to do." The words came out in such a low voice that I barely heard them myself. He clearly did, though.

"Good," he said. "I'll look forward to seeing it on Josephine tomorrow," he said. "And after that . . ."

The carriage was coming to a stop. "After that?" I repeated tonelessly.

Reaching for his cane, he rapped on the roof twice, sharply. The vehicle rocked as the driver climbed off his seat. A moment later the landau's door was flung open, the servant's burly form appearing before us.

"And after that," the marquis said, "you wait."

He studied me again, with an expression that fell somewhere between pity and mild amusement. "You're a very lucky girl, you know," he added. "You might have gone to prison. Instead, you have a fine new bracelet."

He nodded at his driver. The man reached in, grasping my wrist with his big hand and almost lifting me from the carriage as expressionlessly as he'd hurled me into it a half hour earlier. After shutting the door behind me, he returned to his perch and, slapping his reins, pulled the vehicle smoothly onto boulevard de l'Hôpital without so much as a backward glance.

Chapter Thirteen

I stumbled back to Hysteria, dazed by how utterly the elation of less than an hour earlier had been supplanted by dragging despair. For a fleeting instant it had seemed all my problems were solved: My theft was undetected, Josephine wasn't mad, and in two days' time we'd be free of this bleak place of white-aproned men and the dark-gowned women they entranced and examined. Now, though, I felt as utterly impotent as I had when I'd first fully woken in Hysteria a little over a year earlier, stripped of my sister, shackled to my bed.

And yet I knew I couldn't give in to that helplessness. Living on here under the marquis's gnarled thumb was unthinkable in and of itself. But willingly collaborating in his plan to turn Josephine into another rich man's plaything was utterly inconceivable. She wouldn't survive it this time; I was certain of it. In the best of scenarios she'd end up in Lunacy, driven into its stark confines by both the dead man who had hurt her and the live one poised to do the same. In the worst, she'd finish the task she'd initiated on the banks of the Seine.

Hastening past the chapel and through the cemetery, with its familiar rows of blank, spartan crosses, I considered going straight to Charcot's office myself. I could confess my theft, tell him about the old nobleman's abhorrent plans. I thought, too, of going to the marquis's infamous wife. After all, the man was clearly as terrified of her as everyone else was. If I showed her the necklace and told her her husband's grotesque intentions, might she be moved to help me thwart them?

And yet even as these ideas began taking shape in my head, I understood that they weren't viable solutions. For the marquis was right; there was no way on earth France's most famous doctor would take the side of a lowly female attendant—much less a former inmate. Not over that of a prominent nobleman with the power to help Charcot realize his ever-expanding plans and projects at the Salpêtrière: The new photography studio he'd just completed. The psychology laboratory he was planning. The German microscopes he'd just ordered in the hopes of finally detecting the hysterical brain lesions he and his protégés were always searching for, the way Ahab sought his elusive white whale. As for approaching the marquise, what she'd done to her husband's last mistress told me everything I needed to know about the noblewoman. She'd make as likely an ally for us against the marquis as a lion would be for a mouse against a feral cat.

No, I realized, the only solution seemed to be to adhere to my original plan: We'd leave Saturday, taking both necklace and bracelet with us. I'd come up with some errand Josephine and I needed to run together that would buy us enough time to slip onto a Dijon-bound train. By the time Babette realized we hadn't returned, we'd be well beyond city limits. And by the time the marquis came to make good on our bargain, we'd be safely—and hopefully untraceably—in Avallon.

By the time I reached Esquirol, my despair had softened into a kind of apprehensive resolve. Realizing dinner had started already, I stopped by Hysteria to see whether Josephine was waiting for me there. But there was no sign of her.

"Have you seen Josephine?" I asked Claudine, who was attending an elderly catatonic who'd recently been dropped off by her son and his new wife.

She shook her head, cursing beneath her breath as the old

woman—who for the past twelve hours had stood motionless by the window, staring outside in what appeared to be mute horror—resisted the girl's efforts to lead her to her bed. "Last I heard she was in Photography," the *fille de service* said. "But if you're going upstairs, can you take a look for Marthe? She's run off somewhere again. No one's seen her since lunch."

I nodded, suppressing a shudder as I recalled the marquis's lewd comments about the girl as I made my way toward the stairwell. As I passed the linen closet, though, I heard a muffled thud, accompanied by a stifled moan. Remembering that I'd found the child hiding in there last time, I stopped, pulling the door open quietly so as not to startle her.

It took a moment for my eyes to adjust to the darkness inside. When they did, there was no sign of Marthe's huddled form. Instead, I made out two fully adult figures. One was a man, tall and broad-shouldered, his trousers around his ankles, and his intern's apron askew. His face was buried in a woman's pale, naked neck, her hands entwined in his thick, curly hair. Though he had his back to me, I recognized him immediately, though at first I couldn't make out his partner's identity.

Then, slowly, she lifted her head.

I gasped: It was Bernadette. She gave me a slow, beatific smile over her lover's straining shoulder. Then she mouthed a single word: *Go.*

Upstairs, I dully stripped off my dust-streaked day dress and bonnet and climbed back into my work clothes. I was half out the door again before I remembered the marquis's necklace was still in my pocket, in those days a muslin pouch I wore tied above my petticoat. Afraid of losing it on the asylum grounds, I went to hide it in my mattress with Rosalie's bracelet. After pulling it from my skirts, though, I hesitated. Then, following an impulse I couldn't explain, I turned and shut our bedroom door.

Crossing over to the window, I took the necklace from the little bag, holding it up in the waning light. For all his repulsiveness, there was no denying the marquis had taste: The piece was even more breathtaking than it had seemed in his carriage. I couldn't help marveling at the fact that something so lovely could be wielded for such wicked purposes.

I want to see it against her skin.

My throat tightened. He wouldn't, of course. I'd make sure of that. By the time he came for Josephine, she and I would be leagues away, happily spending the proceeds from this sordid gift—and that cursed bracelet—with Amèlie.

I was returning the bauble to its sack when I heard the knob behind me rattle. Whirling around, I was just in time to see the door burst open. Josephine stood at the threshold, her cheeks flushed. I quickly pushed both necklace and pouch back into my pocket, aghast at having been so swallowed by my own gloomy ruminations that I'd failed to hear her approach.

"Where have you been?" she exclaimed, shutting the door behind her as she limped into our room. "You were supposed to come for me before dinner!"

"In traffic," I said a little breathlessly. "I only just got back."

Oblivious to my confusion, she threw herself down on my cot. I sank down next to her, trying to arrange my expression into something approaching nonchalance.

"Monsieur Londe made that skinny assistant of his walk me back," she went on. "The one with the anchovy breath." She made a wry face. "I don't know why they insist I always have an attendant with me. It's not as if someone will steal me away in broad daylight."

Little do you know, I thought grimly. "Rosalie's put them all on edge," I said. "How was the session?"

"Who knows?" She shrugged wearily. "I was entranced for almost all of it, as usual. And when I wasn't, I was worried half sick by what you said last night, looking for signs that they were making me mad. It didn't help that when Charcot woke me they were all staring at me as though I'd grown an extra head. Especially that man he invited."

"Who was he?" I asked, curious despite myself. "Another news-man from London?" Two weeks earlier Charcot had invited a jour-nalist from *The Times* to observe a session in which he'd had the doctors manipulate Josephine's facial features with the use of electri-cal probes, making her involuntarily scowl, grimace, grin, an exercise supposedly meant to study the correlation between emotion and phys-ical expression. I don't know if the reporter actually wrote about it, though it was clear by the end of the session that he was at least as infatuated with Josephine as Paris's newsmen seemed to be.

She gave me a teasing smile. "You'll never guess. He's a *novelist*. Can you believe it?" Her lips twisted into one of her small, amused smiles. "His name is Monsieur Claretie. He's writing about a ro-mance set right here, at the asylum, between a hysteric and an in-tern. He even said he'd create a character in it inspired by me! Can you imagine?" She laughed. "I'll be like Thomas Edison—a real per-son inside a made-up story."

I winced a little, the startling scene in the linen closet playing out again in my mind. "And Charcot approves of this?"

"He made it sound like it was his idea in the first place." She snorted. "Strange, isn't it? He may not want his hysterics reading novels. But he apparently has no issue with novels being written *about* them."

"It is strange," I agreed, though even in my discombobulated state it did make a sort of sense. I'd heard the *Times* journalist had been invited by Charcot, at least in part, to counter the increasingly criti-cal scrutiny under which his hysteria work was coming. Was it so far-fetched that he'd enlist a novelist as well?

"Anyway," Josephine was saying, "that's not important. What's important is what *you* saw. At . . . that is, did you . . ."

She trailed off, the smile fading from her face, as though she were bracing herself for bad news. Her apprehension was so evident I found myself leaning over, taking her hands in my own.

"You were right," I said. "About everything."

She went very still. "*Everything?*" Her voice was barely a whisper.

"Right down to the wallpaper in his office," I said. There seemed no point in mentioning the Bernadette of Lourdes on the music box to her. After all, she'd been right about the Virgin.

Her eyes widened. "You got inside?"

I nodded. "A window was open, just as you'd said. The place was deserted—I'm not sure why—so I had time to check the whole house. It was just as you described it, Josephine. The furniture, rooms, portraits—the whole cursed house." I gave her hands a squeeze.

Her gaze was still wary. "And . . . him?" she asked.

I checked to make sure she'd closed the door fully. "He's dead," I said, lowering my voice. "You really did it. You killed him."

She held my gaze for a long moment, not moving, not even blinking. "How do you know?" she whispered at last.

"I found this." I handed her the *Pompes Funèbres* notice. "It's from the company that handles burials for the city. They clearly arranged his—though it sounds as if it hasn't been paid for yet."

"They were always behind," she murmured absently, lifting the note closer to her face. "In everything." Biting her lip, she studied the smudged missive before looking back up at me. "Where did you find it?"

"It had been in the mail slot of the service entrance. And there's more: There was blood on the floor, exactly where you'd said you stabbed him. Right by the corner of his desk. Here. I rubbed some up."

Pulling my handkerchief from my pocket, I handed it to her as well. Her expression unreadable, she examined it as well before slowly looking up at me again. "It was on the carpet as well?"

"There was no carpet—they'd pulled it up. It must have been too bloodstained to salvage." Reaching over, I took hold of her shoulders. "But don't you see? I couldn't have found all this if your memories weren't real. But they are. You can't possibly be mad."

"So why am I still seeing him?" She still looked dazed, unconvinced.

"Because of what he *did* to you," I said. "And because you're exhausted, and anxious. And perhaps, in part, because they keep hypnotizing you. But you can remember what I'm telling you now when you see him again—*if* you see him again. That can be your fixed spot on the horizon. And once we leave Paris, and you're no longer being entranced, the visions will stop."

"You're sure?" she asked.

"I am. Absolutely. As sure as you were that my dreams would come back."

Setting the note and cloth down, she took my hands in hers and moved them to her lap. "You're *sure* there was no one there?" she asked. "Not even in the servants' quarters?"

I shook my head. "It was as empty as a morgue."

"So my mother . . ." I couldn't tell whether the quiver in her voice signaled longing or rage.

"She wasn't there either," I said quietly.

Shutting her eyes, she exhaled in a way that sounded like a sob. A succession of emotions seemed to play over her pale face: disbelief, relief, grief. But when she opened her eyes again she looked mainly confused.

"I still don't understand why they haven't come for me," she said. "The police."

"There could be a thousand reasons. Perhaps there aren't enough detectives to put on the case—I've read that's becoming a problem." This was true: The city was in the throes of a vicious crime wave at the time, mostly at the hands of roaming hooligans and street gangs. "Perhaps his wife didn't *want* an investigation, because she wanted to avoid a scandal. After all, she must have known what he was. My guess is that she was relieved to be rid of him. Either way," I went on, giving her hands a little shake, "we can go now, can't we? We'll take a train to Dijon on Saturday, first thing, and be in Vault-de-Lugny by Sunday evening, if we're lucky. And you'll meet my sister—I know you'll like her. And Madame Granger will help us look for a flat of our own. Or even a little house. Houses must be cheap in Avallon, don't you think? At least compared to Paris . . ."

I was speaking too quickly, too eagerly; I could hear it in my voice. But I was so desperate to finally hear her say it, for her to finally confirm that she'd *leave* with me, and leave behind the dangers she knew of as well as those she did not. At least, not yet.

For I would tell her about the marquis once he no longer posed a threat—in Vault-de-Lugny, or Dijon, or even on the train. It wouldn't be a lie that way, I reasoned. It would only be a truth postponed.

Josephine stared down at her pale, picked-at fingers, oblivious to my racing thoughts. When she looked up again her eyes were damp and dark, like moss in the wake of a rainstorm.

"I can't believe it." Her tone was almost awed. "I'm really leaving this place."

"*We* are," I said, correcting her. "We are leaving. Together."

Her face seemed to glow in that instant, as though she'd absorbed and stored some of the spotlight from Charcot's stage and was emanating it back through her skin. It made her look even younger than she was, almost luminous. For a moment I felt as dazzled by her beauty as I'd been when I'd first seen her in the softs.

"Thank you," she said. "I—" Then she stopped, dropping her gaze. She was looking down at my skirts. "What is that?"

Following her gaze, I saw with dismay that a length of slender silver chain was trailing from the pocket slash in my skirt: the necklace. It had clearly come dislodged when I pulled out the handkerchief and notice.

"It's nothing," I said, covering it with my hand.

"If it's nothing, why can't you show it to me?" She seemed amused at first. Then, though, her gaze grew serious. "You promised," she said. "*No lies.*"

I watched mutely as she pushed my hand away, sliding the necklace from my pocket and holding it between us, the pendant swinging and twirling like Charcot's pocket watch when he used it for entrancement.

"Is this for me?" she asked, astonished.

I hesitated for the briefest of moments before nodding. In the end, it was the truth.

"Oh, *Laure*," she exclaimed, lifting it to the light. "Where did you get it?"

I swallowed. *No lies.* And yet I knew what would happen if I told her the truth now. She was finally free of the last man who'd trapped and abused her. Could I really tell her another now lay in wait? A temporary lie might annoy her. The truth, however, might destroy her. And then I'd never get her to come with me.

"In a little shop," I managed to say. "One not far from the judge's house. I was able to sell my books and things for more money than I'd expected. And I remembered what you'd said about Rosalie's bracelet. How it would have made you happy to—to have someone give you something so lovely."

"Is it real?" She turned the pendant over to study the back. "It can't be real. It must be glass—like in de Maupassant's story."

You can tell Charcot's people it's paste.

"Of course it's glass." I kept my eyes fixed on the pendant as I forced out the words, strangely certain that if I met her gaze I'd shatter like glass myself.

And then her arms were wrapped around my neck. "Thank you," she whispered. "I don't care if it's glass. It's the most beautiful thing I've ever owned."

Her fragrance—faintly floral, faintly sour, an undernote of something deep and richly bitter—flooded my senses. Struggling to breathe, I broke away.

"I'm glad you like it," I said numbly.

"*Like* it?" She laughed. "I *love* it! Here. Help me put it on—I want to see how it looks."

Handing the thing back to me, she turned away, sweeping up a few fiery strands that had fallen free from her chignon to expose the slim stalk of her neck.

There was nothing I wanted less in that instant than to comply. I would rather have swallowed the thing whole myself, felt its sharp edges and glittering points gouge the soft insides of my throat. Seeing no way out, however, I set my jaw, carefully draping the silver chain around her throat. The closure was one of those box clasps that even in the best of circumstances required good light, steady hands, and keen attention to secure. Not surprisingly, it took me several attempts. Finally, though, I fit the tiny silver tongue into the groove. As the little mechanism locked into place, I had a sudden

vision of myself, fastening Josephine into one of the rusted neck restraints Pinel had famously done away with, repellent devices that
the interns now used to demonstrate to their tour groups how much
kinder asylum care had become.

"There," I whispered.

Springing to her feet, Josephine crossed over to the little mirror
Charcot had permitted us. The elated smile I saw reflected in its
mottled surface seemed to slice straight through my gut.

"Oh," she breathed. "It's perfect."

"It looks lovely." The compliment felt strangely false, the way prais-
ing her "new dress" had that day in Charcot's office. Climbing to my
feet, I made my way to stand behind her. "But we should take it off
and go to dinner."

I reached again for the clasp. But she was faster, intercepting me
by catching my wrists before I'd even touched the cursed thing.

"I'm not hungry," she said. "And I don't *ever* want to take it off."

She met my eyes in the glass as she spoke. Combined with the
warm pressure of her fingers, the tenderness of her gaze was like a
sweet, deep blow to my belly.

"But—Babette will confiscate it," I protested.

"I don't care." She was still holding my wrists. Lifting them above
her head, she did a slow, waltzlike twirl until we were standing face-
to-face. "I don't *care*," she repeated, more softly.

We were standing close enough now that our noses all but brushed.
I felt her nearness like some invisible charge between our skins,
something that seemed to melt away my confusion and guilt like sunlight burning off morning mist. Staring into her eyes, I saw her pupils
quiver and dilate slightly, as though she'd just been given one of the
morphine shots the Salpêtrière doctors prescribed for headaches and
seizures.

And then she was kissing me, our lips not merely meeting but fitting together with the precision of fine watchworks. And it was as
though the floor had fallen away from beneath my feet.

I was aware, at that point, that there were women who took other
women as lovers; I had been to the so-called *saphique* areas of Mont-

martre, where some ladies lived openly together as man and wife. And I was as conscious as anyone that Salpêtrière inmates often visited one another's cots after lights-down. Sometimes this was to seek solace in the wake of a night terror, as Josephine had so often with me. Sometimes, though, it was in search of a more complex sort of comfort, as was made clear by the cottony rustlings and quiet moanings that echoed through those dimly lit wards in the early hours. Nor did these sounds come exclusively from the beds of those inmates committed for this very proclivity, whom the doctors called *sexual inverts* and the hysterics called by cruder names. They came from everywhere: the beds of women who had fiancés or husbands or children alive in the outside world, of women who had lost one or the other to disease, death, or misfortune. Initially, of course, I'd been shocked. As the months had passed, however, I'd come to consider these covert couplings as something outside moral dualities— *good* or *bad*, *sinful* or *virtuous*. I saw them, rather, in the same way I saw hysterics' visceral need to tell the world what had happened to them: as an attempt to reclaim their tortured bodies and minds for themselves. Until this moment, though, I'd never considered them in the context of my own longings and desires. Or at least, I had never done so consciously.

I pulled back, almost painfully aware of the damp saltiness her lips had left on my own, of my pulse roaring in my ears. Josephine seemed thrown as well, her color high again and her eyes almost too bright, too full of questions, to bear. Turning away, I hurried back to the bed and busied myself smoothing out the coverlet, as cognizant of her gaze as I would have been her warm palms against the small of my back.

"You should eat," I said unsteadily. "I'll put an order in with the kitchen—I need to go fetch your dress from Laundry anyway. And you should probably bathe, if we're leaving on Saturday."

"I'm *tired*," she said, as though I were proposing she spend several hours scrubbing the bathhouse floor. "Can't we just rest for a little bit?" Crossing the room to me, she dropped back onto the bed in front of me. "Tell a story first," she coaxed, like a child putting off bedtime. She patted the spot beside her. Neither her expression nor her voice hinted that anything unusual had just happened. But I was still tingling from the unexpected press of her lips, still buffeted by confused crosscurrents of emotions: Jubilation and shame. Apprehension and excitement. And underrunning all of them, a taut and almost aching sense of expectancy—though for what, I wasn't at all sure.

"What sort of story?" I asked, lowering myself down beside her but keeping a careful three or four centimeters of space between us.

"Oh, I don't know. Perhaps a story about two girls who have an adventure together." She leaned back against the wall, toying with the marquis's pendant as it glimmered greenly against her throat. "But a happy story," she added. "A story without men."

I was tempted to laugh. "I don't know any stories like that."

"You can make one up, can't you? After all, you write about the women here. In your journals."

I'd told her about my secret project of putting the desperate and disregarded narratives of Charcot's hysterics onto the page. She'd been the one to come up with the term by which I still think about them today: *Hystoires.*

Have you done mine? she'd asked.

No, I'd laughed. *Do you want me to?*

She'd thought about this somberly, chewing her lower lip. Then she nodded. *Yes,* she'd said. *Eventually. When it's safe.*

"They aren't really stories," I said now. "They're just my impressions about what might have happened to them. What it was that made them sick. But none of them are happy. And almost all of them involve men." The truth was that I could no more have made up a "happy story without men" at that moment than I could have recited *The Odyssey* in the original Greek. "I can read more from *L'Ève future,*" I offered instead. "We've got four chapters of that left."

She grimaced. "That book's crawling with men. Most of them loathsome."

I couldn't argue with this, though I felt a faint stab of indignation on Villiers de l'Isle-Adam's behalf. He may have been a man, but I admired his imagination, his audacity. The way he blended fact and fiction into his characters and their worlds, with neither apology nor explanation. It was something I'd have liked to try myself, if I'd had the time and the courage to push my journalistic scribblings in more novelistic directions—though as a woman, I doubted those efforts would have been received with the same pomp and admiration.

"I'm sure it's still better than whatever your Monsieur Claretie will write about *this* place," I added. "Even if he puts you in his book."

She laughed. "I think you're jealous, Laure!"

"Of who?"

"Of Monsieur Claretie."

I snorted. "Why on earth would I be jealous of *him*?"

"Perhaps because *you* want to be the one to write my story," she countered lightly. "And not him."

"I already told you I would. When it's safe."

"I know you did." Wiggling herself back to lean against the wall, she hugged her knees to her chest. "Maybe when we go to Vault-de-Lugny you'll write it. Maybe you'll write a whole book." She smiled, a little mischievously. "Maybe someday you'll become an even more famous writer than Monsieur Claretie."

"Not if I write stories without men," I replied dryly. "Besides. It's impossible. Everything's about men in the end."

"Not everything," she said, with surprising sharpness. "And it can't be *impossible*. Nothing's impossible."

"Then why don't you tell one?" I said, challenging her.

"I will, then." Pursing her lips thoughtfully, she folded her arms behind her head. "There were once two girls who lived in an old, gloomy castle that was ruled by an old, gloomy wizard—"

"No men," I interjected.

"A wizard's not a man."

"Of course he is. A wizard is a male witch."

"Well, *this* one isn't a man. He's just a wizard," she insisted stubbornly. "Now be quiet." She touched a finger to my lips, and again I seemed to feel its slight, warm pressure everywhere—in my belly, my throat. In the tingling roots of my hair.

"The old, gloomy castle," she continued, "was ruled by an old, gloomy wizard who put both girls under his spell. One day, though, they discovered how to break the spell together. Then they decided to escape. Taking a magic necklace that belonged to one girl and a magic bracelet that belonged to the other, they ran away from that wicked place. They sailed all the way to Omaha—"

"*Omaha?*" I couldn't help laughing. "In America?"

"Why not? It was in that story you told me. About the eighty-day journey around the world."

"But why not New York, or San Francisco?"

"Omaha sounds more exciting," she said firmly. "But hush—you're not letting me finish."

"Sorry. Please continue." I leaned back next to her, suppressing a smile and folding my hands in my lap.

"They moved to Omaha," she went on, "and found a little cottage in the countryside, with a pretty garden. And they lived there happily ever after together, with lots of lovely books and empty journals and a little white cat named Mimi."

I looked at her. "That's it?"

She shrugged. "A happy story. No men. What more do you want?"

I laughed again. "Perhaps something a little . . . longer?"

"I've no energy for longer." Yawning, she settled onto her back. "I can barely keep my eyes open as it is. I think the doctors must have had me run a footrace while I was under."

I glanced at her again sidelong, realizing that it was the first time she'd been entranced by them without me with her. "Did Charcot not say *anything* about today's exercise?"

"Only that tomorrow's audience would find it 'most instructive.'" She yawned again. "I'm sure it's just some variation on what they always do. Magnets, or lights, or scribbling things on my skin, or poking electrodes into my face. Either way, Monsieur Claretie seemed very excited."

I bit my lip, hoping Charcot wasn't planning another demonstration involving aphrodisiacal substances. Then again, I told myself, it really didn't matter what he did. Just so long as it was his last time in her mind.

I closed my eyes and pressed my knuckles against my temple. A dull ache was starting to build there, the result of lack of sleep, the day's exertions, and anxiety over all I still had to do. What story could I invent to explain our disappearance Saturday? I could say Josephine needed new stockings; that was plausible, since hers really had been ruined by her clambering around on all fours on the stage floor. To buy us more time, I could perhaps say her corset had broken too—or better yet, that she had to be fitted for an entirely new one because she'd gained weight. That would please Charcot; he was still concerned Josephine wasn't eating enough. Then again, knowing him he could probably tell exactly how much Josephine weighed simply by looking at her with those piercing eyes of his. . . .

"Laure." I felt Josephine shift toward me. "You must stop worrying so much."

"I'll stop worrying when we're on the train," I said wearily.

I felt her hand on my knee. "Whatever happens, we'll be together. That's what matters."

"I know," I said, aware that my pulse was racing again. She'd touched me like this hundreds of times these past weeks. After our kiss, though, it somehow felt different, as though an entirely new Josephine was curling into my side now, lightly stroking the rough weave of my skirt.

I was suddenly afraid to open my eyes.

"*Look* at me," she said quietly, as if hearing the thought.

I did. Her face was so close to mine that our noses brushed; I could feel her damp breath against my lips. I was paralyzed by her proximity, her intensity, combined with a confused urge to retreat from her, from whatever edge we were peering over together.

But then her hand moved to my thigh, and her eyes bored into mine, as warm and deep as a gold-flecked, green sea, and it all fell into place. I felt my limbs soften, felt the center of me melt. I felt my emptiness and somehow knew she could fill it.

Catching my breath, I pressed my palms against her chest. My mouth was dry, my skin tingling as though touched by the honeyed tips of a million minuscule needles.

"Are you certain?" I whispered.

In answer, she plucked my arms from between us and, with her ever-startling strength, used them to pull me close.

And after that no words were spoken for some time.

Chapter Fourteen

We sat together in the little garden behind the midwife's cottage in Vault-de-Lugny. The air around us was heavy with sun and pollen, the heady fragrance of a dozen-odd flowering herbs. Cicadas droned in the distance, the sound drowsily interrupted by the occasional knock of a woodpecker against a tree. "And this one," Amélie was saying, pointing to a graceful stalk bursting with small, snowy blossoms, "is angelica. You can use all of it—even the stem—and it's good for all sorts of things. Heartburn, and arthritis, and joint pain, and the sniffles." Lowering her voice, she added: "If your monthly menses won't come, it sometimes helps with that too. Though Madame Granger says not to talk too much about that use."

My sister was taller than I remembered her being, her face fuller. Her round cheeks glowed with health. I could tell that her new foster mother had been taking good care of her these past months, for there was a lightness to her as she laughed and chattered that I hadn't seen since before our father's death.

"I can't believe you're finally *here,*" she went on joyfully. Plucking one of the stems, she held it out to me, her eyes wide and bright, brown like mine but a little lighter, a little larger. "Here," she said. "It's for you."

"What should I use this for?" I laughed. "I don't have arthritis or the sniffles."

"Oh," she said gaily, "but you will. You'll have all sorts of ailments in prison."

"Prison?" I frowned.

In answer she held up her hand, the gesture accompanied by a faintly metallic jingling sound. I saw that she was wearing a bracelet: a delicate gold chain, richly studded with sapphires. "*Amélie!*" I caught her wrist. "Where did you get that?"

"From your friend," she said, tilting her chin to indicate something—or someone—behind me.

I turned, expecting to see Josephine. But to my horror it was the marquis who stood there, his top hat glinting like gunmetal, his horse-faced groomsman at his elbow.

"I see you've failed to uphold your side of our agreement," he said, his lips curving into a gloating, triumphant smile. "I'm afraid you leave me with no alternative." He nodded at his manservant, who stepped forward with a smirk. I shrank back—but it wasn't me he was reaching for. It was Amélie.

"Laure!" my sister cried as the man's large red hand closed around her forearm. Behind us the cicadas' buzzing chorus suddenly swelled into a roar, the woodpecker's desultory knocking into an insistent pounding. "*Laure!*" Amélie cried again, but it wasn't Amélie anymore.

"Laure!" Julienne was rapping on the door. "Babette says to make sure you're both up. Charcot wants her in the amphitheater at nine today."

I sat up slowly, my mouth gluey and sour, my ears still ringing with the phantom drone of dreamed insects.

"Are you two up?" Julienne huffed. "I need to get the loonies to breakfast."

Hysterics, I thought reflexively. "We're up." I shook my head groggily as the *fille de service*'s footsteps clicked off down the corridor, then glanced at the carriage clock on our bedside table. Instantly, I was jerked awake: It was already past eight.

Panicked, I threw my coverlet off. Since we'd moved to the second floor, Babette had sent someone up to wake us every morning at seven, like clockwork. Had she forgotten today? But the old woman never forgot a thing. More likely Julienne had deliberately let us oversleep. "I'll have to get you a breakfast tray from the kitchen," I said, turning toward Josephine's cot. "Otherwise we'll barely—"

But the rest of the words dried in my mouth—Josephine's cot was empty.

Leaping from my own bed, I yanked her counterpane from the mattress, as though she might have somehow hidden herself there without my noticing. She hadn't, of course. But as I stared frantically around the room, I saw her hospital dress had disappeared from its hook. And her clogs—a replacement pair for those we'd lost on the omnibus—were gone from beneath her bed.

Moving to the window, I saw the hysterics from downstairs straggling out onto the gravel pathway, chattering and laughing, Julienne first chiding Marthe for racing ahead, and then Louise for attempting to slip back into the ward so as to avoid the misery of putting food in her mouth. But there was no sign of Josephine. Not in the group, and not anywhere else on the grounds that I could see. Had she gone to breakfast early, and without me? She'd never done that before. But then again, she'd never been able to do it before, since I now slept in front of the doorway to prevent her nocturnal wanderings. I just hadn't bothered to last night, not wanting to wake her when she was sleeping so peacefully in my arms. Not when it meant leaving her side.

A thousand worries washed over me: The marquis had crept in over the course of the night and taken her. She'd had another night terror and wandered boulevard de l'Hôpital, been hit by some late-traveling hansom. Worst of all was the fear that, regretting what we'd done together a few hours earlier, she'd rushed off from me in a fit of loathing and revulsion.

Pushing the thought away, I scrambled into my work gown, stockings, and boots and haphazardly pinned up my hair, barely glancing at my reflection. Not bothering to wash, I raced downstairs to Hysteria, poking my head in just to confirm Josephine wasn't there, which (of course) she wasn't. Babette was, however, working on one of her ledgers. Upon seeing her I quickly whirled away. But I was too late; my name was already being called out in that raspy caw of hers: "*Bissonnet!*"

Reluctantly, I turned back around.

"Where is Josephine?" she snapped, beckoning me over.

"She wants to eat in her room," I lied. "I'm getting her a tray."

The old nurse rolled her eyes. "Becoming quite the queen, isn't she. Next she'll want to be driven over in a golden chariot. You've fetched her dress from Laundry?"

"Yes," I lied again, though between being swept into the marquis's smoke-filled carriage yesterday and then into Josephine's warm arms, this was something else I'd completely forgotten to do.

"Well, then, don't just stand there," Babette exclaimed. "It's getting late. Charcot wants her in the wings early today—no later than nine. Did Julienne tell you?"

"She did," I said tightly, briefly considering also telling her that Julienne had all but ensured we'd miss that deadline. But I quickly dismissed that idea. Babette had little tolerance for snitches as it was—and even less if that snitch happened to be me.

"Why so early?" I asked instead. "Is she going on first?" Charcot almost always scheduled his hysteria lectures last, I suspect because he feared that if he started his lesson with them he'd lose half his audience for the other half of his presentation.

"The director doesn't tell me his plans," Babette said coldly. "Go get the girl's food."

By the time I reached the dining hall, the other inmates were already well into their meal. Madame Chambon was pretending to feed her doll-daughter with a spoon, while Bernadette—who, I noticed, had a new *suçon* just above the dark border of her bodice—had her hands clasped, her long-lashed eyes closed in remorseful prayer. Both Julienne and Claudine were busy refilling cups with the weak sludge the kitchen insisted was coffee, while Marthe was taking advantage of their lapsed attention by quietly switching her emptied porridge bowl with Louise's untouched one. Félicie sat at the table's end, scratching violently at her neck with one hand while nibbling daintily at a brioche.

I made my way to Claudine. "Have you seen Josephine?"

She looked up from Clotilde's cup. "She's not with you?"

On the other side of the table, Julienne looked up as well. "Who's not with her?"

"Josephine," Claudine said.

Julienne turned to me, her dark eyes snapping with delight. "You've *lost* her?" she crowed.

"I haven't *lost* her," I said quickly. "I was supposed to meet her here. After she'd gone to the washroom. Perhaps she—got detained."

"Perhaps," Julienne said gleefully. "Or perhaps she decided she was better off getting herself onto Charcot's stage. Given how late you seem to be running today."

The spiteful smile on her lips confirmed for me that she'd set us up. It also sparked a fleeting but powerful urge to slap her smug, fetching face. I forced myself to turn away and make my way back toward the kitchen. Even if Josephine wasn't there—and there was no reason to assume she would be—I could at least put in an order for her breakfast. Neither of us had eaten dinner, and she'd barely eaten lunch. Today of all days, we couldn't risk having her faint on-stage. Not if we were trying to leave tomorrow.

No one in the kitchen had seen Josephine either, though Céline agreed to have some coffee, bread, and jam sent to our room, along with a slice of cold pork left over from the dinner we'd both missed. Thanking her, I turned and hurried back toward Esquirol, hoping Josephine would somehow already be back when I arrived there. But I'd barely taken three steps when another unwelcome voice boomed my name from behind me.

Glancing over my shoulder, I saw Claude leading a line of lunatics back from their own breakfast with Jacques bringing up the rear. Between them they clutched a length of coarse rope, to which the dozen disheveled women clung as to a lifeline. Most of them were silent and dull eyed, though the one nearest Jacques was chattering animatedly to herself, waving her free hand like an orchestral conductor. As the group drew closer I realized she was simply spewing out numbers—*un, vingt-six, quatre cent vingt-trois*—albeit with a surprisingly conversational inflection.

"Looking for someone, Princesse?" the Basque drawled over his charge's numeric monologue (*soixante-douze, cinquante-neuf*).

"That's none of your business," I replied.

"I only ask," he said, "because I just saw that little *rousse* of yours larking about in one of the gardens."

"*Six cent quarante-neuf!*" the *folle* shouted indignantly.

"Shut up, you," Claude growled. "It's too early for your nonsense."

"*Trois mille deux,*" the woman retorted under her breath.

The Basque turned on her, his black eyes flashing. "I mean it," he growled, reaching menacingly toward his pocket. "I'll stuff another rag in that toothless old mouth of yours."

The woman cowered back. "*Zéro,*" she whispered.

"That's right," he said, nodding.

I eyed him with disgust, remembering the marquis's offhand aside: *the chap who runs my little errands over there.* Would he really have chosen this ham-fisted brute for an accomplice? I could barely picture the two in conversation, let alone in alliance. "Which garden?" I asked tightly.

"The one between the promenade and rue de l'Église. She's picking posies like a bride on her wedding day. Which, actually—"

I didn't wait for him to finish whatever revolting observation he'd been about to relate. I bolted back toward the chapel, all but running.

I wouldn't have put it past the scoundrel to lie to me, any more than I'd have put it past Julienne to try to get me in trouble. As he'd predicted, though, I found Josephine in the garden between the chapel and the kitchen. She was sitting on one of the stone benches, staring thoughtfully at the little fountain in the enclosure's center, her red hair loose around her shoulders and the marquis's pendant gleaming in the morning sunlight.

I hadn't yet had time to fully process the astounding thing that had happened between us a few hours earlier, the way she'd drawn me into her and eased herself into me in ways that seemed at once violent and yet ineffably tender. The way I'd somehow known how to respond to and return each stroke and caress with an assuredness that later left me bewildered. The way her freckles had tasted like not cocoa but a mix of earth and lemons. The softness of her skin, as taut and smooth as a ripe peach but for the fleshly script on her arms: *L'hystérie. L'hypnose.*

The culmination of those few, sweet hours was beyond anything I'd imagined possible, a tremulous clenching, a miraculous release. I'd felt tossed upon hot waves of honey, washed up onto her warm form. Filled, for once, not with regret and fear but with an almost unbearable sense of well-being. It was as if this girl—this remarkable, exquisite, vulnerable girl—was the cipher that unlocked who I truly was, a Rosetta stone decoding my own body's meaning. There had been one flickering instant of doubt just before falling asleep, a vague awareness that what we'd just done went against everything I'd been taught was right, both morally and medically. But it had faded away as we fell asleep, still entwined.

And seeing her again now, I felt only wonder.

"*There* you are, Laure," she called brightly, as though I and not she were the one who'd been missing. She lifted her hands, clasping a somewhat bedraggled-looking bouquet of yellow roses and blush-pink dahlias. "Look! Most of the roses are dried up now. But the dahlias have only just bloomed."

"What on earth possessed you?" Weak-kneed with relief, I sank down beside her on the bench. "Running off like that? I've been looking everywhere!"

She gave me a puzzled look. "You didn't see my note?"

"You wrote me a note?"

She nodded. "I left it by your pillow. You seemed so restless last night that I hated to disturb you."

"What did it say?" I asked, bemused by this reversal of our roles.

"Just that I woke early and needed some air. Here." She offered me a rose.

For an instant my dream of Amélie swept back to me: *Here. It's for you.* I shook the memory off.

"What's it for?"

"To press in your journal. For a souvenir."

"A souvenir of what?"

"Of this *place*," she said, as if this should have been obvious. "So we have something to remember our life as madwomen by."

"We're not mad," I said, more from reflex than anything else.

"It doesn't matter what we are," she said. "By tomorrow night, we'll be nothing but free."

I touched her cheek, wanting to kiss her again, right then and there. As I did, though, I heard the Basque's group. The old *folle* was screeching now, the numbers still jumbled and out of sequence: "*Trois!*" she howled. "*Soixante-huit! Deux millions!*"

"You old twat!" the Basque bellowed back. "I *warned* you! Open your mouth!"

"We should go," I said, dropping the rose into my apron pocket. "He wants us there by nine for some reason. If we hurry, we'll have just enough time to get ready."

"Why can't we just leave now?" she asked, not moving. "Today?"

"Because if we don't show up in the amphitheater, they'll know for sure something is off. We wouldn't even make it to the station." I took her arm. "Just one last time. One more day. And then you'll never be entranced again."

She still held back, her jaw tightening. "I'm never being entranced again, regardless."

"What?" I blinked at her, not sure I'd heard properly.

"I'm through with it. I'm through with *them*." Picking up one of the roses in her lap, Josephine toyed with it, heedless of the shining, sharp thorns. "I was thinking about it this morning," she went on. "While you were still sleeping. I won't risk it anymore—not at this point. Not when we're so close to getting away."

"What are you saying? Risk what?"

"My *sanity*," she said. "I'm already too close to losing it as it is. I won't let them hypnotize me again."

I looked at her, aghast. "But how will you keep them from doing it?"

Josephine laughed at my expression. "You really don't understand how it works at all, do you?"

"No," I said, flushing. "You know I don't." I swallowed. "But I do know that if Charcot can't hypnotize you, he won't be able to do his lecture."

She rolled her eyes. "He won't *know* he hasn't hypnotized me, of course. Heaven knows I've been entranced enough times to know how to pretend."

"Pretend?" Now I stared at her. "Josephine, you *can't*. That's what Rosalie tried to do. It's why he sent her to Lunacy. He always knows the difference. Always."

"He won't with me."

"But . . ." I caught my breath, overcome by a creeping sense of déjà vu as I recalled Rosalie that last morning, right before she was exiled from the glow of Charcot's footlights. "But what if he does? He'll put you in the softs, like he did Rosalie. We won't be able to leave. It will ruin everything."

"He won't find out," she said. She was beginning to sound annoyed. "I've kept track of everything he's done to me, and know exactly how I've always responded. And he thinks he has me wrapped around his little finger. It wouldn't even occur to him that I'd dare to defy him. Any more than it occurred to Guillaume."

I shivered, though whether at the casualness with which she'd referred to her rapist's slaughter or at the catastrophic risk she seemed determined to take I wasn't sure. *Don't do this,* I wanted to cry. *Not now. Not when we're so close.*

But I knew her well enough by that point to know that once she'd decided upon a course of action, she rarely wavered from it, no matter what the risk. For someone of our sex—not to mention someone of her class, age, and medical condition—she had an astonishing confidence in her abilities. I think that's why she'd been able to not only survive her employer's abuse but to channel her rage over it into revenge.

"Please, Josephine," I began haltingly. "Just think about it."

"Thinking about it is all I've done this morning," she said wearily, reaching up to brush a loose hair strand out of her eyes. As she did, something on the back of her hand caught my eye: a bead of blood, almost startlingly bright and red.

"Oh," I exclaimed. "The thorns. You must have pierced yourself." Pulling out the fresh handkerchief I'd picked up on my way out of the room, I reached out to stanch the flow. Curiously, though, rather than soaking into the white cloth, the spot shifted a millimeter or two away from it.

Then, to my amazement, it grew wings and whirred away.

"Ah," Josephine exclaimed. "A *coccinelle*! You see? That's good luck! It means my plan will work."

Shading her eyes, she gazed after the ladybug as it zigzagged its way to a nearby rose leaf. Behind us, the chapel struck the quarter hour, pulling me out of my daze. *Eight forty-five.* If we stopped by Laundry en route back to the room, and I did her hair while she ate breakfast, we'd still be late—but not by much.

I stood. "We have to go."

For a moment she continued squinting after the insect. Then, sighing, she accepted my outstretched hand. "Did you see how many spots it had?" she asked, climbing unevenly to her feet.

"What?"

"The ladybug. When they land on you like that, each spot represents a year of good fortune you're to have."

I shook my head. "I didn't see," I said, though this wasn't true.

The reason I'd confused the insect with blood was that it hadn't had any spots on it at all.

Chapter Fifteen

A little under an hour later we sat in the amphitheater, staring out into the already smoke-hazed auditorium. The timing had been tight, but we'd made it a little before nine-fifteen. As I'd pinned up the last of Josephine's curls, I'd made one final attempt to get her to reconsider her plan to trick Charcot. "I just don't think it's . . . wise," I offered, glancing furtively at the reflection of the emerald pendant in the little mirror. It seemed to stare back at me, an incriminating green eye.

"You're not the one who's been poked and pierced and magnetized for weeks on end, while having her brains scrambled like eggs in a skillet," she retorted.

Then, seeing my expression, she softened. "I'm sorry," she said, turning and wrapping her arms around my neck. "I'm anxious too. About everything." She pressed her lips to my cheek, and I felt it again—that strange sense of being at once achingly empty and painfully overfull. I pulled her closer, turning my face so her lips met mine, amazed once more by how easy, how *natural*, it felt. By the way a mere connection of flesh could counter the cold unease I'd felt these past few hours, replacing it with something looser, lighter, something deliciously warm. Josephine seemed to feel it too, for it took several moments before we finally disentangled from each other, laughing as if we'd just shared some unspoken joke, our faces flushed and damp.

Now, just a mere five minutes before the first lesson's scheduled start, we sat in the darkened corridor leading to the stage. For all the fuss about getting there early, we'd been left completely alone. I was tempted at first to wonder if Babette had been toying with us as Julienne had. But the doctors seemed thrown off by something as well. The interns clustered around their *maître*, animatedly discussing what sounded like a last-minute schedule change. Edging closer, I was able to discern that Charcot's first lecture—on amyotrophic lateral sclerosis, a disease that would one day come to bear his own name—was being revised, as the patient he'd planned to use as its subject had passed away the prior night. After fielding competing suggestions on how to fill the hour, Charcot finally nodded.

"*C'est assez!*" he barked with all the imperious urgency of Napoléon on the battlefield. Turning to his secretary, he motioned toward the door. "Fetch that other one from Botarde's ward—the one with subcutaneous pruritus. We'll use her today and find a different subject for next week's lecture."

The younger doctor nodded and scurried off.

I turned back to Josephine, who seemed too focused on the swelling audience to notice anything amiss. "Look," she exclaimed suddenly, brightening. "There's Monsieur Claretie—the one who's going to put me in his novel!" She pointed toward a sallow man who was sitting in the last row of the professional section, seemingly taking notes on the crowd. "He's rather handsome, isn't he?" she whispered teasingly. "In a sad and droopy sort of way."

Unlike Guy de Maupassant (who'd had a kind of square-jawed, intense-eyed virility to him) I actually didn't find this writer attractive in the least, with his houndlike eyes and foppishly forked beard. But I nodded, distractedly scanning the rows before the author for the marquis's groomsman. I didn't spot him, though I knew better than to read anything into his absence. Presuming the nobleman followed his usual pattern, he'd have his servant slip into place just as Charcot began his first lesson, which the man would then sit through with a look of aggrieved disinterest. The marquis would show up an hour later for the hysteria portion of the lecture. Apparently, the old aristocrat had little interest in neurological talks that didn't feature contorting young women and didn't want his seat taken by someone who did.

The rest of the gallery seats, meanwhile, were already nearly filled, and there seemed to be even more civilians than had come during Rosalie's peak popularity. I also spotted at least a dozen women in the mix, far more than I recalled having seen in that overwhelmingly masculine space. A few of the more soberly attired of these might have been medical students, for the École de Médecine had been open to our sex for nearly a decade by that point. But others seemed dressed up as if they were attending the actual theater, in beribboned summer dresses and hats adorned with bright plumes, or even entire exotic-looking stuffed birds. Toward the back, I also spotted a group of shabbily dandyish young men—hooligans, really—who'd have looked more at home at the city's lower-end cabarets than at one of Europe's leading research hospitals. Several of them weren't even wearing shirt collars.

"Odd," Josephine said. "*He* doesn't look like a doctor, does he."

I nodded, thinking she was looking at the same unkempt bunch I'd been studying. But she was actually contemplating the professional section, where Claretie was sitting. Following her gaze, I felt my heart flop in my chest.

For there he was, right in the front: the marquis's groomsman, casually cleaning his fingernails with a penknife. I'd missed him because in place of his usual blue-and-yellow uniform he was sporting a brown suit of balding corduroy, and he wore a derby instead of his usual top hat. But I would have known those horsey features anywhere. I realized only then how fervently I'd been hoping *not* to see them, to be spared the two men's loathsome presence as a parting gift.

Josephine touched my arm. "What is it?"

"It's nothing," I said, quickly shifting my gaze. *Not a lie*, I reminded myself. *A truth postponed.* And yet the jewels at her clavicle seemed to glintingly contradict me. And the thought that that old man would see them as proof he'd already won his prize all but turned my blood to bile in my veins.

"I still think you should take the necklace off," I said tensely. "In case Charcot asks about it."

"So what if he does? It's only paste!" Covering the pendant protectively with one hand, she squeezed my knee with the other. "You must stop *worrying*. It is all going to be all right."

"I know," I said, though I didn't. Not at all.

Leaning over, she pressed her soft lips against my ear. "Remember what you told me in the garden," she breathed. "One more day."

I don't know if it was the words themselves or the warmth of her breath, the way it seemed to send cascading shivers across the entire span of my skin. But when I opened my mouth to reply, what I'd intended to say—*I know*—became something else:

I love you.

And once more, I almost said it—just as I'd almost said it after telling her my plans to flee to Morvan. But then the amphitheater's double doors burst open with a theatrical bang. Charcot appeared between them, his stocky form briefly thrown into a shadowed silhouette by the morning sunlight behind him.

He stood there a long beat, surveying the packed chamber like a monarch surveying his realm. Then he made his way down the aisle, cane thumping against the floor, interns trailing after him like white-aproned ducklings.

An expectant hush fell over the room as the group—eleven in all—made their way solemnly to the front of the stage. When they reached it, Charcot nodded at Monsieur Londe, who switched on his device. As usual, this broke the spell: The audience stirred and murmured in response to whatever startling image it was projecting, though from where I sat I couldn't yet see it.

Pulling himself up the stairs, Charcot hobbled to his lectern, where he removed his hat and placed it next to him on a stool. Pulling out his pocket watch, he frowned, looking from it to the pendu-

lum wall clock as though debating which one to believe, until the iron
minute hand clicked into place on the *XII*. He stood there sternly
through the clock's twelve short, metallic chimes. Then he replaced
his watch in his vest pocket.

"Gentlemen," he began, as always. "As I've noted in the past, hysteria is a neurological illness, in the same extended family as multiple
sclerosis, amyotrophic lateral sclerosis, and Parkinson's disease. With
its myriad symptoms, however, and startling propensity to mimic any
number of medical afflictions, it might perhaps be seen as the 'black
sheep' member of that family—one that, to date, remains stubbornly
resistant to clinical definition."

He spoke with his usual sonorous authority, each word as honed
and polished as the stones that dangled from Josephine's neck. All of
his interns and most of those in the professional section listened with
their usual breathless attentiveness. In the back rows, though, I was
already beginning to detect a restless rustling: Women inclining their
heads toward one another, whispering. The hooligans passing a cigarette tin and lighter among themselves. For my part, I was confused:
Was he planning on starting the lecture with Josephine? And if so,
who was the subject of the second hour of the lesson?

As if in answer, I heard a door close quietly behind us, followed by
footsteps quickly approaching from the back corridor. A few seconds
later Marie appeared along with Claudine and Félicie. The hysteric's
wiry hair had been piled hastily atop her head, and the angry spot
she'd been scraping at over breakfast was freshly plastered.

Guiding the two women over to us, Marie sat Félicie next to Josephine and gave her an awkward pat on the shoulder. "Keep her
quiet," he told Claudine. "Dr. Charcot will let you know to bring her
out." And with that, he hurried back to the interns' section.

Félicie stared around the backstage area curiously, sliding her fingers beneath her neckline so she could rake at the spot where the
secretary's hand had just been.

"Never been back *here* before," she observed.

"Shhhh," Claudine hissed. "And stop that!" Catching Félicie's wrist, she enfolded it tightly between her hands before shooting me a beleaguered look. "They don't pay us enough for this nonsense," she said.

This, of course, was such an understatement it didn't merit a reply. "What's happened?" I asked instead.

"All of twenty minutes ago they decided they needed this one here, today. *Now.*" She rolled her eyes. "And of course, Babette acted as though it was *my* fault the girl's neck looked like she'd hacked it with an axe. We barely had time to bandage it before Marie herded us here like two goats."

I looked back at Charcot, who was still addressing his audience. Was he really going to devote the entire two full hours to hysteria, then? I'd never heard of his doing it before—though it would doubtlessly be a popular decision with the audience.

"As I've also discussed in past lectures," he was continuing, "and as we've been able to demonstrate conclusively in my work here at the Salpêtrière, mesmerism can be a powerful clinical tool in the identification and examination of hysterical symptoms. According to some of our recent findings, in fact, it may prove to be the key to eliminating hysteria altogether."

He paused portentously, turning back to catch my eye. Still absorbing his last pronouncement—were they *really* about to cure hysteria?—it took me a moment to realize that he was cueing me to bring Josephine onstage. Not for the second hour of the lecture as he usually did, but now. It was an unsettling turn of events, but I was relieved at least that the marquis still wasn't in his seat. It felt like a tiny blessing—perhaps even a good omen after all of the morning's dark harbingers: My terrifying dream. Josephine's disappearance. The spotless *bête à bon Dieu* I'd brushed from her arm.

"Let's go," I told her.

Turning back toward the gallery, Charcot surveyed his viewers. "I believe," he said, "that some of you may be familiar with the morning's first subject."

In a heartbeat the room fell silent, four hundred faces turning expectantly toward the brightly lit stage like pale blossoms turning toward the sun. Standing, I reached down to help Josephine from her seat, thinking to make one last plea that she not risk destroying our future together. But she'd already risen on her own. As she limped onstage beside me, the audience erupted into its usual furor, heightened by the whoops and whistles of the hooligans. Bonnet feathers trembled and swayed like storm flags ahead of a summer squall. A whispered chorus arose: *That's her! That's the* rousse *I read about! Josephine!*

"This patient," Charcot continued, lifting his voice slightly to be heard over the din, "presents us with a classic example of hysteria triggered by emotional and physical trauma. She was brought to the Salpêtrière a little over a month ago, after trying to drown herself in the Seine."

I settled Josephine into her seat, straightening her skirts for her as I usually did. Then, leaning over, I pretended to adjust her dress's neckline. "You don't need to do this," I whispered. "One last time surely won't hurt."

"It might," she murmured back. "And so I do." Her green eyes remained stubbornly fixed on one of the plaster figurines displayed at the foot of the stage: an old woman with Parkinson's, so severely stooped by her disease that she appeared almost folded in half. Sighing, I straightened back up and began the return trip to the wings.

"As some of you may also know," Charcot went on, "our asylum has recently installed a new photography studio, since the camera can be another useful tool for capturing hysteria's vagaries and symptoms." He waved a hand toward the image Londe had projected onto his screen. Curious, I glanced over to finally see what it was. I nearly tripped over the hem of my gown in surprise.

Not one photograph but two were shimmering on the white canvas, side by side. I'd seen the one on the left before—had, in fact, been present when it was taken. In it, Josephine appeared fully dressed in her hospital gown, on her knees, with her hands and eyes lifted toward Londe's glass ceiling. It was one of the stances she sometimes affected during the "passionate poses" phase of her fits, and while it looked as though she was lost in pious prayer, I knew she was tearfully begging her judge for mercy.

It was clearly the other image, however—the one I hadn't seen before—that had caused the stir. In it, Josephine appeared on the hospital bed Londe had set up in his studio, the sheets (black, as Charcot believed this set off Josephine's luminous skin better) a dark rumpled ocean around her. She was wearing only a shift, her hair tumbling down her bare shoulders in tousled disarray.

But her demeanor in this one differed dramatically from the older photograph. She'd turned her head toward the camera and was gazing at it directly, almost coyly, her pointed chin tucked and her expression at once challenging and amused. Something about that look snagged in my memory like a loose thread catching on a thorn, though in my distracted state it didn't occur to me what it was until I'd once more taken my seat next to Félicie.

It was *Olympia*, the painting that had caused shock waves at the Paris Salon when it debuted there over two decades earlier. I'd never seen the original—it was still deemed too scandalous to be displayed in any of the city's public museums. But I'd come across an image of it in one of my father's books, and he'd told me the story behind it. He'd described the public outcry the work had sparked. Not just because it unapologetically portrayed a naked prostitute, or because Manet had refused to romanticize either his subject's body or her profession, but because of Olympia herself—the way she gazed unrepentantly back out at her viewers from the depths of her boudoir.

"It caused such a scandal," my father had told me, "that I heard some Salon visitors tried to attack the canvas on the spot." He'd chuckled. "In the end, though, the joke was on them. The model isn't even a real *prostituée* but a talented painter herself. In fact, her work was selected for last year's Salon, and poor old Manet's was rejected."

The remembered rumble of my father's voice made my throat tighten. I couldn't help recalling the marquis's snide speculation: *What would your late father think of you now?*

And what would he think, I wondered miserably. For what was I now? A former asylum inmate. A thief twice over. A lecher's potential henchwoman. And as of last night, I was also the lover of another woman—a revelation that would surely have had both my mother and my *grande-mére* rolling in their graves. And yet—perhaps strangely—I somehow thought Papa would have understood about Josephine if he'd had a chance to meet her. He would certainly have liked her, with her fierce determination to better herself, her thoughtful insights, and her blade-sharp wit.

"Oooh," Félicie was whispering. "She looks like a *talonneur* in that one. Does her mother know they're taking such pictures?"

I'd been so lost in my thoughts I'd almost forgotten she and Claudine were still there. Turning to look at them now, I saw Félicie twitching and wriggling in the way she did when she desperately wanted to scratch—though she couldn't, as Claudine still had her fingers clamped around the girl's skinny wrists like fleshly manacles.

"Upon admission," Charcot was booming, "the patient presented with a cluster of classic hysterical symptoms, including a case of hysterical amnesia, anesthesia on the right side of the body, and a moderate contraction of her left foot. The hemianesthesia has since resolved. Despite our best efforts to cure them, the amnesia and contraction have not, though the contraction eases during hypnosis and natural sleep. Such things are not uncommon."

He paused, running a hand over his well-oiled white hair. "But there is one more aspect of this case which we've only recently discovered—one which may not only shed light on the mysterious appearance and disappearance of certain symptoms but even offer a route to curing them altogether. For as we have recently discovered here, hypnosis can also be used to uncover a somewhat less explored manifestation of this disease: that is, the presence of a second—or as it is often called, 'double'—personality."

A second personality?

Jolted, I glanced at Josephine. I'd heard of double personalities before, of course. The papers had been obsessed with them after a case was discovered in Bordeaux: a seamstress who'd in one life been glum, lonely, and perpetually ill, and in another healthy, happy, and—ultimately—married with a child. But I'd never heard of the phenomenon's being studied here at the Salpêtrière—much less with Josephine as its subject. This, I realized, must have been what Charcot and the other doctors had been doing with her yesterday, the exercise Charcot predicted would be "most instructive" for today's audience.

As the repercussions of this sank in, my surprise shaped itself into something else: a cold fist that seemed to close around my lungs. Charcot was clearly planning to reproduce whatever had happened in his clinic yesterday for today's audience. But Josephine had no memory of that session, and I hadn't been there to tell her about it.

In short, she was going to have to replicate a "personality" Charcot had met—and she had not.

"Little is known about what causes personalities to 'split,'" Charcot went on, "though they appear to do so across the world, regardless of gender, race, or nationality. There is also some evidence that the phenomenon occurs more often in hysterical patients than in those who are not hysterical."

She can't still plan on going through with it now, I thought numbly. I stared at Josephine, willing her to look at me, to confirm that she understood the colossal mistake she might be about to make. But she was staring into the audience, her features fixed and unchanged but for a faint shifting of her eyes. I turned my own gaze back to the gallery, reflexively checking the groomsman's seat once more, expecting to see him picking his teeth, or perhaps pulling a hair from his nose.

This time, though, it was empty.

For a single, fleeting instant I allowed myself an utterly illogical hope: That the servant had simply taken a washroom break. Or that the marquis's plans had changed, and they both had simply . . . left. Then I heard footsteps, and a quiet round of indignant murmurs and sighs. The marquis was working his way down the row, his wiry figure unmistakable in a summer tailcoat of pale green and a straw hat with a matching band. When he reached his seat, he settled into it with the proprietorship of an Opéra patron settling into his box, popping his monocle into his right eye socket and clasping his gloved hands expectantly atop the ornate handle of his walking stick. I averted my eyes—but not quickly enough to miss it: the slow, cold smile as he spotted the necklace that was the mark of his ownership.

There was a wild urge to race back onto Charcot's stage, to yank Josephine from her seat and drag her back out the way we'd come, off the stage, off the grounds, out of Paris altogether. Once more, however, I forced myself to stay where I was, as helplessly trapped as Félicie's wrists in Claudine's fists.

"As those of you who have encountered her on my stage before will know," Charcot continued, "Mademoiselle Josephine is a girl of a sweet, modest, and somewhat nervous nature. While eager to please, she is also very shy and proper when it comes to the opposite sex."

Despite myself I suppressed a smile as Josephine's dry observation in the garden came back to me: *He thinks he has me wrapped around his little finger.*

"If I may direct your attention to the two photographs my colleague has just displayed," Charcot went on, "the one on the left is a good representation of that persona."

Up until this point, Josephine hadn't so much as glanced at Londe's screen. Now her eyes darted toward it along with every other gaze in the audience, studying it briefly before returning to Rosalie's portrait. Once more, nothing in her expression seemed to shift.

"Her secondary personality," Charcot went on, "though subservient to her primary one, is significantly more assertive. This personality calls herself 'Jeanne.' Like Josephine, she exhibits hysterical symptoms clearly derived from emotional trauma. Interestingly, though, these symptoms are not the *same* symptoms as Josephine currently suffers. Jeanne has no contraction of the left foot, for instance. She does, however, manifest anesthesia of the right side of her body—which, as I've noted, Josephine also suffered from initially upon arriving at the asylum. From what we have deduced, this symptom—which in Josephine's case appeared to mysteriously 'disappear' overnight—did not, in fact, disappear. It simply moved to a new host—Jeanne. And it is this fluidity—the possibility of 'shifting' hysterical symptoms back and forth between different personalities in one body—that leads us to hope that we may one day cure the hysteric of her disease altogether. How, you ask? In the past we've had some success, here at the Salpêtrière, in transferring symptoms *between* hysterics with the use of magnets. Our thinking is that similarly, we might shift symptoms between hysterical personalities; or more specifically, from the dominant personality to the subservient. If we could then manage to keep that secondary personality permanently suppressed, we would effectively have rid the patient of her malady. At present, of course, this is only a theory. But I believe it is one that shows intriguing promise."

He had come to a stop directly in front of Josephine as he spoke. "For now, however," he said, "I shall let you witness the workings of a dual personality yourselves. Are you ready, mademoiselle?"

No, I thought numbly. *She is not ready. She will never be ready.*

Josephine smiled up at him sunnily. "Yes, Docteur."

Charcot looked out at the audience, one dark brow quirked as he pulled his tuning fork and stylus from his apron pocket. "As I've said," he noted. "Eager to please."

It wouldn't even occur to him that I'd dare to defy him, she'd said.

For some reason, I found myself shivering again, though the crowd rippled with excited-sounding laughter. Then Charcot lifted his stylus. The room fell silent again as, rapping the metal rod against his tuning fork, the doctor held the vibrating instrument to Josephine's pale ear.

"*Sleep,*" he intoned.

Immediately, Josephine's chin sank onto her chest.

"I am going to ask you some questions now," Charcot went on. "I want you to answer them honestly and directly."

"Yes, Docteur," she said. Like her posture, her voice was the one she always used in the lethargic stage of hypnosis: slow and heavy, its consonants thick. As though she were speaking around a mouthful of cotton. If she was feigning, she was doing an exceptional job of it.

"What," he asked, "is your name?"

"Josephine," she slurred.

"And where are you from?"

She shook her head. "I can't remember," she said. "I can't remember a lot of things."

"That is perfectly fine," Charcot replied. "Can you tell us a little about yourself from what you do remember? What, for instance, is your favorite color?"

"Green," she said without hesitation, smoothing the fabric of her skirt. "Emerald green. Like my dress."

"It's lovely indeed," he told her in a tone he might have used to compliment Madame Chambon on her doll-daughter. "Very becoming."

"Thank you, Docteur." Josephine dropped her gaze modestly.

"I'm sure," he went on, "that your sweethearts must like you very well in that dress."

"Sweethearts?" Josephine's brow puckered. "Oh, I don't have any sweethearts."

"Really?" Charcot feigned consternation. "Surely such a pretty young lady as yourself has scores of suitors!" He paused, studying her for an extra moment. "Perhaps," he said, "one even gave you that necklace."

I felt my heart skip. But Josephine merely shook her head, laughing a little. "Oh no. It is only paste, you see. Like the one in that story. I have no suitors. I have no interest in such things."

I glanced back at the marquis. His wet, red smile had widened in satisfaction, as though Josephine had just declared her passion for him directly. Charcot, however, seemed to think nothing of the response. "No suitors?" he repeated. "Ah, I see. Perhaps I was confusing you with someone else." He gave his audience a knowing glance before continuing: "One more request, if you please, mademoiselle."

"Of course."

"I would like," he said, "for you to give me your hand. Your right one, if you please."

Josephine dutifully extended her hand. Charcot took it, examining it in the light as if searching for some sign of illness. Then, lifting his stylus, he pressed its point into the skin of her palm.

"Ah!" she exclaimed, snatching the hand back and holding it protectively across her chest.

"Did that hurt you?"

"It—startled me," Josephine replied. "I wasn't expecting it."

"I apologize," he said crisply. "But I wanted to establish that you have full sensation in that extremity, and this was the most direct way to do it. And now, mademoiselle, I am going to count to five. When I reach three, you will fall into a deep sleep. I will then snap my fingers. When I do so, you—Josephine—will remain asleep. But you will allow Mademoiselle Jeanne to be introduced to our audience."

So far, he seemed to see nothing awry with Josephine's responses—and to be truthful, even I still couldn't tell whether she was actually hypnotized. But if she wasn't, he was sure to know within the next few seconds. I wanted nothing more than to shut my eyes and cover my ears during that interim, to block out whatever was coming next. But Charcot was already counting—*Un . . . deux . . .* By the time he'd intoned "*Cinq*," Josephine's head had fallen forward, her eyes fluttered shut. She looked as serene and untroubled as she had last night, asleep in my arms.

Charcot stared down at her almost fondly. For a moment, he almost looked like a father gazing down at a sleeping daughter. Then, placing his hand by her ear, he snapped his fingers.

At first Josephine didn't move. Then, drowsily, she lifted her head. Opening her eyes, she stretched her arms languorously toward the ceiling, her hands clenching tightly into fists.

"Oh," she drawled. "I must have fallen asleep. How rude of me."

Her face still had that strange, almost preternatural flatness to it. But her posture was more relaxed, her voice lower, huskier. Her countenance had changed as well, the chin slightly tucked. I glanced back at Londe's screen. I hadn't imagined it; she looked uncannily like the second image now. Like *Olympia*.

"You did indeed," Charcot was saying. He was once more circling her chair, examining her minutely with his hawk's eye, as if she were an entirely new patient to him. "Can you give us your name, please?"

A low, purring laugh. "My *name*, monsieur?" Josephine repeated. "Why, you know my name. It's Jeanne. We spent the afternoon together yesterday, you and I. Along with your merry little band of interns." She turned slightly in her chair, appearing to survey the amphitheater with unfocused eyes. "And that fascinating visitor of yours. The *author*. Is he here now?"

"He is, in fact." Looking bemused, Charcot indicated the man Josephine had pointed out to me at the beginning of the lecture.

"Oh! *Bonjouuuur*, monsieur," Josephine called, fluttering her pale fingers as if greeting a neighbor from a window.

The audience rippled again with amusement as the writer offered a self-conscious smile, politely touching the rim of his hat.

"Now that we've established that," Charcot said dryly, "I would like to ask you a few questions. Please answer them as honestly and directly as you can."

Josephine quirked a brow. "I'll try," she said. There was a distinct hint of sarcasm in her voice, though if Charcot noticed it he chose to disregard it.

"You say your first name is Jeanne," he continued. "What is your family name?"

"We discussed this yesterday. I couldn't recall it then, and I can't recall it now. Why, Doctor, I half believe you weren't *listening*! Do you make a practice of that—of not *listening* to your patients?"

Now she sounded as though she was taunting him outright. Still, Charcot appeared unruffled as always. "As I said," he told his audience, "Mademoiselle Jeanne is more assertive than her dominant counterpart—with a significantly quicker temper. Such temperamental differences are not unusual in these cases. Perhaps, at least," he said, turning back to Josephine, "you can recall your favorite color for us? Is it green?"

Josephine shuddered. "I can't stand green. It makes me think of frogs. *Slimy* frogs."

"What *is* your favorite color, then?"

"My favorite?" Reaching up, Josephine touched her necklace with her forefinger. "It depends. On some days it's silver. Some days, gold."

I shot another look at the marquis—and immediately wished I had not. He was chuckling along with the audience, eyes gleaming, perhaps at the thought of having two Josephines to summon at whim, rather than one.

"Do you get jewelry from your sweethearts, then?" Charcot was continuing. "Surely a lovely girl such as yourself has an admirer or two."

"Admirers?" Tipping her head back, Josephine let loose a throaty laugh. "Perhaps one or two," she said coyly, her eyes darting to where I sat. "But I wouldn't want to get anyone in trouble."

I felt my face flush. Charcot, however, just nodded again, as if she'd passed a test to his satisfaction. "As you can see," he said, briefly directing his gaze toward the audience, "Mademoiselle Jeanne is more overtly flirtatious than Josephine. Such coquettishness is another trait often found in hysterics, along with the sort of vanity we're also witnessing. Very well," he said, addressing Josephine. "Now, mademoiselle. I would like you to lift your right arm for us."

With a faint shrug, Josephine extended her arm like a queen proffering her hand to be kissed. My unease stirred again, a brittle shift in my gut.

"Thank you," Charcot said. He patted his pocket, frowning slightly. "If you'll recall," he told his viewers, "I mentioned earlier that Josephine arrived at the Salpêtrière with pronounced hemianesthesia—that is, a lack of physical sensation on the right side of her body. She also presented with a reduced ability to smell with her right nostril and to taste on the right side of her tongue. She has since regained feeling in that part of her body, as well as full olfactory and gustative sensibilities. Note, however, that these symptoms have not *disappeared*. They have merely been transferred to her subservient personality—

Jeanne. In a moment we shall have her take a little stroll for us, to confirm her left foot is no longer contracted. First, however, we will once more test her hand. As you will recall, Josephine presented with full physical sensitivity on her right side. Jeanne, as we will see, will not."

He patted his pocket again, fumbling once more for his stylus—or so I assumed. The truth is, I was so fixated on the prospect of Josephine's having to walk without limping that I was staring at her skirts, trying to discern whether her ankle was straight or torqued. It was only when I looked back at Charcot that I saw that he *wasn't* taking out his stylus, but the black roll of felt in which he kept his surgical needles. To my horror, he selected one that was easily the length of my own hand.

"This needle," he said, holding it up so it glinted in the stage light, "could cause a person with normal neural responses significant pain. In the case of a patient suffering from anesthesia, however— including hysterically induced anesthesia—it can be introduced from the top of the hand, between the second and third metacarpals, and back out through the palm without causing the slightest discomfort. As you shall see."

Josephine seemed to register none of this; her gaze had returned to somewhere past the audience, and it remained there as Charcot took her hand in his, poising the needle directly below the ridge of her knuckles. Then, all of a sudden, she gave a violent start, leaping to her feet.

"No!" she exclaimed. *"No!"*

"What are you doing?" Claudine whispered, and only then did I realize I'd leapt to my feet as well.

"He's *hurting* her," I hissed. "Can't you hear her?"

"He's not!" Claudine retorted indignantly. "He's a *doctor*! Besides, he's not even touching her!"

And in fact, when I turned back to the stage, Charcot was no longer holding Josephine's hand. But she was still shaking her head frantically, her fingers clutching at her waist, her protest now a full-throated cry of protest. *"No!"* she screamed. *"No no no,* leave me *alone!"* Taking a step back, she landed fully on her contracted foot, staggering precariously before catching herself, her terror-glazed gaze still fixed on the back of the auditorium.

Throughout her outburst, Charcot had stood motionless, needle glinting in his grip. I saw him following her gaze, briefly scanning the back of the amphitheater as well. Heart pounding in my throat, I did the same. I saw nothing unusual, only a handful of ordinary-looking spectators who'd arrived too late to find seats.

I glanced back at Josephine apprehensively. She'd sunk to her knees by this point, and was gripping at her hair with both her hands, as though trying desperately to rip it from her skull. Then, abruptly, her body went rigid, and her eyes rolled up into her head. Falling onto the floor, she began to convulse and vibrate with such force it seemed she was being shaken by some unseen being, the emerald pendant jerking and bouncing against her skin like a thing possessed.

"My God," I cried. "*Help* her! Somebody, help her!" Unable to bear it any longer, I ran to her at last, kneeling, pulling her trembling head onto my lap. I was vaguely aware of Babinski hurrying over as well. Pushing me aside, he knelt beside the seizing girl, plunging a fist into her abdominal area. Usually this stopped Josephine's seizures within a few seconds. But she continued grunting and thrashing, the back of her skull slamming against the floor until I pulled it into my lap again.

"Josephine," I said, desperately. "*Josephine*. It's all right. It's all right—stop. *Stop!*"

I couldn't tell if she heard me. But as I continued crooning and Babinski continued pressing her abdomen, the convulsions slowed, and then finally stopped. She lay limp-limbed in their wake, her face gray, her hair matted and darkened with perspiration. For a second or two I feared she'd fallen unconscious.

Then her lashes fluttered. With a low moan, she opened her eyes. She reached for her pendant, clutching it as though it were a talisman.

"It's him, Laure," she gasped, peering up at me. "He's here."

"Who?" I asked, though I already knew who—knew the only "he" it could be.

I looked back again toward the auditorium's rear, the spot where she'd claimed to have seen the judge "melting into the wall" in the past. There was still no one there.

I leaned over, feeling my scalp prickle slightly as I did. "There's no one," I said quietly, my lips close to her ear. "It's only your mind playing tricks again. Remember what we talked about—what is *true*."

"It *is* true," she said, her tone shrill with fear. Her expression was terrified, stricken. "I *saw* him, Laure. He's really here. He's come for me at last."

Chapter Sixteen

"Who's come? What's she saying?"

Babinski had been holding on to Josephine's wrist, concentratedly monitoring her pulse. Now, though, he was staring at me, his dark eyes narrowed.

"Who?" he repeated. "What's she talking about?"

"Nothing," I said, throwing Josephine a warning glance. "She's dazed from the fit. She's not making any sense."

She truly wasn't, and it was beginning to frighten me almost as much as her recurring delusion was clearly frightening her. *How could this be happening?* I thought. She'd seemed so confident last night, assuring me that my findings at the judge's house were just what she needed, that she knew now how to keep her head when and if she saw him. And yet she wasn't keeping her head at all now. In fact, she looked more distraught than I'd ever seen her outside of her fits. Almost as though she was going—

I stopped myself. *No. Don't even think it.*

"Listen," she was gasping as I helped her as she struggled to sit up, her back warm and damp from her involuntary exertions. "You must listen, Laure. I saw him. He's here."

Struggling to tamp down my panic, I turned to Babinski. "I need to get her back to her room. She didn't sleep last night. Nightmares again."

The rest of the amphitheater had erupted into pandemonium, a chaotic jumble of urgent whispers, excited chatter, scattered laughter. A few people appeared to be leaving, in either confusion or disgust. Charcot, however, remained where he'd been, staring out over the sea of bobbing heads. His expression struck me as both baleful and appalled, as if he were taking in the sight of his fifth-arrondissement mansion after someone set it ablaze.

"Stay here," Babinski instructed. "Let me see how he wants to proceed." Dropping Josephine's wrist, he climbed to his feet and hurried over to join his mentor.

I nodded. But the minute the tall intern's back was turned, I helped Josephine to her feet. With a cautious glance over my shoulder, I began walking her away, my spine tingling in anticipation of being stopped and summoned back. By some miracle, though, we weren't, and over the next few minutes I managed to get Josephine off the stage, past a bewildered-looking Claudine and Félicie ("Is it always like this?" Félicie asked as I passed), and into the darkened corridor to the back exit. Josephine stumbled beside me without protest, her eyes unfocused and her face still that frightening shade of grayish white as I struggled to think of what was likely to happen next, what we should do. This had to be Charcot's biggest stage disaster yet—far worse than the debacle Rosalie had sparked. At minimum he'd want to examine Josephine now, question her as he had Rosalie. And in Josephine's current state, that could prove catastrophic—even if she wasn't, as I feared, going mad before my eyes. For Charcot would find out she'd feigned her trance. In fact, he almost certainly knew already—he couldn't have missed the fact that her foot had still been contracted, even when she was supposedly being "Jeanne."

Glancing at her damp, wan face, I wracked my brain for a solution—or at least a plan. Should we simply flee now? Could I even consider taking her through the streets of Paris in this condition? Babette and the doctors would notice our disappearance almost immediately; there was no way around that now. But I could see no other options, beyond confessing everything to Charcot and praying for a mercy that he'd almost certainly withhold.

We'd have to try, I decided. There'd be no time to get Josephine out of her eye-catching stage dress—no time to disguise her in any way at all, other than perhaps by having her wear my bonnet to cover her hair. But if I could get her back to the room, retrieve the hat, bracelet, and my savings, and we were lucky enough to catch a hansom right outside the gate, we might have a chance of getting to the station. Once we did, the midday Friday rush might provide enough cover to board a train together—if not one to Dijon, then one going somewhere else, somewhere far enough from the city that we'd have a chance to catch our breath and regroup.

Behind us, Charcot seemed to have recovered himself enough to speak again. "Gentlemen!" I heard him boom. "While this development has been . . . unexpected, I ask you to keep in mind that hysteria by its very *nature* is a disease that defies expectation. The experienced clinician must train himself to seek out the order within the chaos, to find the one diagnosis that makes sense of a thousand seemingly nonsensical symptoms."

Something about his voice sounded strangely desperate to me, like that of a hawker at a market stall at the end of the day, trying to rid himself of surplus product. It was a thought so completely at odds with the great man's genius that—as always—my instinct was to dismiss it. But fast on its heels came another realization, this one so outright treasonous it nearly stopped me in my tracks. As we continued stumbling toward the exit I turned it over in my head, stunned as much by its audacity as by my absolute certainty that it was true: Jean-Martin Charcot may well have been the most brilliant mind in France, if not the world. He may have solved the mysteries of myriad baffling diseases. But when it came to hysteria, he was wrong—completely, utterly wrong.

He had no idea what he was talking about at all.

Josephine was still trembling as we made our way down the gravel path, past the garden where barely three hours earlier she'd announced her disastrous plan. I still had no better plan myself than somehow getting her to the train station, once we'd collected our things from our room. Thankfully, she let me hurry her along to the extent that I could. But when we reached Esquirol she balked.

"No," she said, hanging back from the double doors and glancing fearfully in the direction of the amphitheater. "I won't be safe there. Don't you see? He'll know that this is where to find me. We have to find somewhere *safe*. Please, Laure!"

"Josephine," I said, slowly, desperately. "I promise you. He's not alive. He can't be. That's why I went back to his house. Remember what I found there—the blood? The funeral notice? He's *dead*. Try to focus on that, like we discussed."

"I *tried*, Laure!" She was all but wailing now. "It didn't help—I still saw him. He's dead, but he's here anyway. Either it's his ghost, or I've really gone mad." She stopped, pressing her palms against her closed eyes as if she might press the heinous hallucination from her memory. "He's making me pay. I know it. He's making me pay for what I did to him."

When she dropped her hands again she was crying, tears spilling onto her cheeks in two wet streams that she made no move to wipe away. "I should have drowned myself when I had the chance. It's so clear what has happened—what was always going to happen. Don't you see? Even here, I was trapped by him from the very beginning— as trapped as I was in that cursed house." Squeezing her eyes shut, she leaned weakly against the sandstone wall of the ancient building. I stared at her, aghast. I'd never seen her cry like this before. Quiet, despairing. Completely lucid.

"It's just your illness," I said at last, struggling to keep the desperation out of my own voice. "It's just—it's just all the mesmerism. Listen to me. *It wasn't him*. We need to—"

We need to go, I was going to tell her. *We need to go right now*. But before I could finish, I heard heavy steps on the gravel behind us. "*Alors, Princesse!*" I heard. "Not so fast!"

Oh no, I thought.

I glanced over my shoulder to see the Basque striding toward us. "Where are you taking the *rousse*?" he asked jovially.

"She needs to rest," I said, reaching protectively for Josephine's arm. "I'm taking her upstairs."

"No, you're not." He stepped deftly around Josephine so he stood between us and the building's entrance. I tried to move past him—first to the left, then the right—but he blocked us each time like a goalkeeper, his infuriating grin never wavering.

"I've no time for this, Claude," I said through gritted teeth.

"This isn't about *your* convenience," he said. "It isn't about you at all." He reached again for Josephine's arm. She flailed away from him, as though his thick fingers burned her skin.

"Don't *touch* me!" she cried. "Laure! Don't let him *touch* me!"

"What's the matter with you?" Trying to keep my voice from shaking, I tried slapping the attendant's hairy hand away, but he didn't loosen his grip. "Have you lost what little mind you might have in that ugly skull of yours? I need to take her to her room."

His grin cinched at the corners, becoming more of a snarl. "I'm to take her to the softs."

"The softs?" My stomach seemed to drop toward my feet. *Of course.* It was what Charcot had done with Rosalie after she'd sabotaged his lecture—he'd kept her there for more than two days. He did know Josephine had tried to trick him. He'd probably known from the start—from the moment her chin dropped to her chest in "sleep." And of course, now he was so determined to punish her that he'd given the order to come after us before the lecture was even officially over.

"Laure!" Josephine's voice was shrill with panic. "Laure, you can't let him take me. You can't. . . ."

"It's all right," I told her unsteadily. "I'll come with you. I'll talk to them. I'll—"

"You'll stay here," the Basque interrupted brusquely. "My orders are to bring her alone."

"Alone?" I repeated. "But Dr. Marie always lets—"

"Marie has nothing to do with it." All but picking Josephine up off the ground, the Basque began half leading, half dragging her toward Lunacy. She struggled against him wildly as she had in Feeding, trying to slip from his grasp, to scratch his face, to plunge her booted toe between his legs. But either she was too weak, or he'd learned enough from that encounter to keep her firmly in hand. Throwing one beefy arm around her, he pinned her arms to her sides and began marching her toward Rambuteau.

"Wait!" I cried, leaping after them. "I'll help you," I said breathlessly. "She'll—she'll go more quietly if I come along. She always does. It'll be easier."

He slapped my fingers off as casually as though slapping away a mosquito or gnat. "Sorry, Princesse. My orders are for one hysteric. Not two. And worst case, I've got enough ether here to keep her in line." He patted his apron pocket. "Besides," he added, winking. "It doesn't really matter if she's quiet or not, does it? It's the softs. No one'll hear her either way."

He held my gaze, a leering smile on his face. Then he dropped his eyes to the marquis's pendant.

"Nice necklace," he said, enunciating each syllable as though it were a spoon he was licking. "Looks expensive."

I stared at him, understanding slamming into me like a wall of ice. He wasn't here for Charcot. His "orders" had come from the marquis.

It was true then; he was in the nobleman's pay. And now he'd come to bring his master what he wanted.

In that instant, it was as if every story I'd told myself—every small, false hope I'd used to keep going, to somehow get us to the very edge of escape—guttered out like so many spent candles. The world went black despite the day's early-summer brightness, and I stood there, sealed into the dark.

For looking from the Basque's arrogant black eyes to Josephine's terrified green ones, I now understood the devastating choice I had to make. It was no longer between staying here with Josephine or going to Amélie with her. It was between Josephine herself—and my sister. Between Josephine, in fact, and the whole life I'd been envisioning for myself with Amélie. And it really was no choice at all. For if I tried to stay, what would it accomplish? Josephine was doubly doomed. Not only was she very possibly losing her mind, but she was squarely in the sights of two powerful men who had different versions of hell for her. One sought to subjugate her body for physical pleasure, the other her mind for professional gain. Inevitably, she would fight them both. Equally inevitably, she would lose. And if I tried to intervene, the marquis would follow through on his threat. I'd end up in prison. And likely as not, I would never see Amélie—or Josephine—again.

"*Laure?*" Josephine was crying now as Claude wrestled her away. "Do something! Why aren't you *doing* something? Don't leave me with him!"

Move, I thought. *I have to help her.*

But I was fixed as firmly in place as if I'd sprouted roots. I stood there like that, hideously immobile, as her screams turned into full-on screeches, that otherworldly mix of falcon and banshee that, years later, I'd always think I'd heard when she first arrived: *No no no don't TOUCH me,* and *I will kill myself,* and *Laure, don't leave me, please don't leave me, please please oh God please. . . .*

And then, abruptly, she went silent. When I looked up again I realized that the Basque must have dosed her, for he had her in his arms like a sleeping child. He gave me one last gloating grin over his shoulder before striding away, a soldier transporting the spoils of battle. I stared after them both mutely until he'd turned onto allée Rambuteau with her, toward the softs. Out of my sight.

Chapter Seventeen

The chapel bells began their dolorous noonday tolling. *Move,* I thought again, *just move, you must move.* And yet still I could not, even as the word *move* became as metallic and meaningless as the chiming, which seemed in that moment to go on forever.

It wasn't until the last ring had echoed into nothingness that I finally pushed my trembling limbs back into motion. I shuffled first toward the Esquirol doors, mainly because they were there. But the thought of encountering Babette—of being questioned, as I surely would be—stopped me after only a few leaden steps. Then I saw Marie rounding the infirmary corner, striding purposefully toward Hysteria.

Turning away, I hurried off in the opposite direction—toward the reformatory school and the kitchen. With each trembling step I reminded myself that I'd had no choice, that I was as caught in the marquis's web as Josephine was. It dawned on me, in fact, that there was no way now for me to even leave for Dijon on my own, for mad or not, Josephine would surely tell someone where I'd gone. Moreover, now that the marquis had his knobby hands on her, he'd assume I was willingly in his service, would want me there to keep delivering her to him on demand. And when he was done with her—probably when she, like Rosalie, had been transferred to Lunacy—he'd have me handle the next hysteric who caught his fancy. The only way to escape him, and prison, was to do his bidding for now. That meant betraying Josephine not just this once, but over and over again, until either she succumbed entirely to her madness or his twisted interest in the damaged women of the hysteria ward was replaced by whatever foul fancy came next.

The idea was nauseating, unthinkable—especially after the revelatory sweetness of the night we'd just spent together, the breathless optimism we'd shared in the garden just a few hours earlier. And yet, I thought wretchedly, I had no choice—not if I was to see Amélie again. *No choice. I have no choice.* The words became a kind of dull drumroll and I a toy soldier, marching mechanically and unthinkingly to their cadence. I don't think I was fully aware of where it was I was heading until I found myself passing through the asylum cemetery, with its unmarked crosses the color of weathered bones, steps away from where Père Julien had left the chapel's heavy oaken door propped open as he often did on warm summer days.

Inside, I found the nave as empty as I'd found the asylum grounds; but for lazily floating dust motes illuminated by the chapel's single stained glass window, all was utterly still. The only other human figures in sight were those of Mary, Christ, and the assorted saints, tucked into their worn sandstone niches. Surveying them from the threshold, I had the passing thought that they actually seemed more alive—and more human—than I felt. I listened. But beyond the faint sounds of conversation outside, the only sound I made out was that of my own thudding heartbeat. Following an urge I had no energy to question, I kicked the lamb-shaped doorstop from the door, watching dully as the latter swung heavily shut.

Then, throwing my gaze up toward the aged and sand-colored cupola, I opened my mouth—and screamed.

I screamed until my head ached, until my throat was raw and tears streamed down my stinging cheeks. I screamed to drown out my searing shame over my helplessness, over the way I'd let a wicked man turn my own cowardice into the very chains that now rendered me helpless. I screamed to fill the scorched abyss of all my losses—

not just my family, but all the failed futures I'd envisioned for myself: Daughter of two loving parents. Daughter of a respected doctor. Sister of Amélie, soon to be living happily with her in Morvan. Along with my best friend—and now lover—Josephine. The most extraordinary girl I'd ever met.

My eyes were still squeezed shut, but I suddenly saw her again: *Josephine*. Not wild and delusional, as I'd just left her. But as she'd looked last night, after our union; lying in my arms, her heart-shaped face limned in moonlight. Her skin coated in my scent, and mine in hers. Just before she'd drifted off, I'd reached a wondering hand up to touch her hair as it lay with mine on the pillow. Iron and copper, intermingled.

"What is it like?" I asked her.

"What?" she murmured.

"To be beautiful."

I'd expected her to protest the compliment, or at least smile self-consciously. She did neither. She thought a moment, seemingly in earnest.

"I hate it, mostly," she said at last.

"*Hate* it?" I repeated. "Why?"

She sighed. "Men want to possess you. Women want to dismiss you. Everyone wants to claim you in some way."

"So you don't want it?" I was incredulous. "You don't want your beauty?"

"I don't want *that*," she said wearily. "To be constantly claimed by strangers."

"What do you want?"

Reaching over, she put a finger on my cheek, stroking down to my jawline, to my chin, to the dimpled hollow of my neck.

"I want *you* to claim me," she'd said. "Only you." And then she'd pulled me to her again.

The memory was so fresh, so close, that at that moment the words seemed to reverberate in the dust-scented air. It was only as they faded that the realization hit me, as devastating and disorienting as the retort of a secretly planted bomb: that all of my losses, and in fact *all of them taken together*, were dwarfed by the catastrophe of losing Josephine.

And I had lost her, of course, utterly, completely. Mad or not, the minute she woke up and saw the marquis, she would know the full extent of my duplicity. He'd tell her about the necklace, and she would realize I'd not only lied to her but had actively collaborated in her violation. That, intentionally or not, I'd served her up to him like a lamb on a platter, exchanging her trust and faith, her husky laughter, her brushing touch and whispered wisdom, for—for what? For a handful of blue jewels.

She'd resist the noble, of course. This might catch him off guard at first; he clearly expected his advances to be as welcomed as they had been with Rosalie. But I doubted Josephine would hold him off for long, given both her ether-weakened state and the ruthlessness I'd sensed during my own abduction by the man. She might end up as bruised and beaten as she'd been when she arrived here. She might even end up dead, her brain and body further desecrated by the doctor's scalpels, before being buried in the cemetery beneath a blank cross. Even if she did survive, though, she would never forgive me. Not ever.

And she'd be right not to.

I don't know how long I stood like that, my eyes shut, my heart aching like a raw wound, and my own scream still ringing in my ears. I listened for Père Julien's heavy footsteps, or the slower shuffle of his half-deaf bell ringer. But no one came. There was only a faint fluttering somewhere in the rafters, some bird or bat startled by my despair.

I made my way to one of the pews, slumping onto the seat and staring up at the various dilapidated versions of Mary ornamenting the altar and nearby alcoves. She'd been captured by her sculptors in all stages of her life: Over Père Julien's confessional, she appeared as a young girl, gazing demurely up at her own mother, Saint Anne. Beneath the sanctuary window she appeared twice: first as a pregnant Virgin, staring down in serene wonderment at her miraculously seeded womb. Then in middle age, kneeling beside her dying Son. The way the two statues had been arranged—the pregnant Mary above the older, her arms extended in a gesture of joyous welcome— it looked as though the younger Virgin was blissfully contemplating her own bereft future, opening her arms to her impending misery. Middle-aged Mary seemed barely more perturbed by her heartrending circumstances, something I'd always found nearly as bewildering as the idea of her immaculate Conception. For surely it had to be excruciating to watch someone you love—a child, no less—die in such a savage and brutal way: nailed to a cross, organs ravaged by spear tips, ears ringing with malicious insults and jeers. It had to be worse—far worse—than facing a few years in Saint-Lazare with the knowledge that your one surviving family member was alive and well.

And yet as she gazed down at her perishing firstborn, the Madone's expression was resigned, even serene. As though she fully accepted the brutal predicament in which she now found herself. As though the loss of her Son was a mere extension of her love for Him, a sacrifice she was more than willing to make so He could return, resplendent in His divinity.

As I stared at her now, the worn mother of God with the blank eyes and the faintly chipped nose, the full extent of my own failure seemed to build within me, a cold, hard boulder of self-loathing and shame. Mary had sacrificed her Son—arguably, the one perfect man in all of humankind's existence—so He could ascend to heaven and mend a broken world. I hadn't even been able to sacrifice my own physical freedom to protect the person I loved most of all. Instead, I'd sent her—a girl who'd brought meaning and purpose and even joy into my bleak and suffocating little universe—to hell. Or at least, to the closest thing to it on earth she herself could have imagined. I'd done it to escape prison, and the prospect of a life alone there, without my sister. Only now did I see that I'd merely consigned myself to a different kind of isolation, a different prison. To the monstrous specter of my own selfishness and treachery.

"What do I do?" I whispered, fixing my gaze on Mary's calm countenance. "How do I save her?"

As if in answer, I heard a burst of throaty cooing somewhere above me, followed by the sound of desperate fluttering. Looking up, I saw something was hurling itself at the window over the younger Mary's head, flailing and scrabbling against the pink-and-purple mosaic before flapping off in the direction of the doorway.

It was a pigeon, one of the many that found their way into the chapel and belfry. As the creature swooped its way across the chamber, though, a ray of sun burst through the small circular window, briefly limning it in tinted light. I saw then that it was the last of Rosalie's *beaux bébés,* the one whose tail feathers she'd dyed a garish purple. Cooing convulsively, it flew to the door I'd shut, hitting it with a *thud* before tumbling to the flagstones. I caught my breath, afraid it had concussed or even killed itself. But it quickly righted itself, stalking to and fro before the threshold as if waiting for an important delivery there.

Another thing I've trapped, I thought miserably.

As if hearing the thought, the bird jerked its gaze up. Then it fluttered back toward the apse, landing squarely on the younger Virgin's veiled head and peering at me with eyes the color of bright copper.

Heaving myself to my feet, I made my way back to the chapel door and pulled it open.

"Come," I said. "You can go now."

The pigeon cocked its head inquisitively, as though weighing this invitation.

"Come," I called again. "Don't you see? You can *leave.*"

With a whir of its wings, it left its virginal post, flapping back through the nave, over my head, out into the daylight. I shielded my eyes as it made a swooping southern arc toward boulevard de l'Hôpital, before abruptly turning north, toward Hysteria.

And just like that, I knew what I had to do.

———

I was back at Esquirol moments later. As I flew by the building's front courtyard, the *reposantes* glanced up from their knitting in bemusement. "Eh, fuck off, Laure," Tante Maubert called genially. "There's no fire in the fucking lake!"

I raced past them, pushing through the double doors of the building, finally stumbling into Hysteria in a clatter of slammed doors and staggering steps. Babette was standing by the nurse's station with Marie. As I burst through the entranceway, the two of them turned to face me. The old nurse's brow creased with displeasure as I drew up short beside them both, the steel of my corset digging damply into the undersides of my breasts.

"Laure," she snapped. "Where on earth have you been? I've had Julienne out looking for you." Craning her neck in a way faintly reminiscent of the pigeon, she peered around me expectantly. "Where is Josephine?"

"He has her," I said, still gasping for air. "He took her from me, and now he has her."

"What?" Babette snapped. "What are you talking about? Who? Where is Josephine? The director wants to see her—see *both* of you—immediately in his office."

"He has her," I repeated, still panting. "The marquis. He *has* her. He was blackmailing me. Over the bracelet."

"What bracelet? What are you going on about now?"

It was my last chance, I realized—I could still take it back, save myself. But I didn't. I barely stopped to take a much-needed breath. "The sapphire bracelet. The one the marquis tried to give Rosalie. I never returned it. I kept it for myself. And the marquis found out. He told me he'd have me thrown in prison if I didn't—if I didn't give him time alone with Josephine."

As what I was saying registered, the old woman's expression shifted from confusion to disgust to a kind of vicious glee. "I *knew* it," she said. "I knew that man was a scoundrel. And *you*—I knew about *you* from the moment I first saw you. Doctor's daughter or not, I told them—"

"Josephine," Marie interjected, roughly pushing the old woman aside. "Where is she *right now*?"

"Claude took her," I said. "He's been in the marquis's pay. He said he was taking her to the softs."

We raced together across the grounds toward Rambuteau, Marie's long thin legs and arms pumping in a way that might in another situation have been almost comical, his apron strings fluttering behind him like small white flags. Babette kept nearly apace with him, her seamed face somehow both grim and gleeful. I stumbled ahead of them both, my lungs aching, the words *I'm sorry* and *Please hold on* and *We're coming, we are coming* and *Please please don't let it be too late* filling my head like unspoken prayer. And yet I remember thinking—as we rushed back past the baths and the *chalets des folles* and the front entrance to the amphitheater, around which a few straggling audience members clustered in small, gossipy groups—that it was taking *too long*, that my feet weren't moving quickly enough, that I was in one of those dreams where the ground slickens like unmarred ice and the air thickens like aspic and it's impossible to get traction or make headway or even breathe.

I flung myself into Lunacy like a shipwreck survivor reaching land, bursting through the weighted double doors and barely noticing that the attendants who normally stood guard by them were nowhere to be found. Stumbling onto the basement level, I careened around the corner, bracing myself for the sight of the Basque. When I reached the corridor, though, it was unexpectedly empty—and so dark that I drew up short again, as if I were about to run into a pitch-black wall.

Normally, the isolation ward was lit by the kerosene lamps that hung at intervals on the walls, flickering at a low flame both day and night. Today, however, someone—Claude, I guessed—had doused them all, save for one faint light that I at first couldn't locate.

I heard Marie's footsteps on the stairwell behind me, Babette following like an off-rhythm echo. The two pulled up short behind me,

Marie exclaiming in consternation as he registered the strange gloom. "What the devil?" he muttered. "Where's—"

"He's not here," I said. "No one is."

And yet as my eyes adjusted further, I realized I didn't know if this was true, for I'd now traced the faintly flickering light to its source. It was coming from within one of the cells, the door to which had been left slightly ajar: number three. The same cell to which I'd brought Josephine's breakfast that first day we met. Which made no sense; the soft cell doors were almost always kept closed and locked and—by Charcot's decree—free of lamps, out of concern that the oilcloth that covered their floors and walls might catch fire.

"Where is she?" Babette rasped, catching up with us both. "Where's Claude?"

Marie and Babette trailing in my wake, I took a trembling step toward the cell, my scalp tingling with a sudden, cold premonition: We *were* too late. I'd failed her. I'd open the door to find Josephine lying on the cell's padded floor, delusional or unconscious. Or worse.

"Josephine?" I called quietly.

There was no answer.

Pulse skittering, I pulled the door all the way open. Once more, it took a moment for my eyes to adjust. When they did, I gasped in dismay. For yes, there she was, stretched out on the floor. A green gleam of silk, lying motionless, arms spread wide.

Then, though, I looked more closely and saw it wasn't Josephine after all. It was her stage dress—the green gown we'd bought at La Samaritaine together. It had been laid out so that the skirt was full and smooth, the flattened arms opened to embrace the low, dirty ceiling. Next to the dress lay her corset, stays, and petticoat, all neatly folded. Beside these was a pair of expensive-looking men's leather boots arranged so that the toes pointed out—like those of a dancer in first position.

I was still processing this bizarre tableau when Marie and Babette caught up with me. "Good God," Marie said in a tone of disgust mixed with confusion. "Who on earth is *that?*"

"No one," I said. "It's her dress."

It was only after I'd said it that I saw where he was looking. Not at the gown, but in the same darkened corner of the cell where I'd first seen Josephine herself.

Only now it wasn't Josephine who was standing there, motionless, flickeringly backlit by a wall lamp that had been set on the floor. It was a man—and not the man I'd expected to find here. His face was familiar but so utterly different from the marquis's that it took me a moment to place its features: The small and piggishly wide-set brown eyes. The crooked nose and sallow skin. The cleft chin beneath the sparse, scraggly beard.

It was Josephine's judge, the same man I'd seen yesterday, in the portrait hanging in that horrible office.

Or rather, it was the same man—and yet not the same. For while the portrait's subject had been finely and fully dressed, the man in front of us was not. There was no sign of his trousers, shirt, or jacket. He wore only a white silk undervest—through which I made out the bumpy outlines of a bandage—and white hose, which he'd apparently soiled. He was also standing awkwardly, with most of his weight on his right leg.

And there was another difference as well: In the painting, the judge's expression had been amused and somewhat haughty, the eyes narrowed, the lips curved in a cold smile. Now, though, his face was as flat and lifeless as if an iron had passed across it. His eyes were wide and unblinking, the pupils dilated. They remained so as Marie cautiously approached him, as the young doctor waved a hand before the man's stone-still face, then pressed two fingers beneath his ear, feeling for his pulse.

When Marie turned back to us, his own expression was shocked, almost disoriented. I knew what he was going to say before he said it.

"My God," he breathed. "He's been hypnotized."

It was true: Josephine's rapist was utterly, helplessly entranced.

Epilogue

It's hard to say who was most shaken by that surreal scene. I heard Babette cry out, a harsh, confused squawk that quickly turned into below-breath mutterings about *rousse* harlots and witchcraft. I saw Marie's confusion turn to alarm as he tried frantically to awaken the judge, murmuring and then cajoling and then outright shouting into the man's ear, clapping his hands, waving his medical mirror before the unseeing little eyes.

For my own part, of all the bizarre sights I witnessed in my time at the Salpêtrière, this was easily the strangest: the man who'd inflicted Josephine's horrific physical and mental injuries standing half naked and fully catatonic, in the same dank and filthy cell in which I'd first met her. Even now, nearly four decades later, having combed meticulously through my memories and journals and the letter I wrote that night to Amélie, I still find myself questioning whether I'm recalling the scene correctly. For what Josephine did to her attacker that afternoon was even more audacious—and less probable—than what she'd done to him in his own house: accomplishing with her mind what she hadn't with her knife.

And yet over the years, I've come to conclude that she'd not only pulled off this extraordinary feat, but that she'd been preparing to do so for weeks. This, at least in part, was why she'd so meticulously probed me on exactly *how* the doctors entranced her during each session ("How far did he count?" she'd ask. "What did his voice sound like? Where was he looking as he said this?") and why she'd listened so intently to my responses. It is also, I now believe, the real reason she resisted—or tried to resist, for to this day I still don't know—Charcot's attempts to entrance her that last day on his stage. She'd wanted to know for sure how the doctors did what they did to her, so she could correctly replicate the sequence herself. Whether she expected the judge to appear as he did is obviously another question, though it strikes me as unlikely. I think she'd believed her sightings of him were, in fact, hallucinatory, and that she was truly going mad. Which makes her escape all the more impressive to me; for even while doubting her own sanity, she'd still planned for the possibility that she *was* sane, and that at least some of those sightings might have been real.

And in the end, she was right to do so. For as Claude later confessed, Josephine really had wounded the judge that day in his office, and fairly badly. But he hadn't died. He'd fallen unconscious on top of her, both from shock and—as happens with some—from the sight of his own blood, though in her terror Josephine obviously hadn't realized this. When the man came to, both he and his wife had (as I'd speculated) wanted to avoid a public scandal. That might have drawn media attention not only to Guillaume's pattern of unsavory encounters with servants but to the staggering debts he'd accrued at Longchamp, and the high-stakes *lansquenet* games then fashionable among certain elites.

So the couple had not notified the police of the incident. They'd called a doctor, and shortly afterward dismissed their help and left for an extended stay in Nice, where Madame Guillaume's parents had a home. It was there that the judge, still recuperating from both his wound and his wounded pride, read of Josephine's improbable rise to Parisian celebrity and hatched his depraved plan to return for her. I'm not sure how he found his way to Claude—perhaps through the marquis, for it seems likely the two men knew each other. Either way, he clearly believed he'd set his trap perfectly. I can only imagine—

and often do, with great relish—how he felt upon realizing it was he who'd instead fallen into hers.

And fall he did, utterly. As it turned out, Josephine had succeeded so completely with her self-taught hypnotic technique that it took hours for the Salpêtrière doctors to bring Guillaume out of it, which they only managed by applying pressure to his left testicle. Even then, he remained disoriented and incoherent, unwilling or unable to answer any questions about what he'd planned to do to Josephine, or what had actually happened between them in their time alone together. Trembling like one of Charcot's Parkinson's patients, he shrugged on an old orderly uniform Babette brought him, refusing Charcot's offer to replace the expensive clothes Josephine had fled in, the rings she'd stripped from his fingers, or the watch and thousand francs she'd taken along with his outfit. He'd simply shuffled off, leaving the doctors in perturbed puzzlement and me wondering how I'd gotten everything so catastrophically wrong.

And I had gotten it wrong—all of it. The disastrous scope of my compounded misassumptions became clear only months later, when I read that Guillaume's bloated body had been dredged from the Seine by the Paris river police. The papers blamed the suicide on the man's aforementioned debts. But they'd also mentioned his young son, who—as is not uncommon—happened to share his father's given name, and who had died from tuberculosis just before the family left the capital. Reading that, I felt as though I myself had been plunged into the chill depths of that river. For it was clearly the son's funeral to which the note I'd found had referred, not—as I'd assumed—that of the judge himself.

None of the papers attributed the suicide to anything other than financial woes and grief. But they all printed a clue that everyone but me seemed to miss; that not only had Josephine's rapist ended his life as Josephine had tried to end hers, but he'd leapt to his death from the very same bridge from which she'd tried to do so: the Pont Neuf. I am all but certain that before fleeing that dank little room in his shirt, waistcoat, topcoat, trousers, and a hat that must have swallowed her own small head, Josephine had rid herself of her attacker—and hopefully, at least some of her own demons—by planting the grim suggestion in his miserable mind. Perhaps—who knows?—she somehow even "transferred" her own foot contraction to him as Charcot claimed to have transferred Rosalie's wrist contraction to Caroline, for I later heard the doctors discussing the fact that he'd been limping as he shambled off toward boulevard de l'Hôpital. If so, it would help explain how she managed to flee the asylum so quickly that day.

But I think it was probably Charcot who was the most stunned by the whole situation. After being summoned to the softs, he took in the strange scene, his face as leached of expression as that of the transfixed judge. I watched the color leave his face as well, as the implications of what he was seeing dawned on him: That not only had his hysterical protégée escaped him, but that she'd used his own hypnotic techniques to do it. In the process, she'd also seemingly controverted his oft-repeated theory that hysterics—and *only* hysterics—could be hypnotized in the first place. Unless, of course, the judge had been an undiagnosed hysteric as well—something we'll obviously never know.

And the marquis? Once his bracelet was returned to him, he agreed not to press charges so long as no one told his wife about his lavish lovemaking efforts. So far as I know, he never mentioned the emerald pendant to Charcot. He merely moved on to his next conquest, a so-called *petit rat* in training at the Opéra de Paris who soon seen sporting a garnet ring and matching earbobs. It's true that for months afterward the sight of a sleek black landau could send my heart straight into my mouth. But I still take immense pleasure in picturing Josephine's face when and if she brought the necklace to a pawnshop, still believing it to be paste. It may be the one lie I told her that, in retrospect, was actually a kind of gift, a happy twist on de Maupassant's bleak little story.

As for myself, the days immediately following Josephine's disappearance were both chaotic and disorienting. Charcot appealed to the police for assistance in tracking her down; "for her own safety," he insisted. After a week or so, though, it became clear that the trail had already gone cold—there was no sign of her, in Paris or anywhere else the detectives reached out to with inquiries. She'd simply vanished, as utterly and completely as Cendrillon's spell-spun ball gowns and pumpkin carriage. Still, I seemed to see her everywhere as I drifted aimlessly about the grounds, waiting to hear my fate: In the baths where I'd washed her freckled back. In the amphitheater corridor where we'd spent so much time waiting, watching, and worrying together. In the bright little garden where I'd finally found her that morning and thought that her blood had sprouted wings. Lying on the cot where we'd spent our last night together, I'd close my eyes and try to remember every exhilarating, ecstatic moment of it. And upon waking in the morning, I'd hold my breath, listening despite myself for her limping footsteps in the hallway. Her breathy voice: There *you are, Laure!*

I never did, obviously. Though I did find the note that she'd left me that last morning, curled and crumpled in a dusty corner beneath my bed: *In the rose garden*, it read in her careful, schoolgirlish script. *Meet me there when you wake.*

And below that, scrawled more hastily, almost as an afterthought: *I love you.*

When they finally dismissed me, it came as little surprise. I had, after all, stolen from one of Charcot's top patrons, collaborated with that same patron, and schemed to run off with his top hysteric. But I always suspected the real reason for my termination was that I simply knew too much—not just about the marquis and the judge, but about Charcot himself as well, how completely he'd been duped by one of his own hysterical subjects, and how wrong he'd been about hysteria in general. He delivered the verdict to me himself, along with severance wages that amounted to more than enough to cover the day-and-a-half journey to Vault-de-Lugny. To my utter amazement, he also wrote me a letter of reference for future employers, signed by the great Jean-Martin Charcot himself. After handing it to me, he gave me his standard, distracted advice (*Here and now, Laure*) and wished me luck.

As I was crossing the threshold of his black-walled office that last time, though, he called out to me: "Laure." Turning, I found him looking at me again.

"You knew her better than most," he said.

I nodded warily, wondering if he was going to fault me for not having warned him about Josephine's unexpectedly subversive—even murderous—capacities. But the expression on his face wasn't the anger with which I was by then so familiar. It wasn't even his usual cold disdain. It was something I'd actually never seen on that chiseled visage before: uncertainty.

"Did she—" he began. "That is, this whole time, was she only—"

It was as though he'd pulled off a mask at the Bal des Folles, revealing a shockingly vulnerable-looking stranger. I stared at him, disoriented—not only by the unprecedented shift in his demeanor, but by the sudden realization that I didn't know myself. *Had* Josephine been feigning it all, all along? Could that even have been a possibility?

Looking back now, of course, I can't imagine it was.

In that moment, though—perhaps absurdly—I wasn't sure.

And thankfully, in the end I wasn't forced to answer either way. Charcot shook his head; the moment passed. "Never mind," he said brusquely, and returned his attention to a new device—a thing that looked like an iron gallows—that he was working on for the treatment of railway spine.

I never saw him again.

After leaving the Salpêtrière, I lived for a time with Amélie and Madame Granger, in the latter's neat little house on rue de Château in Vault-de-Lugny. My sister and I shared a room upstairs there, and there were some nights when—just as I'd fantasized—it almost felt as though we were back home together again, reading to each other by lamplight at the end of the day, or scribbling in our respective journals, or sharing increasingly slurred stories as we slid into sleep. By day, when I wasn't at one of the tutoring positions Madame Granger helped me secure (aided immeasurably, of course, by Charcot's rec-ommendation), I distracted myself from my searing grief and regret by helping with the housework and the midwife's business accounts and correspondences.

For a time, I placed regular notices in all the major Paris papers as well, the message simple and direct: *Josephine, I am sorry. Please contact me c/o Midwife Granger, in Vault-de-Lugny.* I meticulously perused those same papers for some indication of where she might have gone. I never got a response, or found any confirmable leads. But in 1890 a *Paris illustré* piece about a string of mesmerism-related thefts that had taken place in a traveling carnival caught my attention. All of the victims were men who'd paid to meet with a somnambulist, a young woman who called herself "Mademoiselle Eve" and claimed to com-municate with the dead. All emerged from her stall dazed and stripped of their valuables, though—strangely—none registered those losses until the carnival had left town. There were no identifying details about the *hypnotiseuse* and no further stories on the subject that I could find, though I combed the papers obsessively for weeks after-ward.

Three years later, my pulse leapt over another *Paris illustré* head-line: *Former Salpêtrière Hysteric Takes "Revenge" on Asylum Doctor.* That piece, however, clearly *was* about another woman, one who'd at-tempted to assassinate Gilles de la Tourette for supposedly "hypno-tizing her from afar." Luckily, her bullet went not through the Gnome's heart but his neck. It later turned out the would-be killer had never been at the Salpêtrière at all, but had become so obsessed with the Charcoterie's hypnotic research that she'd convinced herself she was one of its victims. She was promptly committed to another Paris asylum, Sainte-Anne. She'd perhaps have been gratified to learn of the Gnome's own psychiatric institutionalization in Switzerland some years later, where he died of one of the diseases in which he'd specialized at the asylum: syphilis.

The same year of that attack, I read of Charcot's death from con-gestive heart failure while on holiday in Nièvre. The *Figaro* headline, *Jean-Martin Charcot, Pioneer of Brain-Related Maladies and World-Renowned*

Hysteria Expert, Dies at Age 67, filled me with an odd mix of grief and relief, as though a window that had allowed both sunlight and danger into my life had been unexpectedly slammed shut. But there was also a sense of almost sheepish amazement that our wizard—like the one in a popular children's book that came out shortly after his death—was not a wizard after all, but a mere mortal man. It was a revelation underscored by the fact that in the wake of his passing, the hysteria "epidemic" that had for years had Paris in its grip more or less simply faded away. Doctors still diagnosed it, of course—I'm told they still do. But Charcot's hard-earned "discoveries" about its nature—its supposed four stages, and defining connection to hypnosis—were, unlike his work with Parkinson's and amyotrophic lateral sclerosis, quickly (and perhaps eagerly) forgotten. I heard that many of the great man's former acolytes—Janet, Babinski, Freud, and even Marie—made a point of distancing themselves from the final chapter of his work while continuing to revere him, as does most of the world now, for laying the foundations of what would become the medical field of neurology.

Even Rosalie—who had triumphantly returned to Charcot's stage shortly after Josephine's disappearance—was mysteriously "cured" of her hysteria after his passing; supposedly, she never suffered another attack. She did stay on at the asylum, working first as an assistant in Monsieur Londe's photography studio before moving with him to the Salpêtrière's new radiology department. She eventually lost both her legs and an arm, and, at the age of fifty-four, her life, to another mysterious malady, one that later came to be recognized as radiation poisoning. It's always struck me as a strangely poignant end, perhaps because I remember her as an almost dangerously radiant being herself, one whose fiery light was too bright for that darkly oppressive place. And so, bit by agonizing bit, the asylum put it out.

But it was well before then that my sister met and married a widower from Avallon, a kind physician who'd lost his first wife and infant daughter to childbirth. He and Amélie went on to have a son and twin girls together, all three of whom became my godchildren. Their home is joyous and chaotic, filled with books and baying dogs and lively phonograph music, with adjoining clinical spaces in the back. They make for a wonderfully collaborative team, assisting and advising each other's practices with affection, mutual respect, and the occasional robust argument in a way I know would have filled our father with both joy and pride.

After the wedding I moved into a home of my own not far from theirs, a small, simple flat just off Avallon's central square. There I've spent the better part of a half century, most of it happily enough. I've a sunny alcove where I can read, write, and meet with my students, or sit in my rocking chair with a cat (I've had two now, both white, both named Mimi) on my lap, its rumbled purring easing my ruminating mind in the way Babette's carefully rationed ether doses did when I was ill. I've learned to enjoy serving Burgundy specialties— slow-cooked pork jowl, garlicky snails, and of course the region's famed wine and cheese—to the few friends and even fewer lovers I've found here. Only one of those approached the kind of wondrous joy and ease that I experienced in Josephine's arms, though it too was cut tragically short—not by madness or a scheming nobleman, but by the unfathomable devastation wrought upon us by the Great War. As painful as the loss was, it somehow made me even more aware of the aching and shame-tinged space left within me by Josephine's departure. That remains to this very day.

But so much else remains too: Josephine's cutting wit and startling insights about the world around her. Her boundless willingness to fight—literally as well as figuratively—for herself. Her furious independence and unwavering demand that those she cared for earn her loyalty. Her unrepentant insistence on being who she knew she was, and on loving—and loathing—accordingly. It's thanks to her that I no longer find myself looking to men for direction in my life—for love or money, for permission or approval. I look only to myself. She taught me that.

And yet in my darker moments, I still curse myself for having failed the bigger lesson she tried to teach me: how to keep her in my life. And glumly, I ponder what I might have done differently. What if I'd thrown caution to the wind and agreed to flee with her sooner?

What if I'd listened to her and fought the Basque as he tried to take her away? What if I'd never gone to my father's lawyer, had never stolen the marquis's bracelet in the first place, had never given that repugnant little man the means or motivation to exert his will over us both?

Most of all, though, I wonder: What if I'd simply *believed* her? If I hadn't brushed off her insistence that her rapist was alive as the delusional ramblings of a soon-to-be madwoman? After all, I started my hysteria journal—the same one I've drawn from to craft these pages—because the women around me needed to be heard. And yet when it came to Josephine herself—the woman who mattered the most to me, the woman I still think of as the greatest love of my life—I didn't listen when she desperately needed me to.

When, ignoring once and for all Charcot's commanding dictate (*Here and now, Laure*), I finally sat down to put this strange tale to paper, I thought I was doing it for myself. After all, so much has happened since Josephine was dragged bloody and fighting into Charcot's *musée pathologique vivant*. The world has been swept by war and deadly disease, by revolution and jazz. Outhouses have moved indoors, and carriages—including omnibuses—now move with the aid of motors instead of jostling horses, though they make me more ill than ever. Men—and now a woman—have flown across the Atlantic. And while Thomas Edison (the real one) has yet to invent the perfect female android, he has brought music into our parlors and made pictures move. Both the corset and the archaic marriage laws Madame Aubert decried in her little paper have been abolished, and women in many countries—though, somehow, not yet in France—have won the vote. Overall, the world seems to be hurtling forward at an even more frenzied speed than it did in those dizzying days in the eighties. The past feels increasingly small and hazy, a blurred and rippling reflection receding rapidly from view. In finally setting this all down, I'd ever more hoped to create a bulwark around my memories, both real and imagined. Now that I'm almost finished, though, I see that it's become much more than that. It's actually a confession of sorts, of all the things I did wrong during that time. Of how my loneliness and impulsivity, my arrogance and selfish need, led me to betray the person I cared about the most.

It's also my way of apologizing, should Josephine ever happen to read these pages.

And if she does—if *you* do—please hear this: I am sorry. And I am grateful. And—all these years later—I still love you. I hope wherever you've ended up, be it Montana or Montpelier, you've found the happy ending you wove into your little story as we lay together, blocked off from the world in our grimy little room, on what would—unbeknownst to either of us—be our last night together.

I think often about that fable. Not just because it seemed to spin its own spell, transforming us from friends into fleeting lovers, but because even though the ending has changed, it somehow feels less fantastic than the fantastical story I've laid out in these pages. It may, in fact, be the truest version of our story together. Which makes sense, given your uncanny ability—even at the very height of your maybe-madness—to distill the world's vagaries and evils into pure goodness and crystalline truths.

And so here it is again. It's not exactly as you narrated it that night. But it's the way I still hear you telling it in my head, your voice graveled with exhaustion, buoyed by hope and relief, and sweetened— if only fleetingly—by love:

There were once two girls who lived in an old, gloomy castle that was ruled by a gloomy wizard. The wizard had both girls under his spell. One day, though, one of them discovered the source of his magic and turned his spell back onto the wizard himself. She flew away to a new life, a magic jewel around her neck. But before taking flight, she broke the wizard's hold on her friend as well.

Her friend remained earthbound, her wealth confined to her family, her books, her words.

They were apart. But at last, both were free.

Author's Note

Though inspired by actual events and historical figures, *The Madwomen of Paris* is a novel, a fictive reimagining of the stranger-than-fiction universe occupied by Jean-Martin Charcot and the women in his care at the Salpêtrière. In order to give readers a full sense of this universe within the relatively narrow scope of the narrative's timeline, I have done what historical novelists can happily (if perhaps uncomfortably for some) do, shifting and omitting some events and chronologies, and entirely inventing others. Some of the "hysterics" I've depicted in these pages are drawn from women who lived, worked, struggled, were studied, and were publicly presented at the Salpêtrière, either in Charcot's larger Friday public lectures or the smaller, less formal ones he held on Tuesdays. Josephine Garreau is partially based on real-life Salpêtrière "star" Augustine Gleizes, whose compelling photographs provided the initial spark for this book, and who really did escape from the asylum in men's clothing. Rosalie Chardon is largely based on Blanche Wittman, whose swooning image was iconically captured in Andre Brouillet's painting "A Clinical Lesson at the Salpêtrière." Similarly, all of the hypnotic "exercises" I've reimagined here were carried out in some form as part of nineteenth-century hysterical research, though not necessarily by Charcot. For those interested in learning more about these extraordinary women, and the Salpêtrière during Charcot's reign, I highly recommend Asti Hustvedt's remarkable book *Medical Muses: Hysteria in Nineteenth-Century Paris*.

The medical luminaries I've referenced—among them Pierre Janet, Georges Gilles de la Tourette, Joseph Babinski, and Sigmund Freud—all studied with Charcot in real life, though I've taken a small liberty in placing them all under his mentorship during the specific span of the novel's narrative. Most worked with Charcot around 1885, though Pierre Janet arrived at the asylum a few years later. In-depth histories of both Charcot and his associates can be found in *Charcot: Constructing Neurology* by Christopher G. Goetz, Michel Bonduelle, and Toby Gelfand. Jonathan Marshall's *Performing Neurology: The Dramaturgy of Dr. Jean-Martin Charcot* contains illuminating insights into how Charcot's dramatically powerful stage presence helped to shape the field of neurology. And fascinating actual transcripts from Charcot's medical lectures, including a lecture on hysteria, can be found in *Charcot the Clinician: The Tuesday Lessons; Excerpts from Nine Case Presentations on General Neurology Delivered at the Salpêtrière Hospital in 1887–88* by Christopher G. Goetz.

Andrew Scull's *Hysteria: The Disturbing History* was among the books to which I referred to try to put hysteria into historical context, tracing the disease from its ancient associations with a "wandering uterus" to Charcot's radical reclassification of it as an identifiable neurological disorder in the nineteenth century. Edward Shorter's *From Paralysis to Fatigue: A History of Psychosomatic Illness in the Modern Era* was helpful in understanding hysteria in terms of nineteenth-century cultural shifts, as well as its evolution into modern diagnoses such as depression, anxiety, PTSD, and dissociative, somatic, and conversion disorders. Explanations for why and how this shift occurred vary, but in 1980, after a decades-long decline in reported cases, hysteria was finally removed from the American Psychiatric Association's *Diagnostic and Statistical Manual of Mental Disorders*, after having been listed there since the manual's 1968 inception.

Hysteria's legacy, however, like Charcot's, remains deeply influential to this day. Though Sigmund Freud spent less than half a year studying under Charcot, he was so powerfully affected by both his *maître*'s practice and teachings and by his own experiences in Charcot's hysteria ward that it shifted the entire course of his career. Upon leaving the Salpêtrière he continued studying hysteria and hypnosis with another mentor, Josef Breuer, eventually coming to the conclusion that the disease was linked not to brain lesions or even heredity, but to trauma—especially sexual trauma—in early childhood. By the turn of the century, however, he'd abandoned this idea in favor of his theory of infantile sexuality. Though he continued for a time using hypnosis therapeutically on patients, he later abandoned that as well, focusing instead on the "free association" technique that would become a cornerstone of modern psychoanalysis. Like most of Charcot's protégés, Freud ultimately distanced himself from his mentor's hysterical theories. But he continued to revere Charcot for the remainder of his life, and named his first son Jean-Martin in his honor.

The Salpêtrière merged with the Hôpital de la Pitié in 1964 to form the Groupe Hospitalier Pitié-Salpêtrière. It is now a sprawling teaching hospital in Paris's thirteenth arrondissement, with departments in all major medical specialties. It continues to be known for its neurology department.

Acknowledgments

A small army of supporters played roles in helping to bring this (at times) impossibly ambitious-seeming project to life. I am deeply indebted to my incredible agent Amelia Atlas at CAA for her literary vision, wisdom, and support, and to Hilary Teeman and Caroline Weishuhn at Penguin Random House for seeing promise in a very strange and somewhat vague story idea about nineteenth-century hysterics and hypnosis, and for guiding me with patience and insight as I found a way to tell it. Thanks, too, to Aja Pollock for her amazing copyedits and for catching everything from hopelessly tangled timelines to haphazard hyphens and comically bad comma splices. Maura Sheehy, Courtney Zoffness, and Michelle Brandt all patiently read through excerpts and chapters as *Madwomen* staggered toward coherence, and Julia Lichtblau also fed me fabulous food and encouragement. Andrea Lafleur, Amy Hopwood, and (again) Alison Lowenstein offered candid thoughts and feedback on several (often ponderous) completed drafts. Karen Decter, Maxime Spinga, and Adele Cosjin were invaluable comrades in the boundless treasure hunt that is historical research; any errors that appear despite their indefatigable efforts remain mine and mine alone. Special thanks to Florian Horrein of the Salpêtrière's Charcot Library for showing me where to find the old Salpêtrière within the new, and for graciously fielding numerous queries about Salpêtrière's history. Thanks to Andrea Lafleur (again, always) for being my personal Paris tour guide, fabulous host, fashion icon, and refreshing voice of reason, wisdom, and much-needed snark. Thanks to Jean-Michel Hirt and Karima Berger for welcoming me into their beautiful Paris home to talk psychology and history, and to the incomparable Mary Morris for introducing me to them after doing the same in Brooklyn.

Writers need writing spaces, and I am so grateful to those who provided them to me over the past four years. Thanks most especially to Scott Adkins and Erin Courtney for creating the Brooklyn Writers Space, now a beloved refuge throughout all four of my novels. I am also deeply indebted in particular to Maura Sheehy, whose extension of an empty therapy suite as a Covid writing oasis was both lifesaving and uncannily appropriate, subject-wise. Dan Ellis, Sarah Bird, Caroline and Rich Peterson, Virginia Terry, and Matt Jacobus were all also extraordinarily generous in opening their beautiful homes to me. Thanks as well to the Catwalk Art Institute and Prospect Street Writers House for offering glorious rural residencies that proved crucial to both my sanity and my book's completion, and to the Jewish Book Council for supporting struggling writers in times of COVID mayhem.

Thanks most of all to my beloved family—Katie and Hannah, for being the gorgeous, thoughtful, and hysterical (in the humorous sense, usually) young women they are, and Michael, for, well, everything, as usual; reading, rereading, and re-rereading, plot-doctoring, co-bourboning, and generally helping me survive this strange journey. You were right. And last but never least, so so much love and gratitude to Steve Epstein and the deeply missed Rozanne Epstein, without whose faith and support this book simply wouldn't exist.

THE MADWOMEN OF PARIS

A Novel

Jennifer Cody Epstein

A BOOK CLUB GUIDE

Questions and Topics for Discussion

1. Did you know how much about the history of hysteria and "mad" women being institutionalized in France before reading *The Madwomen of Paris*? Did anything in this lesser-known bit of history surprise you?

2. While much of the story examines women's rights (or lack thereof) in the medical arena, Laure also at one point encounters a women's rights advocate being arrested. How are the topics of feminism and equality represented in the story, both inside and outside the medical field? What has changed since the 1800s? What hasn't?

3. Dr. Charcot is a real historical figure who contributed much to the medical field, particularly to modern neurology. However, as we come to find out in the novel, his methods for treating hysteria were less successful. What did you make of his methodologies for treating his patients? How culpable do you think he is for the harm his patients endured, since he truly believed he was helping them?

4. Think of the men in the novel and their behaviors toward women, especially the vulnerable women in their care. Do you think that if hysteria primarily affected men instead of women they would have treated male patients in the same way? Do you think that there are social norms of the time that contributed to the way these respected doctors viewed their patients?

5. Mental health and its treatment, particularly for women, are key themes of the novel. How has society's view of mental ill-

ness changed over time? How much do you think the female-oriented hysteria affected this change versus male-oriented mental health issues like shell shock?

6. Think about the line: "A friend. In this place. The idea seemed strangely fantastical." Why do you think the women of the hysteria ward were so competitive with one another and reluctant to be one another's allies? Do you think this is a result of the hospital's practices, the time's attitudes toward gender, or something else? Do you think this sense of competition still exists today?

7. As Laure and Josephine grow closer and learn to rely on each other, their friendship deepens into something more. What do you think it says about humanity that relationships can form and flourish even in the darkest of places? What do you think it says about Laure's and Josephine's resilience?

8. How does the theme of family present itself in the story, in both "found" family and "blood" family?

9. In the book, both Charcot and Laure's late father consider "nervous disorders" like hysteria to be responses to the overwhelming speed of modernization and change in the late nineteenth century. Do you see parallels to this "modernity-induced trauma" in today's world? How does it manifest itself today and how have attitudes toward it changed?

10. *The Madwomen of Paris* is told from the perspective of Laure, as though she is writing it several years after the events and looking back on her experiences. How does this format impact the plot? Do you think that Laure is a reliable narrator, or do her own biases and hindsight have an effect on the accuracy of her tale?

11. What did you think of the twist at the end of the novel? Were you able to predict it, or did it take you by surprise? How surprised do you think the other characters were to find themselves in that situation?

12. When Laure writes her recollections about life at the Salpêtrière, she is doing so in a world that her younger self would hardly have recognized. What astonishing changes do you think she's seen over the course of the novel's timeline, roughly 1880 through 1930? Do those changes seem more or less remarkable than those people have witnessed over other periods?

Jennifer Cody Epstein: On Finding the Bravery to Write Critically About the Past in Fiction

Q: What prompted you to write this book?

A: It started with an old photo I stumbled upon while researching *Memento Mori,* or Victorian death photography. But the subject of this picture was clearly, almost startlingly alive: a young woman, scantily clad, with tousled hair and one arm held at an unnatural angle. I was struck most of all by her expression: Locking gazes with the camera, she was staring at it in a way that was both provocative and challenging.

Intrigued, I followed the link and learned her name: Augustine Gleizes. A working-class girl in nineteenth-century Paris, she'd survived a violent sexual assault at the hands of her mother's employer and was subsequently diagnosed with hysteria. She was committed to the Salpêtrière women's asylum, where she joined a handful of women who were studied, photographed, and publicly displayed by Dr. Jean-Martin Charcot, widely considered the father of modern-day neurology. Charcot used hypnosis to draw hysterical "symptoms" out of his patients, often before huge audiences in his popular weekly lectures.

Augustine, as it turned out, was so highly sensitive to hypnosis that she quickly became one of Charcot's "star hysterics," young women who were followed by the tabloids, featured in chocolate advertisements, and even depicted in a famous Salon painting. After years of being continually hypnotized, photographed, and put through bizarre experiments, though, she'd clearly had enough, and after a few failed attempts fled the asylum disguised as a man.

I was utterly fascinated by all of this: the woman, the story, the stranger-than-fiction setting. And, of course, that final, role-inverting act of rebellion, which seemed presaged in that dramatic first photograph.

Q: How long did it take to go from idea to publication? And did the idea change during the process?

A: I first found Augustine's photograph in 2017. The book comes out this July. So, about six years in total. Though at points it felt much, much longer—particularly during Covid.

In terms of the idea: I knew from the beginning where I wanted the story to end up, so overall I guess the answer is no. But figuring out how to get there took numerous iterations. I'm a heavy rewriter/editor in general, but this novel took more writing and whittling and rethinking/restructuring than any of my others.

Initially it was going to have a modern-day thread as well as a historical one, like my last novel *Wunderland*. But as the historical side of *Madwomen* began taking shape, I realized that what it really felt like to me was a classic nineteenth-century Gothic/ horror novel. So that was how I ended up writing it: scrapping the contemporary narrative, tweaking the tone to evoke that of *Jane Eyre* or *Wuthering Heights*, and playing up the grim and dark aspects of asylum life (not that that was hard!).

Q: Were there any surprises or learning moments in the publishing process for this title?

A: Certainly one surprise was having my first editorial review run in *Science Magazine*, which I hadn't anticipated. It does make sense, since Charcot is such a gargantuan figure in scientific and medical history. But seeing a novel I'd written featured alongside books on things like "permeable micro electrodes for bioelectronic implants" and "stem cells releasing oncologic HSV and anti-PD-1 target brain metastases"—all as "summer reading" suggestions, mind you—really tickled me. I'm sure Mr. Muldoon, the middle school chemistry teacher who (very generously) gave me a C in his class, would find it amusing as well.

Q: Were there any surprises in the writing process for this book?

A: A lot of the things I uncovered in my research about nineteenth-century hysteria and its supposed symptoms and treatments were pretty surprising. For instance, I'd never heard of dermography, a condition that allowed physicians to "write" on their patients' skin by lightly tracing it with pointed instruments, which in turn left raised, bright red lines. Even more weird was the assertion that these lines could be prompted to bleed at a specified later time through hypnotic suggestion.

Other belief-defying conditions associated with the disease included women blistering through hypnotic suggestion or bleeding stigmatically from their feet, palms, and over the heart. There is also a record of a woman losing the ability to speak her native tongue and having to resort to another she didn't know particularly well.

But I think the biggest surprise was just how difficult it was for me, as a woman and a novelist, to write critically about Charcot—even now, a full century-and-a-half later. He is still so revered, and so much of that reverence is so absolutely deserved. For the first year or so of this project I really grappled with how to portray him, not wanting to detract from the very real contributions he made in areas like Parkinson's and ALS.

I think that's why so much of him ended up in those early drafts: I was unconsciously giving him the kind of hallowed spotlight that famous men are usually given in historical narrative. In retrospect, though, I was actually falling into the very trap I'd set about dismantling in the novel: allotting him outsized merit and authority simply because he was a famous man who dominated the historical record, unlike the vulnerable women he diagnosed, studied, and (ostensibly) treated.

Even in a work of fiction it felt surprisingly scary to call him and the other famous men he worked with (Freud, Gilles de la Tourette, Babinski, Janet) out for the damage they did during this last, strange chapter of Charcot's career, and to give the women they damaged the same kind of dimensionality, autonomy, and authority. But once I did, the story became far less of a struggle to write.

Q: What do you hope readers will get out of your book?

A: First and foremost, I hope that they find it interesting, unexpected, and compelling; a chance not just to learn about a little-known chapter in medical and feminist history but to get a sense of what it might have been like to live and breathe in that moment.

But I'd also like *Madwomen* to offer readers an opportunity to consider some of the novel's themes in a modern-day context; for instance, the ways in which society views mental health in general, and women's mental health in particular. Or the ways in which a male-dominated medical establishment simultaneously overlooks, downplays, and fetishizes women's health issues. And, of course, what we really mean when we use terms like "hysterical."

As an author, I'm drawn to historical fiction because I believe the past can provide a powerful lens through which to examine the present—and in the process learn new things about ourselves. So I hope readers are able to appreciate my work in that way as well.

Q: If you could share one piece of advice with other writers, what would it be?

A: Write what you know, but also don't be afraid to leap into the great unknown! Taking that leap can feel daunting—even paralyzing. But it also offers unparalleled opportunities to learn, to challenge yourself and your readers, and to explore, exercise, and encourage the kind of empathy that is more crucial than ever in today's world.

This interview was conducted by Robert Brewer and originally appeared on WritersDigest.com.

PHOTO: ALEXANDER BERG

JENNIFER CODY EPSTEIN is the internationally bestselling author of *The Painter from Shanghai, Wunderland,* and *The Gods of Heavenly Punishment,* which won the Asian/Pacific American Honor Award for Literature for Adult Fiction. She has written for *The Wall Street Journal, Vogue, Self, Mademoiselle,* and many other publications. She has an MFA in fiction from Columbia University and an MA in international affairs from the Johns Hopkins School of Advanced International Studies. Epstein lives in Brooklyn with her husband and two daughters.

JenniferCodyEpstein.com
Threads: @Jennepstein
Instagram: @jennepstein

About the Type

This book was set in Baskerville, a typeface designed by John Baskerville (1706–75), an amateur printer and typefounder, and cut for him by John Handy in 1750. The type became popular again when the Lanston Monotype Corporation of London revived the classic roman face in 1923. The Mergenthaler Linotype Company in England and the United States cut a version of Baskerville in 1931, making it one of the most widely used typefaces today.

RANDOM HOUSE BOOK CLUB

Because Stories Are Better Shared

Discover

Exciting new books that spark conversation every week.

Connect

With authors on tour—or in your living room. (Request an Author Chat for your book club!)

Discuss

Stories that move you with fellow book lovers on Facebook, on Goodreads, or at in-person meet-ups.

Enhance

Your reading experience with discussion prompts, digital book club kits, and more, available on our website.

Join our online book club community!

f **g** randomhousebookclub.com

Random House Book Club ™

Because Stories Are Better Shared

 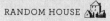